As The Darkness Falls

Things Are Not What They Seem

DANIEL HOLDINGS

For The Watchmen,
People Still Listen... I Did

∞

Acknowledgements

I am so grateful to my wife Vickie for her constant patience, inspiration and assistance with this work. She's way too smart for me. I'm also thankful to my daughter Sarrah, inspiration for Bryce's Sarrah, and always my favorite daughter in the whole world!

A very special thanks to my Pop, Lyle, who has encouraged and assisted me more than I can say. For his unconditional love and support, I am truly blessed.

I'd like to thank the fellas around the room on Monday nights, Merle, Dave, Stan, Ken, Steve, Jeff and Eli. I've learned a lot over the last few years and I credit a great deal of that learning to this group.

I'm also grateful for my friend Larry Taylor on his mountain top in Oklahoma. His belief in my work has been crucial for its exposure to a larger audience. He was also kind enough to look at this novel's manuscript and give me his honest opinion prior to publishing. His website is www.larrywtaylor.org.

A huge thank you to Steve Quayle at www.stevequayle.com. He is not only a wealth of knowledge and information, but passionate about what God has given him to do. He was extremely generous in allowing my use of any of his research and also permitted my portraying him as a vital character in the book.

To that end, I'm also grateful to Romy Zarit for her assistance in helping get the "Quayle" character right and for her proofreading skills.

A big thank you to Sue Bradley for her writing the Foreword and her "quiet corrections" that has helped me present my work in a more professional manner.

The Watchers Series mentioned in the book is indeed a creation of L.A. Marzulli. Dr. Roger Leir is a prominent guest in them. L.A. has done some first rate research on a variety of subjects. He also coined the phrase "The Great Deception" a few years back and I've taken the liberty to use the term often. He's a prolific writer and speaker and his blog site is www.lamarzulli.wordpress.com.

Special thanks to Barry S. Roffman at www.arkcode.com. Barry is a devout Orthodox Jew who does not believe that the Messiah has come. His work on finding the Ark of the Covenant is fascinating and factual. You can check out his theory on the location of the Ark using the Torah Code and his interesting track of current events at his website.

A couple points of clarification are needed. The idea of numerous Sun spots giving it the appearance as described by John in Revelation 6:12 is not mine. I heard Stan Deyo talk about such a possibility on a radio show one time. Stan's a brilliant, out of the box, thinker. His website is www.standeyo.com.

In the same vein, the phrase "black ubiquitous membrane" is from either Augusto Perez, www.theappearance.com, or Rick Wiles at www.trunews.com. I don't remember who said it first, but both of these men are worth checking out.

A scene has "Quayle" being interviewed with Tom Horn, www.raidersnewsupdate.com. The conversation did indeed occur. I've found Tom to be a terrific research source and I'm grateful for his ongoing efforts on the behalf of truth.

Heartfelt thanks to Ed and Manaya Warkentin, Alvaro, Zoraida, Stephanie, Vanessa and Azlynn Mora, Doug and Lisa Hemphill, and Dave and Lisa Duckett. All of which are inspirations for characters and for letting me use their names and personalities. And no, Alvaro is not a scientist, but he is a great friend. I am grateful for all of their love and support.

Special thanks to Tom Schlitz and Dorothy Crothers for their proofreading skills and encouragement.

Last, but in no way least, I am grateful to Yeshua; for His love, care, direction and provision at all times. I couldn't live without Him.

Foreword

As *The Darkness Falls* moves front and center into the sophisticated genre of multi-dimensional scientific techno-*fiction.*

The implications and conclusions realized are beyond the realm of recommended reading and should be required reading for anyone sensing a foreboding, looming and imminent transition.

Settle in and sit tight as Nobel Laureate and physicist Dr. Bryce Obadiah Cooper returns in a compelling odyssey encompassing prehistoric civilizations; Nephilim; current geopolitical events; crop circles; extradimensional life forms; CERN's *"Cathedral of Science"* where particles themselves are deconfined; vibrational harmonic refractors; HAARP and other ionospheric heaters; solar and galactic physics; dimensional-time theory and electromagnetic ramifications.

Propelled by a conversation with historian/author/adventurer Steve Quayle in Bozeman, MT, Bryce Cooper ultimately finds himself swept 7,000 miles away for a face-to-face meeting in Jerusalem with the High Priest of the sacred Temple Mount.

Ambitious but uncluttered, *As The Darkness Falls* runs a marathon of cataclysms which become infinitely more horrific as life is consumed in an accelerating, spiraling descent.

In an exquisitely compelling sequel to *Three Days In the Belly of the Beast*, Daniel Holdings once again capably and commendably provides a universally appealing odyssey that is staggering in scope and nearly incapacitating in consequence.

The depth and accuracy of the research will ultimately require the reader to suspend any level of comfort as the disturbing message at the heart of *As The Darkness Falls* is strikingly prescient and more relevant today than any other time in history.

As Dr. Bryce Cooper laments, *"Sometimes I wish it wasn't true …. there were times that I doubted my own sanity."*

As The Darkness Falls brings us up to date and right to the edge: if it makes us edgy, it's because that's exactly where we are. If we are to survive, we must be engaged.

Sue Bradley
Research Journalist

There are things known and there are things unknown, and in between... are the doors of perception.

Aldous Huxley

∞

As The Darkness Falls

∞

Direct descendent of
Aaron Priest of Levi

(Aunt Ruby)
UNCLE JOE –
SURROGATE DAD

BRYCE OBADIAH COOPER   5'10"
DIED @ 17 < GRACE ANN COOPER   SOME   BROAD SHOULDERED
                                 JEWISH   TAN (INDIAN)
DIED @ 8 < JEREMIAH OBADIAH COOPER   SANDY
                              BLACKFOOT   BROWN HAIR
PhD @ 17   INDIAN
DIMENSIONAL THEORY
PARTICLE PHYSICIST   (M THEORY)
NOBEL PRIZE WINNER   ↓
                                        @ 24

LHC — LARGE HALDRON COLLIDER
CERN — EUROPEAN ORGANIZATION 4 NUCLEAR
                                  RESEARCH
HAARP – High FREQUENCY ACTIVE
     AURORAL RESEARCH PROGRAM – ALASKA
CASIMIR EFFECT   Pg 80
DR GROVER WASHINGTON McNABB – "MAC"
     BLACK 290 6'6" NBA + NFL MATERIAL
     ASTRO PHYSICIST   12 YRS SR. TO BRYCE
MIT — MET   GREW UP IN PHILY
     MAC ≈ 29
     BRYCE ≈ 17

BRYCE — PICKED AS TEAM LEADER — LHC
MAC — PICKED BY BRYCE TO JOIN

     FROM THE FRENCH: CONSEIL EUROPEEN pour
              la RECHERCHE NUCLEAIRE

GERMAN
GABRIELE COOPER - "GABBY" - WIFE
    MARRIED 7 YRS '84 BASELINE SHOT
    DARK HAIR; COBALT BLUE EYES
DIGBY STANFORD WILLIAMSON - "DIGGS"
    COOPER'S RESEARCH ASSISTANT
    DISTANT RELATIVE OF THE QUEEN
    BRITISH
    ABOUT ≈ 25

LJ - SON 5 YRS OLD CURRENT TIME
    Little Joe

ATLAS 7 - COOPER'S EXPERIMENT   Pg 43

LHC - NICKNAMED "THE BEAST"

SSgt Danny Mendez - Mendez
    met @ HAARP

HARMONIC PARTICLE REFRACTOR - fabric
        gold & precious gems
Pg 59 - ABBOT = NEPHLIM

RESEARCH

GAKONA, AK   (Pg 65)

HAARP

Pg 111   LHC Process

Pg 262
266

Urim   Thummim

293
320

Chapter 1

Lazy Hoof – Present Day

*S*hooting stars of color sprayed in all directions like celebratory Independence Day festivities. The colors faded into hot white sprigs that diminished and melted into his peripheral view.

He found himself floating above the outskirts of Geneva, Switzerland. In the distance the snowcapped Alps glistened under the Sun. The breeze was cool, but not cold. This was a perfect vantage point: A clear day in the crisp blue sky.

Hovering at a couple thousand feet, he had a clear field of view of the CERN facility and the surrounding farmlands. Those empty farmlands were equally as important as the CERN campus itself.

Buried at almost six-hundred feet below ground was The Large Hadron Collider, an atom-smasher and the world's biggest machine. And the accompanying seventeen mile circular beam tunnel was also entombed under all of that farmland. The reason that he knew these things was because he worked there as a lead physicist for many years.

As he mused about his former life, something strange began to happen on the ground. Wanting to get a better look, he willed himself to go lower and he slowly floated down. Closer to the ground now, he could barely make out what looked like ants moving to and fro. He realized that they weren't ants, but people coming and going from the main building, L1, of CERN.

A dark blur of movement caught his eye. Without warning, like a giant spinning drain, the whole seventeen mile LHC circle above ground began to rotate counterclockwise. As it spun, the natural colors of white, brown and green began to smudge and bleed together, making everything in this vortex look the color of a dull gray.

The area spun like a washing machine on its spin cycle. But it wasn't a drain like he first thought. It was an opening or portal of some kind, turning and churning with power generated from deep beneath the earth.

Without warning, black vapor began to spit out from the center of the swirling hole. The blackness continued to pour out from the center like a torrent. This vapor slowly thickened and became a black membrane. It was so thick that within a few moments, he could no longer see any other distinctive colors... save black.

As he floated high above the turning below, movement in the corner of his eye caught his attention. He looked up and saw a white light speeding down toward Earth, almost like a falling star. Rather than resembling a meteor, it looked like lightning striking in the middle of the day. Its destination appeared to be the exact center of the churning black membrane. When it finally hit, it was instantly sucked in and covered over, without a trace.

After the lightning strike, the blackness grew and expanded even faster. It kept rising and spreading out in all directions from whence it came. As the black circle rose to his height, he realized that it was not a liquid or solid mass. It was the joining of individual parts, too numerous to count. These individual parts were giant beings whose color was dark and black as midnight.

As the creatures rose higher they reached his level in the sky. From this vantage point, he could clearly see them for what they were. They were soot covered, black winged creatures that looked like giant humans, but were a mass of muscle. With eyes that were blood red and faces contorted with rage, he knew exactly who and what they were.

Then, with unexpected and sudden violence, he was jerked from that place to a different location. All at once he was floating in front of a massive huge ball of fire. He knew it to be the Sun.

As he looked to either side of the orange and yellow ball, he could see billions of stars in the distance. Like above Geneva, he floated there in space without the need of oxygen or protective clothing. He was now so close to the Sun that it took up his whole field of view.

In awe, he watched the Sun's violent eruptions of molten plasma. They looked like flaming fingers dancing in a choreographed ballet over its surface. It was beautiful. But as he watched, it began to change into something much less impressive right before his eyes.

Where there was once orange and yellow burning plasma, holes began to appear all over the Sun. But that wasn't right he thought. They weren't holes. They were more like dents of darkness with no color. Dent after dent appeared until the Sun looked like a honeycomb sphere, rather than a solid mass of fire.

But around the edges of the black dents, there was still orange and yellow fire. Those areas began to fester and grow what looked to be long strings of flapping and swaying fire. String upon string grew out and were joined together all around the sphere. Finally, when the connections were done, he was amazed that around the honeycomb sphere there had now been woven what looked to be a fiery giant spider web.

As he watched the web being formed, sometimes he would see red and orange hot fibers snap off the Sun and be hurled into space. When the web was done, it too became alive, flapping and whipping across the surface of the Sun. So active was the new web structure that more and more long filaments of string began to snap off and be slung in every direction.

He watched one particular active region just below the flaming honeycomb's equator. Churning and burning plasma bubbled in rage, arcing and spitting. The region spat sprays of fire as if they jumped off the Sun, trying to escape.

Turning his head, he watched one particular filament being whipped into space. But before he could turn his head back, from behind him he heard a disconnected fiery string snap off the Sun with a "crack". He turned just time to see that it was aimed right for him.

Automatically he floated to the side, moving easily out of the path of the red hot finger. With amazement, he watched the orange and red string zip past him and expand in width as it rushed forward. Tracking it with his eyes, he realized that it was heading directly for a small blue dot in the distance: Earth.

Instantly he bolted from his perch aside the Sun and accelerated enough to easily overtake the finger of death. Now finding himself well ahead of the burning emission, he stopped to hover above the Earth. So beautiful and blue, it looked like a spinning globe in history class.

He looked over his shoulder and saw that the hot plasma was still a long way off. Turning back to face the blue planet, he noticed something. The black midnight that he saw coming out of the LHC's spinning circle had not yet covered the globe. But now he also saw smaller spinning circles of darkness form in other places, all around the Earth.

He was thinking it wouldn't be long, before the whole planet was covered in darkness. But as he pondered this, he saw the Earth begin to wobble and shake. From his vantage point, it almost looked like a drunkard stumbling. As if the scene couldn't get any stranger, he then saw what looked like plumes and pillars of gray and black smoke belching up into the Earth's atmosphere. Following those puffs, he saw spraying fire coming out of the source of the smoke.

As a detached spectator, he realized that the Earth's crust had destabilized and began to shift violently. At the same time he knew that the Earth's core became super-heated and started expanding. The result playing out before his eyes was severe volcanic activity and mega earthquakes all around the globe.

Wishing that the scene would end, he was caught off guard as a huge wall of water swelled up from the area of the Alaskan Aleutian Islands. The wave kept building and building until finally it was so huge that when it reached the coast of the Pacific, it wiped out everything and everyone in its path.

He looked over his shoulder to see where the finger of fire from the Sun was. It was much closer and he knew it would be only a matter of time before it hit. He turned back to the scene before him.

As he did so, he floated closer to the ground. From this perspective, he could see that war and death broke out on every continent. He saw civilians looting and killing each other. He saw civilians killing the military and the military killing civilians. He saw militaries under the same flag killing and fighting amongst themselves. And worse, in every part of the globe, he saw major conflicts breaking out between countries. Death wrought by war consumed the planet.

He floated back up to get a better look at the globe. Just as he did, he saw pillars of red fiery smoke explode in various countries throughout the globe. From those pillars rose huge mushroom clouds of death.

Closing his eyes he shouted, "NO! STOP!" speaking for the first time.

But when he opened his eyes again, he saw that the darkness that originated from the LHC had now enveloped the whole Earth. He watched as a last mushroom cloud towered above South Korea, and then disappeared as the darkness enveloped it.

Now the ubiquitous darkness was complete and it wrapped the whole Earth.

A roar from behind him caused him to jerk to the side automatically.

And then he watched as the immense burst of plasma that the Sun spewed like a blow torch, burn and boil his home: the Earth.

He hovered, lamenting with tearing eyes when all of a sudden, a piercing loud ringing in his ears caused him to reach for them in pain. Then he became aware that the back of his head felt like it was on fire.

He closed his eyes and when he opened them again, the colors and lines of the scene became blurry. He didn't understand what was happening as his vision went white. Slowly the whiteness dissipated and a myriad of shooting stars consumed his whole field of view. Eventually the stars began to evaporate and a sudden jarring pain at the back of his head screamed for attention.

His ears were still ringing when through the haze; he noticed muffled sounds like someone running through puddles of water. Adding to his confusion, the sounds amplified the pain that he felt at the back of his head.

Ever so slowly, the mass of shooting stars started to blend away. In their place came colors and blurry lines, blended together with indistinctive shapes. Gradually his eyes began to focus. As the shooting stars disappeared; the ringing subsided and then he realized that he was looking up... at familiar faces etched with concern.

"Coop! Come on buddy... don't you die on me! You're too ugly to give mouth to mouth!"

He coughed a few times. He realized that he was lying in the dirt, in the middle of his horse corral.

Carefully he lifted his neck. He looked down at his feet and saw his favorite cowboy boots. Slowly he twirled each foot to make sure he could move. He flexed his fingers and fists. Aside from a headache and a bruised backside, he realized that he was okay.

He coughed again, "MM... Mac? What are you doing here?"

As he looked at his longtime friend, he noticed a few fleeting shooting stars. He also noted the queasy feeling in his stomach and that he felt woozy.

Seeing his old friend made him feel even more confused.

Ranch foreman, Danny Mendez, had Bryce's cowboy hat in hand. As he helped him sit up, he said, "Boss... that was a nasty fall! Anything broken?"

Bryce coughed again. "Ah... no, I don't think so. But I haven't been laid out like that since Uncle Joe threw me across the dojo." Bryce rubbed the back of his head and winced, "How long was I out for?"

Danny and Mac exchanged a confused look.

"Out Boss?" Mendez asked, as he handed his hat back to him. "You were never out. You fell off and we ran right over."

Bryce slowly got to his feet. As he did so, he smacked his black Stetson Cowboy hat against his jeans trying to get the dust off.

Turning to Danny, he said, "Mendez! Whad-a-ya mean I was never out? I had a whole science fiction movie playing out in my head. When I was in dreamland..." then he remembered they weren't alone. Turning back to Mac he said, "Wait a minute..."

With a big Cheshire Cat grin, he grabbed the six-six black man and gave him a massive bear hug.

"What are you doing here?" he said as they broke. Looking around behind Mac, he asked, "You bring Diggs with you?"

"Naw," Mac said as he slapped Bryce on the back. "You're stuck with only me. Made the trip on short notice. He's all caught up at Diamond Light Source in Oxfordshire. You know Diggs. I called him, but he said he was too busy to break away right now. Said he'd try coming out over the summer."

"Yeah, I know Diggs," Bryce said. "Sometimes I think he's a worse workaholic than I ever was!"

Mac shook his head, "Who'd of guessed. Ol' Diggs a big shot Ph.D. running his own atom smasher in England? Makes me a proud papa!"

Bryce knew exactly how Mac felt. He was proud of the young Brit too. And it was more than the Montanan recommending Diggs to Mac. He and Diggs went way back... even though the new Ph.D. Diggs didn't remember.

Putting on his Stetson, Bryce nodded at his friend and said, "Well, it's good to see you just the same. But what in the world are you doing here? Who's running the LHC while you're gone?"

Mac chuckled, "I'll tell you what I'm doing here. I pulled in just in time to see the great Nobel Prize winning Dr. Bryce Obadiah, redneck, Cooper, turned cowboy, fall off of his horse! Man you should've seen yourself!"

Bryce started gimpily walking toward the corral gate with Mac in tow, "Yeah... well, it ain't the first time."

Danny chuckled, "And it probably won't be the last either!"

Bryce gave the twenty-something Hispanic a playful sideways glance, "Who asked you anyway Snowbird? Now get Gabe cleaned up and settled back in the barn. That's enough for me for one day. I'm gonna go take a couple of ibuprofen and show Gabby what the cat drug in."

"You got it Boss," Mendez said lightly with a smile.

Walking straighter, Bryce slapped his friend on the back again, "Seriously Mac, what brings you way out here? In the middle of Montana? You coming from Geneva is a bit out of your way for the entertainment of seeing me fall on my butt? What gives?"

Mac stopped his steady gait. His smile and jovialness disappeared and he looked hard into his friend's eyes. With the worry lines of a distraught man evident all over his face, he said, "We made the modifications to the LHC that you left for me..." and he stopped and dropped his head.

Bryce rolled his hand, as if to say keep going. "Sooooooo..."

Looking at his friend again, he bit his lip and said, "Coop... something happened.... The Collider..." spontaneously the words flooded out of his mouth in a torrent, "The CERN higher-ups directed us to reconfigure the experiment. They wanted us to retrace the steps of an older experiment conducted even before you got there!" he paused with a horrified look in his eyes.

"Whaaattt?" Bryce asked.

Mac was his best friend. But even for him, Bryce wouldn't provide specifications that duplicated his experiment four years ago - before the Reset. The Montanan's fear was palatable. He'd seen what the world's largest machine could do. He wouldn't let that happen again.

So his promise to help Mac with improvements to the collider, and the experiment, had ulterior motives. Yes, it was the least he could do, because he was the one that recommended Mac for the Director's job. But beyond that, as a consultant he could keep tabs on the work and ensure that they didn't venture into a dangerous dimension as he himself did four years before. He'd given Mac just enough information to make the Collider slightly more powerful and efficient. But the news that the big man brought was totally unexpected.

"The thing is...," Mac said, "I know it sounds crazy! But the LHC opened up some kind of portal... an opening or door, or gate... whatever you want to call it. And..." he visibly shivered, "we saw things... creatures, entities... I don't know... beings of some sort. And at the center of them was this bright light that swooped in. It looked to be the leader of these... these things," he shook his head.

"We didn't have a choice. We shut it down. At least until we could figure out what it was. I was going to call you, but I had to notify CERN first. That's when..." he stopped abruptly and hung his head.

The hair on the back of Bryce's neck stood on end. He was a Heinz 57 mix of Spanish, Jewish and American Indian as well as other DNA. His Native American senses saved his life more than once. At present, his built in alarm for self-preservation was tingling.

He knew firsthand about the things that lived on the other side of the dimensional demarcation line. There were good entities... and bad entities. He'd seen them; interacted with them; and was almost killed by a couple of the bad ones. Judging by the look on his friend's face, Mac saw the bad ones.

"That's when what? What happened when you called CERN?" Bryce prompted.

Mac raised his head to reveal misty eyes, "Shortly after I called - a bunch of government types in black suits showed up. They said that the experiment was being terminated immediately. Said it was because of the economic collapse of the European Union a few weeks ago. They said that there weren't enough funds to keep the experiment going. But then..." he paused.

"What?"

The look on Mac's face turned to one of anger, "That's when they evacuated all of the scientists and technicians. My whole team! They demanded that we leave the premises immediately and also that we leave everything just as it was. Heck, they wouldn't even allow us to clean out our desks!

"And get this... a huge contingent of military personnel showed up at the same time. They were wearing UN uniforms for crying out loud! They told us that our services were no longer needed and that we were to vacate the facility immediately. They treated us like criminals! They even revoked our visas!"

Bryce's mouth was open in shock. He and his friend joked all the time. But searching Mac's face, he could see that he wasn't kidding. As long as he'd known Grover Washington McNabb, he'd never seen this look on his face. He was angry and he was scared.

Something was twirling in the back of Bryce's mind as Mac told his story. It was a subconscious thought that was trying to come to the surface. As he grabbed onto the thought, instantly all of the color drained from his face. Looking very pale, he asked a question to which he already knew the answer: "Maaaccc... what was the earlier experiment that CERN had you reconfigure to?"

Mac's eyebrows knitted in confusion, "Operation Falling Star, why?"

Bryce winced, "I was afraid you were going to say that..."

PART ONE

IN THE DAYS

"MAKE THEE AN ARK OF GOPHER WOOD"

THE BOOK OF GENESIS VERSE 6:14

∞

Chapter 2

Bozeman, Montana – Three And A Half Years Earlier

"*C lump, Clump…Clump, Clump*" bounced off of the wooden floor and then died in the aisle. It was the sound that his boots and cane made as he hobbled toward the counter.

Bryce used his cane to support his previously busted leg. Each day he went through a regimen of strenuous physical therapy and Pilates. And, with each day, he could put more weight on it. It was the physicist's hope that soon he wouldn't need the cane it all. He was looking forward to going for a long run.

But his wife, Gabrielle, said that he was trying to do too much, too soon. She might be right, but that didn't stop Bryce from pushing his recovery. Take this trip for example. The doctor just cleared him to drive. And where was his first trip? It was a drive over three hours, and two-hundred plus miles, to Bozeman, Montana of all places.

His wife did vigorously protest. She was angry and called it foolishness. But rather than shrinking at her rebukes, he enjoyed her civilized tirade. Her sing-songy German accent would thickly come out when she was mad… or if she'd been drinking.

Finally calming her down with reason, he told her he was getting cabin fever being struck around the ranch. He promised to take breaks and bring his cell phone. In the end, she saw the determined look on his face and knew she would not prevail. He was going and that was final.

Three hours and many road miles later, he found himself in this very strange store. Despite his protests to his wife, he really didn't know why he came or what he'd find. But something in his gut told him that he needed to prepare. Prepare for what, he didn't know. But from what he heard, this was the place to start.

The sign over the store said, "Safe-Trek Renaissance" and as he approached the counter, Bryce did a double take.

"Naw..." he said under his breath.

"Hi!" said the serious, but friendly looking man from behind the counter, "Can I help you find something?"

Bryce scratched his head and said, "Well, maybe. But can I ask you something first?"

The serious eyed man sized up the physicist. With a quizzical look on his face, he said, "Sure."

"Anyone ever tell you that you look like Jack Nicolson?" Bryce asked.

The serious eyed man, who looked like a fit sixty plus, chuckled. "All the time... Steve Quayle," he said as he stuck out his hand to shake.

Bryce took the man's firm grip and shook. "Bryce Cooper."

Recognition crossed Quayle's serious eyes and they softened, "You mean the physicist Dr. Bryce Cooper?"

"Yeah," Bryce said sheepishly, "that'd be me."

"Ha, I heard you came back to Montana. I was even told to expect you. I just didn't think it'd be so soon."

Told to expect me, Bryce thought? *Who would know I was coming this way?*

In a poker face, belaying his surprise, he tilted his head and asked, "Told? Told by who?"

Quayle shrugged his shoulders and waved his hand, "Ah... long story. Not important." Then changing the subject, he asked, "Didn't you have a ranch up near Missoula?"

This stranger knew an awful lot about him. While normally this kind of thing would make him feel uneasy, he didn't take Quayle as a threat. It was almost like he was supposed to know about him. He got the feeling that this man was an important part of his new life.

Shaking off the thoughts, he said, "Moved back bout six months ago. Decided to make it a permanent stay this time."

"Well... welcome home," Quayle said warmly.

"You know," he continued, "it's funny, I don't usually help at the store. But one of my girls called out sick and they were shorthanded. Thought I'd chip in today. I'm glad I did."

"Yeah? Me too..." Bryce said distractedly, as he looked around.

The establishment appeared to be a cross between a military surplus outlet and an outdoor sports store. In the mix was what looked like organic and dried foods and supplies.

Bryce turned back to Quayle. "Sunglasses"

Quayle pointed and said, "Aisle twelve."

"No, no," Bryce said, "Sunglasses! That's what you're missin. If you were wearing Sunglasses, you'd be a dead ringer for ol' Jack."

Quayle shook his head and smiled, "Boy if I had a dollar every time somebody told me that! So what brings you in today?"

Bryce grinned with embarrassment, "To tell you the truth, I don't really know," he said honestly. "Saw something about your store online. Visited a few chat rooms. Asked around. People had good stuff to say about you... so I decided that I'd come and check it out for myself."

"Is that right?" Quayle said coming around the counter. "So are you a Prepper?"

Bryce shook his head, "Who me? Naw... I'm just an ol' cowboy who came home. Those city folks down in L.A. All flashy. Now they're preppers."

Quayle chuckled, "No, no... I didn't ask if you were a preppy. I was wondering if you were a Prepper. As in Preeee-par-er."

Bryce dropped his head feeling like a dunce, "Oh... of course. That's what this store is all about isn't it?" he said shaking his head at himself.

Bryce looked around the contents of the huge store's shelves and observed the bustling shoppers in its aisles, "Can I ask you a silly question?"

"Sure..."

"People really buy all this stuff?"

Quayle grinned, "Well, it brought you here didn't it?"

Bryce turned back to the man and smiled, "Touché."

"Come on, I'll show you around," Quayle said.

Quayle liked Cooper. A prolific researcher, writer, blogger, talk show guest and at times host, he'd come across Dr. Bryce Cooper's name many times. He'd heard that he was down to earth. The storeowner wasn't disappointed.

Quayle called out to the back room, "Scooter! Can you watch the counter please?"

A tall stocky kid came out from behind a drawn curtain. He had a rag in his hands, wiping them off, "Sure thing Steve."

"Thanks," Steve said.

The two men started down an aisle. With his thumb, Quayle pointed behind them, "Kid plays football at MSU (Montana State University) and works here part time. Big guy like that is great for moving around stock. And he's not a bad bodyguard either."

"Bodyguard?" Bryce asked shocked. "Whad a you need a bodyguard for?"

Quayle smirked and shook his head, "You'd be surprised."

The storekeeper looked down at Bryce's cane, "Was that a horsing accident?"

Bryce chuckled, "You might say that. Looks worse than it is. I'll be back runnin in no time. Almost healed now."

"Glad to hear it," Quayle said sincerely. Turning his attention back to the store, "You wanna grab a cup of tea before we get started?"

It was only nine-thirty in the morning. Bryce got an early start on the long drive and only drank one cup of coffee before he hit the road, "You wouldn't happen to have a cup of coffee would you?"

Quayle shook his head, "Sorry, not a coffee drinker. Just tea, but

I'll make it extra strong if you'd like."

"Sounds good," Bryce said, "Thank you."

"Great... I want to pick your brain anyway," Quayle said like an old friend.

Bryce couldn't put his finger on it. He felt the same way. It was as if Quayle and him were two of a kind.

"Pick my brain?" Bryce asked with a sideways look, "Bout what?"

Quayle stopped in the middle of the aisle and faced Bryce. Looking around to make sure no one was in earshot, he dropped his voice to just above a whisper, and asked seriously, "Do you remember that statue out in front of the CERN facility?"

"Statue?"

"Yeah, you know the one. Just out front. You probably passed it every day."

Bryce held his hand to his chin trying to remember, "I think so."

"Did you ever look at it?"

He shook his head, "No... can't say I did."

"Not in the whole time you worked there?"

Scratching his head, "No... no, what's this about?"

"So if you never looked at it, you probably can't tell me whose likeness it is?"

"Alright Mr. Quayle, just..."

"Steve please"

"Alright Steve... what are you getting at? It's way too early in the morning for twenty questions."

"That stature is the image of CERN's mascot."

"Yeah? So?"

"Since you never really looked at it, you might be interested to know that it is a representation of the Hindu god Shiva."

"Okayyyy"

"Do you know what Shiva is known for?"

"I really hope you're gonna tell me before you give me a cup of tea."

Quayle smiled. *Yes, down to earth*, he thought.

"Shiva," Quayle said, "is also known as... The Destroyer of Worlds."

Bryce's mouth dropped open, "Huh?"

After a few beats, the physicist said, "There must be some mistake."

"No, no mistake my friend. He has other jobs, but that's the one that sticks out to me. So let me ask you this question:" Quayle looked around again to make sure they weren't being overheard, "Why would a world-class organization like CERN have The Destroyer of Worlds as a mascot?"

Bryce scrunched his forehead as he racked his brain. He quickly thought of several reasons, but they were all lame. Shaking his head, he gave up. He couldn't think of one good reason for the choice. After a moment, he said, "I have no idea."

Again Quayle looked around. Then he leaned into Bryce's ear and said, "Three words..." and then dropping his voice to a whisper, he said, "Operation Falling Star."

Bryce's eyes grew wide and he looked like he'd just been slapped. *How could this Bozeman storekeeper know about one of the most closely held secrets of the CERN facility?*

And more importantly... why did he care?

Georgia Guidestones, Elbert County, Georgia – Summer Before

"What are they?" six year old LJ (Little Joe) asked his father.

With a bewildered look on his face, and travel guide in hand, Bryce answered, "I don't rightly know son."

In her sing-songy German accent, his wife Gabrielle, with baby Sarrah on her hip, added "And what are they doing way out here? In the middle of..." she gave a deliberate look around, and then said, "nowhere?"

This was the middle leg of the family's vacation. In the last three and a half years since he returned to the ranch, Bryce gave many lectures on physics and science. A couple of those were in Washington D.C.

But the problem with business travel was that you never got to stop and smell the roses. So with this year's invitation to be the Keynote Speaker at the National Science & Technology Medals Awards Banquet, he brought his family along. And smell they would.

The day after the lecture was over, The Coopers headed out to see the sights of the Nation's capital. After a few days in the city, they rented a car and headed down to Florida.

Bryce had family all over the country. A few of them lived in the southernmost state of the continental U.S. So he decided to pay them a visit. And... while he and his small clan were there, it was a good time to lie around on the white sand beaches.

The physicist meticulously mapped out the three day journey. Included were stops at various sightseeing locations along the way. The Georgia Guidestones was the half-way mark between D.C. and their hotel in Florida. He'd never heard of them, so he thought it was worth a look.

"It says here that somebody by the name of Robert C. Christian went into the Elberton Granite Finishing Company in June of 1979. He told the president of the company that he represented a small group of loyal Americans who believed in god. He then gave the president the specifications for the monument," Bryce flipped the travel guide page, "and interestingly he gave the measurements in metric."

Gabby shrugged her shoulders, "So?"

Bryce smiled at his German wife of almost ten years, "In Europe you've been using the metric system for some time but..."

"They use inches and feet in America... right," she said in understanding.

"Yup. Why someone would come to a small town in Georgia, back in the late seventies, and order a big fancy monument using metric specs, is very strange."

Bryce looked back at the brochure. Reading to himself a little further, he let out a long high whistle.

"What?" Gabby asked curiously.

"Says here that when he asked how much it would cost, it was over six-figures."

"So"

"So apparently the man didn't even flinch. This guy Christian, which was only a pseudonym as it turned out, went..."

"What's a suuu-doe..." LJ asked.

Bryce smiled at his son. He didn't miss much. "It means that it wasn't his real name, fake. It was... kinda like a code name that meant something. Understand?"

"Yeah, I think so," LJ said.

"Anyway, it says here that this guy Christian went right down to the bank and had the full amount wired to the company's account... that same day! Then he insisted on secrecy. Apparently, even to this day, no one really knows who this guy was. Nor does anyone know what the purpose is behind the structure."

Gabrielle shrugged off an involuntary shiver even though the family was baking in the hot Georgia Sun. "Kind of creepy if you ask me," she said.

LJ walked up to the structure. He ran his hand over the words carved in the stone. "Dad, are these all different languages?"

"Yeah..." Bryce consulted the travel guide again, "Says here that each side has a different language, but they all say the same thing."

"What does it say?" the boy asked inquisitively.

Bryce traded a look with his wife, "If you think the story behind this thing is creepy, get a load of this."

She simply shrugged her shoulders as if to say "go ahead".

Bryce walked up next to his son. Reading from the top he told him:

> *"It says, 1) Maintain humanity under 500,000,000 in perpetual balance with nature, 2) Guide reproduction wisely - improving fitness and diversity, 3) Unite humanity with a living new language, 4) Rule passion - faith - tradition - and all things with tempered reason, 5) Protect people and nations with fair laws and just courts, 6) Let all nations rule internally resolving external disputes in a world court, 7) Avoid petty laws and useless officials, 8) Balance personal rights with social duties, 9) Prize truth - beauty - love - seeking harmony with the infinite, 10) Be not a cancer on the earth - Leave room for nature - Leave room for nature."* When he finished he gave his wife a wary look and shook his head.

LJ broke their knowing stare. With head cocked and a confused look, he asked, "Dad... that doesn't sound like very many?"

"Very many what son?" his dad asked.

He looked up in his father's eyes, "People. How many people do we have on the Earth now?"

Again Bryce traded a look with his wife. His son was every bit as bright as he was at that age and he did know his math.

Bryce cleared his throat, "We ah... crossed the seven billion mark a few years ago."

LJ whistled just like his dad, "Boy, five-hundred million is a lot less than that," he pointed to the words on the stone high above his head, "How are they going to get down to that number?"

Again, Bryce traded a look with his wife and shook his head. He looked back at his son's intelligent eyes. For the first time he could remember, he was scared for his future. "I don't know son... I don't know."

After a moment of silence between all of them, Gabrielle cut in with a jovial tone, "Okay, how bout... we hit the road. The white sands of Florida are calling us! Besides," she chuckled with forced humor, "this place gives me the creeps!"

Sarrah clapped and cooed.

Gabby turned tail to head back down the hill to the car.

Bryce put his arm around LJ's shoulder, "Come on son. We got a lot of road to go," he dropped his voice, "and if we find a long straight country road, maybe I'll give you that drivin lesson I promised! But don't tell Mom!"

"Cool!"

Chapter 3

Bozeman, Montana – Three and a Half Years Earlier

*B*ryce had a light sheen of perspiration on his forehead, even though the Fall weather was cool. He could feel his hands twitching. He feared that Steve Quayle would notice the tremble.

Operation Falling Star was an experiment conducted before Bryce ever got to the LHC (Large Hadron Collider) in Geneva, Switzerland. The disinformation generated by CERN's people had diluted the story so much that it was now considered only a fable. CERN , or the European Organization for Nuclear Research, was in charge of the facility. The old acronym CERN came from the previous organization's structure before integration with the European Union. Though now defunct, the acronym stuck.

It was only after his experience of six months ago that Bryce dug into what really happened. In that experiment a portal or hole opened up. This portal allowed an entity, or life form, to be seen through the machine. The story went to say that as soon as people saw it, all of the systems crashed with a computer virus. Later experiments were reconfigured so that the hole could not open again until... Bryce's ATLAS 7 experiment.

Whenever he thought about it, Bryce's gut churned. He'd been used... fooled... duped. The Fallen and the Nephilim, knew exactly what would happen when Cooper made his modifications and boosted power. He knew this because they did it once before with Operation Falling Star.

Falling Star looked like a trial run, perhaps even a mistake. But his experiment six months ago, before the Reset, was different. He was told as much. They wanted to make an opening. And he knew that even though the Reset had occurred, they wouldn't stop trying.

"The Reset" was how Bryce came to think of his second chance. Instead of driving the world toward Armageddon, history had been Reset to the time period of three years before his ATLAS 7 experiment. With that Reset came a new lease on life. He'd become a Believer, recommitted himself to his family, and walked away from his dream job at the LHC to live at his boyhood home, the Lazy Hoof Ranch in Missoula, Montana.

They took their tea outside. Bryce had previously heard Quayle on various radio shows. From what he gathered, he'd been at this conspiracy and Prepper business for at least thirty years.

The man was extremely intelligent, well-spoken and widely versed on many subjects, although certainly not a mainstream media type. From all appearances, he was genuine. If Bryce could learn to sift through the man's extensive research, Quayle could become a treasure-trove of pertinent information. But before he'd believe anything he said, there was one thing he needed to clear up.

He and the storekeeper went out back to a picnic table behind the store. The air was crisp, even cold. They could see white translucent puffs of breath as each of them spoke. Steam curled up off the top of their hot mugs of tea. Bryce's back was to the storekeeper, as he held the warm mug in his hands and looked down a lush ravine with a creek at the bottom.

"Come on Steve, whad-a-ya mean a mutual friend told you I'd be here? Heck I didn't even know that I'd be here," Bryce asked candidly.

Quayle was sitting on the picnic table bench. He dropped his head at the question, "You're going to think I'm crazy. Not that that's unusual. Nearly everyone who hears me for the first time does," he said with grin.

Bryce turned around to face him, "Try me," he said keenly.

"Okay... but don't say I didn't warn you."

Bryce nodded.

"I was in my office this morning before the store opened, having some quiet time."

Bryce knew the phrase to be used by Believers for a time set aside for Bible reading, prayer and meditation.

"The thing is, this time is special. I have it in the morning so I can focus. I never want to be disturbed. So I always lock the door."

Bryce sipped his tea, "Always?"

"Always" Quayle said with certainty. "Anyway, my feet were up on my desk, with my back to the door, and I was reading quietly when all of a sudden..." he paused.

"Go on," Bryce prompted.

Quayle shook his head and got to his feet, "All of a sudden I heard this voice behind me! I was so surprised, it about knocked me out of my chair."

"A voice?"

"Yes, that's right... a voice. And it belonged to someone."

Quayle rounded the table and leaned on its edge with his arms crossed. "I whipped my head around and I saw this young guy standing there!"

"But I thought you said the door was locked?"

Quayle leveled his serious eyes on Bryce, "It was."

"Sooo, what'd this guy look like?"

Quayle looked hard at Bryce. That wouldn't have been the first question he asked. Cooper didn't seem surprised.

"He was approximately six three or four, big broad shoulders, blonde hair and... blue, and I mean really blue, eyes. He was stocky, solid muscle. I'd say he was in his early twenties."

Bryce's head dropped at the news. He took a deep breath.

"Are you okay?" Quayle asked.

Looking up again, "I'm fine. What'd he sound like?"

Quayle cocked his head. He thought the question unusual. The physicist didn't ask what the visitor said... he asked what he sounded like.

"Now that you mention it, I hadn't really thought about that," holding his chin, "His voice was pleasant. And as I think about it, even though he just showed up in my office... and I'd never seen him... I didn't feel threatened, shocked, or nervous. It had to be his voice. The way he spoke... it was in a sing-songy way. Kind of..."

"Melodious?" Bryce posed.

Quayle's eyes narrowed, "Yes... that's right. Melodious is a good description." he paused, "You know this guy?"

Ignoring the question, Bryce asked, "Did he happen to say what his name was?"

Eyeing Bryce suspiciously, Quayle said "As a matter of fact. When he got done telling me what he told me, he said his name was Gabe."

Bryce staggered back like he was hit in the jaw at hearing the name. Quayle reached out to steady him, "Are you okay? Here, sit down before you fall down."

Bryce sat. He looked like he was going to throw up.

The physicist cleared his throat, "What did he say?"

"Here's the thing," Quayle, in a rapid-fire delivery, said, "when he left, I checked the door. It was locked! I've had some crazy experiences in my life, but this one was..."

"What did he say," Bryce asked more forcefully.

"Right," Quayle said, "He gave me your exact description. He said Bryce Cooper was coming to see me. He told me to answer all of your questions. And he stressed that word ALL. Then he told me I was supposed to teach you what you needed to know."

Bryce looked like he was going to start hyperventilating, "What do I need to know? I don't even know what I don't know!"

"I asked him that too... what you needed to know. All he said was that I would know when the time came."

Bryce's head dropped and he shook it, "Grreaaattt... That sounds just like him."

Quayle asked again incredulously, "You know this guy?"

Recovering, "You might say that," Bryce said. He looked up, "What else did he say?"

Quayle sighed, "Even though I'd known about it before, he's the one that told me to talk to you about Operation Falling Star."

Bryce stood abruptly up in anger. "Great! That's just great! Why didn't he say anything about it before?" he said to himself.

"Before?"

Bryce looked over at Quayle. He remembered he wasn't alone, "He say anything else? Anything at all?!"

Quayle shook his head, not quite understanding what was going on, "Only one other thing. He said... and I quote - he's coming."

"He's coming?" Bryce asked with a scrunched up face, "Who's coming?"

The storekeeper shrugging his shoulders, "I don't know. He didn't say. Just that: He's coming. Then I dropped my feet off my desk and spun around and... he was gone!"

"He's coming?" Bryce said under his breath.

"So who was this guy anyway?"

Bryce was slowly pacing with his cane – thinking.

Finally he looked over at Quayle's questioning gaze, "I guess you could call him my Guardian Angel."

SURF, Dorking Surrey, UK – Present Day

Dr. Alvaro Mora was a world renowned Helio Astronomer. His specialty was all things to do with the Sun.

He was a naturalized American citizen originally from Costa Rica. Remembering those humble beginnings, regardless of the awards and accolades he'd received, kept him balanced and level headed. Admittedly it was that, and his beautiful, but stern wife Zoraida.

Zoraida was also Costa Rican, although from a much smaller city than Alvaro. They'd been married nearly fifty blissful years. He'd sired five wonderful daughters and two great sons. Adding to their joy, they were blessed with nearly too many grandchildren to count. And their oldest granddaughter, Azlynn and her husband just gave them their first great-grandchild.

In his mid-sixties, the not quite average height Dr. Mora had gray thinning hair, a friendly wit and a thick Spanish accent. His close longtime friend Daniel in California often joked that he looked like a Latin Mr. Magoo... especially when he was driving.

A hard worker all of his life, he was looking forward to retirement by this time next year. In preparation, he'd arrested his high blood pressure and cholesterol. If he could finally take it easy, he wanted to enjoy a long life with good health. On late work nights like this, he would daydream about spending more time with his family in the land of his birth. He wanted desperately to go fishing for marlin with his cousin in the blue Caribbean waters off the east coast of Costa Rica.

Concentrating again, he pushed aside the wistful thoughts that attempted to distract him from the pressing duties of the night. His current assignment was at SURF, The Solar UK Research Facility, just outside of London. This final posting of his career may be less glamorous than earlier positions, but it afforded him the opportunity to teach. Educating young up and coming scientists was a longtime passion. And with Oxford University only an hour and a half away, he had the best of both worlds: practical science and instruction.

When they came to England four years ago, he and Zoraida were fortunate to find a small, yet comfortable thatched roof cottage in Gerrards Cross. They were only forty minutes by train to London and half way between SURF and Oxford. Dr. Mora, or The Professor as he was called, split his time between lecturing at the university two days a week and working at his SURF office the other three days.

Lost in thought, he was sitting in front of his SURF computer observing in real time the views from the aging SOHO A and SOHO B satellites (SOHO - Solar and Heliospheric Observatory). The two satellites were placed in orbit around the Sun, ahead and behind the Earth. "A" was the one in front of the Earth's orbit and "B" was behind the Earth's orbit. Their jobs were to give a constant, uninterrupted view of the Sun from its deep core to the outer corona and also to observe the solar wind.

In recent years, The Professor gained international recognition for his observations of increased solar activity. While not earthshattering, these observations were done during a time that the Sun should have been less active. This peculiar behavior of Earth's solar system's star, and Dr. Mora's hypothesis regarding the increased activity, ruffled more than a few feathers.

He observed that although the Sun was on an eleven year cycle, it appeared to be unusually active during the waning years of the cycle. Mora noted that on November 4, 2003, when the cycle should have been relatively calm, a massive CME (Coronal Mass Ejection) or Solar Flare, popped off the Sun. The flare was one of the largest and longest on record. It rated at an estimated X45 flare. So strong was the aberration, that it prompted Helio Astronomers like himself to add additional strength ratings to the solar flare rating system.

If the CME occurred three months later, the Earth's orbit around the Sun would have taken the blue planet directly into the on-coming flare. The thought made Dr. Mora shudder.

He studied a series of solar storms in the 1870's. At a time before the advent of modern electronics or communications, some of those storms were so strong that they caused fires to break out at telegraph offices all over the world. It was said that because of the intense inductive current in the air, operators no longer needed to connect their bases to batteries to send messages.

"Amazing," The Professor whispered to himself.

One could only imagine what would happen to a modern Earth that depended on electricity, should a storm of that magnitude ever strike the planet now. *Bad things...* he thought.

Bringing his thoughts to the present, he shook his head as he viewed tonight's data. The Sun had been belching huge CMEs over the last few days. Given the lateness of the cycle, the activity was both unusual and alarming. Fortunately thus far all of the eruptions were directed away from the Earth. But Mora knew it was only a matter of time. And the massive explosions from the star were building.

With the size of the eruptions, the danger to life on planet Earth was extreme. Should such a flare hit Earth... the world would be thrown back into the Stone Age... if not much worse.

The Professor scratched his thinning gray head. In addition to the problems with the Sun, there was some other data, seemingly unassociated with the CMEs, which called to him.

He had a theory bouncing around in the back of his mind; one that he only voiced to one other person. That was because it was just too crazy to discuss openly. Nonetheless, he was quickly coming to the conclusion that there were no other explanations for the increased solar activity, and the degradation of the Earth's magnetic field. There had to be a correlation

Dr. Mora couldn't shake the burning feeling in the pit of his stomach. He opened the top drawer of his desk. Pulling out a half empty bottle of Pepto-Bismol, he took a giant gulp. Tossing the bottle back in the drawer, he wiped his mouth with the back of his hand.

A massive X flare, pointed directly at Earth, could erode, if not erase, the Earth's protective plasma clouds that surround her. If that were to happen, satellites, power grids and other technology based on electricity would fail.

It would be the end of modern civilization.

Chapter 4

SURF, Dorking Surrey, UK – Present Day

*H*is theory all fell into place for him a week ago. The latest round of solar flares, coupled with new information on FTEs (Flux Transfer Events), provided the necessary remaining pieces of the puzzle.

A FTE, or Flux Transfer Event, opens every eight minutes over the Earth. It is a literal magnetic portal, or conduit, that connects the Sun to the Earth's Magnetosphere. Through this conduit, simple high energy particles would flow to the planet from the Sun.

While the solar flares could potentially fry the planet and were disturbing on their own, he thought that he'd seen something in the FTEs that was even more alarming. As he was reviewing the data last week, he'd inadvertently slowed down the data feeds coming from the European Space Agency's (ESA) four Cluster spacecraft and NASA's THEMIS probes. Both of these programs were responsible for observing and reporting FTEs.

He was stunned by what he thought he'd glimpsed. Little by little, Mora put together a mosaic of unbelievable results. As he dug deep, he found that something nefarious was riding the FTE conduits, to and from the Sun. Those "something"s were so disconcerting that at first he'd dare not mention his suspicions to anyone, lest they think he was crazy.

Preparing to leave for the evening, he went to load fresh data for his weeklong vacation. Shaking his head, he mumbled, "That's not right!"

After a few clicks of the mouse and additional keys punched, the results were the same.

"What?!" he said aloud.

Again, the bile in his stomach began to creep up his esophagus. He ignored it as his hands flew over the keyboard and mouse. Each time he came up with the same results. He checked and rechecked.

He knew that systems and data bases all over the world were redundant. He visited several sites and looked into their archives. If real-time data was corrupted, they should at least have correct data on their backup. Yet, the data that he knew should be there... was gone.

Over an hour later, he flopped back in his chair, mentally exhausted. He tried to think of all the reasons why the data would be missing from all the databases throughout the science community. Nothing made sense. He sat perplexed, distressed and spent in front of the computer.

He felt a burning pain in his gut and he grabbed his stomach. Opening the desk's top drawer again, he reached for the pink bottle of medicine. This time he tilted it straight up in the air and drained it. Empty bottle in hand, he stood abruptly. Angrily he threw the plastic bottle at the trash can. It hit the rim and ricocheted across his office floor before coming to a spinning rest in the middle of the floor.

Standing behind his desk, he leaned on it with locked elbows. He needed to figure out what was going on. He'd double checked the Deep Space Network, the Goddard Space Flight Center archives, NASA's archives and even the ESA's info. All of the data from every single database pertaining to his observations and hypothesis, and subsequent data on the FTEs, were gone. Worse, now the images and data showed only normal solar activity with no increase!

Impossible, he thought! *Data and visual records didn't just vanish!*

He leaned back down to look at his screen again. He clicked the mouse a couple of times to show a recent video capture from

SOHO A - That's when he saw it.

To his trained eye, he saw the recording jump. He ran it again. The same result.

"Qué es esto?! (What is this?!)," he asked bitterly.

Someone switched the film. He knew it! They replaced it with observations of normal activity. Quickly he checked other sites. The same results!

He again sat back in his chair. Scratching his head, in a low purposeful voice, he asked, "Why would someone do that?"

Such a charade would be no small task, he thought. *The Deep Space Network was a high profile and highly secure agency. Action of this type would not be done by mistake...*

"It was deliberate?" he asked himself in his Spanish accent, stunned at his own words. He thought back to the events surrounding the discoveries.

He followed protocol. It required him to notify his superior prior to any announcement to the media. Now that he thought about it, he was still waiting to hear back. That's what he'd been doing this evening: preparing a statement to go public.

Then it hit him: The data disappeared after he alerted his superior.

"Why?"

His agency was currently being very tight lipped with information being leaked to the public. Given the potential for a global disaster caused by a rogue solar flare, he could understand their caution. They, nor he, wanted to start a world-wide panic. But this... removing the data... it was unconscionable.

And why now? It would only give them a few days at the most. Eventually the news would get out. Some amateur astronomer would see what was happening with the Sun and make a YouTube video of it. It would probably go viral and they would have to answer for the cover-up. It made no sense.

What to do next, he wondered as he strummed his fingers on his desk.

He could speak to his superior again, but he was a government type, likely to tell him that he made a mistake. Worse, he could suggest that he was growing senile in his advanced age. Then he would suggest, perhaps even demand that Alvaro retire. Retirement sounded good, but he didn't want to go out like that. And he sure didn't want to leave things undone. He had to try to get the information out some way.

Then it came to him.

He picked up his battered old briefcase from the floor. Hands moving quickly, he set it on the desk and opened it, rifling through the thick wad of papers and files. Near the bottom, he pulled out the DVD on which he'd recorded his first observations and data.

Most young scientists on the network didn't take the time to record a hardcopy of observations. They'd rather use the storage in cyberspace. Not him; he was old school. He wanted to touch, feel and examine those things that he thought were important.

He opened his laptop and put in the disc. Then he zipped the file to his hard drive. Next, he encoded the file in an old algorithm that he was sure only the recipient would know. He started to sign into his email, when he promptly stopped himself.

He closed his eyes and placed his finger over his lips in deep concentration. His laptop was at the moment connected to the building's wireless network. If he sent the file from his office, those who erased the data would know his recipient.

His eyes snapped opened.

He looked at his watch: seven-thirty. It was the Friday night before the official start of his vacation. He and Zoraida rented an out of the way cottage in Cornwall on the water. His daughters

Stephanie and Vanessa flew in with Vanessa's daughter Delilah. His granddaughter Azlynn also made the trip with her two year old.

The plan called for Zoraida and the girls to head to the Cornwall vacation cottage that afternoon. He promised her that he would finish early and meet them all there that evening. He already worked longer than he intended by a couple of hours. She called again a short while ago and he promised he would be leaving soon.

Cornwall was a good four hour trip from where he was. If he didn't leave now, he wouldn't arrive until after midnight. He didn't like driving at night because of deteriorating night vision. And the narrow, winding road that traversed the last ten miles of the trip was treacherous even in the daytime. He sighed, he had to leave now.

Quickly he reached for his laptop and switched the machine to hibernate, then slid it in its case. Next he crammed more work in his already overstuffed briefcase. After all, he wasn't retired yet.

Lastly, he threw his cell phone on top of everything and closed the case. He stood to his feet and patted himself down, looking for his keys. As he was doing so, he spied them on his desk where he dumped them after lunch.

Lunch? Snatching them up, he suddenly realized he was famished. He hadn't eaten for a good twelve hours. No wonder the acid in his stomach burned.

He snapped the metal briefcase clasps down with a "click". Once more he scanned his desk. Finding that he had everything, he threw the laptop strap over his shoulder, picked up his briefcase and headed for the door.

The thought of conspiracies would have to wait.

Down in the lobby, the slightly overweight guard sat in

front of a bank of security screens. The displays showed different vantage points from both inside and outside the facility. Down the corridor from Dr. Mora's office was a camera installed high in the corner. Clearly Dr. Mora could be seen with his laptop and briefcase. The guard knew that he was finally leaving for the evening.

Silently he snatched up the phone and dialed the number. It rang twice before the other end picked up.

Without introductions, in a Cockney accent, the guard said, "It looks like 'e's leavin' for the evenin'. 'e 'as 'is briefcase and laptop in St. Martins-Le-Grand. (It looks like he's leaving for the evening. He has his briefcase and laptop in hand.)"

A cold voice on the other end replied, "Have you been monitoring his calls this evening?"

"Yeah, there 'aven't any outside calls on the chuffin' landline. The bleedin' only incomin' call on 'is Flowery Dell was from 'is trouble and strife Bo-le Of Glue 'ours ago. (Yes, there haven't any outside calls on the landline. The only incoming call was on his cell from his wife two hours ago.)"

"And his network activity?" the voice asked.

The guard pecked a few keys on the console. He studied the screen and said, "It looks loike there were nah emails sent or video conferencin' done. 'e 'as accessed 'is usual sites a few times this evenin'. (It looks like there were no emails sent or video conferencing done. He has accessed his usual sites a few times this evening.)"

"I see..." the cold voice said lost in thought.

"Wot do ya want me ter do? (What do you want me to do?)" the guard asked.

"Nothing. This call never happened," and the line went dead.

The guard's rather thick lower lip curled down in irritation. He slowly replaced the phone handset.

About a week ago, he was approached by the cold voice and

offered a large sum of money to keep tabs on Dr. Mora's activities and schedule. While he liked the old man, with the economy crashing, the guard like everyone in Europe was desperate. Besides, these people paid in gold coin. At the time, the guard didn't see any harm in watching the scientist. It wasn't like he was being hired to kill him or anything.

The ding of the elevator reaching the lobby pulled the guard out of his thoughts. He looked up.

"'eadin' aahhht earlier than usual professor? (Heading out earlier than usual Professor?)" the guard asked in his friendly way.

Mora was walking at a good clip. He was obviously in a hurry.

"Yes, yes," he said to the guard. As he passed the high guard counter, he rapped twice on its top quickly. "Heading out on holiday George. Wife's waiting for me. Gonna have to do a little work while I'm away," he said while still on the move and not looking back.

Of course the guard George knew that Dr. Mora was going on holiday (vacation). He'd already reported this information to the cold voice.

But that wasn't enough. The voice insisted that George find out where The Professor was staying, and exactly when he would be leaving. As extra incentive, he was given a nice bonus for his efforts. Somehow the guard knew that the voice was monitoring the good doctor's departure even now. The thought made him shudder.

Calling to The Professor's back with a smile, he shouted, "Doc, don't ya kna that you're supposed ta sla daahhhn before ya retire? (Doc, don't you know that you're supposed to slow down before you retire?)"

"Wouldn't that be nice?" Mora called back. He briefly paused, turned and saluted, as he said, "Night George!" Then he spun around and pushed through the glass doors.

Staring as the glass doors slowly swung shut, the guard said, "Night Doc... be safe."

George continued to stare at the now closed glass doors for a long time. He pondered the reasons why someone would want to keep tabs on The Professor. The thought caused all of the blood to drain from his face.

Slowly his eyes drifted down to the phone on the desk, "What have I done?"

Chapter 5

__Tel Aviv, Israel – Present Day__

Zac emerged from his front door and paused to take in a deep breath through his nostrils. The warm air blowing off the nearby water immediately filled his lungs with the salty sweetness of the Mediterranean Sea. He smiled to himself.

"Good morning Zac!" his neighbor called to him from his porch next door.

Jostled out of his reverie, he looked over, smiled, and said in a guttural Yiddish/English accent, "And Good morning to you Josiah! And to you as well Eleazar," he added, greeting the ancient looking man sitting next to Josiah in a chair.

Josiah was his neighbor's full name. It also happened to be of Hebrew origin. The two men, neighbors for the last three years, had developed a cordial friendship. His neighbor, Joe, took to calling the Israeli "Zac", as the American substitute for his given Hebrew name. In turn, Zac would call Joe, by his Hebrew name. It was a running joke between the two men.

Joe and his wife Ruby immigrated to Israel three years ago from Montana. Joe was a Gentile (non-Jewish by blood or practice), but Ruby had distinct Jewish blood running through her veins. And that was all that was needed for the charming couple to be welcomed back to her homeland.

Joe and Ruby grew up on the hard work of ranch life. Joe's best friend, Jerry Cooper, married Ruby's sister Grace Ann. The four of them were nearly inseparable. And when Jerry and Grace Ann decided to turn their fledging cattle operation outside of Missoula, Montana to a horse breeding ranch, Joe and Ruby joined in the labor pro bono.

Little did they know that Jerry would be killed in a horse accident, and Ruby's sister Grace Ann, would die of cancer only a few years later. Those tragedies made an orphan out of Joe's genius adolescent nephew, Bryce Cooper. The couple loved Bryce like he was their own. But soon, the brilliant teen would graduate school early and run off to college.

Even after Bryce left, Joe and Ruby made the most of the situation. They managed to turn the ranch around by putting out more than a few champions. But the hard work of ranch life took its toll on Joe's body. These days, his back gave him fits. He figured that whatever easy life he had now, like sitting on the porch and drinking coffee, he'd earned.

Eleazar was the elderly man sitting next to Joe and was Joe's neighbor on the other side. The old man was more Jewish than most of the people who lived in Tel Aviv. A survivor of the Nazi concentration camps during World War II, his was a full Hebrew heritage.

The Jeweler migrated to Israel almost four years ago. He had a shop in Geneva, Switzerland for decades. As the old man told the story, he had an epiphany regarding his life and beliefs. That experience prompted him to finally move to the Eretz (the Land of Israel).

Tel Aviv was right on the Mediterranean. It was ideal for retirement and Joe and Eleazar would spend countless hours talking, drinking strong coffee, and eating.

I wish I could enjoy life as much as these two, Zac thought wistfully.

But such was not his lot in life. In his late fifties, he and his wife were married almost thirty years. This was his second marriage. His first wife and infant young daughter were killed in the 1976 Yom Kippur War.

While he loved his current wife dearly, he'd never gotten over losing his first family. He fought hard to stifle the bitterness in his belly he felt toward his Arab neighbors. But persevere he did.

Like all men in Israel, as a young teenager until his early twenties, he spent time as a conscript in the IDF (Israeli Defense Force). But even after his compulsory time was done, he found himself fighting again in his late-twenties, when Israel was attacked by her Arab neighbors.

That conflict taught him much. It taught him to never let his guard down. It also taught him that things were rarely as they appeared. As testament to that, his current life was a good example.

He was a successful Finance Minister for the present Israeli administration. But, because of his Jewish Orthodox faith and government position, he developed significant religious contacts in the Temple Reconstruction Movement (TRM). Such affiliations were unusual given the secular state of the government and most people who lived in Israel.

His countrymen's perspective of him was that of a man behind the scene in politics; a mover and shaker. Very few knew of his religious affiliations and absolutely no one knew of his third, most secretive, position that he held. So secret was this work, that even his wife was clueless about it.

"And what does this beautiful day hold for you two?"

"...and around Europe, the dire financial conditions have contributed to an increased suicide rate. In other news, soaring temperatures around the globe have touched off numerous wildfires and violent thunderstorms..."

Joe held his hand to his ear. Then he reached down and turned off the radio he and Eleazar were listening to while sipping their morning coffee.

"What was that?" Joe asked, hand still to his ear.

Smiling and shaking his head, Zac repeated himself, "So what are you two up to today?"

"Well..." Joe said in his deliberate Montanan drawl, "seems to me that my pal here and I may just need to go to the market today. Think we need to rustle up some desert for dinner tonight."

He looked to the older man, "Sound good?"

Eleazar, in the best cowboy impression he could muster, gave a long drawn out, "Yee-upp."

Redirecting to Zac, he said, "You're still comin over right? Made sure it's all kosher. No babybacks. Just beef."

"Yes, yes of course. I need to make a quick trip to Jerusalem. But I should be back for your famous barbeque ribs."

"Good... cause if you weren't, I'm afraid my friend here," Joe pointed to Eleazar with his thumb, "would feel the need to eat your portion."

With a warm smile, and rubbing exaggerated circles on his stomach, the old man said, "Yee-upp."

"And how's the arm?" Joe asked as he pointed to the sling around Zac's neck.

Zac looked down. His left arm was still heavily bandaged. He shrugged, and then grimaced as punishment for the absent minded gesture. "It's fine, just a flesh wound. I'll be using it again in no time."

The "flesh would" that he was referring to was the 7.62x39mm round of an Egyptian AK-47 that ripped through his muscle. He was very fortunate that the bullet didn't break the bone or hit his artery. In that sense, he was telling the truth, it was only a flesh wound, though not the kind he alluded to.

Along with that wound, Zac had cuts and scrapes on his face from spraying rocks and sand kicked up during last week's firefight. He was very fortunate to have walked away from such a dangerous op.

However, this was of course, not what he told people. When asked what happened, he'd simply said that he got in a car wreck last week when he was out of country.

"I guess I'll just have to eat one handed!," Zac said. "I probably need to get going so as to get back in time. "Talk to you two later... and Josiah?"

"Yeah?"

"Stay out of trouble will you?"

"Ha! Son, trouble's my middle name! See you tonight!"

Zac waved to the two men and grimaced as he slid behind the wheel of his specially enhanced Mazda 3. Truth be told, his arm hurt like heck. He turned the key and the car, along with the radio instantly came to life:

"...but the American Ambassador has assured his Israeli counterpart that regardless of financial stresses on the American financial system, the United States' commitment to Israel would remain steadfast. In other news, seismic activity around the world has spiked drastically, leaving scientists to wonder if the latest increased Sun activity has affected the Earth's magnetic field..."

He reached over and turned down the radio. Zac smiled to himself as he took a last look at the men reclining on the porch. As he backed out of his parking space, he thought to himself: *I do believe you are telling the truth Josiah; trouble could be your middle name.*

Shaking his head, he put the car in drive. Although the American was nearly 70, he carried himself like much more than a country boy. Zac had no doubt that Joe could take care of himself.

Zac liked him. He was unpretentious and down to earth. Those were two qualities that were sorely lacking in his world. But more than anything, he trusted him... so he owed him the truth.

Zac's training taught him how to surveil anyone. He used this skill just after Joe and Ruby moved next to him. It didn't take long for him to figure out that Joe was exactly who he represented himself to be: Honest and hardworking.

Normally things would have dropped there. But something surfaced in that short investigation that turned out to be of paramount importance to his country. This was reported back to his religious contacts at TRM. The information was filed away and forgotten... until last week's op.

The use of this information would not directly affect Josiah. But the truth would come out. It was better if it came from Zac. The Israeli owed him that much.

To tell the American the truth, Zac would have to take him into his confidence. That alone made him uneasy. He just hoped that when Joe found out what his neighbor learned and how, he would be forgiving. Zac hated to think of the consequences of escalation.

Time was running out. The call might have already been placed. Soon, an unexpected visitor would show up on Josiah's doorstep. And then things could get ugly.

"I'll talk to him tonight," he said aloud, as he merged onto the road to Jerusalem.

Then he reached over and turned up the news again:

> "...Tabak, Syria's Prime Minister, has called a press conference for tomorrow promising a very important announcement that is said to change the shape of the Middle East forever..."

With furrowed brow, Zac looked at his dashboard radio. Speaking to the unseen newscaster, he said, "Not before we change it first."

Bozeman, Montana – Three And A Half Years Earlier

Shaking his head, Bryce said under his breath, "That guy sure gets around..."

Not quite hearing him, Quayle said, "Scuse me?"

"Nothing," Bryce answered blowing out a heavy breath. "So I guess you're supposed to be my Sensei?"

"Your what?"

"You know... my Sensei. Like a master martial arts instructor teaching a student?"

Quayle smirked, "I like that."

Changing the subject, Bryce asked, "Didn't I see a book that you wrote on giants?" .

"Yes, it's called Genesis 6 Giants."

Bryce's eyes got big, "Hold on... you mean Genesis 6 giants like the Nephilim?"

"That's right... You know about the Nephilim?"

Bryce gaffed, "Been up close and personal! What can you tell me about 'em?"

Quayle shook his head, "You are a strange one Dr. Cooper."

"Yeah, I've been told. Coop, please. It's what's all my friends call me."

"So what do you want to know about them?" Quayle asked. "You want to hear about ancient giants or do you want to know about modern giants? Should I tell you about giant skeletal remains in the Middle East and Europe, or do you want to know about giant skeletal remains right here," he said waving his arms, "in North America? There are..."

"Hold on," Bryce's eyes lit, "skeletal giant remains here?"

Quayle's smirk disappeared. He pointed to the southwest, and in a breathless, continuous sounding run-on sentence, he said, "In 1833, soldiers digging at Lompock Rancho, California discovered a male skeleton 12 feet tall. It had double rows of upper and lower teeth. Unfortunately, the body was secretly buried because the local Indians became upset about the remains." He pointed to the east, "Large mounds in Illinois were discovered in 1835 to contain huge skeletons, one of which was over eight feet in length with a correspondingly large skull, with many other skeletons measuring at least seven feet tall." He pointed to the southeast, "Large bones in stone graves in Williamson County and White Country Tennessee were discovered in the early 1800's. The average stature of these giants was seven feet tall."

He started counting on his fingers without breaking stride, "Several giant skeletons were found in the mid-1800's in New

York State near Rutland and Rodman." He went to another finger, "A giant skull and vertebrae was found in Wisconsin and Kansas City," and another finger, "A giant found off the California coast on Santa Rosa Island in the 1800's was distinguished by its double rows of teeth," and another finger, "In Ohio in 1872, an earthen mound was discovered to contain three skeletons that in life would have stood at least eight feet tall. Each also had double teeth in front as well as in back of their mouth and in both upper and lower jaws."

Then he stopped using his fingers and continued in rapid-fire succession, "A nine-foot, eight-inch skeleton excavated from a mound near Brewersville, Indiana, in 1879. Skeletons of, and I quote, enormous dimensions, end quote, were found in mounds near Zanesville, Ohio and Warren Minnesota in the 1880's. Miners in Lovestock Cave, California, discovered a very tall, red-haired mummy in 1911. This mummy eventually went to..."

Holding his hands up against the barrage of facts, Bryce said, "Okay! Okay! I get it! Giants roamed North America! How do you keep all those facts in your... hold on," he paused, "did you say that some giants had red hair?"

"Yes..." Quayle said, wondering why, out of everything he just spit out that Cooper lit on red hair.

Bryce turned his back on Quayle and leaned on the picnic table top. Shaking his head, he said, "So did mine..."

Chapter 6

Pasadena, California – Present Day

𝒯 he career of a scientist, particularly a geophysicist, was afforded to only those individuals who had a deliberate mindset. Scientists and the scientific method, did not lend itself to emotion. One must gather information and, based upon the facts, render a logical hypothesis that was supported by said facts. At least that is what a scientist was supposed to do.

But Evan Young was scared. As irrational as it sounded, even to him, he couldn't shake the feeling that this was beyond human capabilities. Beyond even earthly possibilities. It just didn't make sense.

Yet, there he stood in his CalTech office, examining the geologic activity from the last two weeks. Almost overnight, the Earth started to rebel as it wobbled and groaned.

The activity started six months ago. At first there were small earthquake swarms. These were only minor tremblers that were followed by days of inactivity. And then straightaway, just two weeks ago, the real shaking started. And then they began to build and become more consistent and severe.

Inexplicably "mega" quakes started popping off all over the globe. Perhaps that was the most troubling thing to Evan; the Earth's activity was not localized to normal trouble spots.

For instance, there had been earthquakes throughout the middle of America. There were also large earthquakes throughout Europe. There had even been earthquakes at both the North and South poles. These were perhaps the most troubling.

America... Evan thought. Most people were familiar with the San Andreas Fault that ran nearly the length of California. That fault was overdue for a significant earthquake.

But hardly anyone knew about the Cascadia Sub-duction Zone off the coast of Washington, Oregon and Northern California. That area was equally overdue for a significant quake. However, should one strike there, a huge tsunami was sure to be generated. Many people would die.

And then of course there was the New Madrid fault. Its power renowned for the late 1800 quakes in which one was so strong, it caused the mighty Mississippi River to run backwards for a time.

Rapidly activity in these areas grew exponentially.

Despite what he was told to report to the public, the opposite was true. As instructed, in interviews he and his people would say that with every quake, pressure was being released from faults. "It was a good thing to have earthquakes. It made for a more stable Earth."

Evan knew it was a crock. Worse, in his gut he felt that the seismic pressure was increasing rather than dissipating. He feared that it would grow to the point where a significant event would occur: a mega quake in America's own backyard. Huge metropolises now resided all along fault lines. The death toll would be massive.

And then there were the quakes off the northwest seaboard of North America and the Aleutian Islands. Those tremors were also building. Add to this the dramatic activity around the "Ring of Fire". Volcanoes that were active became even more active; long dormant volcanoes were beginning to roar to life; even ancient extinct volcanoes were now showing activity.

The "Ring of Fire" was the name of an oblong circular area of the Pacific where various tectonic plates of the Earth's crust met. This area stretched from the Aleutian Islands all the way down to New Zealand, and as far east as Japan and as far west as California. Historically it had always been known for its seismic and volcanic activity. But of late, the Ring of Fire became alarmingly alive.

Of course the dreaded Yellowstone Caldera and little known Canary Island volcanoes even showed increased tremors over the last couple of weeks. These two volcanoes were perhaps to be feared most of all. If either of them were to go, a lot of people would die.

He scratched his bald head in confusion. "This makes no sense..." he said to himself in frustration. It was as if, some unknown force... some outside influence, was causing the Earth's molten core to expand; to force its way to the surface.

The Earth's crust, the outer most surface, was anywhere between 3 to 50 miles thick, depending on where it was measured. It was also made up of approximately 47% oxygen. *That's not a lot of protection for what lies underneath the surface,* Evan mused.

The monster beneath was the almost 2000 mile thick mantel. This mantel was made up of boiling and churning lava, or magma. Should the monster decide to roar, it could eject super-heated silicate melted rocks, rich iron and magnesium and catapult them from volcanoes all over the Earth.

The center of the monster was the core. It was made up of two parts. The solid inner core was hypothesized to be about seven-hundred and fifty miles thick. The liquid outer core was thought to be over two-thousand miles thick and made up of eighty percent iron.

Evan shook his head. Even the best efforts of mankind could only drill down a little more than two miles. That happened at the Kola Superdeep Borehole in Murmansk, Russia. All of this was guess work. Sometimes he felt like an accountant, just making up numbers to make them fit together. How could any simple human fathom what was going on beneath the Earth's surface, especially now.

And in the midst of all this craziness, the USGS, a government agency, was ordered not to accurately report this activity. Seismic activity was routinely omitted from their websites. Where a trembler couldn't be ignored, it was severely downgraded.

Inexplicably, he, the Director of the world's leading organization on geological matters, was being muzzled. He was told that it was for the greater good... to avoid a world-wide panic. His superiors lamely assured him that it was just an active period in the Earth's history and, just as it always did, it would settle down soon enough.

"Ridiculous..." he said quietly to himself in disgust.

He wondered if his bureaucratic supervisors were that foolish or if they suffered from "Normalcy Bias".

Normalcy Bias referred to a certain mental state that people found themselves in, in the face of a disaster. Normalcy Bias according to Wikipedia often resulted in situations where people failed to adequately prepare for a disaster, especially on a larger scale. There was documented evidence where governments failed to include the populace in its disaster preparations.

Worse, Normalcy Bias was the assumption that since a disaster had never occurred; it would never occur. This was especially dangerous because it resulted in the inability of people to cope with a disaster once it did occur.

People with a Normalcy Bias had difficulties reacting to something they never experienced before. These people tended to interpret warnings in the most optimistic way possible. Often they would seize on any ambiguities to infer a less serious situation.

Evan shook his head again. It sure sounded like his bosses. But privately he wondered if their non-disclosure was for more nefarious reasons. He heard his youngest sister's new husband speak about conspiracy theories and the New World Order. Over last Thanksgiving, he told of how a shadow government wanted to significantly reduce the population.

Evan wrote it off as insane, tactfully changing the subject. But now, watching how his supposed sane bosses were ignoring the problems staring them in the face, his brother-in-law sounded more sane with each passing hour.

They were in such denial, that he couldn't even speak to them about what he thought was a worse case scenario. It was, to put it bluntly, that Earth was about to enter into its latest pole shift.

Pole shifts occurred throughout Earth's history, and in most cases, violently. It was the literal flipping of the north to south and south to north poles, or anywhere in between. Clues of sudden pole shifts could be found in geological samples all around the Earth. He again shook his head.

Breaking his mental lament was a knock on his office doorframe. "Excuse me Dr. Young," a tall fair haired man said in a proper eastern accent.

"Xavier... I'm sorry, I didn't see you standing there," Evan said in a daze.

"That's perfectly alright sir," the tall man replied crisply. Evan knew that his number two went to Harvard. His accent could only have been cultivated at such an Ivy-League school. "I just wanted to give you the latest activity reports. Here you go," he said, handing him a thick sheaf of paper.

"Not more bad news I hope," Evan asked sullenly.

"I'm afraid so sir. We have four volcanoes going off in Costa Rica alone, and Chile has had another seismic event. That makes a total of ninety-six active volcanoes at this time. I dare say that the data would suggest that the crust is becoming unstable," he said with cold disassociation.

Dr. Young, who was a man in his mid-sixties, short and squat with a bump of a stomach from too much time spent behind a desk, deliberately flipped open the wad of papers. Quickly he ran his finger across page after page, looking at the numbers. Three quarters through the report he slowed down, and then settled at a spot on a page.

Xavier watched as Young's face turned ashen. He looked up dumbfounded at his second in charge. Nervously he pushed his thick rimmed glasses up on the bridge of his nose. He was clenching the paper so tight, his fingers were turning pink and his hands were shaking.

"Why... this is stunning Xavier... stunning. It makes no sense. For some unknown reason, it appears that the Earth's mantle is expanding at an alarming rate. But why?" he asked rhetorically.

"Sir, is there any evidence that this has happened before?"

In a daze and still looking down at the papers, Evan, shaking his head said, "No... no, not this. I mean, not that I know of. Pole Reversals yes, but the core... the mantle?"

Xavier was quiet, almost emotionless, watching his mentor. He'd never seen the scientist so distraught.

Suddenly, Young abruptly stood to his feet. Then he wound up and violently threw the report against the wall with a loud thud.

Xavier didn't flinch.

"BLAST!" Young shouted, "Just what am I supposed to do about it?! Those pencil necks in Washington have tied my hands! I can't even put out an alert!! Meanwhile we are getting flooded with calls from around the world! I'm just supposed to say everything is normal? We look like fools!"

Surprised by the outburst, but not entirely shocked, Dr. Xavier Maximilian Black didn't know what to say. He'd always known Dr. Young to be a mild mannered man. He was a brilliant scientist, and an excellent politician. Yet, to see his frustration boil over was very much out of character.

"I am sorry Dr. Young... I just thought..."

Regaining his composure, Evan remembered his junior colleague. "No Xavier. I'm sorry. I don't mean to shoot the messenger," he said as he reached to grasp the younger man's hand and shook it while patting him on the back.

Xavier returned the grip, "Yes sir. Quite alright. I know you're frustrated. I wish I could help."

"I do too Xavier... I do too. We have to warn them."

"Yes sir. I hope we can too." With that he slowly turned to go back to his pressing duties.

As he was walking down the hall, his cell phone rang. Looking at the caller I.D. he saw that it was his wife Ivy.

He hit the answer button, "Hel...

"Xavier!" his wife said in an urgent whisper, "You are not going to believe what I just heard!"

"Ivy this isn't..."

"Something is going on!"

Xavier stopped in his tracks. He knew his wife. She wasn't one for melodramatics. He looked up and down the hall. No one was around. "What are you talking about?"

"I can't really say on the phone. But I will tell you this. I think this is worse than what I feared."

"How could it be..."

"It just is. You'll understand when I talk to you. Right now I need to make the call."

"Make the call? Are you sure? I mean, he's all the way in Geneva. I don't know what help..."

"He's back in the States."

"What?"

"I tried calling him at his office. Some government type answered and said he was returning to the U.S."

"Ivy we talked about this..."

"It's the only way Xavier. Maybe his friend can even help you with your ah... non-disclosure issue."

He pulled the phone from his ear and stared it in anger while his nostrils flared. Getting back on the line he said, "Ivy, we need to think this..."

"There's no more time Xavier. If you're going to go public and I am going to find out what's going on, we have to do it now! Are you with me? Or am I gonna have to do this on my own? Xavier was squeezing his phone so tight, he thought it might break. "Honey, of course I'm with you," he said. But he didn't add what he was thinking: *Where else would I be?*

"Good, I'll make the call. I'll let you know."

"Okay, I have to clear it with Young. Please call me right back."

"Kay," and the line went dead.

"Where else would I be," he said under his breath."

Chapter 7

*A*bdullah Abbas Tabak stared intently at the huge map of the Middle East. He closed his eyes for a moment and imagined what it was like to lead the Ottoman Empire of old. He could hear the shouts of the brave soldiers of Allah, as they captured inch upon inch of land until it was all theirs. The coppery aroma of blood filled his nostrils as it ran freely on the battlefield. Charged electricity filled the air with excitement like waves of the ocean rolling over his mighty warriors.

A quiet rap on the door brought him back to the present.

His eyes snapped open and he sighed. "Come," he said in Syrian Arabic.

In entered his aide Farouk.

The balding, beady eyed, bespectacled man noted that his Charge was seated in the same position that he'd seen him many times before. He was in his big overstuffed leather desk chair, facing the Middle East map that stretched over the entire wall behind his desk.

He smiled thinly. *Someday soon this great man will restore Syria to her rightful place at the head of the new Ottoman Empire,* he thought.

In truth, the Ottoman Empire was the offspring of the Seljuq Empire of Persian heritage. It was the rise of this empire that began the spread of Islam across the region that was once dominated by Christian European influence.

Farouk Yilmaz was a small unimpressive man with a beak for a nose and shiny head ringed with dark hair. He was brilliant in his own right, but was better known for being cold heartedly ruthless. Stories abounded on how he marshaled the silent might of the Syrian secret police, the Mukhabarat, to silence anyone who would stand in the way of his President.

He quietly walked over to Tabak's desk and waited for the President to swivel his chair around. After a moment, Tabak sighed heavily, cleared his throat and turned to face forward.

"It is done Your Excellency," Farouk said.

'Done' was the official withdrawal of Turkey from NATO (North Atlantic Treaty Organization). Turkey was the last Arab country to leave the organization and was historically a long-standing member of the alliance. However, its resignation from the treaty was no surprise to anyone.

In recent months, Turkey closed American and NATO bases in their country. They also imposed a strict no fly zone. No longer was their government a western leaning one. With its latest elections, a hard lined Muslim had come to power from the Brotherhood. And the country recently instituted Sharia Law (moral code and religious law of Islam).

Since the Arab Spring of 2011, the falling of the governments in Egypt, Syria, Libya and a whole host of others, prompted the ascension to power of leaders like Tabak. These new leaders were either directly, or indirectly, part of the political movement of the Muslim Brotherhood.

As a consequence, Western influence in the region had seriously eroded. In its place was a power vacuum eagerly filled by surging radical Islam. No friend to their former rulers, these leaders privately sought death to America, the West and the Zionist State of Israel.

Tabak was a Syrian by birth. He had an Iranian mother and Syrian father and rocketed to power from virtual anonymity. The charismatic leader came from outside political circles, and was supported by a grassroots movement. And a rumor surfaced that he literally rose out of a well as a baby. Thus indirectly the story compared him to the prophesied Caliph (Islamic Messiah) prompting many to say that he was destined to lead the Arab nations to greatness.

Tabak's elbows were on his desk with his fingers making the shape of a triangle. "That is very good news," he said to the subordinate. "And what, if anything, do we hear from our former captors, the Americans?"

Farouk considered the question. He pushed his round lensed glasses up on his nose and said, "They responded as you said they would Excellency. With their economy collapsing, and the EU (European Union) now defunct, all of the Zionist supporting nations are struggling with their own civil unrest. They are hardly in the position to do anything other than ask them to reconsider."

"Quite..." Tabak said, as he stared off beyond Farouk in thought. Focusing back on his aide, he said, "With the might of the Turkish forces now firmly with the Brotherhood, we now have the strength to proceed with our next step.

Tabak paused a moment, "And our press conference tomorrow?"

A look of mirth played across Farouk's eyes. "The new leaders from all across the region have been told to expect a glorious announcement. It would seem that given the new world dynamic, all Arabs are willing to unite behind the Brotherhood. We can look forward to many wearing the Shahada. Truly we shall have the cooperation we need to destroy the Zionist's pathetic little country Israel."

The Shahada is the first of the Five Pillars of Islam, expressing the two fundamental beliefs that make a person a Muslim: There is no god but Allah, and Muhammad is Allah's prophet.

"Yes, but we must practice patience Farouk," he hissed

like a snake, "first they must all be willing to truly serve the cause and be part of our New Ottoman Empire."

With head slightly bowed at the gentle rebuke, the beady eyed man said, "Yes Your Excellency."

Lazy Hoof – Present Day

Bryce, still smarting after falling off his horse, gimpily walked Mac in the direction of the main house. He and his old friend were in deep conversation when another man, mid-sixties, six-two, with his own cowboy boots on and a head full of greying red hair intercepted them.

"Dr. Cooper, you got a sec?" Ed Warkentin sheepishly asked.

Turning around to see the ranch guest, Bryce said, "Oh Mr. Warkentin. Hi. Please, just Coop." Bryce and Mac stopped, giving Ed his full attention.

Ed Warkentin looked and sounded like a cowboy, but Bryce knew that he and his wife Manaya were native Southern Californians. They showed up unannounced at the ranch the day before. Accommodating them was no problem. Most of the guest cabins were empty anyway because of the new "Great Depression".

The expected collapse of the Dollar, and Europe's problems, was all anyone talked about. Real unemployment numbers in the U.S. hit twenty-five percent. Jobs were nonexistent. Civil unrest and riots were a regular occurrence, even in Montana.

The drought of the last few years also snow balled into a food shortage. Store shelves were emptying and water was even becoming scare. When the citizenry was desperate, the thin line between civilization and anarchy quickly faded.

Bryce, with Steve Quayle's help, had the forethought to develop a plan for the Lazy Hoof. He envisioned it becoming a "city of refuge" if things went sour. For instance, he'd overbuilt the guest cabins and bunkhouses. Realistically, they could house hundreds of people until things settled down. Food storage and a sufficient water supply were also part of the plan.

Included with those essentials was ample armament and ammunition for security purposes. The physicist even went so far as to bury huge gasoline and diesel fuel tanks on the property to ensure the ranch's vehicles could still function if there was a fuel shortage.

But Bryce considered the crown jewel of the work, the cavernous underground shelter that he managed to build under the main ranch house. While not the Hilton, it would be sufficient if things really got bad. But Cooper hoped that they'd never need any of it.

Bryce focused his thoughts on his ranch guest. Although the Warkentins didn't have a reservation at the Dude Ranch, his staff happily accepted them. But coming with no reservation is not what stuck out to him about the couple from California. What stuck out to him was what Manaya Warkentin said to him when they checked in.

Yesterday he happened to be walking by in the main house when one of his staff stopped him to introduce him to the new guests. He immediately noted that Manaya was legally blind. At her side was Ed and her harnessed Seeing Eye Dog, Koffee.

Upon greeting him, the woman warmly grasped his hand. Then she told him that they'd come all the way up to Montana to tell him what she "saw". He thought it a very strange comment given her optical disadvantage, but didn't say anything. She said it would only take a few minutes, but that it was urgent. He'd yet to get back to her.

He traded a knowing look with Mac who nodded. "You

go head. I'll find my way," the big man said as he headed off in the direction of the lodge.

"What can I do for you Mr. Warkentin?" Bryce asked.

"First," Ed said in a warm tone, "I'll call you Coop, if you call me Ed. Deal?"

Bryce smiled, "Deal."

"Manaya sent me over. She's very agitated. She said that she needs to tell you what she saw. She said it would make sense to you and that you would understand."

Hand on chin, Bryce said, "Huh... okay. I have a few minutes. Where is she now?"

"I left her down by the river. That little spot where the water slows. Said you'd know exactly the place. Said it meant a lot to your mother."

Bryce's mouth dropped open and he turned white. He knew exactly the spot. But how in the world did a blind woman from Southern California, who he didn't know, know where....

Grace Ann Cooper's favorite spot was before she died?

Bozeman, Montana – Three and a Half Years Earlier

By the end of that first meeting with Quayle, Bryce gained a world of knowledge that he didn't even know he was looking for. It was only six months before that he was nearly killed by an angry red-headed giant Nephilim. He now had a reference point for the experience. In addition, Quayle was a resource for the numerous crazy questions running through his head.

As Quayle walked him out to his car, he carried a stack of books that he gave Bryce for homework. In the stack were many of his own; *Angel Wars, Genesis 6 Giants, Genetic Armageddon,* but there were also books from other writers pertinent to the subject matter that Bryce asked about.

There was a book by someone named Stan Deyo called *The*

Cosmic Conspiracy. Bryce never heard of him, but Quayle said his brilliance would impress him. Steve also threw in a copy of *Dare to Prepare* from, Holly Deyo. Bryce wouldn't know until much later how important that book would become to him as he got his house in order.

Just before walking out the door, Quayle went back for a few more books. One by Tom Horn called *Forbidden Gates* was about transhumanism and genetic manipulation. And on the top of the stack, he threw a book by someone named L.A. Marzulli, entitled *The Cosmic Chess Match.*

Bryce was hobbled with a bad leg so Quayle brought out the stack of books himself and placed them on the front passenger seat. Scooter brought out boxes and bags of supplies that Bryce bought. It was the beginning of making the Lazy Hoof, a safe haven.

The new friends made an appointment for Quayle to come over to The Lazy Hoof in a consultant capacity. The intent was for Bryce to show him the whole layout so he could, for a fee Bryce insisted, write up an action plan to get the ranch ready for whatever may come.

Shaking hands and slapping each other on the back, Cooper and Quayle said goodbye to each other. As Bryce cranked the truck and drove away, he looked down at the books now spread out on the front seat.

In addition to the books, Quayle gave the physicist a list of websites to check out. What the man with the serious eyes didn't know was that Dr. Bryce Obadiah Cooper was a speed reader with a photographic memory. Thus, it wouldn't take him long to go through the information.

And what Bryce didn't know, nor could have guessed, were the connections he would find between the crazy conspiracy, pseudo-science world of Steve Quayle and his own passion for physics, or his harrowing experience before the Reset.

Within the week he began to understand the nightmare of six months earlier. And he also understood that it wasn't over. He didn't know when or how, but he believed that he would have to wrestle with that same evil again.

And he feared that... so would the world.

Chapter 8

Outside SURF, Surrey England – Present Day

Dr. Mora noted how beautiful the English evening was. A breeze blew lightly through the parking lot and the moon was full. Nonetheless, he had no time to appreciate it as his quick pace hurried him to his old black Mercedes coupe. In his haste, he failed to see the car that sat watching him from a dark corner.

The car's driver had a small pair of night vision binoculars to his eyes watching Mora get into his car. To his surprise, rather than starting the engine, Mora just sat there. Although the Observer's position kept him from being noticed, from his vantage point he couldn't see what The Professor was doing either. So he waited.

Inside the Mercedes, The Professor slipped the laptop out of its case and laid it on top of the seat. He opened it and hit the "on" button. Since it was only in hibernate, it came right up. Next, he opened his briefcase and began fishing for something. He knew it was there, he just didn't know where.

Finally, in one of the large pockets that he seldom used, he felt the item's unique shape and pulled it out. In his hand he held a "Hotspot." It was a device like a wireless modem that gave the user the ability to access the internet anyplace on the planet via satellite. His grandkids gave it to him last Christmas. They told him that from then on, he didn't have any excuse not to call or write them. He had yet to use the device and long since forgotten about it, until now.

He plugged the device into the USB port. Next he pulled up the network connections screen and made sure that he disabled the facility network and enabled the hotspot. Then, he pulled up an old email account that he hadn't used since his early days teaching at Oxford. "I hope he remembers," he whispered to himself.

Eyes closed he said, "God... please let this work," and then he uploaded the entire file with the algorithm. He took a deep breath, paused, and hit send.

"Email sent" read across the top of the account. The Professor breathed a sigh of relief. With the mission accomplished, he shook his head at his own paranoia.

But sitting there in the quiet, he thought deeper about the issue. He realized that no small feat had been accomplished. *To erase and change all of the data... he corrected himself... evidence... to change all of the evidence that was compiled for the last few months was virtually impossible.*

No... these were deliberate acts. But why? Why would someone ignore what was coming. And more importantly, why would someone try to cover it up? They had to know that they couldn't hide it indefinitely. Someone would find out, if not in days then at least in weeks. They were only buying themselves time before the world knew the truth!

He shook his head again in frustration.

At that moment, his stomach let out a loud, animalistic growl, and again it burned. His train of thought was broken and he was brought back to the present. "I need to eat," he said to himself, suddenly feeling weak and tired.

With the information going to a man whom he knew he could trust, he'd done all he could do tonight. He would follow-up in the morning.

He needed to get on the road if he was going to make it to the cottage in Cornwall before midnight. Zoraida was going to kill him. He didn't want to start his vacation by making her angry. He turned off and stowed his laptop, closed up his briefcase and started his engine.

One of Britain's only twenty-four hour news radio channels roared to life:

"With the recent collapse of the European Union and

the Euro, country's leaders are scrambling to come to terms with the loss of the currency and rising shortages of food. The United Kingdom, who resisted the temptation of joining the currency experiment by keeping British Sterling, has been the one bastion of safety for our continental neighbors. This has brought new pressures of inflation to Britain and is being vigorously battled by the current government. Meanwhile high-tech joint projects on the mainland such as CERN's Large Hadron Collider experiment in Geneva have been traded for bread lines. This is especially curios because the Swiss also kept their currency rather than switching to the Euro. Nonetheless, the masses are now growing hungry and the disillusioned are rioting. Violence has broken out in many countries. America is also on the cusp..."

The Professor shook his head upon hearing the distress of nations. "I guess things can always get worse," he said to himself, as he reached over and turned off the radio.

As his car backed out of its space, the Observer in the dark corner, made a call in his cold voice; "He's just pulling away now. It will be at least four hours until he is at the spot. Make sure you're ready."

Lazy Hoof Ranch – Three and a Half Years Earlier

Sitting on a hill, in the cab of Bryce's F-350 4x4 truck, parked under a shade tree, the two men had a clear view of the lodge and area where the new guest houses would be built. Quayle asked his host, "And what's that," pointing, "over there in the distance. Construction?"

"That is the beginnings of our new Dude Ranch."

"Dude Ranch? I guess the physicist has gone all cowboy?"

Bryce just hung his head and shook it smiling.

"How many people will each of those buildings hold?"

"Most of them bunk four," Bryce said, "There are a few units that can bunk eight for bigger groups. And those," he pointed to another section, "are smaller studio cabins that hold two."

"Is that the maximum capacity for each?"

Bryce smiled, "I knew you'd ask that. That's the comfortable vacation capacity. We'll have extra cots and sleeping bags in storage. We can cram people in like sardines if we have to.

"Okay... Do they all have water and electricity?"

"Yeah, water comes from our own artesian well," he pointed, "and over there. It also recirculates underground through a baffle for the fishing pond there..."

"Can you cap it off?"

Bryce looked at Quayle, "You mean for worst case?"

"Yes... worst case. That is what we need to prep for. If it doesn't happen, that's great. If it does, then we are ready."

"Not only can it be capped off, but I have someone doing plumbing to rout the water away from the surface if we need to."

Steve pointed at him, "I like the way you think. Are those electricity wires there?"

Bryce squinted, "Yeah, run over from the house."

"We're going to have to bury those at least three feet."

"Got it."

"How serious are you about this," Quayle made quote marks with his fingers, "City of Refuge?"

Bryce thought for a moment, "Seems to me that God gave us this land for a reason. We have plenty of it. I want to do what's right. If things go south, a lot of people are gonna be hurtin. We want to help."

"I like it! How many people do you think you're going to be able to put up?"

"Well as far as the cabins go, there's," Bryce stopped to count, "right around thirty-five. Like I said, we can have people in sleeping bags and on roll-away cots. So in all," he scratched his head in thought, "probably a little shy of two hundred if we pack them in. That doesn't count the main lodge house, the barn, the guest house and the other places that we can squeeze people into. All in all, we probably can sleep and feed about eight hundred."

Quayle shook his head, "That's a lot of mouths. You need a decent size kitchen, storage for extra food, long term food," he said, as he added the items to his growing list on the yellow pad in his hands. "What about emergency shelter... you know, underground?"

"Yes, I saw that kind of thing in Holly Deyo's book. By the way, thanks for suggesting all of those. I found each of them helpful in their own way."

Quayle looked at Bryce surprised, "You mean you've finished them?" It'd only been a week and a half since he gave them to him.

Bryce shrugged, "Yeah, I speed read. No big deal."

Shaking his head, Quayle said, "Well... I speed read too, but even I couldn't have gotten through all those that quick. You'll probably need to go back over them to make sure you have a good grasp."

Bryce shrugged again, "Naw," he tapped on his head, "I got it. Photographic memory."

"Photographic what?"

Changing the subject, Bryce asked, "So do you know a good contractor that can help with the underground shelter? And I stress good. I want to get it as close to under the house as possible so we can get to it from our basement. And it needs to be inconspicuous."

Hand on his chin, Quayle said, "Yes... I know of a company. They'll give you a fair price, they do excellent work and they'll make the construction as inconspicuous as possible. I'll make a call."

"Great"

"Now how are you set for weapons and protection?"

Bryce looked at Quayle with a big grin on his face, "Steve... you're from Montana. How do you think I'm fixed for weapons?"

Quayle smiled back, "I thought you would say that. But if that day ever comes, you'll need to make sure you have some heavy firepower. Plus you want to think about reloading your own ammo. Let's take an inventory."

"Okay, no problem."

"Now, can you take me along the perimeter? We'll need to find out where to place some guard towers, cameras and other security measures... oh... I almost forgot, we need to scope out a place for some fuel storage tanks that can be buried without people knowing they're there."

"Fuel storage tanks?"

"Yes, you told me to be thorough and..."

"And what?" Bryce asked.

Steve grinned and said, "You said money was no object. But brother, I'm telling you, all this is going to set you back a few dollars."

When Quayle asked how much he was willing to spend, his actual reply was "whatever it takes". The Prepper expert was taking him at his word. It looked like he was going to help Bryce make a fortress; a very pleasing to the eye, comfortable and functional fortress, but a fortress nonetheless.

Bryce nodded and started the truck, "That's fine. I just want to do it right. You're the expert."

Looking down at a map, Quayle asked, "How many acres do you have here?"

Bryce took the toothpick out of his mouth and threw it out the window, "Ten-thousand."

Quayle exhaled, "It's a good thing I'm spending the night. I think this is going to take us a couple of days."

Bryce put it in drive and pulled out, "Look at the bright side."

"What's that?"

"My wife is not only beautiful; she's also an excellent a cook!"

Chapter 9

Jerusalem, Israel – Present Day

*T*el Aviv was a little more than seventy kilometers from Jerusalem. It should have taken less than an hour of travel time to the ancient city. But because of snarled traffic, travel by car was just as treacherous and laborious as driving in New York. Zac finally arrived for his clandestine meeting two hours later.

Before him, a man that looked as old as Jerusalem itself, stood.

"Shalom Zechariah," the Rabbi said.

"Shalom Rabbi," Zac responded.

Rabbi, as Zac had simply come to know him, was one of Rabbi Shlomo Goren's most trusted students. Rabbi Goren was a strong proponent of the Third Temple being built right up until his death in 1994.

But because of politics, and the tensions surrounding the Mount, it seemed that the planned ceremony for tomorrow might never occur.

"Are our neighbors behaving themselves?" Rabbi asked?

"For now," Zac said candidly.

"Do you know what their announcement is about tomorrow?"

Zac knew what he'd been told, but rather than divulging the confidence, he simply said, "Does it matter Rabbi. Whatever they are planning, our card trumps theirs. Do they not?"

The Rabbi nodded stoically, "Truly."

"But," Zac said, "I will say that I do not believe we have much time."

This statement caught the Rabbi off guard, "Oh? I'm sure that they are well aware of our ceremony tomorrow. Yet they have made no moves to stop it, nor have they raised a complaint?"

Zac smiled, "And doesn't that seem a little odd to you?"

The Rabbi thought for a moment, "Yes, I suppose it does. I just assumed that it was Hashem's (God's) blessing."

"It is, at the very least, that. However, could it be that they are not worried about what will occur tomorrow because they intend to come and take the Mount back?"

"Hum," was all that the Rabbi said. "And what of our venture last week?" he pointed to Zac's arm, "A provocation in the making?"

Zac snickered, "As if they need one Rabbi? They hate us already."

The Rabbi nodded, "You are right of course, but I was referring to any movements by the Egyptians to try to get the article back."

Zac pursed his lips. He thought about how much he could say. "No, they have not made any... how should I say... out of the ordinary moves as a result of the raid. But, the Syrians seem to be moving troops in our direction. And the Russians were already been massing on Iran's borders. Since they are allies, I doubt that they have hostile intent toward the Iranians.

"There is much talk about this joint military exercise that they are conducting. As a result of the repositioning of forces, the whole Arab military contingent is very active right now. I don't know if we could differentiate between hostile intent by the Egyptians for last week's operation or movement for the exercise."

"Ah... yes, quite," the Rabbi agreed.

"And how about here? Is everything prepared?" Zac ventured.

"Yes, everything is ready. Hashem (God) has seen fit to provide us a Red Heifer. The wall has been built and cleansed per the instructions in The Law. The last of the Temple implements have been completed. The Cohen (priests) have been trained."

The Red Heifer is critical to Orthodox Judaism. Tradition says that it must be provided by Hashem Himself. The ashes of the Red Heifer, after it has been properly sacrificed and burnt, are used according to The Law to cleanse the Levitical Priesthood for Temple work. In addition, there are other necessary cleansing rituals that require these ashes. According to Jewish tradition, there had only been nine Red Heifers in Israel's history. Mamonides, the Jewish Sage, said that in the days of the tenth Red Heifer, the Messiah would come.

"And there is no sign of the two other items?" Zac asked.

"No Zechariah, I'm afraid we must depend on the Package. Time is very short. We need our answers. In his wisdom, Hashem has also seen fit to provide those; albeit through an unexpected source."

The "unexpected source" was a direct result of what Zac inadvertently found out by bugging Joe and Ruby's home. While he understood the items were needed, he was not comfortable on how the information came about. To his consternation, it made him cheap and dishonest.

Reading the look on his face, the Rabbi put his hand on Zac's good shoulder, "Adonai's (God's) ways are not always easily understood. There are larger issues here. I am sure you will be forgiven for what you've had to do in providing for tomorrow's festivities. Soon our friend will arrive with the Package and your misgivings will be forgotten. You will see."

The thought of his betrayal disturbed Zac greatly. He considered himself an honorable man. There did not seem to be any honor in betraying a friend. He looked down at the dirt, and asked "How soon before the Package arrives?"

Fingers interlocked at his mid-section with a placid look, the Rabbi said, "I believe the call will be made shortly."

"And what if he does not agree to bring it?" Zac asked, with laced concern.

The Rabbi paused in thought about how to answer. Finally he said, "We believe that Hashem brought this to our attention because he knew that our new friend would be willing to turn over the Package. Exactly how we will convince him, I do not know. That is for Adonai (God) to decide. Our job is to trust him."

"That doesn't answer my question Rabbi," Zac said

deadpanned.

The Rabbi's look betrayed his confidence, "If need be, we can take an extra couple of days to try to convince our friend. If he still does not agree to surrender it then..." he let the sentence hang in the air.

"How long before you can actually use that arm," he asked, pointing to Zac's arm in the sling.

Zac breathed out heavily. He knew what the Rabbi was getting at. "Should only be a few days," he said flexing his hand in the sling. It really is only a minor wound and it is not my shooting hand."

"Then you would be available to travel in a few days to retrieve the item by force if need be?"

Zac, a man not given to emotion, felt a pang of fear at the thought. This was not due to his going in harm's way. He'd done so many times in the past and in much more difficult circumstances. Rather, the Package rested in the hands of a friend's loved one. It would be very unfortunate if he had to divest that person of the Package through violence.

"I will do what I must Rabbi," he said.

"Good, those two items are very important to what we are trying to accomplish Zechariah. And if Adonai continues to bless our efforts, we will be able to ask our questions of him within the next day or two."

Zac blew out a tired breath, "That's good. Because frankly I do not know if we have much longer than that."

Changing the subject, Zac asked, "And the ceremony for tomorrow? Are we ready?"

"Yes, cleansing of the Cohen will be completed tonight. We must follow the guidelines in the Torah (First five books of the Bible – The Law). Only then can the Mishkan (Tabernacle) be set up on the top of the Temple Mount."

Zac was still amazed at how all of this came about. After all of these years, Israel was finally given use of part of the Temple Mount. It was the one and only condition to a peace for land swap with the Palestinians. While Zac did not like the idea of negotiating with terrorists, the recovery of the Mount was worth the compromise.

It was planned to use the Mishkah (Tabernacle) as a temporary Temple. A wall was built between the Dome of the Rock and the location where the Tabernacle and soon to be constructed Third Temple was.

According to The Law, The Red Heifer had already been sacrificed as a burnt offering. The ashes of the Red Heifer were collected and placed in water to make it clean. And in turn, that water was then sprinkled with a Hyssop branch on the wall, temple implements, priest and all other items to make them clean.

And what of your news," the Rabbi pressed. "They are surrounding us. Do you think that they are getting ready to move?"

He looked at his teacher for a moment with serious eyes. Then finally he said, "It would seem so. There is a lot of chatter. We believe that they are positioning themselves for war without outside interference."

The Rabbi smirked, "You mean without our Gentile friends the Americans coming to our aid?"

"Of course. And they are right. It will not be long before we are totally on our own. The world..." he paused trying to find the right words, "is spinning out of control.

"Europe has collapsed and now food and water supplies are getting dangerously low. Civil unrest is growing. The American economy is hanging on by a thread. We have reports that the United States has already began to call back their military. You are correct that we will soon be on our own."

"All the more reason to move on the Temple and Tabernacle. Doing so will bring the Messiah. And He will bring peace," the Rabbi said assuredly.

"Yes... of course," Zac said, not quite as certain as the Rabbi.

A concerned look crossed his teacher's face, "You doubt this? You believe Hashem will abandon us?"

Realizing the misunderstanding, Zac quickly added, "No, no. Of course not. I..."

"Then what is it then Zechariah?"

Pausing in thought, Zac offered, "We have been getting reports of troop movements from all over the world. It appears that the armies of Earth have reached the conclusion that it is better to fight, than have peace.

"China is ready to engage in Taiwan, North and South Korea have massed at the DMZ, Russia has massed on the border of Iran and now there is very quiet talk of a new Arab alliance. Soon, I fear, the world will be at war."

Then looking deep in his teacher's eyes, he said, "I just hope that the Messiah comes quickly."

The Rabbi nodded in understanding, "Have faith Zechariah. Soon the Messiah will come and everyone will have peace. That is why we are pushing so hard to get this done. The world needs Him. You will see."

"I hope you are right Rabbi... for all of our sakes."

Lazy Hoof Ranch – Three and a Half Years Earlier

It was a long three days. Quayle needed to extend his stay at the Lazy Hoof by an extra half day.

At the end of the third day, his evaluation of the Lazy Hoof was finally complete. But because he extended his stay until the morning, he juggled his schedule. As a consequence, Quayle had to do a late-night talk show interview from Bryce's office Skype.

Watching Steve Quayle in his professional element was something that Bryce will never forget:

> *"And now," Quayle said to the interviewer, "they're talking almost gleefully about the end of what was created, and in creating a triple helix, not a double helix, a triple helix DNA strand where now anything they can imagine they can manufacture in a laboratory. So this is why the whole issue of quantum entanglement is so*

fascinating. You've got seventy-two HAARP like ionosphereic heaters..."

Bryce sat straight up. *Seventy what,* he thought?

"...and by the way, HAARP is only one form of technology, I don't know if you remember seeing the article where thirteen almost coherent neutron beams were seen going into the reactor?"

The radio talk show host replied, *"Yes, right."*

"Okay now," Quayle continued, *"what people don't understand is, and I was taught this by Sam Cohen, the inventor of the Neutron Bomb okay, he just passed away God bless him..."*

Bryce was sitting behind Quayle, out of sight, so he wouldn't distract him. The physicist just shook his head in disbelief. He met Sam Cohen a few years ago at a conference. But he was a physicist! He was supposed to know other people in his chosen discipline. *Steve Quayle, was well educated, well spoken and well traveled. He was widely versed on numerous subjects and very interesting to speak to. But he was still an uncredentialed intellect, out of the mainstream, from Bozeman, Montana. But he knew Sam Cohen. Amazing,* Bryce thought. *There's more to Mr. Steve Quayle than meets the eye.*

"...but the point is, is that years ago I interviewed him on the radio. And off the radio, he and I had fascinating talks. The point is that you cannot have those neutron beams without something generating the neutron beams and what you're seeing in the reactor, which would be called a neutron flux, this is as it was explained to me, I'm not a nuclear physicist, is neutrons are flushing over the ah... radioactive rods that are in there, that's what's called neutron flux, but... the point is those beams are intersecting. They had to originate from something above the reactor. Now a lot of people don't believe in electrogravitics and they don't understand how the

*military... and I've been told basically that they're not
fifty years in advance, they're literally, they're using alien
technology, they have stuff that's thousands of years in
advancement. Solomon said, 'There's nothing new under
the Sun. That which will be has already been.' So in
adopting that whole... whole chain of thought, if there is
something that is initiating a form of ah..."*

Double and triple helixes? DNA? Quantum entanglement?
HAARP technology? Fallen angles? Sam Cohen? The Neutron Bomb!
Electrogravitics? Alien Technology? *Who is this guy? I thought he
was just some sort of knowledgeable conspiracy theorist!*

Bryce had to admit: during the thousands, if not tens of
thousands of lectures and interviews that he sat through or given,
he'd never seen anyone put out as much rapid fire information as
Steve Quayle did that night.

As a man of science, Cooper took issue with some of Quayle's
conclusions, but could not deny the man's intellectual honesty and
veracity. That night he took away many things from listening to him
up close and personal.

Because of his leg's ongoing recovery, he had lots of downtime.
He used it wisely by reading continually... about more than just
physics. He consumed all of the books that Quayle gave him - like a
man who hadn't eaten in weeks. He obtained other books on
numerous subjects. He went to thousands of websites, listened to
dozens of interviews and even made a few phone calls to people to
ask questions.

His paradigm of the 3D world changed almost overnight.
Through many of the things he'd learned, he began to understand
what was really going on in the unseen world. Those things were far
from the standard scientific model that he learned as a physicist.

And just like before his Reset, he was in the thick of it again. He
hoped he was up to the task. Because somehow he knew: he would
have to be willing to sacrifice everything...

To keep the Fallen from destroying mankind.

Chapter 10

Lazy Hoof Ranch, Missoula, Montana – Present Day

$\mathcal{A}$s Mac turned away from Bryce to head to the main house, he took in the beautiful surroundings of the 10,000 acre Lazy Hoof ranch. Hands on hips, he sucked in a big breath of clean air.

Exhaling slowly, he gazed with appreciation at the jutting Bitterroot Mountains standing guard around the property. He had to admit, if a guy had to give up his life's dream, this was the place to do it.

"Big Sky Country," he said to himself, as he glanced over his shoulder to see Bryce and Ed Warkentin ride off on horseback.

Dr. Grover Washington McNabb, or Mac as his friends called him, was Bryce Cooper's best friend. And since their days at MIT together, they were nearly inseparable.

Mac grew up a poor black kid in Philly. His physical prowess and stature saved him many a time, as he fought to survive Philadelphia's mean streets. An unlikely candidate for higher education, to get himself out of the projects, he used those same physical attributes to land his first athletic scholarship to college.

He was big and talented enough to play in either the NFL or the NBA. Instead, he saw the value of a sustainable working vocation rather than the short-term duration of a professional athlete's career.

He continued to play intercollegiately in his undergraduate and then graduate school because he enjoyed it. But the truth was that he was so smart, he could have gotten a "full boat" academic scholarship anytime he pleased. But like his friend "Coop" as he called Bryce, he liked to be underestimated. It was during his basketball scholarship at MIT that he and Bryce met.

The two were an odd pair. Bryce was 5'11", broad shouldered and fit, but not overly athletic and a quiet, unassuming white guy.

Mac called him a redneck, from the rurals of Montana. Bryce's wavy sandy brown hair was a dead give-a-way to his genetic heritage. Down the line, his mother came from Jewish ancestors who came over to the New World with Christopher Columbus. And Bryce's great grandfather, on his father's side, was a Blackfoot Indian whose Indian name was Wolf Eyes.

Because of his distant Indian heritage, Bryce looked to have an ever-present tan. His native gene pool also spoke to the sure dexterity he displayed in the outdoors and his even temperament. He had an easygoing nature, which was in stark contrast to Mac's innocent upstart baritone bravado.

When the two met in Massachusetts, Mac had already been in school working on his doctorate. Bryce was twelve years Mac's junior, and had been blazing a trail through the PhD program. Regardless of the age difference, they both had something in common; they were both misfits in the world of physics in their own way.

Bryce was a boy genius; serious, shy, quiet and reserved. Everyone else in the program was at least fifteen years older than he. Mac was a humongous black guy, with a happy-go-lucky, jovial attitude who looked like he was more at home on a football field than in a laboratory wearing a pocket protector.

Regardless of the differences, the two hit it off immediately. Their personalities played off one another easily and although Bryce academically excelled, they were equals when it came to their own disciplines.

Mac was the starry-eyed astrophysicist gazing out to the heavens, trying to piece together information applicable to the human existence, while Bryce was the serious particle physicist with a bent toward dimensional theory.

Looking at the two in the middle of a group of their peers would make someone do a double take. The rugged outdoors looking cowboy and the big black athlete always stood out in a group of serious looking top scientists from around the world.

Even though their careers had taken different paths, when Bryce was handpicked for the LHC experiment by CERN a few years ago, he insisted that CERN also employ the smartest astrophysicist he knew, Mac, to come along so they could work together.

And work together they did... until. Four years ago, Bryce unexpectedly resigned from his duties at the LHC for personal reasons. Though shocked and dismayed at his departure, Mac saw that his friend had had some sort of life changing paradigm shift. Where Bryce was always haunted by his past and working himself into an early grave, he abruptly came to grips with where he came from and embraced it - and his family.

He was happier now than Mac ever seen him. He moved Gabby and his then three year old son, LJ, back to his successful Quarter Horse ranch, The Lazy Hoof, in Montana.

Mac visited the ranch many times before. He also brought his onetime research assistant, Diggs, along to enjoy the scenery. That was before Diggs headed off to Oxford University to finish his Ph.D.

Mac shook his head. When Diggs was still at the LHC, although he was a subordinate, he'd come to view him as a friend. He missed the thinning, redheaded Brit with his dry sense of humor and more than capable intellect. Professionally, he learned to depend on him because he recognized that he was almost as smart as Bryce. Thus, he was a key to the LHC modifications that Bryce had left for Mac.

Diggs' insights had become so important that Mac managed to have him, although he had yet to finish his Ph.D., put on staff as a consultant. Hence, since his departure, Mac spoke often with both he and Bryce via regular conference calls. McNabb knew that Bryce's modifications to the Collider were critical for the success of the experiment.

But it wasn't the same. Truth be told, the last three years at the LHC without either Bryce or Diggs left him feeling deserted.

They were more than colleagues. For the long ago divorced Mac, who had no children, they were family. And Mac felt the pain of their loss. It was good, despite the circumstances, to spend time with at least one of them.

The ringing of his cell phone brought him out of his revere.

Looking at the caller I.D., he was surprised to see that it was his x-wife's kid sister, Ivelisse Estefani Black.

Lazy Hoof – Three and a Half Years Earlier

Quayle threw his bag in the back of the old pickup. "Thanks for the hospitality!"

"Well it wasn't a leisure trip, that's for sure. But I hope you found your stay comfortable," Bryce quipped.

"Quite," Quayle said. "I'll get those final plans together and shoot you over an email?"

"Sounds good, but... ah," Bryce paused, uncertain how to proceed.

Seeing the look on Bryce's face, Steve asked, "Something wrong?"

Scratching the stubble on his chin, Bryce said, "Not wrong, but I do owe you some info."

Leaning with his back against the truck cab and arms crossed, Quayle tilted his head. Thinking he'd forgot something, he racked his brain. Then, with a small shake of his head, said, "Nooo, I think we covered it all. But if I remember anything, I'll just drop you a line."

Bryce was leaning on his cane, with his other hand in his jeans pocket. "No, it's not about the Ranch," he said.

"Not about the ranch? What then?"

"Two weeks ago... when we first met. You were wondering about Operation Falling Star."

Recognition crossed Quayle's face, "I remember, but don't worry about it. I only asked because," he chuckled, "because your guardian angel told me to. I know it's classified information. That's why I didn't press you."

Bryce looked around to see if anyone was in earshot. Seeing it was safe, he said, "You know what you were telling me about the Nephilim?"

"Yes"

Thinking about his life before the Reset, Bryce smirked, shook his head and looked down. When he looked up, the smile was gone and he had a dead serious look in his eyes, "I've had firsthand experience with them."

Steve could tell that Cooper wasn't kidding, "Really? Would you care to elaborate?"

Bryce looked hard at his new friend then slightly shook his head, "Can't... not now. It's a long and drawn-out story and not one that I care to talk about. But after hearing what you said about CERN, Shiva and other stuff, I've given some more thought to Operation Falling Star and specifically its relation to what I went through."

Quayle's forehead compressed as he was trying to figure out what Bryce was trying to tell him, "What you went through? I thought that experiment was conducted before you arrived at the LHC?"

"It was," Bryce swallowed hard. "The thing is, while it was conducted before I got there, everyone on staff heard about the incident in one form or another."

"Okay..."

"CERN put out so much disinformation, that it was relegated to little more than a fairytale."

"That sounds like them. It's not surprising."

"But the kind of stuff that didn't get out to the public was what I wanted to tell you about.

"I'm listening."

"I've thought about the timetable. It was just after that incident that something happened with the old LHC Director. He kind of... disappeared."

"Disappeared?" Quayle said surprised.

"Well... not into thin air. The rumor was that he had some

sort of mental breakdown. But now that I think about it, that was right after Operation Falling Star."

"Well, that's intriguing and all, but what does that have to do with Operation Falling Star?"

"As I said, he disappeared after Falling Star. But now I wonder if it was because he might have freaked out at what they saw?"

"What they saw?"

"Yeah... what they saw. This information was held very close, but I suppose because I was the ATLAS 7 Team Leader, some of those rumors naturally made their way to me."

"And?"

"And apparently the LHC opened some sort of..." he made quote marks with his fingers, "portal within the collision chamber."

"I did hear something like that. That confirms it then," Quayle said.

Bryce's face was contorted in confusion, "Confirms it?"

"I heard about Operation Falling Star long before your friend Gabe told me to ask you about it."

"You did?"

Nodding Quayle asked, "Does the number seventy-two mean anything to you?"

"No... should it?"

"Probably, but we'll talk about that later. What kind of portal opened during that experiment?"

"I don't really know. The whispers were never that detailed. And when the old Director disappeared, much of the previous staff was let go. I was brought on with a new tasking along with a majority of green researchers and scientists."

"And what was your tasking?"

Bryce stared at him for a moment. "I was working on increasing the speed of the collision to beyond the Speed of Light with my own emphasis in dimensional ther..."

"A beyond the Speed of Light collision? That's impossible! Einstein's said that mass equals m divided by..."

Bryce just looked at him, "Steve, of course I know the theory."

Quayle said, "Sorry... please go on. Were you successful?"

Bryce looked at him intently, "You might say that."

"What?! This is the first I've heard of it!"

"You wouldn't," then Bryce added, "No one has. But my experiment's not the point."

"So what are you trying to tell me?"

"The point is that during Operation Falling Star, they opened a portal and they saw something."

"Yes, I've heard that."

"They saw entities... horrific entities."

"That coincides with my information."

"And out of shear paranoia, they shut the experiment down. Right after that the Director was replaced with a new Director, my Director, and the staff was cycled. I came on board shortly after with a different emphasis... or so I thought."

"What do you mean – so you thought?"

Bryce scratched his head, "Alright... I'm not comfortable sharing this, but I have to talk to somebody. I've been giving this some thought. I think Operation Falling Star might have been a fluke, a mistake, or it could have been a trial run. And when they saw the potential, they brought me in to boost the collision. My specialty was dimensional theory so it only makes sense."

"And what happened with you?" Quayle asked. "Did you open a portal too?"

"Steve, this is stuff you can never repeat. Agreed?"

Quayle paused, then nodded curtly.

"Not only did I open a portal, I've seen what's on the other side. I stopped them once."

"Stopped them? Stopped who?" Quayle asked tensely.

Bryce set his jaw and he looked seriously into the man from Bozeman's eyes, "The Fallen."

"The... the fallen. You mean like..."

Bryce nodded, "As in fallen angels, or..."

"Demons" Quayle said with his hand to his mouth.

"That's right and they are trying to breech our dimensions and break out into our physical world."

Steve was quiet for a moment, letting the news sink in. He always believed in angels and demons. He'd had vivid visions and dreams himself. But this news brought in a different dynamic. It meant that Evil was no longer content with harassing mankind through a crack. They wanted to come over and play. And he knew that they played for keeps.

"I... I don't understand. Why did you walk away if you knew what they were doing?"

Bryce pursed his lips, "I didn't walk away... I have the battle scars..." he tapped his leg with his cane, "to prove it. I just thought I was done. But I still keep my finger on what's going on. My best friend is now the Director there. I consult with him on a regular basis. They're using my designs. And trust me; nowhere in those designs did I make it possible to open that dimensional bridge again. Besides, seeing what I saw and knowing what I know, I couldn't be part of it anymore. I had to walk away... for the sake of my family at least. And because I couldn't trust myself to not push the envelope."

With laser insight, Quayle said, "But they won't stop trying."

Bryce sighed, "No... you're right. They won't. And thanks to you, I think I know what they're planning."

"Me?"

"Yeah, who did you say Shiva was?" Bryce asked.

Both men in unison said, "The Destroyer of Worlds."

Chapter 11

Tele Aviv, Israel – Present Day

*H*e stood up from the couch and angrily tossed the remote onto the cushions. Sighing heavily, he wiped the sheen of perspiration from his brow. "That's it then!" he declared.

"With Turkey out of NATO, we're surrounded by Muslim extremists!"

"Hon, don't you think you're being a little melodramatic?" she asked in her no nonsense way.

Joe and Ruby were married for over forty-five years. As a former Marine, Joe was the gruff, rough and tumble man that grew up huntin and fishin, busting cattle and working the land. Ruby was a strong, self-assured woman with a tender heart. Theirs was a long love story with highs and lows, just as in any marriage. After many years of hard labor on their nephew's ranch in Montana, they finally retired to Israel.

"Come on Sweetie," Joe said, "do I have to spell it out for you? Turkey's ties to the West are now all but broken. With America's economic crises, they're staring down the barrel of China who insists on taking back Taiwan. And with the withdrawal of U.S. troops from South Korea, they've left the door wide open for a resumption of that conflict. America's virtually naked in the South Pacific! And you know what I heard this morning?"

Ruby was busy dusting and cleaning in anticipation of their guests that evening. With rag in hand, her back was to Joe.

"No dear... what did you hear," she said in a less than

- 85 -

enthusiastic tone.

"Now Germany's threatening to invade Greece unless the Greeks pay back the loans that the EU gave them!"

Over her shoulder, she said, "The EU's defunct. How can one country make that kind of demand? Besides, Greece went bankrupt. Can't get blood out of a turnip," and she went back to dusting.

"That's not the point," Joe said with frustration.

She stopped and turned around, "Just what is the point Josiah?" Then she turned back around and continued dusting.

"The point is... now we hear that Russia has formed," he held up quote marks with his fingers, 'The Euroasian Economic Union!' Economic Union my..."

"Joe!" Ruby snapped, scolding him before he used an expletive describing his backside. She stood there with her hands on her hips scowling at him.

"Well nuts!" he said in his own defense, "You know what I mean! Just look at them," he pointed to the flat screen TV, "Their latest victim is Azerbaijan. That poor country was too weak to defend themselves. The Russians never stopped developing their military in all the years since the Cold War ended. America was duped! Meanwhile, all we did was get fat, dumb and happy. Only worrying about ourselves! All the while, the world was going down the toilet! Now that we're broke and can't afford our military, we leave our friends alone to fend for themselves," he said with disgust. "Taiwan... South Korea... annnnddd," he said exaggeratedly, "now Israel! They've abandoned us too!"

Ruby was tapping her foot and her chin was scrunched up. Over the years Joe saw the look many times before. It meant that he was in trouble.

"Don't forget Josiah that you are American too," Ruby said with irritation. She knew her husband to be a passionate man.

It was one of the things that endeared him to her. But she didn't like hearing pessimism.

She walked over and put her hands on his shoulders. Looking him in the eye, she said sternly, "Our strength was never in America... or our Dollar... or our military. Our strength was and is in God. This is His land. He's not gonna let anyone take it from Him. You know that."

He looked down.

She put her hand to his chin and lifted it so she could see his eye, "So what's really bothering you?"

Looking into her green eyes, he melted. He put his hands on her hips and pulled her close. Whispering in her ear, he said, "Ah honey... I know you're right. It's just so doggone frustrating. How did we ever get to the place where Israel was surrounded by wolves?

"And..." he paused, "I'm thinking about back home. If the civil unrest continues... I hear Martial Law isn't far off. Then there's all kinds of weird seismic stuff going on. Someone was saying on the internet that there's been earthquake swarms along the west coast. Add to that this New Ma... Madrid... the New Madrid fault line that runs down through St. Louis... in the east. It's even acting up now. We have Earth changes all around us and now we've been abandoned by our own country. Plus..." he stopped himself. He didn't want to scare her.

After so many years together, Ruby knew how her man thought. They even often thought in unison, not having to speak what they were thinking, just knowing what the other was thinking.

"Yellowstone?" she asked, solemnly.

Joe nodded, "Yellowstone."

The Yellowstone Caldera was a long dormant "Supervolcano" in Yellowstone National Park. Although the caldera is located in the northwest corner of Wyoming, if the monster decided to blow, Joe and Ruby's beloved Lazy Hoof was way too close to the epicenter. They'd talked about it before. They were fearful for Bryce and his family. They were fearful for their extended family that lived throughout the area. A full-scale eruption could result in millions of deaths in the immediate areas surrounding the park. In addition, some experts said that such an eruption could produce a "nuclear winter" and catastrophic climactic effects globally.

She looked deeply into his eyes. She had the same concerns. They may now be Israelis, living in the Eretz (The Land), but they were also still Americans. And they were Montanan by birth. Both of them loved America and they loved their home. The thought of something as devastating as Yellowstone exploding was frightening.

A tear rolled down her cheek. In a low determined voice, she said, "I know... but you know we're here for a reason... for a purpose. And anyway, Bryce can take care of himself. He has all his life. He has a purpose. And I don't think it was just for what happened four years ago. I think it may be for what's coming. Four years ago..." she paused searching for the right words, "Four years ago he found out who he really was. What did he call it? A Reset?

"Now..." she said firmly, changing the subject and stepping back, "Isn't your partner in crime waiting for you? Aren't you and Eleazar going into the Market today?"

Slowly a mischievous grin spread across Joe's face. "Why yes... yes we are," he said boyishly. "In fact, he's probably waiting for me now," and he leaned to peck Ruby on the cheek. As he turned to head out of the door, she said, "And Josiah, don't forget we have company tonight. You boys don't eat too much strudel or, you won't have enough room for dinner."

"Ahhh honey, would I do that," he said, escaping through

the door without any further debate.

The door closed with a "swoosh" and she was left standing lost in thought. Finally, she picked up her dusting rag to get back to work. She also turned the TV back on for background noise:

> "...and it appears that Russian troops are massing along the borders of Azerbaijan and Iran. Russia has stated uncategorically that the moves are not aggressive, but rather are part of a larger joint military exercise with the new Eurasian cooperative and their Arab allies.
>
> However, closely held sources have shared with us that Egypt's and Syria's political and military differences with Israel have prompted the former Soviet State to take a more active role in the region. It is unclear what..."

She turned down the television.

She thought about the man she loved like a son. And in a quiet voice, she said, "Bryce... I hope you know your purpose in all of this. For all of our sakes."

Lazy Hoof – Three and a Half Years Earlier

After Quayle left for home, Bryce spent the day, mulling over the intense conversation of the morning.

He felt like he was missing something. An important detail was tugging at the shirt tail of his mind, vying for attention. Through lunch, then dinner, he was preoccupied, trying to remember. Finally it hit him. He grabbed his laptop and went out to the front patio.

His wireless router was a strong one in order to provide adequate internet coverage for ranch guests. Out on the broad wooded, knotty oak porch, he fired up the computer and signed into his email.

He addressed the note to the recipient and typed out his thoughts:

"Steve,

Thanks again for all the hard work the last couple of days. I appreciate it more than you know.

I know you're busy and probably trying to catch up. But you said something that's niggling at my mind.

You asked me if the number seventy-two meant anything to me. I know we went off on a tangent before you left and you didn't fill me in.

When you have a sec, you think you can tell me what you were talking about?

> *Thanks,*
> *Bryce Cooper"*

He hit send, and the email shot off into cyberspace. He sat his open laptop on the bench beside him.

It was only six in the evening and this time of year, the Montana Sun was already being put to bed. Bryce loved the twilight at Sunset. The air was crisp and he pulled up the collar on his light jacket. He blew into his hands and then reached for his steaming cup of after dinner coffee.

The crickets were out in force this night. Millions of the things were rattling all up and down the valley. The occasional bird would trumpet the end of another beautiful Montana day. He heard a couple of coyotes in the distance. Here, after so many years of running from it, Bryce felt balanced. He was at peace.

Swiftly, breaking his calm, five year old LJ bounded through the screen door.

"Hi Dad!"

"Hey buddy!"

"Wacha doin?"

"Ah... sitting here letting my food settle. You?"

"Just got done helpin mom with dishes. I'll be glad when Sarrah's old enough. That's a girl's job anyway!"

"Is that right?"

"Yup! Hey, you wanna throw the football?"

Bryce looked down at his mending leg, "Son, you know I can't..."

"No, no. You sit here on the porch and I'll go down there," he pointed to the grass a couple of feet away, "and we can toss it easy. Pleeeease?"

Bryce grinned, "Okay... sure!"

"Great! I'll be right back!" LJ said, as he took off through the screen door again.

Bryce smiled big. This was such a fun age. He missed it the first time before the Reset. Now he promised himself he would stop and smell the roses. As he was thinking about how much his life had changed, his computer beeped with an incoming email. It was from Quayle:

> *"Seventy-two is a very important number in the Kabbalah, Jewish mysticism. For your purposes, it is interesting to note that there are seventy-two ionospheric heaters, HAARPs, and seventy-two stargates or portals around the world.*
>
> *If you go to my website, www.stevequayle.com, do a search for a paper entitled Planet X – Nibiru – Gabriel's Fist, something like that. I think that should help.*
>
> *I believe that the LHC is like a main lock in a worldwide locking mechanism. If the main lock is unlocked, then all the other locks, portals, can be unlocked. Could that be what they were trying to do with you and your experiment?*

I hope that helps. Talk to you soon.

Steve"

Bryce turned off the laptop and closed it in shock. "The Abyss... I knew it!" he whispered, as he set the laptop down on the bench.

Just then LJ tore out of the house. "You ready?! You ready?!" he said as he jumped off of the porch to his spot.

Cooper sat stunned by what he just learned, in a whisper, he said, "I hope I'm ready..."

Chapter 12

__Outskirts of Cornwall, England – Present Day__

*H*e'd been driving for over three and a half hours straight. After leaving his office in Dorking, he decided, although it was farther, to head up to the M25 that ran around London.

Country roads in the UK were notoriously slow and the M25 was more like the freeways back home in America. On that road, even with the traffic, he made decent time. As it merged with the M4 in Slough, he got off and stopped at a small diner to have a much needed bite.

Before he got back on the road, he called Zoraida. As expected, she chastised him for not leaving work sooner. But she could hear the urgency and concern in his voice when he told her he was looking into something very important. She graciously let him off the hook by telling him how much she appreciated him taking the time off from work.

Over the years, he tried to speak with her about his job. But she wasn't really science minded and she didn't understand. Take his most recent effort last night. When he tried to tell her what he figured out about what might be riding the FTEs, she looked at him like he was speaking Chinese.

If she couldn't grasp even the basics, how could she understand the crazy stuff he'd found? Even he thought it was crazy. That's why he'd already determined to send his whole theory and data to his confidant.

Back in the day, he was his most prized student. It also helped that they both shared the same faith. Plus, the confidant was removed from his immediate professional sphere. That gave The Professor the confidence needed to disclose his thoughts, and even worst fears, free from judgment by his peers.

His full bladder wrestled him from his thoughts. He went to

the "loo" when he left the restaurant. But that was hours ago. With sudden urgency, his head swiveled around, looking for any sign of a public restroom.

All he saw was the semi-dark countryside slightly illuminated by a full moon. He sighed. He didn't want to stop and lose more time.

He hadn't seen another car for a long time. After he got off the M4, he caught the M5 out of Bristol. His GPS led him down the road he was currently on, the A38. A while back, he passed a huge nature preserve called Dartmoor National Park. If he was going to take a leak in nature, that would have been the place. He knew that up ahead was more populated areas. He didn't want to stop there and get tangled in traffic.

All of a sudden he saw a sign that read "Marsh Mills". It was a small town and given the late hour, it was deserted. Even if he wanted to use the loo here, he was out of luck.

Then, as he passed through the area, he went by what looked like an old windmill. "Hum..." he sounded, as he reached over and touched the GPS screen. His non-accelerator foot was involuntarily tapping to the urgent tune of his bladder. He knew that if he didn't go now, he was gonna go anyway!

"There," he whispered, as the map showed a river and a turnout. He punched the accelerator and another five minutes passed. Finally, he spied the turn out into an empty clearing illuminated by the moonlight. He pulled off, and swung his car around in a big "U-Turn" so he could leave in a hurry.

The car barely stopped, when he slammed it into park. He was out the door and rounding the car's backside while the gasoline in the tank still sloshed. He planted his feet on the far side of the car between the car and a sheer drop off down to the river. He barely managed to unzip his pants in time.

He breathed out a heavy sigh of relief as the pressure dissipated. Finally, he zipped up and straightened his belt. Only now did he look over the edge that he'd nearly drove off of. It was a good hundred and fifty feet to the bottom.

He whistled. "That was close. Gracias Padre!"

Still looking over the edge, without warning he heard a thunderous rumbling sound from behind him. He turned just in time to see two huge truck headlights bearing down on his Mercedes.

In an explosive crash that sounded through the gully below, the behemoth dump truck broadsided the car pushing it and him over the cliff to a sure death.

Lazy Hoof – Present Day

"Well hello Ivy! What a pleasant surprise." Mac said with a smile into the phone as he watched Bryce and Ed ride off.

Ivy was Ivelisse Estefani Black, Mac's first and only ex-wife's kid sister. Ivy and her sister were from a large, passionate Puerto Rican family. Mac's relationship with his ex-wife was stormy from the beginning. But Ivy, a full fifteen years younger than her sister, always looked up to him.

When they divorced all those years ago, Ivy was devastated and vowed to keep in touch with the brother-in-law that she liked better than her sister. And keep in touch she did.

Through the years, she would always remember Mac's birthday and send him a card. Around the holiday's he'd always get a call. And she even went out of her way to see him once in a while.

One such trip took her out to Massachusetts when he was attending Harvard and working on his Masters. It was the strangest time. She called him up out of the blue and said that she'd won a trip to Boston from a contest she forgot entering. She asked if he would show her around.

He was more than twenty years older than her and a father figure. He said he'd love to, but the day she drove in, he had a basketball game. She happily attended and that's where he introduced her to her present husband.

Xavier, or "X" as Mac called him, was a young upstart kid

studying geophysics. They were teammates on the basketball team. X was a six-six, blonde haired, blue eyed bull. One time during a game, a fight broke out and the kid was so upset that when Mac went to pull him off the bloodied other guy, he threw big Mac off like he was a ragdoll. He used to tease the kid that he growled at him like a wild animal. From that day forward, Mac was glad that X was on his side. He'd hate to make him mad.

After taking one look at Ivy, Xavier asked Mac to introduce him. Instantly they fell for each other. She was a savvy upstart from the Spanish Harlem of New York. Mac heard that he was from Boston and came from old money, lots of it.

Mac thought it strange seeing them together. There has always been a natural competitiveness between New Yorkers and Bostonians, i.e. the Yanks and the RedSox. In spite of X's reserved personality, the two would playfully banter with one another over many a meal.

He always thought Ivy was stunningly beautiful. She was a mixture, as many Puerto Ricans are, of Caribbean African with Spanish highlights. But that combination also nurtured a passion for life that bled out of her with both generous displays of grace and volatile fits of temper.

Mac thought they were an odd couple: The tall, blue eyed, blonde haired white guy and the fiery light skinned Puerto Rican. Their relationship was a testament to the saying "opposites attract". X brought temperament to Ivy's passion. And she brought passion to his drabness. The two were madly in love. Somehow, it worked.

Ivy was behind X in school. But both of them went on to finish their educations. Ivy did her doctorate in Medicinal and Pharmaceutical Chemistry at USC. X graduated with his Ph.D. in geophysics. From there, X landed a top job with the USGS in Pasadena, California where he'd been ever since.

A couple of years later, out of the blue, a headhunter type called Ivy and offered her a prestigious position at a leading pharmaceutical company. Coincidently, the company's headquarters was also in

Pasadena.

It didn't take long for the two to pick up where they left off; soon after they were married. Mac went to their wedding seven years ago. He didn't hear from her as often, but she was part of a family that he'd long since lost. And he cared for her like his own kid sister.

"How are you Mac?" she asked lightly. She always called him Mac, even when he was married to her sister.

"Ah, could be better, could be worse. Right now I'm in Montana cooling my heels with my buddy Coop."

"You're with him right now?!" she asked excitedly.

Everyone in the science community knew who the famous Dr. Bryce Obadiah Cooper was. Mac shared long stories about Dr. Cooper nearly every, albeit seldom, time he and Ivy talked.

One of the things that Ivy gleaned from those conversations was how well Cooper was connected. Apparently he had relationships with the media, the White House, world leaders and other heavyweights in the science community. If anybody could hear hers and Xavier's concerns and get it to the people, it was Dr. Bryce Cooper.

"Well, no I'm not with him at this very..."

"I need your help," she blurted out in a low determined voice.

"My help?" Mac asked, now hearing the urgency in her voice. "You okay? Is X okay?"

"Yes, we're fine. I can't go into it over the phone. They might be listening," she whispered. "Do you think it'd be okay if X and I come up to see you guys?"

"Who might be listening," he asked immediately alarmed.

"I can't go into it, but... we need to talk. It's really important. In fact, it's urgent."

"Urgent? We? What-da-ya mean urgent?"

Mac took the phone from his ear and looked at it questioningly. Putting it back to his ear, he said, "Sure... sure. I don't think there's a problem. When do you think you'll make the trip?"

She was quiet for a moment.

"Ivy? You still there?"

She bit her lip, "Yes, I'm here. The thing is... can... can we come up right away?"

"Right away?" Mac asked bewildered, "You mean tonight?"

"No... I mean like... the next flight out."

"What?" Now Mac was really concerned. "Alright... what's going on Ivy," he asked firmly. "It's not like you to skip out on work. And how the heck did you get that stiff necked husband of yours to agree on such a spur of the moment trip? Are you in trouble with the law... do you owe someone money... how much do you need?"

"No, no really," she said with a giggle. "It's nothing like that. Call it professional advice... that's all. Like I said, I can't really go into it on the phone. But Mac... it is very, very important."

Ivy was never one for being over dramatic. If she said she needed to speak with them, he knew it was serious.

"Okay," he said quietly. "You need me to send one of Coops planes for you?"

"He's got a plane too?!" Ivy asked with surprise. Then recovering she said, "No, no... we're fine. We can fly out of LAX direct. We'll be there early evening."

"Okay... sounds good. And give me a call when you land. We'll send a car for you."

"Okay Mac, I appreciate it. Love ya."

"And Ivy?" he said sternly.

"Yes"

"Be careful... I'll see you when you get here."

"Okay, see you soon," she said, and severed the connection.

Slowly renewing his stroll to the lodge house, Mac stored his phone.

Shaking his head, he asked aloud, "What was that all about?"

Chapter 13

__Lazy Hoof – Three and a Half Years Earlier__

Bryce plopped down at his computer chair like a thirsty man wandering in the desert. He briefly looked at Quayle's site, but had yet to do any real digging.

Sometimes there just weren't enough hours in the day. Between writing the numerous scientific papers on everything from M Theory to his own dimensional theory and settling into his new position as owner/operator of the Lazy Hoof, he hardly had time for anything else.

He often had to remind himself that scientific papers and articles that he'd written before the Reset were wiped out. Thus, to his frustration, he had to write them again.

But, as with everything he read or wrote, he remembered every crossed "t" or dotted "i". His photographic memory would never let him forget something once he read it.

His memory and his ability to consume large amounts of data quickly, and definitively analyze it, gave him an advantage over most mere mortals.

His brain capacity had launched him ahead of all of his peers in his chosen discipline of physics and also provided for opportunities not afforded to the average scientist.

But despite this success, he tried very hard to keep a low profile. He had spent his life trying to be underestimated. For instance, because he was so well read, his vocabulary was almost as extensive as a modern supercomputer. Yet, he often spoke like one of his ranch hands that he employed.

His mother always told him to "never forget where you came from". He took the admonition to heart. He never wanted to appear like a super-intellect.

But with a growing number of public appearances and the extensive writing of scientific papers and books since his Reset, he thought that his days of being an underestimated genius in relative anonymity were gone forever.

With a sigh, he did a search on Quayle's site for the title he was given. Up came a list of papers, the first being the paper in question. He clicked on the link; only thirteen pages. He figured that he could speed read it in a few seconds.

He started through the paper, shaking his head at one point because he thought the conspiratory tone over the top. There was a bit in there on CERN and some science fiction show that he'd never seen. But as he raced through the document, he stopped dead on page six.

This section was talking about HAARP; a subject that he was uncomfortably intimate with. He read through the part once and stopped to ponder the astonishing claim that lay there in. He shook his head as if to say, "No way!" Then he read it again, slowly this time. "HAARP? Come on Quayle!"

He read again, aloud this time:

> *"This tuning of frequencies would in fact align with the very real phenomenon of Ley lines, properly described by Alfred Watkins as lines of electromagnetic energy crossing grids of the Earth and forming 72 nodal points, which frequently archaeological evidence of layering cultures and time periods over specific areas. The concept of the planetary energetics explains the role of electromagnetism attraction from the consistency of ancient Neolithic structures as stone circles, barrows, chalk hill figures and ancient monuments.*
>
> *Within the realm of quantum theory which examines matter at a subatomic level, this would then apply to the micro and the macro: from the smallest of discreet units,*

to a hierarchy of quanta of similarly shaped and electrically powered clusters at a galactic and cosmic level."

"Come on! You can't be serious! Galactic and cosmic level?"

"The logical conclusion of fractal self-similarity should (and could), lead only to the acknowledgement of a purposeful and organized original creation, which, at some point in the temporal past, was interrupted by deliberate action precipitating multiple catastrophisms and the subsequent descent of not only the human species but the creation as a whole, which again points to both Genesis 3 and the Days of Jared as the antecedent events.

Similarly, in a January, 2011 broadcast of Coast to Coast AM, guest Steve Quayle noted that there are 72 ionospheric heaters similar to the HAARP facility in Gakona, Alaska. This number would correspond with the 72 nations of Genesis 10 as being under the influence of [powers] of the 72 regents of the fallen hierarchy and the 72 quinaries of the degrees of the zodiac in Kabbalistic teaching!"

Bryce sat back in his chair and considered what he just read. As crazy as the paper might sound, it touched a nerve with him in several places. Then his mind drifted back to a time before his Reset.

Geneva, LHC (Topside) – Four Years Earlier

"So you're saying that... that these Nephilim are the half breed offspring of fallen angels and humans?" Bryce asked incredulously.

"That's right doctor. That's exactly what I'm saying... if you can accept it."

Intensely staring at his mentor, Diggs said, "And there are other places in the bible where they show up. But I understand how you feel about the bible, so let me defer to other writings."

"Such as?"

"There are other writings called the Book of Enoch, the Book of Jubilees and the Book of Jasher. These are ancient texts, pseudo-books, found with the Dead Sea Scrolls. Each, describe huge beings that were massively strong. There were accounts of them having six fingers and six toes. Most were said to have blonde hair, the precursors to the 'Aryan Master Race' that Hitler was trying to duplicate. Other stories said that they had flaming red hair. But the one constant to all of the tales is that the Nephilim were easily provoked to anger. They were also known to have huge appetites and eventually became so blood thirsty that they had to leave the Earth, or go into hiding."

"Honestly Diggs, I don't have time for fairy tales. We have a news..."

"Speaking of fairy tales, do you remember all of the Greek myths of gods and such?"

"Sure, but I don't see..."

"And do you remember hearing the urban legends of werewolves, vampires and Big Foot?"

"Son, did you hit your head or something? What are..."

Diggs made a few other keystrokes and swung his flat screen monitor around for Bryce to see. "Take a look at these."

"What in the world?"

"No Dr. Cooper... not of this world is my point.

"These are skeletal remains found in and around Greece. There is no explanation for them, nor do archeologists know from what time period they came. And there are similar findings in other parts of the world."

Bryce was suddenly intrigued.

Diggs, made a few more clicks with his mouse. "These are ancient axes recovered from the Sumerian era of ancient Babylon."

"They're huge! How could anyone swing one of those?"

"That's the point doctor. No 'man' could swing them, but it was said that the Nephilim were over twenty feet tall."

"Come on Diggs, if there were creatures like that roaming the Earth, why didn't they leave their mark on history."

"Dr. Cooper, they left their mark more than you know." Diggs changed the screen. "These are some hieroglyphics from the pyramids.

"The pyramids? That looks like..."

"So let's talk about the building of those same pyramids. Despite the best efforts of archeologists, no one can give a satisfactory explanation of how ancient peoples, with simple tools, could build such great monuments. The precision alone was beyond the knowledge of those people. Even with our technology, we would be hard pressed to duplicate them.

"Just look at the physical aspects of cutting stone. And, what of moving those massive stones over great distances with people who barely discovered the wheel? It would take our generation, with all of our technology, and huge machinery, many years to build those structures. And yet, they did it with rickety wooden carts? What's harder to believe? That they accomplished all of this on their own, or that they had outside help?"

Diggs made a few more keystrokes. "These are the Abydos-Hieroglyphs depicted on the walls of the ancient temple of Abydos in Egypt."

"Holy moly! That looks like a helicopter," Bryce said

taken aback. "And that looks like a plane... hold on... is that a spaceship?" he asked dumbfounded.

"And these glyphs are not just in Egypt. There are plenty on Mayan temples as well. Look here," Diggs said with a few more keystrokes and a couple of clicks with the mouse.

"What in the world?" Bryce said shell shocked.

Giving Bryce no reprieve, Diggs pressed on, "And you know how the Mayan's made human sacrifices?"

"Sure..." Bryce said, still staring at the computer screen.

"What if the Nephilim left because they were blood thirsty as I've mentioned? And what if, because those primitive people knew the Nephilim, or gods as they called them, to be blood thirsty, so they sacrificed humans, spilling their blood like chum for sharks, to draw them back?

"And look at this," Diggs said, as he made a few more clicks that pulled up a map of the world with various ancient ruins listed on it.

"The pyramids are located at the very geographic center of the world. How did the Egyptians figure that out? But wait, there's more.

"And look at these. These are ancient ruins all around the world whose builders are also questionable." Diggs pointed to the screen, which showed a topographical map of the Earth, with ancient ruins superimposed all over it.

"Okay," Bryce said.

"Now watch," Diggs made a few keystrokes and a line appeared connecting all of the sites, all over the world.

Those lines on the map formed a mirror image of the constellations in the sky.

Bryce's mouth was agape, "No way..."

Diggs now rammed his point home, "I believe... that these creatures still interact with us on a regular basis. I believe that these and others are interdimensional creatures that are not bound by our physical laws. As such, I believe that they operate in that spatial dimension right below our own in your theorized dimensional stack. And, I believe that they move with impunity in and out of human sensory range."

"I'll be a... So are you saying that these... these... angelic beings mentioned in the bible are really Nephilim?"

"No, those angelic beings are not Nephilim. Remember, Nephilim are half breeds with human DNA. I believe that that is why they need to travel around in 'space ships'. Because unlike their angelic cousins, they are somewhat bound by the same physical laws that we are. The difference is that they have the technology to overcome the dimensional barrier.

"Angels on the other hand can move back and forth with impunity without such assistance. In addition, I believe that the Nephilim are relegated to the shallower dimensions in the stack. From what I've read, angels are able to travel into the stack relatively deep."

"Hold on a second. Are you telling me that you think the stack of dimensions lead to heaven... and... and... God?" he said skeptically.

"I promised you doctor that we would keep this discussion scientific. Let's just say that whatever is over there... in the other dimensions... isn't us, and leave it at that.

"But getting back to the Nephilim and UFO's," Diggs said, spinning his monitor back toward him. "The ancient depictions of these creatures have them disappearing up into the sky. As crazy as it sounds, it seems that UFO sightings have increased over the last few years. The UFO craze has even been made popular and acceptable by Hollywood science fiction movies.

"As you know, through your own research, the

investigation of UFO sightings has become a quasi-science. I've read instances where astrophysicists go into flattened down crop circles looking for evidence of electromagnetic residue that..."

"Hold on a sec. Did you say... electromagnetic residue?"

"Yes... amongst other things..."

Bryce picked up a pencil on the desk and started twirling it in his fingers. Diggs knew this to be a sign that his mentor was thinking and digesting. As crazy as the story might be, he knew that Dr. Cooper as a Dimensional Theorist didn't automatically dismiss things that were out of the ordinary. He weighed all factors and tried to postulate an answer or reason.

Bryce, now fully engaged, seriously asked Diggs, "Have you given some thought as to what the reason was behind this magnetic residue?"

"As a matter of fact, I have given it some thought. It could be something to do with the changing of electromagnetic fields that enables them to move between dimensions. The bigger the magnet, the deeper in the stack they are able to go."

Bryce went white as a ghost. He looked as if he were going to be sick.

"Are you okay Dr. Cooper? You don't look so good."

"I was afraid you were going to say that; the bigger the magnet, the deeper the penetration..."

Bryce was stunned into silence by the revelation. Slowly a look of recognition came across his face. He was holding the pencil in his hands so tightly that it snapped in half with a "crack".

"Uh-oh."

Chapter 14

Surrey Countryside, UK – Two Weeks Ago

*T*he Mullard Space Science Laboratory (MSSL) was the headquarters for SURF and was located in the Surrey countryside, in the center of the Guildford/Dorking/Horsham 'triangle'. It was there that the Director of MSSL maintained his office.

The Director came to the project out of the blue as an outsider three years ago. His science discipline was not in astronomy. This was a sore point with many would-be directors from within the organization. He was a Ph.D. with superb credentials, but nonetheless, people were bitter. And his heavy handed management style didn't help.

The one small reprieve for the staff was that he wasn't around much. MSSL was a small facility. It was true that the organization maintained many professional working relationships with other research facilities throughout the world. However, such a posting would be characterized as "low-key" at best. And it was this juxtaposition of the Director's activity that baffled many.

He was often away on business; flying out of Gatwick, the nearest airport, at a moment's notice. He practically lived with a phone in his ear. And it was rumored that he'd even counseled with kings and world leaders. The question on everyone's lips, but none dared to ask, was: Just why is he so important?

The extremely large man had an odd shaped oblong head. He rested his excessively big feet, matched to his stature, on the corner of his desk. As was his habit, he rubbed the top of his bald skull with sides full of white hair, which long ago changed from its original fiery red.

His Scottish brogue boomed into the telephone's handset, "Och aye Mr. Secretary, we ur oan schedule. aam pushin' mah fowk as stoaner as Ah daur. they ur only human ye ken (Yes Mr. Secretary, we are on schedule. I'm pushing my people as hard as I dare. They are only human you know.) "

That was the problem with diplomats: They may be ruthless, but they lacked common sense. Even the best plans needed time to bring them to fruition. The end game was close now. The Scott could taste it.

The Secretary of the United Nations was very anxious about "The Arrival". He was a member of The Group, the Kings of the Earth that the Director and his kind put into power. But the truth was that he, nor any human, really understood the full implications of what The Arrival would mean for mankind. But, as with all subservants, he was promised position, wealth and power. That was always enough for the greedy.

"We hae tae stick tae th' security protocols 'at we've established. tay much exposure main compromise th' plan. ye dornt want tae ta happen dae ye? (We have to stick to the security protocols that we've established. Too much exposure will compromise The Plan. You don't want that to happen do you?)"

The big man listened and nodded.

"Och aye, och aye. th' arrival ay uir guests is still scheduled fur th' sam time. but much needs tae be accomplished afair noo an' 'en. thes dimen... Ah pure techt 'at th' atmosphaur main be cultivated in sic' a way 'at when they dae arrife, they will be received wi' open arms. 'en we wulnae need disclosure, they can disclose themselves. ye an' yer colleagues will jist need tae be surprised (Yes, yes. The arrival of our guests is still scheduled for the same time. But much needs to be accomplished before now and then. This dimen... I mean that the atmosphere must be cultivated in such a way that when they do arrive, they will be received with open arms. Then we will not need Disclosure, they can disclose themselves. You and your colleagues will just need to be surprised).”

Listening, he nodded again, chuckling.

“Och aye mr. secretary, ye ur reit. most ay them will be genuinely surprised! 'at will be a secht. okay, Ah main say cheerio th' noo. Ah hae an appointment comin' in shortly (Yes Mr. Secretary, you are right. Most of them will be genuinely surprised! That will be a sight. Okay, I must say goodbye. I have an appointment coming in shortly).”

In closing, he exchanged superficial and unfelt pleasantries with the man and replaced the handset.

Absent the Scottish accent, he said in an ominous tone, “Yes,” through a slit of a smile, “there will be lots of surprises in the very near future.”

A knock at his office door broke his reflection.

“Enter,” he boomed.

Through the door came Dr. Alvaro Mora, lead researcher of SURF.

“Director,” Mora said with his thick Spanish accent, “thank you for seeing me on such short notice.” The Professor reached over and shook the large man’s hand. Alvaro’s hand was enveloped by the Scott’s as if it was swallowed by a large fish looking for a meal.

In a pleasant but business like tone, the Scottish brogue was back as he said, “Ay coorse Ah woods make time fur mah leid researcher ay a body ay th' most important projects in th' organization. (Of course I would make time for my lead researcher of one of the most important projects in the organization.)” Then he gestured for The Professor to take a seat.

“Thank you,” The Professor said. “As I said on the phone, it is a rather urgent matter. I believe the Earth could be in grave danger."

After Mora was settled, the Director leaned forward on his elbows and said, "Wa don't ye teel me aw abit it? (Why don't you tell me all about it?)"

It was then that Dr. Alvaro Mora began to talk about the soon rampaging Sun and the anomalies that he believed to be riding in the Flux Transfer Events.

Taking notes and listening with rapt attention was physicist Dr. Lynn Abbott, former Director of the LHC.

Lazy Hoof – Present Day

After Bryce and Ed climbed off their horses, Ed tied them to a nearby tree. Koffee, the Seeing Eye Dog, sat head down at Manaya's feet. His eyes followed Bryce as he walked up, but the animal did not so much as twitch.

Manaya was sitting on a rock, facing the river. Bryce knew the rock well... before she died, his mother sat there often.

As Bryce walked up to Manaya, Ed meandered over to the calm river, within earshot. He picked up some smooth stones and started skipping them across the water.

"Thank you for coming Dr. Cooper," Manaya said facing the water.

"Bryce, please," he said.

"Thank you again, Bryce."

As the Montanan studied her face, he thought that there was something... unique, special about her. Instantly, although he didn't know why, he liked her.

"So how did you two find the Lazy Hoof," Bryce asked with genuine interest. "No offense, but despite Ed's cowboy boots there, ya'll don't look the ranch type."

Ed, a bit on the shy side, stopped throwing rocks and chuckled. He knew that the comment was more geared toward his wife than he. He was comfortable enough, but Manaya was a different story.

Even now, her make-up was impeccable, her brunette hair was perfect, she was adorned with jewelry, had on a cashmere sweater and a nice pair of slacks. Her shoes were flat, but Bryce guessed that they probably came from one of those fancy department stores on the west coast like Macy's or Nordstroms. He guessed that the couple was probably in their sixties.

Ignoring the question for the moment, she said, "This is a beautiful spot. Your mother's favorite."

Ed looked over at Bryce curiously. Although Bryce didn't return the look, he felt the man's eyes on him. Cooper kept his gaze on his wife.

"Yeah... that's what your husband said. Since I remember every name I read, and I've never read your names until yesterday, it's a forgone conclusion that you've never been here. So just how did you know about that," he asked pointedly.

For the first time, the woman turned her face to Bryce. She had a hint of a smile. Then the blind woman said:

"I saw it"

Lazy Hoof – Three and a Half Years Earlier

Bryce looked at the clock. It was late. The kids were tucked in. His pregnant wife already came down and said she was headed to bed early. All was quiet at the Lazy Hoof. It was the perfect time for Bryce to get lost in the online community of Steve Quayle.

Bryce continued to devour the website, along with the substantial links to other "alternative media" sites. One such link led him to an audio interview with Steve Quayle and Tom Horn. He immediately recognized Horn as the same author who wrote Forbidden Gates, a book that Quayle gave him.

He found the book a fascinating read. It discussed transhumanism and the use of Nephilim technology in genetics. Sprinkled throughout were scientific proofs that Cooper could dig his teeth into. So he guessed that any interview with those two men would be worth a listen. The subject was the mysterious number seventy-two.

The interview was a few years old and entitled, "Steve Quayle & Tom Horn: Inter-Dimensional Stargates Opening, Fallen Angels, Demons, Djinn, Nephilim Coming...." He'd already listened to it once. This was his second time through, fast-forwarding to the parts he wanted to focus on as he took copious notes.

> Quayle - *"Well let's talk about seventy-two. And obviously, seventy-two... and thank God for every bit of research that Sue Bradley and others have done... yourself, myself and all those who've contributed, but the thing that's interesting is that we're talking about a number that is so significant to the end times, so significant to the occultists..."*

Bryce shook his head, "Occultists?"

Inside the recesses of his brain, a red warning light flashed. His gut told him that an important part of his personal history and mankind's future was about to fit together like precision puzzle pieces.

> Quayle - *"...so much emblazoned in symbology... ah... from the number of bricks on the back of the Great Seal, to seventy-two ladder rungs on Jacob's ladder. Let's talk from your perspective from all of the research that you've done, why is seventy-two so important?"*

Bryce skipped a long preamble where Horn spoke about certain and imminent genetic manipulation to the human race, including, but not limited to, the rerouting of people's DNA.

While Bryce found that part of the discussion was enlightening, he was particularly interested in information that may, or may not have a direct relationship to his work in physics. He kept fast forwarding until he found the spot he wanted:

> Tom - "...*after the sacking of Admiral Poindextor, they went in and found appropriations to DARPA (Defense Advanced Research Projects Agency) for the creation... this is a quote! For the creation for a master race of superhumans! Well... Steve, when later in 2005, DARPA admitted that what we are doing now is even bolder, we just got smarter about how to hide it and call it by different names... what would be bolder than a master race of superhumans? Joel Golder has said that he was told several times not to ask about certain things. And they said specifically not to ask about, quote: time reversal methods and the special focus area at DARPA, end quote. What? Time reversal methods? What could that possibly mean? It really does sound like our pals at DARPA have for years Steve have been preparing to open these seventy-two stargates that you mentioned in the last show!*"

Bryce stopped the audio and sat back. His head was spinning. He felt like Alice in Wonderland. And this rabbit hole was insanely deep.

"Seventy-two stargates?" he asked his computer. "Seventy-two HAARPs? What is going on here? Have I just jumped onto the loony wagon? These guys are saying that the government... our government has been trying to open seventy-two stargates?"

He believed that they were using the word stargate interchangeably with portal. But to be sure, he opened another tab in his Internet Explorer and Googled "stargates".

Many references dealt with a science fiction show, but as he continued to search he found several discussions where pseudo-science believers thought that stargates were simply interdimensional portals that allowed people, or... *entities*, he thought, to cross between dimensions.

So Quayle and Horn are talking about real stargates or portals... but not just one or two. Quayle seems to think there are seventy-two of them. And seventy-two HAARPs? But what could the connection be? He started to twirl a chewed up yellow pencil between his fingers as he thought.

Horn said that DARPA was using advanced technology to make superhumans! Advanced technology, as in... Nephilim technology?

Quayle said there was a... he looked down at the notes he'd been taking... *an occultist connection? Seventy ionospheric heaters, HAARPs he reminded himself... seventy-two portals, stargates... Nephilim technology...*

Abruptly he sat straight up as the pieces clicked into place.

"Not only are they trying to open the Abyss and let all the Fallen out, they're making an army!"

Chapter 15

Damascus, Syria – Present Day

"That is very good news Mr. Secretary," Tabak said into the telephone handset. "Yes... we are ready on our end."

A quiet rap on the door drew the Prime Minister's attention. He hit the mute button and said, "Come!"

Beady-eyed Farouk slithered through the door. Tabak pointed to the opulent red velvet chairs in front of his desk. Like an obedient dog, Farouk hurried and sat.

"I thought the same thing Mr. President."

Farouk gave a quizzical look to Tabak.

Tabak wrote a note on the yellow pad on his desk, tapped it and slid it over to Farouk: "Group Conference Call."

Farouk nodded and wrote his own note. Tabak acknowledged it with a wink.

"That's right Director. I've just received a report from my most trusted advisor," he smiled at Farouk, stroking his ego, "Everything is in place."

Farouk knew everyone who was supposed to be on the call: The new King of England, The King of Saudi Arabia, The President of the U.S., other world leaders from kingdoms and governments. The Banker and Director, important players behind the scenes, were also privy to the call.

This was as close as Farouk had ever gotten to a conversation with any of them. While he'd on occasion spoken to the principal's representatives, direct conversation was reserved for the principals themselves.

"Very well then. Thank you all. We will speak face to face in Tehran day after tomorrow." With a look of irritation, he replaced the handset.

"Something wrong Your Excellency?" Farouk asked upon seeing his Charge's look.

Tabak was tapping his lips with his index finger. "I would not say wrong... just curious."

"Curious sir?"

"Curious that The Banker has become far more assertive with The Group than in times past."

"And this disturbs you Your Excellency?"

"Not disturbs Farouk. Just... interests."

Tabak knew the look from his second. The man would be more than willing to take The Banker out if asked. He'd done so many times before.

"Surely a Commoner like The Banker would not dare to usurp leadership roles from royals and leaders like yourself?" Farouk asked indignantly.

The Prime Minister smiled and condescendingly explained, "Your loyalty is very much appreciated. But there is much you do not understand. I may lead this country and..." he gestured to the wall map with his chin, "...will lead the New Ottoman Empire one day, but men like The Banker provide the gold for such exploits. I am not," then he nodded to Farouk, "and thus you should not, be offended by his actions. It is just curious."

Taking the gentle rebuke, Farouk changed the subject and said, "All is ready for your trip to Tehran."

"There is much to do before now and then, yes?" Tabak smiled leanly, "The Tehran trip will be the first real opportunity for all of us to get together. These exercises are as much for unity as they are for training."

The multinational, multicultural joint military exercise was one that had been scheduled for months. However, since its humble beginnings of an exercise with just Syria and Iran, virtually all the Arab countries in the Middle East had joined. In addition, Russia with their new Eurasian contingent would also be attending. No more was the United States the lone military powerhouse.

"Will there be anything else Your Excellency?" Farouk asked, wanting to get back to his duties.

"That will be all for now," Tabak replied.

"Yes sir," with that, the loyal servant got to his feet and slithered out the door quietly.

Tabak sat brooding and thinking about The Banker and the things that were to be.

As The Plan progressed, the world would change forever. Just how much, even the future ruler of the would-be New Ottoman Empire could not have ever guessed.

Tel Aviv, Israel – Present Day

The meeting with the Rabbi made Zac feel uneasy. While he was absolutely dedicated to what the TRM wanted to do, he questioned the event's timing. Such a provocative move by the State of Israel, especially in times like these, did not seem prudent.

However, he reminded himself that Adonai was still in charge, regardless of man's efforts. If he allowed the Tabernacle, and then Temple, to be restored to the Temple Mount, who was Zac to question the timing?

The Israeli had to admit that given the long duration since the second Temple was destroyed on Tisha B'Av (the ninth day of the Hebrew month Av) in the year 3830 (70 A.D.), the Temple's restoration was a miracle.

And the Rabbi was right on one other count: The Tanakh (Jewish Bible) said that when the Messiah came, he would bring peace. Zac saw the sit-rep (situation report) this morning. He left out some details in his discussion with the Rabbi – Israel was being surrounded. And this time, the government feared it was not simply for a show of force. If Israel ever needed peace... it was now.

The meeting Zac just left was additional evidence to that fact. From his meeting with the Rabbi, he'd driven back to Tel Aviv for his afternoon briefing. The news was not good. Turkey, as expected, formally withdrew from NATO this morning. That didn't surprise anyone. Turkey had long ago become an Islamic fundamentalist State. What was unsettling were the reports of Russian troops massing along the Iranian and Azerbaijani borders.

There were also reports of ship and submarine movements flowing into the Strait of Hormuz, the world's vital sea choke point for oil shipping. "Chatter" had spiked and it indicated that something very big was afoot. Things could escalate very quickly.

As he drove the streets of Tel Aviv, he wondered what would become of this city... his home. Many of his fellow Orthodox Jews were reviled by the city. They said that since its founding in 1909, it'd become a modern day Sodom and Gomorrah. Worse, he couldn't dispute the claim.

Placed on the beautiful Mediterranean Sea, it boasted a population of over four-hundred thousand. Unfortunately, despite Israel's heritage, that population was by far, mostly secular. Its twenty-four hour culture earned it the title of "The City That Never Sleeps" and its reputation rivaled New York and Las Vegas. Here, the cosmopolitan lifestyle distracted Israelis from the sober reality that Jews were hated by the Arabs who surrounded them.

To avoid this dire truth, the average Israeli would say that the Middle East was by its nature a tremulous region. History showed that Muslims would just as soon fight amongst themselves, than conduct an orchestrated attack on Israel.

Even now, Saudi Arabia was in the middle of a gruesome crackdown on its people. The Wahhabis, Osama bin Laden's radical sect, were trying to wrestle the throne from the House of Saud. The result was death in mass. Thousands were killed, and as a last resort, the Throne used chemical weapons on its own people. Zac knew this because it was his job to know. However, neither the state controlled media, nor western mainstream media reported on the violence, and thus the world continued in blissful ignorance of the atrocities. But Israel knew what her enemies were capable of.

Then of course there was the sectarian violence that spread throughout Iraq, Afghanistan, Libya, Egypt, Syria and other countries after the Arab Spring in 2011. Many longtime Arab leaders had been deposed. In their place the vacuum was filled by still other despots and evil men.

Many of these new leaders, like Tabak of Syria, were far worse than the originals that they'd removed. There was simply no end in sight to the violence, unless they could focus their anger somewhere else: a common enemy. Zac feared that that common enemy would soon be Israel.

As a precaution to the pending violence, Israel already began the distribution of gas masks, M-16s and ammo. The Reserves were put on a war footing and all of the civilian population was reminded where their emergency shelters were. War was in the air.

Driving back home, he shook his head to himself and mumbled, "It's Nazi Germany all over again." He sighed. Such was Israel's lot in life.

Zac realized that such thinking could easily drive him into depression. To avoid it, he purposed the shifting of gears in his mind. He fixated on Josiah's American barbeque ribs and instantly his mouth began to water.

He didn't know what the man's secret was, but he was certain that if he wanted to open a barbeque restaurant, he would be the wealthiest man in all of Tel Aviv. "But without the pork," he said aloud and chuckled.

Suddenly very hungry, he pushed the accelerator down and sped toward home.

Lazy Hoof – Three and a Half Years Earlier

Bryce's night sleep was fitful. He tossed and turned, unable to get comfortable. He had thought about going downstairs in the middle of the night to resume his research. But he knew better. He used to do that often. And he knew that if he started back down that road, he would build a habit that was hard to break.

Finally, in the wee hours of the morning, sleep found him. But his dreams were haunted with shape-shifting Fallen and angry Nephilim, HAARPs burning the atmosphere and portals opening. His abbreviated sleep was eventually interrupted by his bedside alarm going off at six a.m.

Still unable to conduct his full morning exercise routine, he went to the walk-in closet, as was his habit, and did his hundred push-ups and an abbreviated crunch routine. By the time he was done, he was winded and his leg hurt like crazy. As he labored to get to his feet in the closet, he purposely punched himself in the stomach, testing the tautness of his one-time six-pack. He noted that his mid-section was still flat, but had diminished to only a four-pack. He could hardly wait to get back to running and a harder work out.

Showered and shaved, he hobbled out to talk to his new ranch hand, Danny Mendez. Danny recently joined the Lazy Hoof after his honorable military discharge. Bryce stole the bright kid by talking him out of another reenlistment with the Air Force.

The physicist saw what the future held for the Staff Sergeant if he stayed at the HAARP facility in Gokona, Alaska. He thought he was doing him a favor by bringing him on. But in the end, the Lazy Hoof was the greater beneficiary of Mendez' skills and abilities. Seeing his potential and loyalty, Bryce quickly made him the Ranch Foreman.

As the morning wore on, he was tired and irritable. But his disposition was less about his nocturnal slumber, or lack thereof, than about his revelations of the previous night.

Gabrielle, as wives often do, sensed that something was bothering the physicist. But when she asked him about it, he'd tell her that he was fine. But he wasn't fine. To her, he looked worried.

When Bryce and family moved back to the ranch, Joe and Ruby moved out of the main house and into a smaller cottage on the grounds. When they came over to show the Coopers their retirement plans, Bryce was fidgety and he'd hardly said two words. Joe eyed him a couple of times, but didn't say anything. He was of the mind that Bryce was a grown man and if he wanted to talk, he would talk. So he let him stew.

By the time that Bryce did get back to his basement computer, it was after lunch. His leg was sore from all the morning's activity. He labored to prop his foot up on his desk corner with a loud "clump" of his cowboy boot.

But instead of launching the browser, he just sat there, deep in thought. He had so many questions and no idea where to find the answers. Quayle's website was helpful, but he was sure that there were other resources out there. He hated the idea of burning time fishing around for info.

After a moment, he finally said, "You can do this yourself Cooper, or you can go straight to the horse's mouth."

With that, he picked up the phone.

Chapter 16

Cornwall, England – Present Day

*N*ow she was worried. Alvaro called nearly six hours ago from a little restaurant off the motorway. He said that he'd be to the Cornwall cottage a little before midnight. It was now almost three-thirty in the morning. She tried calling him on his cell... No answer.

Seated with her in the front room of the quaint little cottage were her daughters Stephanie and Vanessa, and her granddaughter Azlynn. They were trying to keep her calm by chatting about old times and drinking strong English tea.

Stephanie was thirty-six, lived in New York and worked as an assistant for Goldman Sachs. She was also married to a tenured and successful Money Manager for the Wall Street firm, until about six months ago.

They met at work. But because of her demanding boss, and her husband's souring mood resulting from a decline in business, the two grew apart. The crevasse was too much to overcome and their five year marriage ended six months ago. Part of her reason for making this trip was to break the sad news to her parents in person. She wasn't comfortable making the announcement via phone call.

Thirty-one year old Vanessa was another story. She lived way over on the other coast in California and recently married a music producer. Mom and her eleven year old daughter Delilah were living the California dream with Vanessa's attentive husband in their multi-million dollar beach front Malibu home. Her husband was at the end of studio work with a big name Pop artist, and promised to join the family in England toward the end of the week.

The Mora's first and oldest granddaughter, Azlynn, also made the trip with her two year old son, Micah, from her home in Texas. Azlynn's husband was a professional Bull Rider and was in the middle of the Rodeo Circuit at the moment.

The life of an up and coming rodeo star didn't pay well. Unable to afford such a trip on her own, her aunts Stephanie and Vanessa, who looked at her as more of a younger sister, chipped in together to bring her and her toddler to England. In doing so, they blessed Alvaro and Zoraida immensely because it was the first time that the couple got to see their only great-grandson, Micah.

The children were fast asleep in their beds, unaware of the drama playing out in the cottage's front room.

"I don't understand... why hasn't he called? It is not like him," Zoraida fretted in her Spanish accent.

The girls wanted to call the police, Zorida declined. Instead, their mother elected to pray, at least for now. The Professor's longtime wife was a woman of faith and it didn't surprise her daughters. But they insisted that if they didn't hear from Dr. Mora by three-thirty a.m., they would indeed call the police. It was now twenty-five after three.

"Mom," Stephanie said firmly while she held her mother's shaking hand, "we need to call someone. This isn't like dad. He could be..." she bit off her words as she looked at her sister. "... he could be broke down somewhere. We need to find him."

Just then they heard a car pull up outside and a car door shut. Then the car drove away. The women jumped to their feet.

As they reached for the door, it flew open. They screamed.

To their amazement, there stood Dr. Alvaro Mora, dirt clad, bloodied and wounded.

He looked at them with wild eyes, as if surprised to see them.

In a raspy voice, he shouted, "WE HAVE TO GET OUT OF HERE! NOW!!!"

The Lazy Hoof – Present Day

"What? Whad-ya-mean you saw it?" Bryce asked dumbfounded. "I thought you were... you know..."

"Blind?" Manaya said finishing the sentence for him.

"Well... yeah. Blind. And besides, like I said, I know you've never been here before. How, could you have..." Bryce made quote marks with his fingers, "seen it, even if you could see."

"Your mother was a beautiful woman. Both inside and out," she said, again ignoring him.

Bryce stood there with a questioning look. Then he took off his hat and scratching his head, he looked over at Ed. The Californian was standing by the river and just shrugged. Then he went back to skipping stones.

Could these people have known my mother, he thought. *They're a little younger than she would have been. But I never remember her talking about them.*

"Bryce," Manaya said, sensing his confusion, "why don't you sit down." She padded a big rock right beside her. He knew the rock. He'd sat there often next to his mom. "I'll explain everything," she cooed.

As if in agreement with her, Koffee, her working Golden Lab, raised his head, gave a little whine and lowered it again.

Begrudgingly Bryce squatted down on the rock. "I wish you would explain, because I don't understand a thing that's going on here."

"I know what beauty is Bryce. I wasn't always totally blind. My mother, when she was pregnant with me, contracted toxoplasmosis."

Bryce gave her a blank look, "I'm ah... not that kind of doctor. I have no idea what that is."

She smiled, "Oh come now. You're bright. Have you've never heard of cat poop disease?"

He shook his head, "What?"

She giggled, "Toxoplasmosis is a parasite that a human can pick up when they come in contact with cat..." she dipped her head and tried to sound more dignified, "feces. My mother was working in the garden when she came into contact with some.

"She caught the parasite when I was in her womb. The disease can give healthy adults flu like symptoms. But those with weakened or low immunity, like an unborn child," she nodded, "it can cause a whole host of nasty problems.

"I was ill as a child as a result of it. That illness slowly stole my sight over the years. Now, it's almost completely gone," she shrugged. Turning her face to the sound of the water, she said, "I see shadows and blurs now, nothing more," she said wistfully.

"I'm sorry, but that still doesn't explain..."

"And besides," she continued, "there are other types of sight than those your physical eyes see."

Bryce instantly had a familiar feeling.

About four years ago, he began to see things differently himself.

USGS, Pasadena, California – Present Day

"You want to do what?" Dr. Young exclaimed. "In the middle of a crises? You've godda be kiddin me?!"

"Dr. Young, you know me well enough to know that I don't joke. And I'm sorry, but I need to leave right away," X said with sincere regret.

"Xavier... what's this all about," Young said less forcefully. He liked Dr. Black and knew him well enough to know that his loyal second in charge wouldn't make such a ridiculous request without good reason.

X locked his eyes with his boss. In a whisper, he said, "Evan... trust me when I tell you, you don't want to know what I'm about to do. But, I promise you, it is going to help with," he pointed to the report on Young's desk, "this. I believe politicians call it plausible deniability," he said in his best Ivy League accent.

"Hummm... I see," Dr. Young said, chin in hand. He was quiet for a moment, thinking about his options.

X knew better than to interrupt his thoughts.

With a sideways glance, Young asked, "How long would you

need?"

"A week."

Young gaffed, "A week! What am I supposed to do without you for a week?! And what about your wife? I know she's tied to her desk. You leaving her here while you play James Bond?"

X had a rare smirk, "Actually, this was her idea."

"You're kidding?"

"Nope, she made the arrangements herself. Not only is she coming with me, we are apparently both on a mission."

Dr. Young cocked his head, "What? I don't understand."

"Evan, I need to go. I don't want to go. But I need to," he said pointing again to the report. "I promise to get back as soon as I can. As soon as..." he let the statement hang in the air.

"As soon as what?" Young asked.

X looked hard at his boss, "As soon as I get results."

Dr. Young returned his look. There was no way he would ever contemplate letting a key staff member take time off during a crises. But Xavier Black was a serious man. He never joked. Hardly smiled. Evan often thought he was too serious and lacked personality. He threw himself fully into every task without complaint. And he always exceeded the Director's expectations. He was one of the smartest men at the USGS. Most importantly, he liked action. For him to be willing to walk away in the middle of all of the excitement, spoke volumes to Evan.

Reluctantly, he said, "Well... alright, but..."

"Thank you!" Xavier said, as he hurriedly rose to go.

He was nearly sprinting for the door when Evan said, "And Dr. Black?"

Xavier stopped at the threshold, "Yes sir?"

"Make sure you give me updates on this thing that... I don't know what you are doing," he said sternly and wagged his finger. "If I have to lose you for a week I want results."

"Yes sir, I will."

"And above everything else."

"Yes sir?"

Dr. Young looked down at the report on his desk, and then back to X, "Be careful. It's going to get bumpy from here."

"Yes sir, I will," and then he was gone.

Young let out a long tense breath. Looking down at the report and shaking his head, he said, "It's going to get bumpy for us all."

Chapter 17

Lazy Hoof – Present Day

*B*rilliant colors streamed in as the morning Sun beamed through the log cabin's high stained glass windows. The filtered crayons of light created whimsical patterns of color on the walls and floors.

The custom home was much more than just the main house, or lodge house. Its walls were well insulated looking timbers, with solid oak wood flooring and high ceilings. The numerous triple pane windows in the expansive home gave it a light and upbeat feel. The converted lodge had numerous bedrooms, almost too many to count. There was also a cinema room, a rec room and a cavernous chef quality kitchen and dining area that Bryce recently expanded significantly by busting out walls and putting on an addition. It was not only comfortable and beautiful, but it also had all the amenities of modern living.

Gabrielle often commented that it would be better to have a revolving door at the entrance instead of the tall, sturdy oak one. The Lazy Hoof Ranch was always bustling with activity. And boy did Lady Cooper like the energy of it all. It made her feel alive and purposeful.

That being said, mornings were her favorite time. Because it was one of the few times that things were quiet. She loved to come to the warm Sunroom, off the kitchen, and sit. She'd allowed herself one cup of coffee a day. At seven and a half months pregnant, she was always concerned about her unborn child. Too much caffeine was a luxury she would not afford herself.

Gabby, as everyone called her, was a stunning woman. She was slight in stature, about five feet seven, with long curly dark hair. And her husband often commented that she had the deepest cobalt blue eyes that he'd ever seen. She was originally from Germany and, although she spoke perfect English, she had a sing songy rhythm to her voice, with a slight German accent.

It was later than usual for her quiet time. As she entered the room, mug of coffee in hand, she stopped at the threshold and leaned on the doorpost. She smiled warmly and the Sun sparkled in her eyes.

In the middle of the room, with their backs to her, almost seven LJ and three year old Sarrah were in deep conversation. Sarrah's bleach blonde head was bobbing up and down as she adamantly spoke to her big brother.

Mom watched undetected from the doorway with a huge smile on her face. Standing there in the gleaming Sun, Gabby unconsciously traced circles around her seven and a half month bump of a tummy. It amazed her that Sarrah, not even four yet, could form such complex sentences.

Most children her age could speak, but they often verbalized disjointed and short concepts. However, Bryce Cooper's little girl inherited his genius genes as did her brother. She often wondered what these two beautiful children would grow up to be. If their father was any indication, the world was in for quite a surprise with the young Cooper clan.

"Whad about all the pretty colors in the sky?" she asked pointing up with her little finger. "Did he paint those too?"

"Of course," LJ replied, "and he made the mountains, and the oceans and alllll, the animals..."

"Even ants? I don't like those ants!" Sarrah said with a grimace on her lily white face.

LJ snickered, "Yeah Pea," using part of her nickname, Sweetpea, "even the ants. But some bugs are good!"

"Yuck! I don't think so."

"Sure! Catapillars turn into butterflies. You like butterflies right?"

"Yeah," she said in a little voice, "I like butterflies... I just don't like them ants," she said with a nod of her head in finality. "Soooo...." she started and stopped.

"So what?" LJ prompted.

"Soooo... where is he?"

"Who Yeshua?" LJ asked.

"Yes, Yeshua. If I can't see him, how do I know he hears me?"

LJ's eyes got big, "Oh... he's right here!"

Sarrah's face lit up and her head began to turn, "Where, where?!"

LJ giggled, "Oh you can't see him Pea. Dad says that he lives in another dimension."

Sarrah's face fell and she pouted a bit, "But I wanna go to that da-min-shin-ian to see him."

Big brother patted little sister on the shoulder reassuringly, and "It's okay. He lives," he pointed to her heart, "inside you too. You can always talk to him."

"Always?" she asked cheerfully.

"Yup, always!"

"Yah!" Sarrah cheered.

Gabby, cleared her throat loudly.

The siblings heads spun around together in unison. With a smile on her face, Sarrah said, "Mommy! We just talking about Yeshua."

"Oh, I see," Gabby said smiling. "Is He right there with you?" already knowing what she was going to say.

Sarrah looked over at her brother who just nodded. Turning back to her mother, she said in a certain sounding little voice, "He's" she pointed to her chest, "always wit me in my heart. But Daddy said he lives in another da-min-shin-ian too, but we can talk to Him anytime... and he even hears us!" she exclaimed excitedly.

Mom put her hand over her mouth to stifle an envious giggle, "That's absolutely true. He always hears us," she said.

Gabby ventured into the center of the room. She set her mug

down on the coffee table. Looking down with hands on hips she said, "Little Joe, I hate to interrupt your conversation, but did you finish your morning chores outside?"

"Yes maam," he said enthusiastically with a nod.

"And did you pick up your room like I asked?"

LJ looked down for a moment at the floor. "Nooooo," he said guiltily. "I was just gonna go do it right..."

"Come on kiddo. Get to it, I've told you four times this morning," she said firmly. She reached down to help Sarrah to her feet. "And take your sister with you. She can help, she's a big girl!"

"Yah!" Sarrah said, clapping her hands.

"Ohh, ol right," LJ said as he got to his feet. He grasped his little sister's hand and begrudgingly headed upstairs.

Calling behind him, Mom shouted, "And call me when you're done so I can check it!"

Hands still on hips and listening intently, she heard from a distance, "Okay..." and then she heard two sets of small feet run up the stairs.

Gabrielle surveyed the floor. There, toys, crayons and colored pictures were strewn all across the rug. She sighed heavily. "So much for a quiet time..." she said wistfully to herself, as she crouched down shaking her head to pick up the mess.

Just then she heard heavy footsteps down the hall. Normally she wouldn't have noticed, but these footsteps sounded like they belonged to some big feet.

She turned just in time to see a huge black man standing at the Sunroom's threshold. He was so big; he could have easily been a linebacker for the Denver Broncos.

He took one look at Gabby, and lunged at her.

"Hey beautiful!" he said in his baritone bravado.

"Mac?!" she said, before being swept off her feet and spun her around.

"Wha... What are you doing here?" she stammered.

He gently put her down and touched her tummy. With a worried look, he said "Oh, I'm sorry... are you okay?"

She laughed and playfully punched him in the arm, "I'm fine silly. I'm pregnant, not made of glass!"

Then out came a barrage of questions. "When did you get here? How long are you staying? Is everything okay back in Geneva? Are you hungry? Did you sleep..."

Mac held up his big paw, "I'm fine Gabs, and you know that I could eat anytime. And as far as Geneva goes... well, let's just say that I think I'll be here awhile."

"I... I don't understand," Gabby said, "Problems at the LHC."

He shrugged, "Can't a guy come visit his best friend, and his beautiful wife, who also happens to be a great cook, and maybe take a horseback..."

"Maaaacccc"

"Okay, okay," No sense in lying to her.

He sighed heavily, "I think the problems are just getting started."

LHC, Geneva – Four Years Earlier

Mac listened to Bryce without interrupting. He seemed to be trying to decide if his best friend needed to be committed to an institution, or if there was really something to what he was telling him.

Finally after a moment of silence he cleared his throat and said, "Holy moley Coop that is sooommme story. And you're right about one thing: it doesn't make any sense." He was again quiet, trying to digest what he'd been told, looking deadpan at his friend.

"Mac, I wouldn't blame you if you didn't believe me. But I swear... on... on my mother's grave, I'm telling you the honest truth."

After a moment he said, "Cooper, I never said I didn't believe you. If I didn't know you as well as I do, I might say that you were on the verge of losing it. But along with knowing you, three things jump out at me, which lend me to believe that you did experience... something."

"Three things? What three things?"

Ticking off his fingers one at a time, Mac said, "One: You disappeared from the Control Room. Two: I saw you without your shoes on and with your feet all muddy and dirty. And three... well three is what I wanted to talk to you about."

"You wanted to talk to me? About what?"

"It's about that four minutes that that reporter asked you about."

"Oh yeah, what was that all about?"

"You have been rather incognito of late, so I'm not surprised you didn't hear. The way you took off out of here yesterday, it's no wonder you were in the dark."

"Yeah... sorry about that, I have been a bit preoccupied. I just didn't think you'd believe me."

"Forget it. Anyway, I've done some checking and it seems that this four minute time difference only happened above and below the beam tunnel."

"Hummm... only within the loop? That's strange..."

"You bet it is, but that's not the only thing."

"Really? What else?"

"You're not going to believe me."

"After what I've been through, I'm telling you buddy, I can believe almost anything."

"Do you know what's on the other side of the world from our little experiment here?"

"Whataya mean; the other side of the world?"

"I mean the exact other side of the globe from the LHC."

Thoughtfully, "Ah... ocean I suppose."

"You are exactly right. To be specific, it is the South Pacific Ocean and roughly 724 miles southeast of Christchurch, New Zealand and about 120 m southwest of something called the Arrow Plateau, a marine protected area in the middle of the ocean."

"Okay... so...?"

"So, there were two ships in that area at the same time as our baseline shot yesterday, a fishing trawler and a tanker."

"I don't understand... what does this have to do with..."

"And do you know what was right above us at the time of the baseline shot?"

"Mac, really... I'm so tired. I have a ton of work to do..."

"Actually there were two things above us. There was a weather satellite in low earth orbit and there was a passenger plane making its final approach to the Geneva Airport."

"What are you trying to tell me?"

"Do you know what those two ships, that satellite and the passenger plane all have in common?"

"Noooo... and I wish you'd tell me while I'm still young."

"They all lost four minutes of time... just like us."

Bryce almost fell over. His mouth dropped open. He sat there stunned by the revelation. "What???" he said."

Lazy Hoof – Three and a Half Years Earlier

"Please leave a detailed message and I'll get back to you as soon as I can... beeeeep."

"Steve, it's Bryce Cooper. When you get a chance, I need to talk with you. I've made some conclusions... should I say... uncomfortable conclusions. Can you give me a call as soon as you can? Thanks," and he hung up. Leaving a message for Quayle did nothing to abate his mounting sense of dread.

His conclusions were leading him down a path that he thought he was done with six months ago. But now, he suspected that what happened six months ago was only a warm-up.

Steve Quayle's website was still up on his monitor. Absentmindedly he began to fiddle with the mouse and inadvertently clicked on a link. Lost in his own pensive thoughts, his eyes slowly began to focus on the screen before him. He read:

"Physicist: HAARP Manipulates Time" from an article dated May 22, 2012 from a website named "Before It's News."

"What????" he questioned, as he started to read.

"A brilliant physicist published a revolutionary paper citing 30 other scientific papers that reveal HAARP has incredible powers far beyond what most investigators of the high frequency energy technology suspect. Dr. Fran De Aquino asserts a fully functional HAARP network, activated globally, can not only affect weather and geophysical events, but influence space and gravity...even time itself! Now the network is almost complete with the activation of the newest HAARP facilities at the bottom of the world: the desolate and alien Antarctic. Will the masters of HAARP become the masters of time too?"

"Masters of time?"

Chapter 18

Tel Aviv – Present Day

*C*he sticky sweet smoke hung in the air, its smell enticing as it combined with the salt water breeze blowing off the nearby Mediterranean. Joe often said that the key to good ribs was indirect heat, and slow cooking over wood chips. He'd been manning the grill for about an hour.

Zac, with his arm in a sling, and Joe settled in a couple of lawn chairs with Israeli Goldstar beers in their hands.

They reached a pause in their conversation when Eleazar slowly appeared through the back door. His progress was slow at his advanced age. And Joe knew better than to try to help him. It would be an affront to the old Swiss Jew. Some things, no matter how old, a man just had to do for himself.

They waited while he hobbled over and plopped down in the chair with a sigh. After he was seated, the retired goldsmith took a sip of the red wine that Ruby brought him.

"So Josiah," Eleazar said with a strange mix of a German and Yiddish accent, "just how is that nephew of yours?"

It was truly a small world. As it turned out, Eleazar knew Bryce from Geneva. Or rather, because of Bryce's Reset, Bryce knew Eleazar much better than Eleazar knew Bryce.

"Oh… he's fine. Expecting his third child you know," Joe said proudly, nodding to his two friends.

The government man smiled.

"Yes… I remember that," Eleazar said looking dolefully off in the distance. He'd lost his wife to the Auschwitz concentration camp during World War II. When they were interned, they were just in their teens. They were only been married a few short months before the Nazi's came. They never had children and he never remarried.

"Do you think he will come for a visit?" the old man asked with a hopeful smile.

"Well, I hope so. But who could blame him for staying away with Israel being surrounded by her enemies?" Joe said.

Zac, with his inside track, nodded his head and said, "Indeed..."

Joe and Eleazar exchanged a brief look. It was the way he said it... like he knew something. The two older men speculated many times about just what their neighbor did for a living. They were pretty sure that he wasn't a simple government Finance Minister.

He didn't carry himself like a government bureaucrat. He was far too fit to have sat behind a desk for years. And, Joe noted that he walked with observant, probing eyes. He didn't miss a thing.

Coming home last week with his arm in a sling and scratches all over his face cinched it for the two men. They were convinced; he was a spy.

"Still, hostile neighbors probably won't keep him away. I suspect that his work will bring him this way eventually," Joe said.

"Work? But I thought he was a... a scientist... a... how do you say..."

"A physicist?" Zac asked.

"That's right," Joe said looking at Zac curiously. *How would he know that?*

"Yes... yes a physicist," Eleazar finished. "At least that's what he was when I met him in Geneva. Nice boy... nice but strange," he finished.

Joe was aware of the story. Eleazar related the two meetings that he'd had with Bryce. Even after four years, that second meeting lingered with the old man.

Bryce ended up telling him things about his wife, Helen that no other mere mortal could ever know: Things about the last days of her life. The retired jeweler confided in Joe that that second meeting with Bryce changed his life. Not because of Bryce's words, but because of a message that Helen gave Bryce for Eleazar. From that point forward he came to the belief that Yeshua was the Messiah. So dramatic was the change that he eventually sold his jewelry shop in Geneva and came to live in the Eretz.

"Did either of you two hear the news of this afternoon?" Eleazar asked earnestly.

"You mean about Turkey leaving NATO?" Zac asked.

"No, more important than that," the elder said with a wave of his hand.

Looking seriously at his friends, he asked, "Have you ever heard of Rabbi Yitzahak Kaduri?"

Joe could swear that he saw Zac flinch. Shaking his head, he said, "No... doesn't ring a bell."

Zac, through a tightened jaw asked, "Yes... of course. Why?" But what he didn't say was that, he knew the name very well.

Joe's searching eyes could see that there was a problem between the two men. He sensed sudden tension. And he immediately attributed it to this Rabbi Kaduri. It wouldn't be until the end of the discussion, that Joe would fully understand the religious dynamics regarding the rabbi.

Zac was Orthodox, noted by the wearing of the traditional kippa (small cap) on the crown of his head. Although he wore Western clothes to work, there were other things, like his kosher diet that indicated his religious beliefs.

Eleazar too wore a kippa. And appeared to be every bit as devout. Bryce told him that with Eleazar's knowledge, he was not only Orthodox, but probably just shy of a rabbi.

His two neighbors looked to be of the same religious persuasion. But the one divide between them was as large as the Grand Canyon.

Eleazar considered himself a Messianic Jew. That was a Jew who believed that the Messiah foretold in the Tanakh and Talmud already came in the form of Yeshua Ha-Mashiach, Jesus Christ. But the position was as volatile as a flame to gasoline in the Orthodox community.

An Orthodox coming to a belief in Yeshua as the Messiah was

considered by the mainstream Orthodox as being an apostate, a turn-coat, a trader, a fool. In their minds, he had fallen for lies of Christians and that was unforgivable.

But the treatment by Zac of the old man was always respectful. The Talmud, an ancient giant collection of doctrines and laws compiled by Jewish teachers throughout the centuries, directed that the Jewish people treat their elders with respect and dignity: Which is exactly how Zac treated Eleazar.

Eleazar continued, "For your benefit Josiah, Yitzahak Kaduri was one of the most revered, most well-respected and influential rabbis of our modern era. He was a spiritual leader to the Jewish people long before we returned back to the Eretz in 1948. He was considered a Tsadik, a righteous man or saint. His followers spoke of many miracles that were done at his hands and also spoke of how he predicted many disasters."

"Allegedly," Zac said shaking his head.

The old man bowed his head slightly and smiled, "Granted. But the point is that Rabbi Kaduri was someone important to the Jewish people," he looked at Zac, "especially to the Orthodox."

"Okay" Joe said.

"When the Rabbi passed away in January of 2006, his age was estimated between one-hundred and six to one-hundred and ten."

"Wow," Joe said. Zac said nothing and sat stone faced.

"And," Eleazar continued, "it was because of his longevity and wisdom concerning The Law, young and old, unorthodox, orthodox and even our non-religious countrymen all revered the Rabbi."

"Of course," Zac chimed in with a hint of sarcasm, "He was, how do you Americans say, a... national treasure."

"But my friend," Zac said somewhat condescending, "this is old news. He died quite some time ago. Why bring it up now?"

"Yes, of course. But for Josiah's benefit," he gestured toward Joe, "I tell this part of the story."

Zac shrugged.

Looking back at Joe, Eleazar said, "Before he passed away, Rabbi

Kaduri said that he had visions and conversations with the Messiah. The Rabbi said that the Messiah came to him."

Zac stood up abruptly. "Please Eleazar, must you go into this?"

Eleazar said something to him in Hebrew, and then the two lapsed into a long diatribe exchange in the language. The men were speaking rapidly and Zac sounded angry. But then again, to Joe, Hebrew always sounded angry when spoken. Nonetheless, he could see that Zac was irritated.

For his part, Eleazar sat meekly in his chair. With index finger raised, in Hebrew he said, "Zechariah, I promise, it is very important for today's news. You will see."

The standing Israeli looked at the confused American and then back to the elder. Still vexed, he shrugged as if to say "go ahead".

When things settled down, Joe asked, "Did I hear you right? He said the Messiah came to him?"

"Ah..." Eleazar said, with a pleased look, "I see you understand the gravity of such a statement by the Rabbi."

Shaking his head, an impatient Zac said "Wait, it gets more interesting."

The old man continued, "Rabbi Kaduri said that he'd written the name of the Messiah on a small note. He gave strict instructions that this note not be opened until one year after his death."

Joe sat up on the edge of his seat and asked, "Well if he died in 2006, they must of opened the note a while ago?"

"Yes they did. And it was done so with much fanfare and media coverage on April 30, 2007."

"Wow. How come I've never heard of this?" Joe asked.

Zac raised his head, "I suppose that it has less interest for Gentiles."

Eleazar offered, "And, because of the shocking revelation behind the note, I believe it was suppressed by the media."

That statement led to a guffaw from Zac. In Hebrew, he said, "Suppressed! He was old. One could hardly take what he left seriously. Surely you must understand that?" At the end of the comment, the two men stared at one another in silence.

Again not catching all of the Hebrew, but sensing tension, Joe briefly changed the subject. Holding up his beer, he asked, "Need another Zac? How bout you El?"

The moment was broken and Zac blew out a long breath. He looked at his beer. Eleazar simply looked down at his lap and said, "No thank you, I still have some."

"You?" Joe asked Zac again.

"Yes... thank you. I would," he said somewhat embarrassed.

Raising his voice to the open back door, Joe shouted, "Honey! Do you think you can bring us a couple of beers?"

The three men sat in silence for a moment. After a couple of seconds, Ruby walked out the door with two beers in hand. "You boys playing nice?" she asked with a smile.

Joe was sure that she heard the raised voices in the kitchen. "We're fine sweetie... just thirsty," he said looking at his friends.

Both neighbors nodded.

"Okay..." she said, but she wasn't buying it.

"Thank you," Joe said.

"You're welcome," and she turned to saunter away.

The little group was quiet for a moment. Chagrinned, Zac held up his beer to Eleazar, who clinked it with his glass. The unspoken message was "sorry" between the two men.

"So," Joe said after a moment, "I don't get it. What's so controversial about any of this?"

"Just wait," Zac said calmly.

"It was... how do you Americans say? A Bombshell," Eleazar said. "When the cryptic note was unsealed, it read as follows: Concerning the letter of abbreviation of the Messiah's name, he will lift the people and prove that his word and law are valid."

Joe's brow crumpled, "That's it? That's what you two almost

came to blows over? Come on, that doesn't sound too ground shaking me," he shrugged. "That's probably why it wasn't reported by the news outlets. A regular non-event."

Zac and Eleazar traded a knowing look.

Eleazar continued, "That is only because you heard it in English. In Hebrew it reads, 'Yarim Ha'Am Weyokhiakh Shedvaro Wetorato Omdim.' This is a typical method used by rabbi's and the Talmud to convey a message. It is an act of reverence."

"Okay, but I still..."

The gentle old man held up his hand, "Wait for it. If one takes the first letters of each of the words in the sentence, the acronym reads..." he paused for effect. "Yehoshua, or Yeshua."

Joe instantly held his hand to his widely opened mouth, "My God..." he said, more out of reverence than shock.

"That's right. One of the greatest Jewish minds of our lifetime told the world that Yeshua, Jesus, was the Messiah," the elder said with a serious tone.

"Unbelievable!" was all Joe could say.

"That's not the only thing," Eleazar said.

"What... there's more?" a dumbfounded Joe replied.

"Ah yes... my friend. The plot, as you say, thickens," Eleazar said with a coy smile. "Rabbi Kaduri gave a message in his synagogue on Yom Kippur, The Day of Atonement, before he died. He said that the Messiah told him that He would appear to Israel... after Ariel Sharon's death."

A look of confusion swept across Joe's face, "Hold on, you mean the former prime minister Ariel Sharon? Didn't he die of a stroke a few years ago?"

"No my friend. You are only half right. He did have a stroke many years ago. But he didn't die. He has been in a coma all of this time."

"Really, I didn't know..." then a look of understanding registered in Joe's eyes. "What a minute... are you telling me that as soon as he dies... the Messiah will come back?" he asked once again in shock.

"Rabbi Kaduri didn't say how long after Sharon's death, or exactly when the Messiah would come. Only that He would come," the elderly man said seriously.

"Again with the Nazarene?" Zac said. "So now we wait for someone who said he came to bring the sword to Israel? Alright, you told the story, can't we just move on."

Ignoring Zac's comment, a contemplative Joe asked, "So, Ariel Sharon has been in a coma for all of these years?"

"Yes," Zac said curtly. "But I don't see why you would have to bring up such a story right before our friend's delicious meal."

Gazing at the younger Israeli without a hint of smugness, Eleazar replied, "You didn't hear then?"

"Hear what?"

With reverence in his eyes, Eleazar said, "Ariel Sharon died this morning."

Chapter 19

*H*is head pounded as he gingerly repositioned in his seat, trying not to reopen the gash on his back. It was hard for him to breathe; he thought he might have broken a couple of ribs. And he was pretty sure his leg was fractured. But none of that mattered right now. He was alive and they must get away. They couldn't stop until they were safe.

"Ah! Mi amor, how much longer are you going to push yourself? Where are we going? Why won't you tell me? We should stop at a motel so you can rest? Why do you not let us take you to a hospital?"

These were the same questions that Mrs. Mora asked him a hundred times since he showed up at the cottage. Within five minutes, his daughters and granddaughter rousted their children. Soon after they were all crammed into the van his wife rented for the trip.

Understandably frightened, they did what they were told anyway. Dr. Mora was far too serious for them to protest. He said he couldn't tell them where they were going. He said it wasn't safe for them to know. The evidence, he said, was his wounds and dirty clothes. He didn't do this to himself. Wild eyed and scared, he did say that if they tried to kill him, they would not hesitate to kill them.

The patriarch told them that they needed to trust him; when they arrived at their destination, he would disclose everything.

He didn't know where that big dump truck came from. He was standing between the car and the cliff, looking down at the river. He just got done relieving himself. The night was dark and deserted. Surely no one would know he was even stopped unless... they followed him.

Alvaro just zipped his fly when he looked up. He saw two huge headlights barreling down on him and hardly had time to react.

The car was in perfect position to be T-Boned by the dump truck. It was at least going fifty. The driver planned it perfectly. It was a straight shot from the highway pull off. He didn't even have to bleed off any speed.

It happened so fast. Just two big lights and a shiny grill was all he saw. It almost crushed him between the wooden handrail and his car. He had no choice. He had to jump.

His momentum took him over the cliff's side with the Mercedes following right behind him. But like an unseen hand grabbing him in the dark, his sport coat snagged on a tree. It changed his angle and slowed his fall, then dumped him on the cliff outcropping.

In stunned disbelief, he watched his beloved classic Mercedes Coupe tumble over the side. It hit the bottom of the gully in a thunderous crash and burst into a ball of flames.

If that weren't surreal enough, after a moment, from the darkness above, he heard a truck door slam. Then saw a single light come to the edge and watched as it was shone down on the burning wreckage. He thought about calling to the light for help, but when he heard the observer light a cigarette and smelled the smoke, he knew that this wasn't a rescuer watching, but a hitman. He was making sure that The Professor was dead.

Mora held his breath and tried to keep his teeth from chattering. He pressed himself hard against the cliff's side, clinging to the darkness.

The assassin stood for a long time, looking down at the wreckage. He watched fire's flames burn down to a smoldering ilk. Finally, the light above him went out and a cigarette butt was flicked over the side. After what seemed like an eternity, he heard a door open and shut, and then the dump truck started up and pulled away.

He let out a heavy breath. But his relief was short lived. He had a terrifying thought. His near death experience was an assassination attempt. And if they tried to kill him, they might also try to kill his family!

Instantly a surge of adrenaline rushed through his body. He must get up that cliff. But how? His phone was in his briefcase. His briefcase was in his car. And his car was at the bottom of the gully, burnt to a crisp. It was dark, save the light from the full moon. He looked at his watch with the hands that glowed in the dark; half-past midnight.

There was barely room to stand on the outcropping. He was stuck. But his life wasn't spared so he could sit there and do nothing. He did the only thing he could do; he prayed.

First he thanked God for sparing his life... he knew he should have been killed. Then he asked Him to give him strength and protect his family. And he also asked that He help him get out of this situation.

When he was done, he carefully turned to face the cliff. He spread his arms out wide like he was embracing it. In the dark, he walked his hands along the cliff side, feeling as he went. Above his head, at arm's length, he could feel a tree branch or root on his right side. He tugged on it. It stuck to the cliff wall. He raised his left foot about two feet off the outcropping and felt for a foot hold. He found one.

"Here goes nothing," he said to himself as he pulled up with his right hand and pushed up with his left foot.

Like climbing an invisible ladder, he alternated finding handholds and places to put his feet. More than a few times, he would slip, or the branches would rip out. He was in excruciating pain and short of breath. But he dare not rest for fear of losing his grip and falling to his death. So he pushed on.

Although it felt like hours, he traversed the twenty five or thirty foot span of cliff in a little more than a half hour.

Finally he crested the edge. He pulled himself up slowly, making sure that no one was lying in wait. Once on solid ground, he staggered a couple of paces away from the edge, bent over and vomited. Much of what came out of his stomach was blood. His ulcer started bleeding again.

When he was done retching, he took a couple more steps and fell to the ground exhausted and in pain. "Gracias Padre (Thank you Father)," he said as he lay there in the dirt. Then he passed out.

His eyes slowly opened and he felt the panic of not realizing where he was. Slowly his brush with death came back to him. He sat up. Immediately his back felt like a jagged knife was plunged into it. His side was on fire and he could only breathe in short breaths. But he realized that he felt somewhat rested. He didn't know how long he'd been out. He looked at his watch; two forty-five.

His eyes went wide. He must get to his family. He slowly got on all fours. That hurt. But when he stood on both legs with his hands on his knees, his brain was greeted with shooting pains from all over his body. He cried out in pain. It didn't matter. He had to go. He stood up. The pain was so great that he thought he was going to pass out again. He tried to ignore it.

As he shuffled to the side of the road, he could feel warm liquid running down his back. He was bleeding. But there was nothing he could do. He looked in both directions. The road was deserted.

He remembered he was about forty-five minutes from Cornwall. He'd have to walk it. He didn't think he could make it, but he had to try.

He took one painful step, and then another. His leg felt like a sledge hammer was brought down on it. He stopped and put his hands on his knees. "Por favor Padre (Please Father)." He knew he couldn't walk any further. He started to cry.

He stood there, by the side of an empty road, in the middle of the night bleeding and in pain, with his hands on his knees, weeping.

Then, out of nowhere, a small, older, sedan pulled up next to him. The window rolled down, and a big, blonde man with a melodious voice asked, "Do you need a ride?"

Alvaro was so grateful. He wiped his eyes with dirty palms. He hobbled over to the car door and without saying a word, he got in. Again, he passed out.

The next thing he knew, he woke up to find the car pulling up in front of the cottage. But the strange thing was that he didn't remember telling the young man where he wanted to go.

He thanked the man, got out of the car and staggered over to the door before he burst in. That was hours ago.

It was about two and a half hours before dawn. He found a sleepy motel not far from their destination. Desperately, he needed food and a couple hours of rest.

The Professor worried that his contact might not have received the email. And even if the contact did get the email, would he be willing to meet at the site. He didn't have any way to make sure. His phone, with his contact's number, was gone. He dare not call him anyway... it was simply too dangerous.

No, he had to trust his instincts. The message was urgent enough. The data was compelling. He had to be there.

He chose it because Tete, his daughter Stephanie, wanted to see it on her trip. At the time, it appeared to be the logical spot for a covert meeting: out of the way, but touristy so he could blend in. But he hoped that his contact wouldn't think it was a joke and not come. That was a real possibility.

After all, it was Stonehenge.

Chapter 20

Lazy Hoof – Three And A Half Years Earlier

*B*ryce clicked on the link to De Aquino's actual scientific paper. It contained detailed mathematical equations and descriptions of De Aquino's theory. After a couple of pages, Bryce hit print. Now this was something he could sink his teeth into.

Out of the printer spit seventeen pages of what was, if true, very disturbing data. He hobbled over to the big white board in his office and haphazardly erased it.

He remembered reading De Aquino's name on a paper that dealt with quantization of gravity. Although he thought it was interesting, the physicist's discipline was different than his own focus of particle physics. He'd never had the occasion to meet him, but now found himself mesmerized that De Aquino theorized about something that Cooper learned firsthand – HAARP manipulating time.

The Montanan started writing row after row of equations onto the board, with plenty of room between lines. When he was done, he stepped back to take in the whole scene. Walking back up to the board, he traded his black felt pen for a blue one and began to make annotations and changes to De Aquino's numbers.

He would write and erase, then re-write and erase. And he would do it again and again and again. This went on for hours. Slowly shadows cast by the Sunlight through the small basement windows shifted with the meandering afternoon Sun.

The phone on his desk rang a few times... he ignored it. His cell phone in his pocket vibrated... he ignored it. At one point, Gabby even came down with a cup of coffee and a sandwich for a snack. She scowled at him and said a few things. Bryce nodded and mumbled something... but he didn't hear her. Gabrielle saw him like this many times throughout the years. She knew that nothing she could say in protest of him standing on his leg too long, would register with his preoccupied mind.

Finally after standing at the board for at least four hours he slowly walked up to it and put down his blue felt tip pen. Then he stepped back to admire his handy work. On the board was a combination of De Aquino's equations and Bryce's blue annotations or changes. To the untrained eye, it looked like gobbily gook. But to the brilliant and dimensionally experienced Dr. Bryce Cooper, it was a flashing red light of danger.

"Not again... only this time worse?" he said to himself shaking his head.

The sound of boots coming down the stairs drew him out of his thoughts. He turned to see Danny Mendez with a burly looking guy in tow behind him.

Sizing him up, he could see that the man was a little shorter than himself. But he was built like tank. His arms were about the size of Mac's and Bryce guessed that he didn't have an ounce of fat on him.

"Boss... I wasn't going to interrupt you, but..." Danny stammered.

"But Gabby told you to please interrupt me?"

Mendez grinned, "Something like that."

Bryce looked at the big armed man next to Danny, "Who do we have here?"

"This is my buddy, Dave Duckett."

"Hi Dave," Bryce said as he reached out and shook the man's hand. The man's handshake was like a vice-grip. You could tell a lot about a man from his handshake.

Bryce took the interruption as an opportunity to pick up the sandwich that Gabby brought him down hours ago. He realized that he was starving.

Chomping down on it with a big bite, he asked with a full mouth, "So what can I do for you boys?"

"Well..." Danny started, "you know... if we're gonna be doing some expanding, you probably want to hire some guys."

Bryce nodded, "You know we are. It's why I brought you on. Dude Ranch," he shook his head, "ring any bells?"

Danny shook his head and smiled, and then looked up, "That's not the kind of expanding that I'm talking about."

"Oh?" Bryce said, devouring the rest of the half sandwich and then reaching for some chips. "What other kind of expanding is there?"

"Word is that you brought that guy over from Bozeman to help..." he searched for the right words, "fortify the Lazy Hoof."

Bryce snickered and shook his head, "My, the grapevine sure does move fast around here."

Danny shrugged with uncomfortableness, "Anyway, I was just wondering," and he gestured with his chin in Duckett's direction, "Goose here would make a pretty good..."

"Goose?" Bryce asked.

"His nickname," Danny shrugged. "Ducks aren't so scary. But when this guy gets mad, now there's an angry Goose."

Bryce thought about the man's grip and nodded.

"Anyway," Danny continued, "Goose and his wife Lisa just moved up here from Southern California. I knew him from the days that I ran the street."

"You from Los Angeles?" Bryce asked with a mouthful of chips.

Shaking his head, Goose said, "Naw, not really. Little area in Riverside County. Bout sixty or seventy miles from L.A."

"That's pretty far from you Danny Boy, isn't it? How'd you know this big guy?" Bryce asked.

Danny's grin said more than his words, "Let's just say I had the unfortunate chance to run into him and his boys one time."

Bryce tilted his head and looked back and forth between the two men. Then he shook it as he reached over for his cold coffee. "I don't wanna know."

"Probably not," Danny said with a smile. "Anyway Boss, I think Goose here would be a great addition to the team. He's a strong... and I mean strong worker, a thinker and a pretty good shooter."

"Shooter?!" Bryce almost spit out coffee. "Just why would you think we'd need a shooter?"

Looking Bryce straight in the eye, "Like I said Boss, people talk... and it sounds like we may need someone who could handle himself."

Bryce looked at the young, light skinned Hispanic with close cropped hair. He shrugged his shoulders and said, "Alright Danny, he's hired."

Goose gaffed, "Hired? You mean you don't want to see a resume or somethin? No referrals?"

Bryce laughed and pointed to Mendez, "He's the Foreman. He's all the referral you need son. I trust him so... therefore I trust you. Welcome aboard!" he said as he stuck out his hand.

This time, in his excitement Goose grabbed Cooper's hand and pumped it wildly. Bryce thought he was going to break it. Goose said, "Thank you Dr. Cooper! Thank you! You won't be sorry! I promise!" and he dropped Bryce's hand.

"I better not be," he said sternly as he tried to flex and shake out his hand behind his back inconspicuously. Then, pointing at Mendez, "But he's your responsibility Danny. Make sure you see to it that he settles in and bring him up to speed."

"No problem Boss, will do."

"Goose, you and your wife have anywhere to stay? Danny said you just got here?"

"Ah... no sir. Lisa's in town looking at some rentals. Staying at a motel in town for now."

Bryce got a scowl on his face. "Not gonna have that," then looking again at Danny, he said, "The old guest quarters open?"

"Yeah, I think so..."

"Good. Put'em up in there. They can stay as long as they need to. Also, go introduce him to Gabby and get him on the payroll... standard beginning wage... that alright with you Goose?" he said looking at the tank.

The big man nodded and smiled, "Sure thing. I don't know what to say. Thank you for the opportunity."

"Well, opportunity's the right word," Bryce said matter-of-factly. "We pay here according to how you work. If you work well, you move up the pay scale. But I always try to pay a fair wage."

Danny nodded his head in agreement.

"Sounds good," Goose said and the two men turned to go as Bryce turned his attention back to the whiteboard.

The men exchanged pleasantries and Bryce walked up to the board again and stopped. "Goose, can your wife cook?"

Confused, Goose asked, "Cook?"

"Yeah," Bryce said, "Can she cook? Does she like to cook?"

"Well... yeah, she's a great cook."

"She want a job?"

"My wife?"

"Yes Dave, your wife. Would she like to help my wife out in the kitchen? I promise we'll pay her for her efforts."

"Well heck yeah Dr. Cooper. Thank you so much..." and he stuck out his hand again to shake Bryce's hand.

This time Bryce waved him off. He didn't want his writing hand crushed again, "Don't worry about. Danny, please let Gabrielle know. Now guys, I got to get back to this."

"Sure, sure Boss. Thanks," Danny said.

"Thank you Dr. Cooper!" Goose said again.

"Thank you guys," Bryce said as the two men bounded up the stairs.

Bryce looked down to his throbbing hand and shook it out. "I believe I wouldn't want to get that goose angry," he chuckled.

Then looking back at the figures on the whiteboard, he thought about his experience with HAARP. He could see what De Aquino was getting at. It all fit.

"So now they can cover the whole earth? They're manipulating time... it's not over. Not by a long shot."

Then he said, glancing back at the empty stairs, "Before this is done, I think we're definitely gonna need people that can handle themselves."

Lazy Hoof – Present Day

"It started," she said, "a few years ago. Only flashes really. Nothing of any detail... just bits and pieces. When I asked God what was going on, I received no answer."

"Huh," Bryce quipped, "I've had that problem before."

She turned her face toward him. Her eyes were deep pools. Although he knew that they were virtually useless to her, Bryce couldn't help but feel like they peered deep into him. "I know you have," she said.

"Let me guess," he said a bit more sarcastically than intended, "you saw it."

Manaya didn't take offense. She simply smiled and said, "Something like that." She turned her face back to the river.

She continued, "I have seen you sitting here many times with your mother."

Bryce could feel a twinge of nostalgia. But he cocked his head as he realized that the old stab of emotional pain he felt before his Reset was gone. He had been mended, healed. He no longer felt deserted by the death of his mother.

What was that mom said to me? "And I have always been with you too."

He felt his eyes glisten. Not from pain, but joy. He was happy. He liked being here. With his busy schedule it was not often that he got to just come here and sit. And sitting here, next to Manaya Warkentin, he realized that she reminded him a lot of his mother: a common sense, strong, woman with an honest heart. He wiped a pooling tear before it rolled down. He looked over at Ed who was busy skipping stones on the river. He was listening, but wasn't looking at them.

Clearing his throat, he asked, "So how did you see us?"

She turned to him again, "Bryce, you above all people know that there aren't answers for us on this side. Your own theories proved only partly right. The other part," she held hands wide, "in the other dimensions, are not fit for words. They are truly other-worldly."

Bryce smiled for the first time. He really did understand that much. She obviously did too. "So you've seen over there?" he asked, now dropping his guard. His gut told him that Manaya was no threat.

She chuckled, "Well... I saw you there, that's for sure. And I guess, as I said, I've seen flashes in," she turned to face him, "the place you couldn't go."

Bryce's mouth dropped open. He never shared that part of the experience with anyone. Only Uncle Joe and Aunt Ruby were privy to much of what happened to him. He hadn't even told Mac about it. No, this woman knew something and he needed to quit dancing around.

"Ok... I'm listening. Tell me what you saw."

Chapter 21

*C*he Banker hung up the phone from the conference call. His eyes settled on something across the room. He rose with purpose from his five-hundred year old antique desk. Traversing the expanse of the spacious office, he stopped in front of the pedestal.

The item was a bit larger than a basketball, but much, much heavier. It was black as night, and highly polished. But in spite of its ultra-smooth surface, it gave off absolutely no reflection. He found that to be its most amusing feature. It was as if this other-worldly stone absorbed all light that it came into contact with.

When he finally delivered the gift to its recipient, he would tell him that it fell from heaven, not unlike the al-Hajr al-Aswad, the Black Stone in the Kaaba, in Mecca. That larger stone was now a centerpiece of worship for Islam.

This was a significant point because Islam's history said that the Kaaba, and the Black Stone, was marked as a place of worship in pre-Islamic pagan times. Such superstition played well for his purposes.

The assumption would be that whoever holds the stone, would be blessed. And thus, the imparter of the gift, favored.

He reached onto the pedestal and picked up the heavy stone with both hands. Holding it in front of him, he stared at it for a long time. Power emanated from its dark beauty, pulsing and vibrating. His hands tingled after a while and he began to feel light headed. On wobbly knees, he replaced the dark stone back on its stand.

This gift was part of a coronation of sorts. With The

Plan proceeding on schedule, it would soon be time to give it to its predetermined recipient: The Prime Minister.

The Banker felt honored to be the one chosen to impart the stone. He was the one charged with pulling the strings behind the scenes. But he was much more than that. No one suspected his background. He was made to fit. He was one of them: Part of The Group.

So he heard the murmurs that came to him. The Others gave The Group its power. They made them the Kings of the Earth. But now... where once they were on the inside, welding power and controlling their own destiny, they felt as if they were on the outside, looking in. The whispers started. They were feeling marginalized, their input ignored and their influence diminished. It was not outright rebellion. None of The Group would be so foolish. But dissent was there. And it was his job to hear it from them.

But this... this token to the Prime Minister was evidence that The Group was still needed... still sought after... still important.

He whispered to the stone, "Soon you will have a resting place."

The buzz of his intercom broke his reverie.

"Sir? The U.S. President is on the line."

He let out an expletive. His assistant Stephanie would never have interrupted him during his Reflective Time; not even for the President!

He set aside one hour out of every day to do nothing but think. He wouldn't write during this time, he wouldn't read anything and... he especially didn't talk to anyone. Particularly impotent leaders with their hands out begging for money! Such interaction would disrupt his flow of meditation.

Walking back across the room to his desk, he stabbed the phone's intercom button. Angrily, he said, "Tell the President that I have yet to hear back from the IMF (International Monetary Fund) Chief. Until then I have no new information to give him."

"Ah... yes sir, but..."

"BUT WHAT?!"

The anger in The Banker's voice frightened the Temp. She didn't know what, but she assumed she'd done something wrong. Mousily she said, "But he's very persistent sir."

Oddly, rather than angering him further, the comment had the opposite effect. He gaffed and chuckled aloud. All of the World's leaders were in the same predicament. The politicians only just began to realize that the end game was near... and they were scared. While they wanted the riches and power that The Others promised, they didn't necessarily want to go through the pain of getting there. This is where the Banker came in: When the time came, he would have to coax them.

"Yes, they all are dear, they all are. I can only help them when I can. Please relay my message." Then he added with serious cold direction, "And... don't bother me again for the rest of the hour... Is that clear?"

She swallowed hard, "Yes sir."

"Good!" he said, and the line went dead.

———————————

Outside of The Banker's door, at her own desk, the Temp's hands were shaking. As she sat there she felt something more than fear. Since being on this assignment the last couple of days, she sensed something was not quite right. She didn't know what that something was. But she did know one thing: He was evil.

This interaction cinched it. She decided: She didn't care how much they offered her, she wouldn't stay. After her shift today, she would have the temp service reassign her. She shook her head. She didn't know how Stephanie Mora dealt with the man.

Steadying her breathing, and calming herself, she slowly picked up the phone. She took a confident breath, hit the line's button and said, "I'm sorry Mr. President but..."

Back in his office, The Banker adjusted his heart rate. He knew he was prone to fits of rage and many times he couldn't help himself. This was in his genetics. Anger and rage was part of who he was. But in this position, amongst these people, he had to maintain a constant air of civility.

Again he walked over to the pedestal that held the black stone. Standing before it in admiration, he said, "Soon."

Lazy Hoof – Present Day

"You must understand," she began, "that I can only tell you what I saw. God didn't show me everything that has happened or that will happen. Only what I need to know to tell you. I believe that he will fill in the rest."

"Okay," Bryce said.

Manaya exhaled loudly, "At first God showed me the face of your mother," she said looking over at the river. "She was beautiful Bryce... really."

"Thank you"

"Then he showed me this place," she said with a wave of her arms. "It is an amazing piece of land."

Bryce nodded, as if she could see him listening.

"And then he showed me that sign above the main entrance."

"Sign? What sign?" Bryce questioned over toward Ed's direction."

Ed was just about to skip another stone. He stopped in mid-throwing motion and looked over his shoulder. He sighed, shrugged and then dropped the remaining rocks to the ground. Walking over, he proceeded to wipe his hands on his jeans.

"Oh Ed..." Manaya scolded at hearing the sound, "those are clean jeans!"

Bryce looked at him shocked.

Ed, who had already rambled over to them, chuckled, "Like the lady said Bryce, there are other ways to see." He patted his wife on the shoulder, "It's okay honey. This is Montana, all the cowboys do that don't they Dr. Cooper?" With a grin he plopped down on the grass next to them.

Bryce chuckled.

"Do boys ever really grow up?" Manaya said with a shake of her head.

Answering Bryce's question, Ed said, "You know that sign that's attached on the timber at the entrance of your place?"

"You mean the one that says Lazy Hoof Ranch?"

"Yeah, that's the one," Ed said. "When she first saw it, she described exactly what she saw. She was so impressed that she made me look it up on the internet."

"Wow"

Ed snickered, "That's not the impressive part."

"It's not?"

Ed wagged his head, "Nope, get a load of this. You know how you have pictures of various buildings on the ranch? The lodge house, guest quarters, barn, etcetera. You also have a picture of the sign in question."

"Yeah?"

"Well, she described every one of them to a tee. And without me telling her anything about them. Plus you have pictures of people that work here? Your picture's there, and your Ranch Foreman... Danny, I think his name is? Anyway, she got them right too... right down to how that Lazy Hoof sign is carved and the wood burnt for effect."

Bryce was nonplussed, "Really?"

"Yup... but that's still not the most amazing part."

"I don't know," Bryce said rocking his head back and

forth, "I'm amazed."

"Well," Ed continued, "out of all those pictures, do you remember ever having put one online that showed this place?" Ed asked, raising his hands.

Bryce put his hand to his chin, "Huh... you know... somebody takes care of that site for me, but no... now that you mention it, I don't think there's one showing this spot."

Ed smiled big, "She told me exactly what this place looked like too."

Chapter 22

Tel Aviv – Present Day

A cool breeze seasoned with the salt of the Mediterranean spread lightly through the backyard. Hand in hand, they sat gliding together on the porch swing, silently lost in their own thoughts. Joe was holding a tepid beer not sampled in at least a half hour and Ruby sipped on red wine.

Zac's expeditious retreat after Eleazar's revelation about Ariel Sharon dampened the evening. The Israeli apologized profusely and said he summarily remembered some "very important business" which needed his attention. Joe couldn't help but wonder if it was because of the displayed animosity between Zac and the elder regarding their differing views of the Messiah. Still, he didn't sense that Zac's skin was that thin.

Eleazar didn't last much longer. The ribs were dished up with all the fixins, "Just like in Montana" Joe bragged. The retiree ate, had a piece of strudel and also left early, forgoing after dinner conversation. Who could blame him, the activity of the day for a man in his ninety's was very taxing.

So Ruby and Joe were left to their own devices. And they welcomed the chance to be alone together. They always did. It wasn't long ago that they retired to the modern Jewish city of Tel Aviv. It was a well-deserved and welcomed retirement after years of building the Lazy Hoof into the success it was today.

When Bryce came home four years ago, it was an answer to prayer. They were tired. It wasn't that they didn't like it on the ranch. To the contrary, they loved it. Ranchin and hard work and it was in their blood. But their bodies were wearing out.

And they loved Bryce like the son they never had. Since Jerry Cooper, Joe's brother-in-law and best friend, died Joe became a surrogate father to the boy-genius. He showed him how to fish, hunt, shoot, ride a horse and how to defend himself using Joe's lifelong appreciation for Aikido.

For her part, Ruby loved and doted over him like a mother. But Bryce's heart was broken by tragedy, wounded. And then in self-preservation, it hardened. He finished his first four years of college at the ripe old age of thirteen. With no time to grieve, and in a hurry to run away, he flew off to Stanford in California for two years and then off to the east coast to MIT. As she remembered, Bryce was one of the youngest people to ever receive a Ph.D. from the top notch school.

It wasn't long after that that he received the Nobel Prize for work on M Theory, whatever that was. Although she didn't understand his work, she did know that it was important and... that he was quite famous. She was very proud of her nephew.

Four years ago, out of the blue, they'd received a call from him telling them that he was coming home for good. Overnight it looked like his personal demons, the real reason for his avoidance of the ranch, were exorcised.

The minute she saw him at the small Missoula airport, she knew he'd changed. His countenance was different. His face was lit up and his step was upbeat. He was happier and more at ease. She hadn't seen him like that since his mother was alive. She and Joe didn't know exactly what happened, but she had her suspicions.

It was only then, that she and Joe began to discuss in earnest their long formulated plan to retire to Israel. She was of Jewish heritage, part of the tribe of Levi, as her sister and Bryce were. Because of this, she knew that she and Joe would be welcomed in the Eretz.

They scheduled their departure for a year after Bryce came home. During that time, his broken leg fully healed and he was solidly brought up to speed on the ranch's management.

Although it was sad for them to leave that part of their lives behind, it wasn't a difficult transition. Despite their love for the Lazy Hoof, it was never theirs. Throughout the years, Bryce wanted to deed over a good portion of the property to them. He also wanted them to take the lion's share of the profits. On both counts they refused. They always told him that they were merely caretakers, waiting for him to come home. And when he did after his Reset, they were overjoyed.

Bryce became a multimillionaire. While he was in school and living on a shoestring budget, Joe stuffed away hundreds of thousands of dollars in ranch profits for Bryce. His uncle invested those profits with a genius Money Manager out of the New York office of Goldman Sachs. The funds grew well beyond expectations.

But her nephew's greatest financial feat occurred shortly after his return home. A friend of his, Steve Quayle from Bozeman, convinced him that he reallocate all of his holdings in physical gold and silver. Which he did to the great dismay of his Money Manager.

To her amazement, in the last couple of years, the crash of the European economy and the near bankruptcy of the U.S. drove the value of hard assets like precious metals through the roof. Ruby marveled at Bryce's foresight. Gold was now over $5,000 an ounce and silver was almost half that amount. The change proved to be one of her nephew's most brilliant moves yet.

Bryce insisted that he pay for everything for their retirement and migration to Israel. Their beautiful upscale home, all of their furnishings and their sporty Mazda 3 out front was paid for by him in cash. He even made sure that they had money in the bank and a monthly retirement check. Not that they needed it; they were more than comfortable. Bryce was as good of a nephew, or son, that any mother could want.

But Ruby also knew that with the potential of war on the horizon, all of these things could be taken from them in a moment.

Breaking the long silence, she asked her husband, "So what do you think will happen now?"

"About what?"

She elbowed him playfully in his side. "You know... the military exercises. And what about that stuff that Eleazar said about Rabbi Kaduri? And didn't you tell me that tomorrow they'll raise the Tabernacle on the Temple Mount. The neighbors can't think well of that."

Joe was quiet for a moment. It was one of her favorite qualities about him. He was slow to speak. She knew that when he did talk, it was always worthwhile.

"Humm... hard ta say. As much as the Arabs hate Israel, they don't like each other too much either. They've been fightin amongst themselves for centuries. Take Jerusalem," he said pointing to the distance. "After all these years, Israel agreed to a two state solution. They gave up more land, the UN recognized Palestine as a nation and in return, Israel got the use of half of the Temple Mount. Now the problem is that Hamas and Fatah are still fighting each other for control of the new country."

He made a big sweep of his hand, "And here's another problem: Muslims are separated into two sects. And even to this day, you have Shiites fighting with Sunnis."

Ruby shook her head, "They're the same people, I just don't understand it."

"You're not the only one," Joe replied, "People through the centuries have been trying to figure them out. All with no luck."

"So what does it all mean to us?"

Joe blew out a long, tired breath, "Well for one, it means that we don't want to be anywhere near that ceremony on the Temple Mount tomorrow. If anti-Israeli people wanted to make a statement, it would be the perfect time to do so."

"You mean a bomb?"

The Montanan man nodded, "Or worse. And here's something else to think about..." he looked sideways at his wife. He didn't want to scare her, but she deserved to know the truth, "They're getting closer to unification."

"The Arabs?"

"The Muslims," he said. "Arabs are people like anyone else. Even the Muslim faith is just another religion. But radical Islamists... that's another story. And there are rumors floating around that someone is pulling the strings from behind the scenes. Someone like that guy from Syria is trying to bring them together and I think..." he stopped in midsentence.

She turned to look at him, "You think what Joe? What do you think?"

He faced her, "I think they're not far off. The Jews will put the Tabernacle up tomorrow and eventually build the Third Temple. Prophecy says they have to. And as far as the whole Rabbi Kaduri thing, that is a very interesting point."

"What do you mean?"

"Well... I hadn't heard the story before. But you have a prominent rabbi saying that when Ariel Sharon died, the Messiah would come back," he held up a finger, "That's strike one. And then... you may not know this, but a Jewish Sage, Mamonides, said that when God provided the tenth Red Heifer for Israel, the Messiah would return shortly. Adonai must have done that because the Jews couldn't erect the Tabernacle tomorrow without it," he held up two fingers. "That's strike two. So look out, because the Muslims believe that when the next Caliph, or the chief Muslim civil and religious ruler came, then the Mahdi will show up just after."

"The Mahdi?"

He eyed her seriously and said, "The Islamic Messiah."

She titled her head in thought and then slowly brought her hand to her mouth, "That's sound like..."

"Yup, it sure does sound like their christ is Christianity's Antichrist." Then he held up three fingers, "That's strike three. Could be we're out."

He continued, "It looks like that all of these things are very close." He shrugged, "So Rabbi Kaduri might have just been right."

It was true then, Zac thought to himself as he shook his head. He slowly placed the phone back into its cradle.

Zac was a man of Orthodox faith, with absolute commitment to the Rabbi's cause. But he was also a practical man.

Thus, here was the crux of his dilemma. In his opinion, the words of Rabbi Kaduri were those of a senile old man. It was true that he was revered by most Jews. But that note was... very troublesome. For Kaduri to publically foretell a specific event which would trigger the Christian Messiah's return was very troublesome indeed.

This in light of tomorrow's ceremonies caused him a great deal of consternation. *It was said that the building of the Third Temple would bring about the Messiah. And on the other hand, you had an old and senile Rabbi Kaduri prophesying that the Messiah would come after Ariel Sharon died. Could both be true? Surely Kaduri could not be right... not with the Nazarene* (Yeshua – Jesus). *Was it not the Nazarene who said he came for the sword. And the sword is what the Jews received from the time of his death until now.*

In the early centuries all in the name of the Nazarene, the Jews were expelled, forced to convert to Christianity, had their Tanakh burned, their property confiscated, their synagogue's burned and were murdered and tortured in droves.

Then of course there was the Spanish Inquisition which sought to again convert them by force or kill them. They were even kicked out of Spain in 1492 and many went to America rather than convert or die.

And how could one forget the Holocaust at the hands of the Nazis. There, in the terrible death camps, the Nazi's said they were "Christians" and by the threat of death, tried to make Jews convert to Christianity. But even with the assurance of a certain death, Jews would not yield to the Nazarene. And now... they are being told that he could be coming back? Ridiculous!

But Kaduri... he was a problem. Even his own Rabbi thought of him as revered. In their conversations, Zac asked him what he thought. The Rabbi also chalked it up to old age and dementia. And now this: The death of Ariel Sharon would either be the misspoken words of a confused and dying old man, or... something else.

Chapter 23

Lazy Hoof – Three and a Half Years Earlier

Quayle returned Bryce's call and gave him a list of portals and stargates to look into. He also touched on the connection between portals and HAARP. The physicist found that he was torn between his logical scientific mind telling him that this was just conspiracy talk and his gut telling him that something much more sinister was afoot.

He found that almost all of these portals were natural phenomena. Not that there was anything normal about a portal opening and closing. It was just that those advents of portals didn't seem to need technology, at least known technology, to open.

However, there were other instances of technology based portals like at the LHC. The problem was that information was very difficult to find on them. They tended to be super-secret military programs or science projects. He thought about using his influence in the science community to gain access to some of those programs; but then thought better of it.

He could be far more effective in his research if he continued to fly under the radar. Should the wrong people find out that he was poking around, they would probably try to hinder his investigation. His experience before his Reset told him that they would just as soon kill him to keep their secrets.

The Gulf of Aden, off the coast of Yemen yielded some very interesting information on an alleged portal. Bryce read that the anomaly was putting off a huge electro-magnetic signature and at times showed a visible vortex on top of the water.

"Electro-magnetic signature?" Bryce said to himself as he read. This sounded very familiar to him. His experience with HAARP six months ago showed the same type of readings. He read on. While the various pages of internet conspiracy theory were jammed with pseudo-science and conjecture, he noted that this particular area in the Gulf of Aden attracted an awful lot of attention from governments around the world.

If the satellite pictures he was looking at were correct, there were ships from almost every navy in the world in that area. The cover story for the build-up was allegedly the policing of "Somali Pirates". Yet, this armada of ships could have easily dissuaded any would-be pirate.

The article that he was reading said that the activity in the area started in 2011. If his recollection was right, that was also the time of the so called Arab-Spring and the huge Japanese earthquake and tsunami.

His mind drifted to another thought. Why did the Fallen and The Others try what they did with the LHC and HAARP? Why then? Those questions had confounded him for the last six months. He still didn't have a satisfactory answer. He shook his head and went back to surfing the internet for clues about stargates.

He came across a few articles that said many of the portals were now opening. One article made a connection between the portals opening and the strange and dangerous weather phenomena that were occurring across the globe. It also noted that a significant spike in violent crime around the world correlated with the timing of portal openings.

"That's interesting..." he said to himself as his mind reached for a still fresh memory from six months ago.

Geneva, LHC (Underground) – Before The Reset

"My ah... cousins and I, can only move in the first two spatial dimensions beyond your 3D world freely. But youuuu... you were chooosennn," he said snidely. "You've been put here on Earth to bridge the gap between dimensions! You're a Levi, and a descendent of Aaron," he said sarcastically.

"We didn't care about this puny little experiment," he said

gesturing with his hand wildly. "We needed you to release the prisoners before their time. By doing it this way..."

Bryce was side stepping again. He noted that the creature had exited the cubicle and circled back around him, blocking his escape route. Now Bryce's back was no more than three feet from the collision chamber. He wasn't planning to escape.

Fifty seconds...

The dimensional rift affects were pummeling Bryce. His head was swimming and he could barely focus. His knees were weak and he felt like he was going to fall over. Just a little longer, he told himself.

The creature was saying, "... by doing it this way, you have given us the ability to open the gate to the Generals and their legions in the Abyss ahead of their time.

"It's quite brilliant you know. It means that we'll be able to launch a surprise attack and, as an added bonus, kill a third, if not more of you humans.

"You have been very helpful you know Dr. Cooper. We couldn't have done it without you."

Bryce bolted upright in his chair: The long elusive "WHY" connection was finally been made.

He remembered the conversation with the monster as if it were yesterday. But he didn't put the pieces together until now.

The creature said, "It means that we'll be able to launch a surprise attack..."

Punching his fist in his palm, Bryce exclaimed, "They were trying to cheat!"

The Others were trying to release the Generals and their minions before they were allowed. They were trying to gain a surprise advantage for the final great battle of Armageddon.

So what just fell into place for Bryce was the understanding that there is a timeline by which they, the Fallen and the Nephilim, were bound. That timeline coincided with our physical laws! The portals were used to break those laws! But even those portals wouldn't be allowed to be opened until the timeline said so.

The Nephilim lied to me! Then he thought: *Surprise, an evil being bent on the destruction of mankind - lying. Well that's a shocker!*

Of course they were concerned with the experiment at the LHC!

I only saw and interacted with one of the Fallen back then. But there's no telling how many of them could have escaped through the portal during my experiments alone! That's why the Reset happened! It was too soon to open the portals!

He sat there, upset with himself that he didn't figure it out sooner.

As he ruminated on that, a new thought floated down and rested on his brain. He recounted his history at the LHC; when he first came on, his unique qualifications and his dimensional theory. He thought about how CERN was more than happy to let him boost the power of the collision. He thought about the unlimited budget that he was given. He thought about the results he attained prior to the Reset. Instantly all the blood drained from his face and he turned white as a ghost.

His pride fooled him into thinking that he was unique in his dimensional pursuits at the LHC. His brilliance in the modification of the systems for his ATLAS 7 experiment caused him to think that no one else could have accomplished what he accomplished. But he finally realized the cold reality of what happened back then and it was like being slapped hard in face.

The truth was almost too horrifying to accept. Even though they didn't call his experiment by the same name, he was always working on Operation Falling Star.

But a new terror instantly replaced his disgust at being used. According to his research, he learned that the portals around the world were now opening.

That could only mean one thing: The timeline's end was almost at hand.

Stonehenge, Wiltshire, England – Present Day

The Professor turned the car off and they sat there. He scanned the parking lot to find any trace that they'd been followed. His daughter Stephanie was next to him. His wife, daughter Vanessa and granddaughter Azlynn were all back at the motel with their children. He would have preferred to come alone, but Stephanie, like her mother, was stubborn and would not let him drive by himself.

He managed to get a couple of hours sleep in his exhausted state. It wasn't hard. He was so tired, he felt like he could sleep a week. With a little sleep to clear his head, and some fresh pan y café, bread and coffee, he was ready to meet his contact.

"Do you see him Dad?" Stephanie asked.

"Nooo," he said in his thick Spanish accent, "but it's really who I do not see that bothers me," he answered distractedly. "They think they killed me... so we shouldn't have been followed."

"Shouldn't have been?" a concerned Stephanie asked.

Stephanie was American by birth. She grew up mostly in the U.S., even though her father's work caused her family to travel extensively, even internationally. When she was old enough, she wanted to make her own life and moved out to New York. She was fluent in Spanish, but unlike her father, she had no discernible accent.

Her big brown eyes rested on him. She was thirty-something now; dark curly hair, light skinned and her father thought that she was still beautiful. *She was always the adventurous one,* he thought; *so self-sufficient.* He was proud of her.

He patted her hands that rested in her lap, "I'm sure we are fine Mija. Just stay close... and keep your eyes open."

He often called his girls "Mija", which meant "my daughter", as a term of endearment.

With concern she looked hard at him, but nodded.

Slowly they got out of the car. Even in these pre-dawn hours, the parking lot was full of cars. This was the morning of the Spring Equinox. Although the ancient ruins of Stonehenge were usually closed at this time, an exception was made on this day so people could participate in the ritual watching of the Sun rise from the site.

This scheduled occasion was what made the environment for the meet with his contact possible. Being a man that paid attention to details, Dr. Mora counted on the gates being opened and the area filled with people.

It was about fifteen minutes before Sunrise and people were still arriving. Most of those that attended looked like throw-backs from the 60's; hippies or pagans. A few of them were dressed as Druids and Witches. But this was neutral ground. It was a place set aside for this observance for centuries.

Being a Helio Astronomer, he studied all things to do with the Sun and Stonehenge was no different. When he was young, he did extensive research on the ruins. He knew that Stonehenge was thought to have been constructed around 3000 BC, well before the wheel was even invented.

Huge Bluestones from rugged South Wales, one-hundred and fifty miles away, were brought to the site for its construction. Construction by... somebody. And that was just one mind-blowing aspect of the ancient site. These stones, some thirty feet long and weighing well over a ton each, were strategically placed in circular patterns, like a hedge. But they were done so in such a way to track the equinoxes and the North Star. Alvaro shook his head at the thought: *Amazing*.

Misinterpreting the shake of his head, Stephanie nervously asked, "What's wrong?"

Pulled from his marveling, he turned to her and smiled. "Nothing Mija. It's just this place. It is amazing don't you think? You said you wanted to see it."

She smiled for the first time, "I did... but not like this. It kind of takes all the fun out of it," she shrugged.

"I know, I know," he whispered. "Come, let's go find my contact."

Chapter 24

Lazy Hoof – Present Day

"Okay... you have my attention," Bryce said.

Manaya smiled big, "Splendid!"

Bryce couldn't help but smile back at her impish attitude. He looked at Ed, who winked, as if to say: "That's Manaya!"

"They started a few weeks ago, these... these things that I started seeing."

"You mean they were visions?" Bryce asked.

"No... not really visions. I mean, they were actual things I saw."

"Okay"

"When they started, it was with some strange abstract picture a country scene with buildings and farmland underneath me."

"Underneath you?"

"Yes, I was flying, or... not really flying, more like floating in the sky. I guessed that I was probably a couple thousand feet off the ground."

"Uh oh," Bryce's mouth dropped open.

"Something wrong Dr. Cooper," Ed asked.

Regaining his composure, Bryce shook his head and said, "No... no, please continue."

"And off in the distance I could see tall white snowcapped mountains jetting up to the sky. It was a beautiful crisp day."

If Manaya had eyes to see, she would have noted that all the blood was now drained from Bryce's face. He was white as a ghost. He swallowed hard.

"Then a curious thing happened."

Bryce cleared his throat and asked, "Oh... what was that?"

"In the center of view, on the ground, there were these buildings. It kind of looked like a college campus, but somehow I knew it wasn't. Beyond that area there was vast farmland. You know open."

"Uh huh..." Bryce was slowly wringing his hands.

"And then a curious thing happened. With the buildings at the center, the whole area started spinning like a top. And when

I say the whole area, I mean the spin stretched out for miles, well into the farmland. The colors started to blur and all of a sudden, a black spray started coming up out of the center, where the buildings used to be. Soon, the spray started taking over everything and all I could eventually see spinning was just this dark blackness. And then, it began to spread out. As I was hanging there, a light from above caught my attention, and then something like a shooting star came roaring down from above and landed right in the middle of that spinning blackness."

"Oh!" Bryce said as he leaped to his feet. "You don't say?"

"Dr. Cooper? Are you okay?" she asked.

Clearing his throat to keep from throwing up, he said, "Yeah... yeah, I'm fine. Just a little cramp is all. Please go on."

She tilted her head up to where he was standing and said, "Okayyy... well, then my view changed all together. I know it sounds crazy, but I started floating in front of our Sun."

"The Sun? Let me guess. It was a huge ball and it took up all your field of view?"

She pursed her lips, "Now how would you know that?"

"Just wondering, please go on."

She cocked her head with a questioning look, but continued, "It, the Sun that is, began to act very strange."

"Strange?"

"Yes. This is difficult to put into words, but... The Sun began to get black spots all over. And then, between the black spots, these long strings of fire began to appear. Eventually the strings connected to each other and it appeared that the Sun was a honeycomb covered by a massive spider web of fire. And then..."

"Let me guess," Bryce interrupted, "A long string like finger snapped off and headed for Earth?"

Now it was Manaya's turn to look surprised, "That's amazing. How did you guess?"

Bryce looked at the surprise on Ed's face, and then back to Manaya. "Ah... I've seen a lot of movies. Please go on."

"Okay..." she said sounding unsure about how to take his answer, "Then I flew back to Earth and saw it begin to wobble and shake. And then I saw a huge wall of water wipe out the west coast of North America and the east coast of Russia and China. And all the islands, including Japan, were washed away!"

Bryce was still listening, but his hands were on his knees and he felt like he was going to puke.

"Dr. Cooper, are you okay?" Ed asked concerned at his distress.

"Yes... yes. I'm fine. Please continue."

"Oh... if you're sure?" Manaya said in a motherly tone.

"Yes... please. But," he made a rolling motion with his hand, "just hit the highlights for me. You know, the important stuff."

"Hum... alright, if you're sure..."

"Yes please"

"Well, without all the gory details, I began to see volcanoes go off all throughout the world. And then everybody was fighting with each other and then..." she paused with tears in her eyes and sniffled.

Ed grasped her hand, "It's alright honey."

Just by her reaction, Bryce knew what was coming.

She wiped the tears from the corners of her eyes with her fingers, and cleared her throat.

Bryce looked at Ed who just nodded, indicating she would be okay.

After a moment she resumed. "And then," she said through a cracking voice, "I saw nuclear explosions all over the planet. Dozens of them. And finally, the blackness that I saw above the spinning circle covered the whole Earth and I couldn't see anything anymore."

Bryce was walking around in little circles with his hands on his waist. He was trying to keep it together. When he finally looked down at her, he saw the sheen of perspiration on her forehead, her eyes were glistening and her breathing rapid. She was scared. Ed was holding her hand, stroking it gently.

"Are you alright?" Bryce asked.

She pursed her lips and pulled her hand from Ed's, "I could ask the same thing of you. You don't sound too good."

"I'm fine," he said defensively. "Must have been something I ate."

"Ah huh..." she said unconvinced. "It was important that I let you know what I saw."

"Why did you think you needed to let me know?"

She undid the scarf around her neck, dabbing her forehead

with it. In a tone of somberness, she said, "Because it was just after all of that that that I saw this place. And... your face. I took it to mean that I needed to contact you."

"What do you mean..." just then Bryce's cell phone rang.

He looked down at the number and all it said was "Jerusalem". "Huh..." he said.

Manaya broke into his thoughts as she spoke rapidly, "Bryce... time is very short... you must answer that call. It is a Rabbi that is working on building the third Temple in Jerusalem. He wants... he needs something that you have, desperately - something that no one else knows about. He's going to ask you to bring it to Jerusalem. I didn't see what this Package was, but you need to do exactly what he says. Time is very short. And you need to personally deliver this package to Jerusalem... right away. There is no time for delays. Time is at an end. You must go," she said almost pleading.

The phone rang for a fourth time.

Bryce was stunned and started to ask "How..."

Manaya interrupted him, "Because I saw that too."

Bryce punched the answer button with his finger to answer: "Dr. Cooper."

"This is Rabbi who?"

Listening

"From Jerusalem?" he said, as he looked at Manaya. "How did you get this number?"

Bryce put his hand over the phone's speaker and whispered to Manaya, "How did you know?"

She shrugged.

Focusing again on the call, he said, "You need me to come where? Tomorrow?! But that means that I'd have to fly..."

Again he looked down at Manaya who, although she couldn't see, returned his gaze with a stern look of warning.

Bryce began to wander off to the distance to chat. When he was about twenty feet from her, Manaya heard him ask angrily, "And just how did you know about that?"

When the call came, Ed got to his feet and wandered back over to the river. Once again he was standing on its edge, skipping stones.

In the solace of her own thoughts, she exhaled a tired breathe, and said, "It is later than we think."

Chapter 25

Lazy Hoof – Present Day

𝒯 he soft sounds of a steel guitar and steady beat bounced rhythmically off the walls of the wood stable. Two long rows of sturdy Quarter Horses looked to be swaying to the old country song.

Former Air Force Staff Sergeant Danny Mendez was sitting on a stool with Dashin Gabe's hoof in his lap. With a hoof pick he scraped out the mud and stones from Gabe's hoof, careful to remove the junk from the frog (the sensitive triangle area in the middle of the hoof) with his fingers. His tan cowboy hat was pushed back on his head, and there was a long piece of straw in his mouth. This task, although menial, was one of his favorites. It made him feel like he was bonding with the horse.

As he cared for his favorite steed on the ranch, he let his mind wander. He thought about the journey that brought him to this: his ideal job. As a streetwise Hispanic kid from Los Angeles, where youth more often than not joined a gang, Mendez escaped the trap by applying himself to education.

He used to joke that he was at least "smart enough not to get shot" on the streets of LA. He'd won several academic awards throughout high school, and was even offered a scholarship to UCLA. But rather than taking the college route, he wanted to "see the world" and travel. Because of his wild side, he also said that military discipline would do him good.

After tech school, instead of seeing the world, he was sent to his first and only assignment in the great white north. There he had a Top Secret job at Gakona, Alaska. He was an RF Transmission Systems Specialist on HAARP (High Frequency Active Auroral Research Program). He liked the position. It was interesting and challenging.

But the assignment did have its drawbacks. No women, and being a remote base there wasn't much to do in winter except drinking at the NCO Club. And other than trying to earn another stripe or two, there wasn't any real vertical mobility. But by far, the biggest drawback to the assignment was the Director of the facility, Dr. Yuri Mikhail Zaslavsky - he gave Mendez the creeps.

So early on, he decided that a good way to kill time was to get his degree. He took online courses and earned his BS in Animal Husbandry with a minor in Equine Science (horse breeding). But the long winters and odd seasons made it hard to gain practical experience. Experience was important if he was to achieve his ultimate goal: Working on a well-known ranch, with a good reputation. Somewhere in that life plan he also wanted to put down roots and then find a wife, in that order.

Just after he got his degree, rather than re-uping for four years, he was considering extending his enlistment for only two. At that point in his career, he didn't know if he wanted to be a "lifer", but he hadn't been presented a better offer. That is, until that fateful day that Dr. Bryce Cooper called him out of the blue.

Just before he signed on the dotted line, the Boss called. He said he'd heard his name from a drinking buddy and he wanted to know if Mendez was interested in a job at the Lazy Hoof. The physicist even sent out a private jet so he could interview for his dream job. He jumped at the chance.

But his ideal job, the private jet and the opportunity to lay down the roots he wanted wasn't what made the decision so easy. In truth, it was Dr. Cooper himself. From the moment he talked to him on the phone, it was like he already knew him and knew him well. From that first day on the job, the Boss always treated him with respect and fairly. Danny knew he had money, that he was probably the smartest guy on the planet and that he was famous in his own right. But to him, he was just "the Boss" and he was his friend.

The ringing of his cell phone broke him away from his thoughts. He gently let Gabe's leg rest on the ground, patted his rump, wiped the sweat off his brow with his sleeve, and yanked the phone from his pocket.

Looking at the caller I.D., he said, "Speak of the devil," he hit the answer button, "Yeah Boss."

"Danny Boy, I need a jet that can get me over to the Middle East in a hurry. What da ya think?"

In the years that Mendez had been with Cooper, he'd become much more than a Ranch Foreman. His other responsibilities were far reaching, and much more complicated. One of those tasks was to personally handle Dr. Cooper's travel arrangements. And the Boss traveled all around the world... frequently.

Bryce had a "Black" charter jet membership card. The card gave Cooper part ownership of a fleet of jets. For a yearly fee, he could fly as much as he wanted, which was a lot for the globetrotting Dr. Bryce Cooper.

Mendez pushed his hat back on his head and whistled. "The Middle East Boss? Where and when do you want to go?"

"Need to leave by nine or ten this evening. And I need a flight plan to Tel Aviv."

Danny didn't say it out loud, but with the news coming out of that region; Israel was one place he wouldn't want to fly to anytime soon.

"Humm... well, either way, you're gonna have to stop off in London to top up the tanks. Private charters don't have smaller jets that go that far. But I think if you got one of the Gulfstream IV-SP's, you'd get plenty of range. And, you'd be flying in style. Dr. McNabb going with you?"

"That's perfect. I want to stop off in London anyway. And yeah, Mac's coming with. Go head and book um Dano!"

Danny smiled. He knew how the Boss liked to quote old lines from TV shows and movies. This was a line that he used often with him. It came from the old show, "Hawaii Five-o".

"No problem Boss. How long do you think you'll be gone? When would you like me to make the return flight for?"

"Humm..." Bryce said in contemplation, "Hard to say. Tell you what, leave it open ended and I'll call you when we're ready."

"Okay, you got it! I'll make the arrangements right now."

"Thanks Danny," and the line went dead.

"Jerusalem?" Mendez said to himself. He knew that Uncle Joe was in Israel, but it didn't sound like a leisure trip. Dr. Cooper was in a hurry and all business.

He turned to Gabe and quickly led him back to his pen. "Sorry boy, gotta go to work," he said, as he stroked the horse's neck. Then he spun and sprinted for his office to charter the plane.

In only a few hours, Dr. Bryce Cooper would be heading to the Middle East. He could not have known how the world would change by the time he reached Tel Aviv.

Bryce asked Ed to lead his horse back to the stables. Cooper needed to walk and gather his thoughts.

He'd worked up a pretty good sweat on his way back to the ranch house. He could feel his leg stiffening up. It was completely healed since one of the Fallen snapped it in half like a twig four years ago. But it still got sore if he did too much. And right now, between getting bucked off a horse in the morning and the long hike that he was practically running on, he felt the limb burn.

But he welcomed the distraction of pain. Mrs. Warkentin's revelations caused him a very familiar sense of dread. He had the same feeling four years ago, and he'd hoped that he'd never have it again. It was like he was the sole person standing on a beach and he could see the tsunami coming, but there was nothing he could do about it.

Unlike his experience back then, his morning's vision told him that the whole world would be affected this time by what was coming. Manaya unknowingly confirmed it. It was a nightmare waiting to happen.

One of the worst things about going through the experience before the Reset, was going through it alone. No one else knew what happened. His near death experience and the near death of millions, including his best friend, haunted him for months after he got back to the ranch.

Finally, after his leg healed and his surrogate parents were ready to retire to Israel, he told them the truth. He even told them about The Package. They took it all well. And most importantly, they believed him.

But then he swore them to secrecy. The things that happened before the Reset, no one could ever know, it was just too dangerous. If the Fallen, or The Others knew what he possessed, or if they figured out how he changed their plans, he, nor the Package, nor his family would be safe.

Bryce shook his head at the thought of the things that Manaya said to him. Initially he was concerned that she might be a plant, or under control of the Fallen. But she knew way too much about him to be anything other than what she appeared. She was a genuine, God fearing lady. And she saw - what he saw - when he fell off his horse. He hadn't spoken about the vision to anyone. He even forgot about it. Yet, she knew. And she knew about The Package.

But his feelings were not the same about the Rabbi who called from Jerusalem. On the phone, this stranger asked him about The Package. He described it to him in detail. How could that be? No one on Earth knew about it except his Uncle Joe and Aunt Ruby. And he knew that they would willingly go to their deaths holding the secret. But something went wrong. And now The Package was in play.

As if that wasn't bad enough, the Rabbi shocked him by telling him that he needed it by tomorrow for a ceremony. When Bryce asked him what ceremony, the physicist almost fell over at the response. It was unbelievable and yet, the Montanan knew it was true.

The Rabbi said that it was "a matter of life and death." He said that the Israelites used the items to talk to God about whether or not they should go to war. And he confided to Bryce that war for Israel was near, and they needed Adonai's guidance now more than ever.

Still, none of this could have persuaded him to turn over The Package. But Manaya saw this man. She knew he was going to call. She knew that he would ask for The Package. He remembered the look on her face. And he remembered what she said, "...you need to do exactly what he says. Time is very short. And you need to personally deliver this package to Jerusalem... right away. There is no time for delays. Time is at an end. You must go." She was pleading with him.

So he agreed. Just like that over the phone. He agreed to turn over The Package to a complete stranger. He shook his head. She said, "Time is at an end." That didn't sound good.

He thought back to Quayle's portals. Were the Fallen ready to open those portals and if so, what would the consequences be? Whatever was going to happen, he was going to Jerusalem.

He came out of a crop of trees and saw the Ranch House looming in the distance. He stopped to catch his breath and rub his aching leg. As he leaned against a tree he stared at the Ranch House. In it was his best friend Mac. And if he had to face the Fallen and the Nephilim, he would only do so with the two men that he trusted more than anyone.

But first, he would have to tell Dr. Grover Washington McNabb what really happened four years ago, and the real reason why he left the LHC.

He had to tell him the truth, or as much of it as he could handle. Since everything was Reset, he didn't remember... about the day he died.

PART TWO

IT BEGINS

"AND THE RAIN WAS ON THE EARTH FOR FORTY DAYS AND FORTY NIGHTS"

THE BOOK OF GENESIS VERSE 7:12

∞

Chapter 26

Lazy Hoof – Present Day

B ryce bounded up the Ranch House steps with urgency. As he came through the front door, he stopped dead in his tracks. A crowd consisting of Gabrielle, Mac, guests, workers and ranch hands were all standing around gawking at a large TV in the expansive lobby area.

He tilted his head and examined the look on their faces. Many of them, including his wife at the far end, had mouths wide open. Still others had a look of worry and dread. But some, like Mac, standing next to Gabrielle, looked starry eyed and in awe.

He walked up to the closest ranch hand and nudged him on the shoulder, "Memphis, What gives?"

Without taking his eyes off the screen, Memphis said in his thick Kentucky accent, "Boss, ain't that the darndest thing?"

"What?" Bryce said, craning his neck to see what all the fuss was about.

With all the people around the TV, he couldn't get a good look, so he walked around the far side to talk to his wife.

"Gabs, what's going on?"

As if jostled from sleep, Gabby briefly glanced up, pointed her finger to the TV, and quietly asked, "Bryce... what do you make of this?" A hint of fear was evident in her voice.

He didn't like being in the dark. With a tone of irritation, he said, "Make of what?"

Mac, who was on the other side of Gabby, slid around, and in awestruck fashion said, "Can you believe this Coop?"

"Believe what?!"

"Those!" Mac said, as he emphatically pointed to the screen.

Finally squinting, he craned his neck around and saw what captured everyone's attention, "What the...?"

"Lisa! Turn that up please," Bryce asked Mrs. Duckett, who was perched on the leather couch, next to the remote.

She did.

A local news affiliate reporter could be seen standing in the sand and pointing up to the sky:

> "That's right Alan. These... these UFO's or Orbs or lights are off the coastline of Washington State and are being seen by thousands... if not tens of thousands of people. There are also reports that the Orbs are hovering above the Aleutian Islands off the coast of Alaska."

"The Aleutian Islands?!" Bryce burst out, remembering his vision.

"SSSHHHHHHHHHH!" the crowd in front of the TV scolded.

On the screen, the cameras cut to a national news desk anchorman, as he excitedly responds:

> "Well, Liz, I know you probably haven't heard, but we're getting reports that these... these anomalies aren't only in Washington State and Alaska. We're getting calls that these lights or UFO's... or... whatever you call them, the English language seems to fail us at the moment, but... ah... these Orbs are also being seen along the west coast of Canada in British Columbia, all along the Gulf of Alaska, annndd..." he looks down to his notes, "on the coasts of Washington and Oregon, as you know, down through Southern California. and..." again he looks down, but then pauses for a stunned second, "... and it also says here, that they can be seen over Japan, and the eastern coast of Russia! Amazing! What do people make of the phenomenon where you are at Liz?"

> "Alan," the local Washington reporter said, "some people are saying that these are aliens, here to help the world and America with our dire situation. Others are saying that they are angels that've come to bring peace to both here and the Middle East... still others are saying..."

The look on Bryce's face betrayed his concern, "How long has this been going on?" he whispered.

"About an hour," Gabby replied, without taking her eyes off the television.

With a big grin, and in a low tone, Mac said, "I heard that the Air Force buzzed a couple of those things. But they didn't even budge."

Bryce didn't hear him. Instead, his mind drifted to a very intense conversation on the same subject, four years before.

Geneva, LHC (Underground) – Four Years Earlier

"Ah, Dr. Cooper it's so nice to see you," the creature shouted over the roar. "Have you come to join your friend Mac? I will shortly be making the trip myself. I figured I'd have a... snack for the road," the creature gestured with fresh kill in his hand, and then bellowed an evil laugh at his own joke.

Two minutes, fifteen seconds...

Overcoming his shock, Bryce said, "So... I... ah..." Bryce was looking at the chamber, he had to get closer, "So you are a... a Nephilim?" he asked.

"That's right human. I am a Nephilim, he said proudly. My ancestors, my cousins, were the fallen angels who took human women and had their way with them. I come from a generation of Nephilim, genetically manipulated to fit right under your noses in your puny little society without notice," the creature said, twirling the meat in his hand for emphasis.

"Some of us 'come down in space ships' or 'UFOs'. You humans are so gullible. One day, you'll welcome us as the solution to all of your earthly problems. And in doing so, you will set up your kind for the Great Deception," he said, as he hideously laughed again.

Bryce reached up and tugged on Mac's shoulder. Through gritted teeth, he said, "Mac, I need you to come down to my office. Now! We need to talk." He glanced back at the TV.

Mac's eyes were locked on the screen, "O... okay Coop, I'll be there in a minute."

"Mac," Bryce whispered, "It's important!"

"Alright... I'll be right there," Mac said with glassy mesmerized eyes fixed on the news report.

Bryce jerked at his big friend's arm, "Now Mac!"

Mac's irritated gaze shifted to Bryce's face, "What's your problem Cooper? I said in a..."

"SSSSHHHHHHHHH!!!!!!" the crowd hissed.

Bryce got in Mac's face, "You're not going to find the truth by watching this on the news. I need you to come with me down to my office... right now. And I'll tell you what's really going on!"

"You can't give me one second to watch history..." Mac started to say a little too loudly.

"SSSSSHHHHHHH," the crowd hissed again with turning heads. Someone on the other side said, "Come on guys!"

Bryce lowered his voice again. Looking Mac in the eye he whispered forcefully, "There's something terrible that's about to happen. I need to talk to you about it! Have I ever lied to you?"

Mac searched his friend's face, then he looked back at the screen. Then he looked around at the crowd and made sure his voice was low, "Why now Coop? Why can't I just finish watch..."

"Because this is just for show. I don't know what's about to happen... but my guess is that we don't have a lot of time!" he whispered with urgency.

Mac sighed heavily, "Alright... But this better be good Cooper! Or you and me are gonna have a problem. This is history we're missin!"

Bryce turned and headed for the stairs to his office with Mac on his heels. Speaking over his shoulder, he said, "Funny thing about history Mac... sometimes it repeats itself."

Chapter 27

Stonehenge, England – Present Day

"*I*t is good to see you Professor. But what happened? You look as though you were run over by an articulated lorry (Semi truck)?"

"Ha, funny you should say that," The Professor said in his Spanish accent. "It's good to see you too. Thank you for coming on such short notice. I really need your help."

"Of course, of course. Whatever I can do," his contact assured him. Then, his blue eyes drifted over to Stephanie, sparkled and lingered for a moment. Shyly he looked away, his face turned red with embarrassment.

"Oh... I'm sorry," The Professor said coyly after seeing the look. "This is my daughter... Stephanie. Mija, this is my prize student that I was telling you about, Dr. Williamson."

"It is a pleasure to meet you," the shy contact said, reaching out to gently shake Stephanie's hand, holding her gaze.

"Thank you. You too," she said, also slightly blushing in the dawn light.

After a moment, The Professor cleared his throat.

The two dropped their long handshake and Dr. Williamson got right down to business, "What have you got yourself into Professor? Meeting here," he gestured with wide arms, "in the middle of all of this craziness. It is a far cry from your office or Oxford's campus."

The Professor smiled. Dr. Williamson was one of the brightest students he'd ever had. He remembered when he first met him during a brief teaching stint at the University of Cambridge a few years ago.

Back then he was very green. At first glance, he appeared uptight and aloof. Later, when Dr. Mora found out about his royal bloodline, he attributed it to upbringing. But when The Professor got to know him, his wonderful dry sense of humor and personable demeanor quickly endeared him to the educator. The two men became fast friends.

Just before his prize student graduated with his Masters in physics, he came to The Professor to ask him for a letter of referral to the Large Hadron Collider Research Assistant Program. Mora happily wrote a stellar recommendation. Although he left before the semester was done, he'd heard that the up and coming physicist was accepted to the program.

By the time he completed his time at the LHC, Alvaro obtained a permanent teaching position at Oxford. When the young Brit heard this, he immediately transferred to Oxford to finish his Ph.D.

That was a few years ago and since then Dr. Williamson matured into a fine physicist. Recently The Professor heard that he'd obtained an important position at the UK's version of the LHC.

"Of course... I can see how it looks," The Professor said, "but it was one of the easiest places to blend in and..." he bit off the last part of the sentence.

"And?" Dr. Williamson prompted.

Dr. Mora shrugged with embarrassment, "And... you can see people approaching from a long way off."

"People approaching? Oh my," Williamson asked with consternation. "Have you people looking for you?"

The Professor simply nodded.

"Perhaps you'd better tell me what is going on."

"Yes," Alvaro said anxiously, "Of course. But first, can I ask if you've brought the data with you?"

"Yes, just as you asked," the student turned Ph.D. said, patting the case over his shoulder, "But I've had no time to review it."

Dr. Mora exhaled a long breath. "Finally... some good news. Come, I'll tell you a story that you're not going to believe," he said as he led Williamson and Stephanie over to a stone bench away from the crowds.

As they settled in, in exact fashion, The Professor began to relate the attempt on his life and the threat he found that could bring about the destruction of Planet Earth.

Digby "Diggs" Stanford Williamson involuntarily shivered at hearing about the potential death of all mankind.

Lazy Hoof – Present Day

"Now... what was so important that you drug me away from the most important news story in history?"

"That?" Bryce said pointing upstairs, "that's not history! That's a show... an illusion... a magic trick designed to suck in the whole of humanity!"

"What? Cooper, I told you... unless you give me something good, I'm going back upstairs," Mac said in frustration.

Walking over to the wall by his desk, Bryce asked, "You ever wondered what was behind this case?" He rubbed his hand over the polished oak cabinet on the wall.

Mac looked at the case confused. It was something akin to a very large dart board or gun case with highly polished wooden doors on front.

"No... but what does..."

"Mac, you've known me a long time. Have you ever known me to quit at anything?" Cooper asked in a melancholy tone.

"Huh? What does..."

Turning back to face his friend, "Just answer the question. Have you ever known me to quit anything?"

Mac narrowed his eyes, "Cooopp what's going on here?"

"Mac?" Bryce said again, waiting for an answer.

Mac sighed in frustration. In a steady cadence, he said, "No, I, have, never, seen, you, quit, anything. There you happy? Can I go now?"

Bryce's arms were crossed across his chest. He could see that his friend wanted to say something, but didn't. Already knowing what Mac was thinking, he motioned with his hand and said, "Come on. Spit it out."

The large man looked embarrassed. Bryce was like his kid-brother. But something still bothered him from when Bryce left the LHC. Mac felt abandoned... dropped. But for the sake of their friendship, he'd never brought it up.

"Well... since you asked... there was your work at the LHC. You quit then," Mac said sheepishly.

"Okayyy... anything else?" Bryce asked, arms still crossed.

"Well... no. That's why it was so out of character for you. You know... being that you're as stubborn as a horse's a..."

"Precisely," Bryce interrupted before his friend could compare him to the backside of a horse. "And I got the feeling that you never really believed the excuse I gave you for my leaving."

"Well," Mac scratched the dark and gray stubble on his chin, "No, not really. But the way you acted..." he said with a far-a-way look, "it was really the way you acted. From the day you told me you were leaving until now, you've been different. I can see the difference. You're happier, less haunted."

"Haunted?"

Mac was leaning on the end of Bryce's desk. He stood straight up, "Cooper, you goofball. Do I need to spell it out for you? About your folks... this place?" he said waving his arms, "You know! You avoided like the plague. And your personality..."

"My personality?" Bryce prompted.

"Come on! I don't know why we have to talk about this now. Let's go back...

"Maaaccc"

Mac shook his head, "You're really gonna make me say this you jerk! Well you were dark... your personality was dark!

"Dark?"

"Cooper, you know what I'm getting at. You didn't have a mean temper or anything, just sad. You were always sad... depressed. Even with that beautiful wife and great kid, and with all your awards and recognition. You were always so unhappy. But now..."

"Now..." Bryce prompted.

Mac shrugged, "Ah I don't know. You're happier. More peaceful. You're still a pain in the..."

"So what's the difference? In me I mean"

"I swear Coop, I'm gonna throw something at you if you keep

dancing with me," Mac said. "You got me down here talking about feelings and all. You know how I hate that. Now you want me to tell how you got religion and now everything's better?! But you dumped me man. Let me swim with the sharks all by myself," Mac said with a dejected look.

"Dumped you?" Bryce never heard this from his friend before. What do you mean I dumped you?"

Mac was back leaning on Bryce's desk. He shook his head, "Ah, I understand and all. First you left and then Diggs. When you guy's left, it just wasn't the same. Even with the job promotion."

"I'm sorry buddy. I didn't know you felt that way. I thought you were too busy to miss me."

Mac shook his head and smiled, "It's okay. Things change. Besides I was happy for you. You made your peace with... God and you were okay after that. Ready to move on. It's cool. But my point is that from that day until this, you've been different. I just assumed that change of heart had something to do with you leaving."

Bryce looked at his friend and cocked his head. He'd never heard Mac talk about how he felt abandoned and he realized that he should have asked sooner.

The reality was that after his Reset, Bryce developed some very definite thoughts and feelings toward his relationship with God. And because he was primarily an agnostic or atheist before his Reset, his belief system now was a hundred and eighty degrees different from the one he had four years ago.

Back then, despite his Christian upbringing and his Jewish Levite lineage, he wouldn't tolerate even a mention of God. But since he stepped over the dimensional divide, everything had changed. He had changed.

However, now he wouldn't classify himself as religious; at least not in the traditional sense of the word. He'd grown to develop a mix of Judaism and Christianity. He read the Bible regularly even though he remembered every letter. His goal was to study the deeper truths in it that would help him to be more of what God wanted him to be.

He also became fluent in Hebrew, Greek and Aramaic so he could read the words in their original language. At the same time, he also read the Jewish Talmud extensively. This too, he committed to memory, but the concepts were a bit tougher for him to grasp.

The Talmud was over sixty-two thousand pages and written in the form of rabbinic discussions. It contained thousands of opinions of rabbis, many of whom are left unnamed. And it covered a variety of subjects, including law, ethics, philosophy, customs, history, theology, lore and many other topics. He thought it was important for him to understand the foundation of Judaism for both personal heritage and his Christian belief system.

He'd come to accept that Yeshua HaMashiach's (Jesus the Messiah's) teaching sprung from the Nazarene's own Jewish roots. Because of this, Bryce now made it a point for he and his family to observe many of the Jewish traditions and festivals. And he often took his family to Saturday services at the Beth Tephila Messianic Congregation in Missoula.

But regardless of his religious practices, he believed that his "relationship" with God was a one on one affair. And because of the unique perspective afforded him four years ago, he didn't think that a church building or temple could replace one walking into Hashem's (God's) presence.

Looking at Mac, a big grin grew on his face, "You really are a knucklehead McNabb. You know that?"

"Oh? I'm a knucklehead Cooper?" Mac said in his big baritone bravado, happy for the change of subjects. "I'm not the one, who brought us down here in the middle of the biggest news on the planet."

"Naw, that's not the biggest news on the planet. This," he said pointing to the wooden cabinet, "is a much bigger, albeit unknown, news. Because, that which lies behind these doors... changed the world forever."

Chapter 28

Lazy Hoof – Many Years Earlier

*A*s the disease progressed, the cancer had stolen her sight. Prior to her illness, she devoured the bible with hungry eyes on a daily basis. Since she had lost her vision, he knew she must have felt a void. A void he could help fill... by reading to her.

This afternoon's reading would be out of the New Testament. He was supposed to pick up where they left off in Revelation. His mother, always the bible teacher, would comment on the various things he'd read.

It amazed him that even with the cancer eating away at her body; she still had an amazing ability to recall religious information and history. Even though he no longer believed, Bryce appreciated his mother's powers of recollection.

Picking up where he left off, in Revelation 9:13-16, he read:

> *"And the sixth angel sounded, and I heard a voice from the four horns of the golden altar which is before God, saying to the sixth angel which had the trumpet, 'Loose the four angels `which are bound in the great river Euphrates.' And the four angels were loosed, which were prepared for an hour, and a day, and a month, and a year, for to slay the third part of men. And the number of the army of the horsemen were two hundred thousand thousand; and I heard the number of them."*

Bryce had been reading from Revelation to his mother for a few days now, and she had explained to him that this section dealt with Armageddon, the end of the world.

She explained earlier that several things had to happen before Armageddon. As he read this, something bothered him. He may no longer believe, but he was a naturally curious youth and he wanted to understand the author's reasoning behind these verses.

He asked in a low quiet voice, "Mom, why were those angels 'bound'?"

Slowly opening her unseeing eyes, she smiled warmly at him, and then winced in pain. In a moment, after the pain subsided, she said in a raspy whisper, "Son... that there is the right question to ask. Remember, at one time..." she started coughing... and she kept coughing. Her body jerked and convulsed. She looked like she was in terrible pain. He held a tissue up to her mouth to catch the bloody mucus and spittle.

He sat there helplessly, holding her hand gently while she tried to catch her breath. Slowly, her coughing subsided and then she started again in a hoarse, even quieter voice, "Remember I told you about... Isaiah 14:12... 14:12-15 I believe..." she coughed again. This time she quickly regained her composure.

Bryce took the break as an opportunity to give her a sip of cold water through a straw. That seemed to help. She continued, "Those verses talk about how the devil was once a beautiful angel who led worship to God. Then he got all high and mighty and decided that he wanted to be like God." She took in a shallow breath. "Well, God wasn't gonna have none of that, and kicked his sorry butt out of heaven. The thing is, Lucifer, that's what his name was back then, managed to get a third of the angels riled up and they followed him.

"Later he would become known as 'the devil' and the angels that followed him would become 'fallen angels' or demons as we call them."

"Some of those fallen angels came to Earth and did some... some very bad things," she hesitated as if searching a memory.

Her eyes heavy now with sleep, as the morphine began to kick in. "Like in the days of Noah..." she said in a dreamy like state. "Those angels you just read... read about," she slurred.

She was quiet for a moment with her eyes closed. Bryce

thought she fell off to sleep. But with a quiet raspy voice, she finished her thought "Those angels were four of the devil's fallen angels, his... generals... they... they will get out of... the aa... abyssss... and kill a third of mankind..."

_____

Lazy Hoof – Present Day

"Coop? Did you hear me?" Mac said with irritation in his voice.

Bryce's back was to him. He was staring at a cabinet on the wall, lost in the memory of his mother's last days.

"Come on Coop," Mac said again in frustration, "quit messin around we're..."

Bryce held up his hand stopping his friend's objection, "And do you know why?"

Wagging his head with annoyance, "Oh alright! I'll bite. What, my hillbilly friend, could be so important to the world, to... to mankind even," he said waving at the cabinet, "that you've hidden it in your basement office?"

"Only this," Bryce said: With a flourish, as he opened the cabinet doors.

Mac squinted. To him it looked like some ceremonial clothes under glass. He could see that there was a sheen to them and were adorned with gold and jewels. Their design appeared to be very old, but the Garments themselves looked to be new and hardly worn. Nonetheless, they were still old clothes.

He erupted, "Doggone it Cooper! You drug me away from the news for this?! What's so important about..."

"Remember how," Bryce interrupted, "when I left the LHC, I told you I found what I was looking for?"

The big man looked confused, "Look Cooper, we just went over that. I said I understood. But what does a... a... toga have to do..."

"This isn't a toga," he said with a smirk.

Mac was standing, hands on hips, fifteen feet from the cabinet. Slowly he walked up to the glass case. He carefully examined the Garments. After a moment, he said, "Well, I s'pose not. So will you please tell me what your point is? So... we can go back upstairs and find out what's going on?"

"The reason that I found what I was looking for is because... I found what I was looking for."

Mac's face was blank and he shook his head. "Cooper," he said measuring his words, "I've had about enough play time. The adults are upstairs watching the real world. I'm going to take my butt..."

"You were there. You just can't remember," Bryce said quickly.

Mac cocked his head, "I was where?"

"The LHC"

McNabb looked at his friend like he was crazy. "Of course I was at the LHC. You got me the Director's job remember? I remember.... Hold on, what do you meeeaann I can't remember?

Bryce looked down searching for how to tell his friend. He knew this day would come. Over the years he thought hard about how to break the truth to Mac. But now... standing in front of him... words failed. He looked up. Sorrow and regret filled his troubled eyes.

"You can't remember, because this you...I mean... this version of you... can't remember."

"This version?"

"Yeah... Mac, this version. You see, this is no toga. This," Bryce said, pointing to the Garments behind the glass, "is an exact duplication of the High Priest's Garments from Solomon's Temple. But of course, if you could remember, you would know them as a different name."

"The High Priest's what? What do you mean I know them? I've never seen them in my life! Cooper..."

"No, this youuu," Bryce said, "hasn't seen them. But you have heard me talk about them."

"Alright Cooper! Enough! I'm going upstairs and..."

"I told you before I quit the LHC that I was thinking about making them. You would know them better as... The Harmonic Particle Refractor."

Mac's mouth dropped open and he was stunned into silence. Bryce let him stew.

When he finally found his voice, Mac said, "The Harmonic Particle Refractor? I... I asked you about that before you left the LHC four years ago! You said you didn't do anything with the idea!" Mac said angrily.

Then Bryce leveled the truth at him. It was like crackin a two by four over his head. "And I used these Garments, and the LHC, to bridge the divide between dimensions. When I did, time and space were forever changed. That's why you can't remember."

Mac was dumbfounded, "You what?"

"That's right," Bryce said nodding, "And you and Diggs helped me."

Mac advanced a couple of steps toward Bryce pointing his big black finger, "Cooper, Diggs was only at the LHC a week before you moved back to Montana! Remember, you're the one who recommended him to me to be my research assistant! You never worked with Diggs!"

Bryce hung his head at the memory, "Not only did I work with him, but he was the best research assistant I ever had. How do you think I knew so much about him?"

Still shaking his head, Mac said in frustration, "I don't know... I thought you looked him up or something. But what does any of this have to do with that!" he said pointing to the cabinet.

Bryce was facing Mac, his back to the cabinet. "That," he said pointing behind him with his thumb, "is how I crossed over time and space. And I did that to try to stop something horrific from happening."

Now the big man looked worried. For a brief moment, he wondered about Bryce's state of mind. Shaking his head gently and in a low soothing voice, he said, "Coop, I don't remember any of that. It didn't happen. If it would have happened, I would remember."

Bryce looked to the ground. After a moment he raised his head. There were tears in his eyes. He choked, "That's because..." He couldn't say it.

Mac gently prompted, "Because why Coop? Why do you think I can't remember?"

Bryce coughed and cleared his throat. He quickly wiped his eyes with his fist. After a second, he looked up, his face steeled with determination, "That's because in that version... you died."

Chapter 29

Lazy Hoof – Present Day

*M*ac sat on the edge of Bryce's desk. He'd been quiet for a time, staring unseeingly at the far wall. Long forgotten was his fascination with the news story upstairs. The two friends talked in the Montanan's office for hours. Cooper was sitting in his beat-up old leather desk chair. His cowboy boot clad feet were up on the corner of the desk. His hands were behind his head with fingers interlocked.

Mac finally broke the latest long silence, still gazing toward the wall. "Coop if... if it wasn't you telling me about this crazy alternate reality, I'd think you were nuts. But if anything, it makes too much sense," he said.

Initially, every time that Mac protested or questioned him, Bryce ploughed on, not wanting to stop the flow of information. Inevitably, the next few sentences would answer Mac's questions or objections.

As Mac began to absorb what the younger physicist was telling him, Bryce would give him details in smaller bites so he could chew on it. The big man might ask a question to clarify or think aloud, but still he listened. Then after a while, Bryce would go over to his white board and write out an equation showing a mathematical proof. Mac would examine the math and find that Bryce's numbers were irrefutable.

Because they'd worked together on Bryce's early LHC work, Mac was intimately familiar with his dimensional theory. By the end of Bryce's tale, all the pieces fit together... especially the science. As fantastic as it sounded, it all made sense to Mac.

Now he was just numb. He was tired and his brain fried. But beyond a shadow of a doubt, one thing was clear to Mac: Dr. Bryce Obadiah Cooper used the LHC four years ago as a bridge to an adjoining dimension. In doing so, both the LHC and HAARP, which

Bryce also told Mac about, were used as a time machine. The outcome to the experience was that the space time continuum was forever altered.

"Sometimes I wish it wasn't true," Bryce said. "There were times that I doubted my own sanity."

Mac shook his head, "All this time... my life... has been a lie."

Shock registered on Bryce's face as his mouth dropped open. He sat up instantly as his boots dropped to the ground with a thud. "What do you mean a lie McNabb?!"

Bryce was flabbergasted. He pointed his finger at Mac, "Are you nuts! You have another God given chance to live. How can that be a mistake?"

"God given" was an interesting choice of words Mac thought. Now he understood the urgency and emphasis in Bryce's voice the day the Montanan told him he found what he was looking for and encouraged Mac to do some real soul searching.

But after Bryce left, Mac hardly thought about the things Bryce said to him: About God and real inner peace. He was far too busy. Being thrust into his new position as the LHC's Director took every ounce of thought and energy he had.

"But I don't get it?" Mac asked confused, "Why tell me now? Why not tell me before? You didn't trust me?"

Bryce considered the question, "Naw, it wasn't that. You know I trust you with my life. I didn't trust myself."

"What do ya mean, you didn't trust yourself?"

"Look..." Bryce said as he jumped to his feet, "You know me. I couldn't trust that I wouldn't jump back into science with both feet once you, or anyone else, knew what happened. This was my chance to live life as I always should have."

"But you're still involved with science. Heck, I see you on TV all the time as the expert," Mac said making quote marks with his fingers. "And I think since you left the LHC you've written more papers than you would have if you were there. And you talk about broader issues even outside of physics. How can you say you stepped away?"

"It's not the same," Bryce said shaking his head. "Writing, or talking about science is not doing science. You know that. When I was in Geneva, or anywhere else I worked, science was all consuming. You know me. I couldn't have all of this," he held his hands wide, "and be involved in the latest experiment. Besides..." he said then stopped himself.

"Besides what?"

Bryce blew out a deep breath. "It wasn't time. This news," he said pointing to the ceiling, "and what Mrs. Warkentin told me, makes me think we have very little time."

"Very little time? Time until what?"

Bryce looked at his friend. Mac appeared exhausted. He hated to dump any more on the astrophysicist. But they had to catch a plane soon. He looked at the clock on the wall. Finally he asked, "What are your thoughts on Operation Falling Star?"

Mac considered the question, hand to chin. "Well... aside from the experiment being shut down just before we got there and... they asked us to reconfigure our experiment to that same experiment... and it shut us down... To tell you the truth, I don't think very much of it at all!"

Bryce nodded his head, "I can understand that. Can you tell me what you saw? What these entities looked like?"

Mac blew out a long breath, "Yeah, I figured you'd ask. I've been thinking about it."

McNabb took five minutes to describe what he saw. At the end of the story, he was visibly sweating.

Bryce was standing with his arms crossed, thinking about what he'd just heard. Finally he said, "Yup, sounds just like what I've seen."

"Hold on, you tellin me that all of this is connected with what you went through?"

Bryce scratched his head, "Mac, that's exactly what I'm going to tell you. Further, based on the results that I just spent the last few hours explaining to you, I believe that we were duped into continuing that experiment under the guise of our ATLAS 7 experiment."

Mac was sitting on the edge of Bryce's desk. He wagged his head, "Why is nothing ever easy with you Cooper. You've given me such," and he pinched his forehead, "a doggone headache. You got any aspirin?"

"Ibuprofen in the medicine cabinet in there," he said pointing to the bathroom on the far side of the room.

Mac breathed out heavily, "I'll be right back."

Bryce smiled for the first time since he started the long disturbing tale. His friend might feel like he'd been through five rounds of an MMA fight, but at least he was on board. Bryce went over to the large coffee bar and made a pot.

Mac came out of the bathroom after freshening up. Bryce poured him a cup of strong black coffee.

For the next few minutes, Bryce related his conversations with Steve Quayle and how the man from Bozeman helped him put the pieces together. He told him about the indirect connection he'd found between HAARP and the LHC. And he shared with him the scientific paper from Dr. Fran De Aquino from Brazil and how he is the one that pointed out there were enough HAARPs on the Earth to wrap the world and manipulate time. He pointed out the anomalies that he found that gave credence to what Quayle said was numerous other portals or stargates.

Although a much shorter barrage than his initial one on Mac, by the time they were done, they downed two pots of coffee. Mac just sat there behind Bryce's desk shaking his head.

"I gotta tell you buddy," the big man said, "when you step in it, it's with both feet!"

"Don't I know it," Bryce agreed.

Mac was quiet for a moment biting his lip, thinking. After a long quiet spell, he said, "So I guess you're gonna tell me that those Orbs aren't what everyone thinks they are?"

"Not by a long shot. Remember what I said about that Nephilim creature? It practically told me this was going to happen."

"Too bad," Mac said with a sad shake of his head, "I was kinda hopin they were. So what now?"

Bryce was quiet for a moment. When he did speak, his tone was an octave lower, "I think all of those portals are ready to open?"

Mac exhaled, "I was afraid you were going to say that. But what the heck can we do about it?"

"For one, that's why we're headed to Israel. After that... I don't know."

Bryce already related what he saw when he fell off his horse that morning. He also told Mac in detail how Manaya confirmed the very same vision. And he disclosed the strange call that happened just as she said it would.

Mac stood in front of the cabinet again, "So you're just gonna hand it over to them just like that?"

Bryce stood next to him looking at the Garments, "What else am I supposed to do? If I don't hand it over, everything that is gonna happen, will happen anyway. If I do hand it over..."

"What?"

"Well, I can only hope that I was told to give it to them for a reason. Maybe they'll make a difference."

"But I don't get it."

"What don't you get?"

"Well," the black man said, "you designed this thing from what you learned from ancient Hebrew history right?"

"Yeah so?"

"Well... why couldn't they do the same thing? I mean, they have the same information that you read right?"

"Yup Mac old boy, you're right. They could. But what they can't duplicate is what's in those two little pockets there," he pointed, "see those?"

Mac squinted, "Huh... I hadn't noticed them before."

"In those pockets are the keys to the whole outfit. Without them, these would be just fancy clothes."

"So what are they?"

Bryce looked up at his friend and then to the clock, "That discussion will take a little more time. We'll talk about it later. You hungry?"

Mac rubbed his stomach, "Well, now that you mention it. Is it just me or did we miss lunch?"

"Come on," Bryce said as he slapped him on the back, "I just happen to know where the kitchen is!"

Following behind the physicist turned cowboy Mac asked, "So we leaving for Israel tonight?"

"Yeah, but before we get there," he started up the stairs, "we need to make a pit stop."

"A pit stop?" Mac asked above the noise of their rumbling feet on the stairs.

"Of course."

Mac stopped on the stairs, "What-da-ya mean?"

"We have to pick up Diggs!"

Chapter 30

*<u>**Wall Street, New York – Present Day**</u>*

C *he human condition, he mused. It's curious that over the
centuries mankind, even with all their technological
advancements, is relatively the same simple creature that emerged
after the Stone Age.*

True, thought the Banker, *it's easy for me to sit in my ivory tower,
looking over the New York skyline, and judge the very culture which
afforded me these luxuries. But because humans were so predictable,
judgment's easy to pass.*

It was a little before eleven at night, and the Banker sat in the
luxurious front room of the most expensive real estate in all of New
York: His penthouse suite at 15 Central Park West.

Nestled in his favorite arm chair, he gazed out the wall of
windows that overlooked the New York skyline and Central Park.
The Banker took a sip, from his tumbler, of one of his favorite
Scotches, an extremely rare Dalmore 62 Single Hiland Malt. It might
have cost a little over $60,000, but was one of the best pleasures for a
man of his discerning palate.

This was a celebration of sorts. And his toast? To the brave new
world that he helped create. He shooed away his two female
companions a few minutes ago. Now he needed to think; to reflect.
Tomorrow was a big day.

His power was derived from control of the world's monetary
system. This was not the banking system or Wall Street that the
public saw. Those were merely tilt-up movie set facades with nothing
behind them. The real monetary system stretched as far back as
Babylon itself and it was where the real money was. Never before had
so much wealth and so much power been placed in the hands of so
few individuals.

As the Chairman of Goldman Sachs, and monetary king of the

United States, he assisted the UN, the IMF, The World Bank, and dozens of Central Banks across the globe. He helped "feed" the countless hungry throughout earth while all the while building his kingdom. It was the money at his command, used here in the U.S. and in third world countries, which kept anarchy at bay. Soon that money would be pulled, and anarchy would reign.

The Others gathered the leaders of the world to themselves through The Group. They were the rich and powerful of the human race that perceived themselves to be in charge. With The Others' help, they consolidated their wealth and power and grew it beyond measure.

He chuckled to himself. The Group went by many names over the years. They were called "The Illuminati", "The Bilderbergs", or the "Free Masons". Most recently, the term "The New World Order" or "NWO" was heard. Whenever kernels of real truth began to surface regarding The Group's identity or intentions, the exposing individuals were always discredited as "conspiracy theorists" or fringe extremists that were unbalanced and fanatical.

But the true horror of what The Group was would not be discovered until it was far too late. The Plan is unfolding just as anticipated. Soon, at The Others' recommendation, the ninety percent depopulation of the Earth, would begin.

And the reason why this was necessary, The Others told The Group, was because more land and less people meant more power and space for them. At least that was the lie The Group was fed. All of them believed that Agenda 21, otherwise known as "Local Governments for Sustainability", was their idea.

This was supposed to be done to preserve the land and its riches for them. Each of The Group was promised a kingdom on the new Earth of his or her own. The Others' convinced them that population reduction was key to their rule.

Nothing could be further from the truth. And after a large majority of the human race was extinguished, The Others and The Fallen would turn their wrath on the pompous and arrogant Group.

Supposedly these were the smartest and most powerful that the human race had to offer, yet they themselves were so gullible, blinded by their own greed and thirst for power.

He shook his head, laughed and said aloud "Maintain humanity under five hundred million in perpetual balance with nature." It was a direct quote from The Georgia Guidestones. Like so many times in the past, The Group would tell the world what they were planning. But the sheep wouldn't listen. They couldn't believe that something so horrible could befall the human race.

He took a drag off of his fine Cuban cigar between his fingertips. *Soon the real "Plan" would unfold just as it was designed... the plan within The Plan. The Group had no idea what was coming.*

And tomorrow was the beginning. This is the eve of a host of events. Earth changes, wars and rumors of wars, neighbor killing neighbor. All of it within the unfolding Plan of The Group.

That Plan was already far advanced. The Group was already in control of every echelon of the world's cultural mountains: the business system, the educational system, the arts and entertainment system, the family system and the media. He snickered again; *they even controlled the world's religions, with some minor pockets of resistance.*

Already nations around the globe were beginning to crumble and darkness was falling. Even right here in America, the bastion of a once mighty democracy was beginning to buckle under the weight of debt, greed and selfishness.

Superior intellectual foresight put The Others in the perfect position to influence everything... right under The Group's noses. And he, The Banker, was in the perfect position to influence The Group. They thought he was just like them. He looked like them. He sounded like them. He enjoyed wealth and power like them. But he was definitely not one of them.

The Group didn't know who, or what, he really was. And by the time they figured him out, it would be far too late. The trap would be sprung. If they had known his true identity, the rumblings whispered to him in private would have never come to him.

The irritating bleating of his cell phone broke his train of thought. Looking at the caller I.D., he scowled at the recognition of that cow of a Temp from the office. He should have let her quit when he found out she was "unhappy" this afternoon. But he didn't want the burdensome task of breaking in another. So he offered her three times her normal pay and dangled the promise of a permanent position in front of her to get her to stay. At such a crucial time, why did he ever let his assistant Stephanie go on vacation anyway?

Nonetheless, he couldn't be upset for the intrusion. He often took business calls late into the evening and early morning. With his genetically advanced metabolism he only needed three hours sleep a night. Even Stephanie called him at home. His assistant's job description required her to be available around the clock. If the Temp was calling this late, he was sure it was for good reason.

He picked up the phone, "Yes?" he said, with a tone of mild irritation.

"Sir," the Temp stammered, "I wanted to remind you about those papers I gave you to sign at home this evening. The courier will be round at seven o'clock in the morning to pick them up. I was told that the deal must be consummated tomorrow by nine a.m. Were you able to get to them?"

Instantly his face turned red and his anger boiled. He did forget to sign the documents. But Stephanie would have certainly found a more tactful way to remind him. He bit off the expletive that he so dearly wanted to shout at her.

Instead, curtly he said, "The documents will be ready for him. Anything else?"

"Yeeesss... yes," she stammered, "one other thing you may find interesting."

"Welllll, I would hope you'd tell me while I am still young," he said, no longer able to hide his seething anger.

In a mouse like voice, she said "There have been reports from out West of..." her voice hung in the air as she thought how to best present the information.

"Reports of what?" the Banker snapped. "Speak up."

"It's just that it is very unusual... not really having to do with business," again she hesitated.

This caught the Banker's attention. Using the remote, he turned down Luciano Pavarotti belting out NesSun Dorma. Then he got up and walked to the windows overlooking Central Park.

With his irritation momentarily abated by his curiosity, he asked, "Unusual? How so?"

"Well sir, as you know, there has been increased seismic activity both in Alaska and all down the West coast of North America."

"Yes, yes. Of course I am aware of the increased seismic and volcanic activity throughout the world. At present count, I seem to recall at least eighty volcanoes currently active on the planet," he said condescendingly to the Temp. "Seismic activity and volcanoes of course have everything to do with business," he said forcefully, "as we have significant interests in Insurers around the world. Should this type of disaster strike, there is a direct affect to our bottom-line. But I wouldn't classify this news as unusual as you've put it," he said, his voice dripping with sarcasm.

"Yes, of course," she plowed on, "It is not the earthquakes or volcanoes that are unusual. But the news media from around the world are reporting..." she struggled to find the right words, "anomalies in the sky. Aircraft of sorts. But no government, including America, is taking responsibility for the aircraft."

The Banker's eyes closed to almost slits. "Ahh... is that so?"

"Yes sir. These UFOs are hovering above the areas of seismic activity that I spoke of. If you turn on the news, you can see it for yourself."

"And... what are the news stations saying that these... these aircraft are there for?"

"They don't really know sir. The Orbs, as they're calling them, have made no hostile movement. Both Canada's and the U.S.'s Air Forces have flown by the craft, yet they were undeterred and stay hovering high over the areas."

The Banker stood quiet for a long moment. So it has indeed started, he thought. He hadn't heard of these plans. It wasn't unusual given the significance of what tomorrow would bring.

Thinking she'd lost the connection in his silence, the Temp asked, "Sir are you still there?"

"Yes, yes of course. Well I suppose that the Calvary has arrived then. Please monitor this situation and let me know if anything changes."

"Yes sir," the Temp said, as the Banker disconnected.

Staring at his own reflection in the glass, he thought about how gullible people were. The Temp, and no doubt all of humanity, was ready to welcome the Orbs, who were really The Others, as championed visitors. And they would come, just not quite yet. As planned, they would wait to interact with this dimension until the World really needed them. Then the trap would be sprung.

He said in a whisper to his reflection, "The human condition indeed."

Chapter 31

Lazy Hoof – Present Day

*M*ac was staring at his bed, trying to figure out what to take with him to Israel. He brought most of his worldly possessions with him since he didn't know how long he would be at the Lazy Hoof. He was... in limbo.

He held out hope that he could get his job back and that they would turn the machine back on. But after what Bryce told him, he didn't want anything to do with the place.

Regardless, he doubted if "The Others" needed his help any longer. He and his team made the modifications they requested. He assumed that they were ready to commence a revived Operation Falling Star without him.

He shook his head in anger and then all of a sudden spit out an expletive and kicked the leg of the bed. Instantly he regretted it. Searing pain shot from his foot to his brain, telling him how stupid the move was. More cussing flowed from his lips, and he hopped around on one foot.

After the pain subsided he flopped down on the bed. He wagged his head as he realized that his hands were shaking. Clasping them together tightly, he tried to get them to stop.

As he stared at the floor, in a voice just above a whisper, he asked, "I died?"

He knew Bryce was telling the truth. But with that understanding, he also knew that everything he thought of before... his self-madeness, his theories of the universe, his life's work, how he lived his life up until now... it was all a lie. And then he thought; *not exactly a lie, just not the truth.*

He felt lost... alone and he feared for his future. He felt like a ship without a rudder, drifting. He felt cheated because they shut him down. He felt used because they played him... and he hated being played. For the first time in his life, he wished he was dead... it would be easier than dealing with this.

And then he remembered what Bryce told him about what he saw...

on the other side. He was sure that if he died, he wouldn't have seen those same things. Not only would he not be allowed "in the place where Bryce could not go" but for the first time ever, he wondered what the alternative might be. And that thought scared him. That's why his hands were shaking.

Tears puddled in his eyes. He hadn't cried in years. But here, behind closed doors, dealing with so many things at once, it was the only thing he could do. Then he did something else he hadn't done since he was a child; he began to pray.

Bryce's "relationship" with God looked straightforward. He didn't use religious language or sound churchy. So the big man thought that if he was going to talk to God, he'd do so without pretense.

He asked God to help him get through this. He asked him to forgive him and said he was sorry for all the things, too many to name, that he'd done. He asked God to be real to him like he was to Bryce. And, he asked God to live inside him.

He sat there on the edge of the bed for a long time. The ringing of his cell phone brought him back to the present. He looked at the caller I.D. and was surprised to see it was from someone he meant to call anyway. He hadn't realized that he cried a bucket of tears. Quickly he wiped them with a tissue and blew his nose.

On the fifth ring, clearing his throat, he choked out, "Diggs, how did you know I needed to talk to you?"

"Mac! It is good to hear your voice. And I need to speak with you as well."

For two years Digby Stanford Williamson was Mac's research assistant, his right hand. And when he finally left the LHC to finish his own Ph.D. at Oxford, the two men would consult on the phone regularly. In addition, Bryce unofficially adopted the much younger Diggs as a kid brother and student.

"Well... if I may," Diggs said solemnly, "mine is an issue of, how do you Americans say... life and death. And I am not exaggerating the point in the least."

Mac's antenna went up. The proper Brit was not one for melodramatics. "Are you alright? What's wrong?" he asked seriously.

"Yes, yes, I'm fine," he replied earnestly, "It's not about me. It concerns a friend of mine. But I... I really can't go over it on the phone. It's... well... let's just say that it's too sensitive for prying ears."

He pulled the phone from his ear and looked at it suspiciously. Putting the phone back to his ear, he asked, "What's going on Digby? This doesn't sound like you."

"I know my friend. But trust me when I tell you; this is a very serious issue," he said in a proper English accent. "I wanted to find out if you've spoken to Dr. Cooper and if all three of us could sit down together."

"Sit down?"

"Yes, I was hoping I could hop over to Geneva with a friend to see you. And perhaps you could do me the huge favor of getting ahold of Dr. Cooper and ask him to join us."

Now Mac knew something was wrong. Diggs might interrupt him at the LHC just to come around and visit... if he had time, but there was no way he would drag Bryce all the way to Europe without good reason.

"Diggs, I'm sorry, I thought you knew."

"Knew what?"

"I'm not in Geneva. They... they shut down the LHC," Mac's sadness dripped through the phone.

"They what?! Why? What happened?" the younger man asked in rapid fire succession.

"Buddy, I can't even begin to go over it on the telephone. It's way too long of a story. Besides, we're headed your way anyway. That's why I needed to talk to you."

"Headed my way?" Diggs asked confused. "Who is we?"

"Oh, I'm sorry. I'm in Montana with Coop. We're hopping on one of his jets in..." he looked at his watch, "about an hour. It'll take us about nine hours to get there."

"Of course, you know that you are always welcome. And it saves me from making the trip. Dare I ask why you and Dr. Cooper are flying all the way to the British Isles?"

Mac chuckled, "Buddy you're not the only one with super spy info. I can't tell you on the phone either. You need to get it from the horse's mouth!"

"I'm sorry??"

"Diggs, what we need to speak to you about is way to... well... crazy.

So Coop wants to take a hop over the pond to come and get you."

"Come and get me?"

Mac winced, "Yeah, that's right. He needs you to clear your schedule for a few days. We're headed to Israel."

"What!" the normally reserved Digby blurted out. "But I... I can't go to Israel! I am in the middle of some very important work! And my calendar is full for few weeks!"

Mac swallowed hard. He knew exactly how Diggs felt. Scientists were creatures of habit and order. What Bryce was asking Diggs to do would be very uncomfortable, even for Mac. But Mac also knew Bryce. He knew he was serious when he said he needed both himself and Diggs.

His voice hardened, "Digby, you know I know how you feel. But it is extremely, and I mean extremely, important. Don't make me remind you that it's Dr. Bryce Obadiah Cooper asking. If he is asking, it is for good reason."

Diggs was quiet for a moment, and then in a low voice said, "Yes, yes of course. It's Dr. Cooper. I would do anything for him, but hold on..."

Mac could hear Diggs cover the phone with his hand. As he did, he could hear him talking in muffled tones to someone in the background.

Coming back on the line, Diggs asked, "Will Dr. Cooper want to leave straight away when he gets here? Or will there be time for him to discuss my... ah... friend's business?"

Mac thought for a second with his hand on his chin, "Well, far as I know he wanted to top off the tanks with fuel and take right back off."

"Right, I thought you might say that. Hold on," Diggs said, once again Mac could hear muffled discussion in the background.

Coming back on the phone, Diggs asked, "Do you think that Dr. Cooper has room on his plane for some company?"

Pausing in thought, Mac said after a couple of beats, "Yeah... I guess so. You and someone else?"

Again more muffled discussion in the background. Back on the line Diggs said, "It shall be myself and seven someone elses."

"What?!" he asked in shock. "I... don't think it's a problem but... I think Cooper's gonna need to get a bigger plane!"

Chapter 32

Missoula Airport – Present Day

"*H*ello doctors Black. I'm Danny Mendez, I work for Dr. Cooper," the Hispanic man said as he cordially shook hands with both Xavier and Ivy. "Is this all your luggage?" Danny asked pointing at the two overnight bags.

"Yes," X responded. "We... ah... left in a hurry."

"That's fine. There are plenty of duty free shops in both London and Israel if you need to pick up anything," Danny said as he took the bags from X.

"Excuse me?" Xavier asked confused. "London? Israel?"

Danny already started leading the way to the private flight side of Missoula Airport. He stopped dead in his tracks. Sheepishly he said, "Oh, I'm sorry. I thought Dr. McNabb told you. Change of plans. He said you two always travel with passports?"

"Tell me what? We need to talk to him now! It's urgent!" X insisted, looking back to his wife who nodded.

"Yes sir, of course," Danny said diplomatically. "He and Dr. Cooper have been called away to Israel on an urgent matter. Dr. McNabb said that you wouldn't mind tagging along. He said you could speak to the both of them on the long flight across the pond. At any point that your business is concluded, I can arrange a direct flight back to California for you.

"For now, I was instructed to take you to the other side of the airport where the private charter lounge is. You can wait there while I go back to the ranch and get doctor's McNabb and Cooper. Your flight leaves," he looked at his watch, "in precisely one hour forty minutes."

Israel, X quickly thought, *that is going to seriously put me out of place.*

Xavier was about to strenuously protest when Ivy's phone rang.

Looking at the caller I.D. she saw that it was Mac. Answering the call, she asked, "Mac? What's this all about?"

Listening to the phone for a moment, she tried to interrupt and said, "But I need..." again she listened. "I know but Xavier has things..." still more she listened. "We're not prepared to..." and with her face softening she said, "Okay, okay. We'll go. I'll just have to take your word on it. We'll see you in a bit," and she hung up the phone.

The shell-shocked Puerto Rican woman said, "Seems that we've won an all-expense paid trip from Dr. Cooper to London and then Tel Aviv."

"What?! Honey, I can't..." was all that Xavier managed to choke out.

"Yes, I know dear," Ivy said reflectively, "Mac said that they needed to deal with matters of life and death."

Then deadpanned she added, "Seems to be a lot of that going around these days."

Lazy Hoof – Present Day

Mac made his way downstairs to Bryce's basement office. He found Bryce hanging up his cell phone. Sitting on the desk in front of him was a Package wrapped in brown paper with twine around it. McNabb looked up at the cabinet on the wall. The doors were open, but the Garments were gone.

The big man said, "I just got off the phone with Ivy and Xavier. They're in for the trip overseas... but under protest."

Bryce smirked, "I hear ya. I hate it when people upset my apple cart too. And Diggs?"

"Talked to him too. Ditto, he's not happy. But because it's you, he agreed. With one caveat," Mac said holding up his index finger.

"Oh? What's that?"

"He called me actually. Said he had somebody that needed to speak with you."

Bryce contorted his face, "Seems I'm a popular guy."

"Don't let it go to your head redneck."

"Did he say what about?"

"Nope, just said he was bringing a little group of seven."

"Seven?"

Mac nodded, "That's what he said."

Bryce thought for a moment, "We might need to get a bigger plane in England."

"That's what I told him."

"That was Danny on the phone," Cooper explained. "He's headed back. You packed."

"Yeah, just an overnight bag," he pointed up, "it's upstairs by the door. You?"

"Gabby's doing it for me. Can't trust myself when it comes to that stuff. I always seem to forget something," he said, shrugging.

Bryce shook his head. He didn't know what he'd do without his "soul mate". The thought of almost losing his wife before his Reset was almost too much to bear. Yahwah, the God of the universe had given him another chance and he wasn't about to squander it.

He loved his family more than life itself and the fact was that this unexpected trip had him feeling uneasy.

Gabrielle was eight months pregnant. Although she was due for another mouth, he had no idea how long he'd be away this time.

When he told LJ that he had to fly out unexpectedly, his son was very concerned. "But what about mom?" he asked. "She could have the baby anytime."

Bryce assured his little man that he would be back before that happened. And he also put him in charge as the man of the house. The assignment seemed to cause his son's shoulders to square and his jaw to set. When he left him a few minutes ago, Little Joe was already trying to figure out what he should be doing as "the man of the house" while his dad was away.

But even though his son was feeling better about Bryce's trip, it did little to diminish the sense of foreboding that the physicist was feeling. Somehow, he knew this trip was different than any of his usual business trips. He could not have guessed just how unusual it would be: both for him and family.

Mac chuckled, "Yeah I remember my absent minded professor friend: Brilliant, but always forgetting the little things. You know... they say that even Einstein couldn't ride a bike."

Bryce was about to protest when he stopped himself. Looking coy, he asked, "Hey, what's up with you?"

Mac scrunched his face, "Who me? Nothin, I feel great."

"You look great... different. That's somethin given how I unloaded on you. Not to mention the considerable odds we're facing."

Mac looked embarrassed, "What?" and held out his hands in protest.

Bryce made a "come" motion with his fingers, "Come on... spill it! What's going on?"

In mock anger, Mac said, "Alright Cooper. You'd find out eventually. I finally took your advice. Me and," he pointed up, "the Man are square."

A big smile formed on Bryce's face, "I'm glad," and he slapped him on the back, "happy for you.

"Alright, alright. Don't get sappy on me."

"I wouldn't dream of it," Bryce said. "I'm just glad you're okay. Given what we might run into, I was concerned about your... ah... status."

Mac smiled, "Like I said: square."

"Good," Bryce said, then quickly changed the subject, "I meant to show you this," and handed Mac a printout of an article.

Mac scanned it quickly and gaffed, "What's this? Bill Gates? Lining the skies with sulfur? Geo-Engineers?"

"That" Bryce said pointing to the paper "first came out in the Guardian in July of 2012. You can read it in detail later, but it describes how Geo-Engineers, with funding from none other than Bill Gates of Microsoft fame, are spraying sulfur in the skies all over the world to combat global warming. It's rumored that Gates is heavily involved in Agenda 21 and his is just another example of how they intend on changing the atmosphere of the planet for their own purposes."

Shaking his head Mac asked, "Well, why doesn't anybody do anything about this? Spraying sulfur in the atmosphere can't be healthy for us land dwellers."

"Nope, I would think not, but Steve Quayle told me that this was just a continuance of a something called Chemtrails. That's the long documented practice of spraying barium, aluminum, pathogens and some have reported that they've found dried human blood cells in the spraying."

"What?! Yuck!"

"Yuck is right. They spray these compounds in a spider web formation in the sky using heavy aircraft at high altitudes. The practice of Chemtrails has been documented all around the whole Earth. As to the why, well I don't really know about that last bit, the human blood cells, but my conspiracy theorist friend in Bozeman makes a direct connection to another project that I, unfortunately, am intimately familiar with."

Mac was standing there with his hands on his hips, shaking his head, "Let me guess... HAARP."

Bryce pointed his finger, "Bingo! And do you know what I think the connection is?"

Mac pursed his lips, "Let me guess: HAARP, or HAARPs around the world, are ionospheric heaters and..." he thought for a moment, "they're bouncing their invisible beams off of these... these Chemtrails and superheating the atmosphere?"

"Two for two McNabb. Care to make it a trifecta?"

Mac nodded.

Bryce continued, "What do you think would be the consequence or result of bouncing those heaters off of say aluminum, barium and even sulfur?"

Mac thought for a moment and then alarm registered in his eyes. He said, "They don't only want to heat up the atmosphere, but...

those chemicals would probably begin to breakdown, thus being absorbed in the atmosphere. So what? They're trying to change the composition of the atmosphere? Hold on, are you trying to tell me that this has nothing to do with global warming, but it is all about changing our atmosphere."

"And he scores!" Bryce said dramatically, "The crowd goes wild!"

Mac wasn't as jovial, "Will you knock it off Cooper! This is serious. Are you telling me that they are trying to change the atmosphere? To what?"

Bryce started stuffing papers in his beat-up old leather briefcase. Looking up at Mac as he worked, he said, "Look, all I can tell you is that their practice of spraying sulfur in the atmosphere has significantly increased since the printing of that article. Why they're trying to change the atmosphere and what they're changing it to is anybody's guess. But let me ask you a question."

"Okay..."

"Where is the one place that the smell and presence of sulfur abounds and it's probably part of the inhabitants DNA?"

Mac scrunched up his face in thought. Suddenly fear registered in his eyes, and he said, "Hell?"

Bryce stopped filling his briefcase and stood up. "That's right Dr. McNabb - Hell. I think they're preparing our atmosphere, or dimension, for the opening of those portals!

"And they're trying to make it as comfortable as possible for whatever will come through those openings. Like I said, time is short, in fact... it's almost up."

Chapter 33

Outside Zuqba, Egypt – Five Days Earlier

2 51.565, 251.565, 251.565... These were the numbers played over and over again in his head.

Pressing themselves into the shadows, he and his men squatted in their dark special ops uniforms with faces painted black. They were waiting for the scout to return.

This was hostile territory, behind enemy lines. They shouldn't be there. Their presence could start an armed conflict sooner rather than later. But they had to retrieve the item. War was coming soon. The Rabbi's connections within the government were strong. He'd convinced the Prime Minister and the Knesset that the benefit far outweighed the risk.

As a testament to the pending conflict, tensions throughout the area were rising. The Arab Spring of 2011 swept Hosni Mubarak from the Egyptian presidency. The leadership void there was filled with radical Islam and the Muslim Brotherhood.

Mubarak, although a despot, adhered to the peace treaty signed between Israel and Egypt in March of 1979. While not exactly friendly, the two countries cooperated with one another for over three decades. But now... now Egypt had received their cruel ruler. The long standing treaty was history and the new President ruled his people with an iron fist.

Egyptian troops and armor were now massed in the Sinai, the long recognized buffer zone between the two countries. The upside, if there was one, was that they left this area guarded by only a skeleton crew. Even the Egyptian naval base at Zuqba, a stone's throw from this location, was practically deserted. It was said that the current multi-national military exercise was all consuming and growing day by day.

Zac knew better. War was coming. This would be their last

and only chance to recover the item. There was no guarantee that when war was brought to Israel, that their push back would be this deep inside Egypt. If it were, they could easily extract the item under the presence of friendly forces. But time was a luxury they didn't have. They needed answers now.

The road leading to this nighttime special op was a long one; nearly twenty-six hundred years long. It was not easy to overcome the bias that the scholars had against this location. The Orthodox and Hasidic rabbis believed that the item never left Jerusalem. And the modern secular Israeli government didn't care if the item even existed. So it remained here... waiting. That is until Zac's Rabbi stumbled upon 251.565.

This was a number found in none other than - The Torah Code. Torah codes were words and phrases, and meaningful clusters of words and phrases that exist intentionally in coded form in the text of the Torah (the first five books of the Bible).

Torah Codes use a primary coding method known as the Equidistant Letter Sequence (ELS). The theory behind the use of these ELSs is to extract one from a text, choose a starting point (any letter) and a skip (a number, possibly negative). Then, beginning at the starting point, one would select letters from the text at equal spacing as given by the skip.

Torah Codes were shunned by mainstream Orthodox teaching. However, Zac's Rabbi found the encoded number 251.565 by accident on a website called Arkcode.com. The site was developed by a brilliant mathematician who was also an American Orthodox Jew. His name? Retired Naval and Coast Guard officer, Barry Roffman.

Roffman dedicated his retirement to the search for truth using the Torah Code. His primary truth of interest was what he believed was located at 251.565. And in search of that truth, Zac and his men now found themselves hoping to extract it.

As an Orthodox Jew, it was the American's belief, as was most Orthodox, that the location and rediscovery of the item would bring to fruition the first advent of the promised Jewish Messiah. That Messiah, Mr. Roffman believed, would bring peace. And peace is what Israel desperately needed.

With enemies surrounding her, the odds of the nation's survival were evermore diminishing with every tank, solider, airplane and ship placed in opposition. To be blunt, the Israelis felt that this daring recovery could very well be their last hope.

The first few peaceful expeditions to 251.565 were conducted by Roffman himself at great personal expense and danger. Although he had significant contacts in Israel, no one would listen to him when he told people what he'd found. Nor would anyone open their purse strings to fund the expeditions – until now: Now they were desperate.

With each and every ELS Map showing the same number, 251.565, the odds against this being a fluke, or mistake or coincidence were astronomical. It could not be a coincidence; it had to be an arrow, a pointer. It was a guide to the spot where Zac and his men now hid themselves in the shadows.

An undeniable guide: 251.565 degrees represented the course from Temple Mount in Jerusalem to the item that he and his men were looking for.

And it was Zac's job to bring it back.

Tel Aviv – Present Day

A creature of habit, Zac was out the door at five a.m. for his morning run. The problem was, his arm was still in a sling from the gunshot wound to his bicep. But that didn't stop him from taking off on a brisk, albeit abbreviated, walk. In the home stretch after five miles, he slowed his pace. During the walk, he pulled the fresh memory from last week's successful operation from the back of his mind.

Seeing Joe walking toward him from the opposite direction after his own morning walk, he noted that the American was also a creature of habit. Zac guessed that he was over sixty, but that didn't stop him from getting his blood flowing. As the two men closed the distance between them, the Israeli couldn't help but notice that the Montanan didn't walk like a senior citizen. His gait was smooth and graceful.

The burden of truth lay heavy on Zac's shoulders. He knew that he would need to speak with Josiah early in the day to keep him from finding out the truth on his own. Tonight was the beginning of the Shabbat and his schedule was clear. This was his opportunity.

As casually as possible, he asked Joe if he'd like to accompany him on a tour of coastal towns in the afternoon. And as an aside, he told him that he needed to speak to him about something important. When Joe asked what it was, Zac cryptically said, "not here". That intrigued Joe: he agreed to go with the Israeli.

In the shower he reflected on the events that would take place that day on the Temple Mount. They were, at the very least, historic. At most: a game changer. His friends at TRM, including the Rabbi, were sure to have a full day. Ready or not, they were about to thrust upon Israel and the world, change that would take the Eretz back to her roots.

He dressed and came down for breakfast.

Although it wasn't prudent for him to attend, he could at least be excited about the ceremonies. Many Orthodox dreamed of this day. But for him, it was bittersweet as he thought about the two men on his team that lost their lives in last week's operation. He hoped that this day marked the beginning of a long lasting peace that the Rabbi said would eventually come. But he feared that before peace would find Israel, many more would die. And that thought put him in a contemplative funk over breakfast.

"Too many," he mumbled in Hebrew.

"What was that dear?" his wife asked from the stove.

"Oh... ah... nothing, just talking to myself."

His wife turned around and smiled. She asked, "And I'm eavesdropping I suppose?"

He smiled back at her. He loved her and his family very much. He wondered what their future held. With armies circling Israel, his concern for their safety was palatable.

Changing the subject he said, "This afternoon," he pointed his chin to the side of the house, "Josiah and I are going to take a drive along the coast. Thought I'd show him a few things."

She was back to cooking on the stove with her back to him. She was quiet for a moment. He couldn't see that the corners of her lips were turned down. But Zac knew what she was thinking. "The coast Zechariah? He and Ruby have lived here for three years... what could you possibly show him that he hasn't already seen? More likely you want to have one of your secretive little chats with the man," she said lightheartedly, but still probing.

He grunted.

Then not so lightheartedly she said, "When will you ever trust me enough to tell me about what is going on in that mind of yours?"

This was a common conversation of theirs. She would tell him "we never talk anymore," or "I never see you". To which he would respond, "we talk all the time, we're talking now...", and "What do you mean you never see me? Do you not sleep in the same bed next to me?"

He supposed that such conversations were universal amongst marriages. If he remembered correctly, though it was many years ago, his first wife said these same kind of things to him.

"As you well know," he smirked and tapped his head with his finger, "this is a scary place. Some things you do not want to know! But I promise; I will be back before Sundown.

It was the day before the Shabbat, the holy day, which meant that all travel and work must stop on Friday at Sunset.

Slowly turning around and playfully wagging her finger at him, she said, "See to it that you do! You have enough to account for without getting Hashem angrier at you!"

Thinking again of last week's gun battle and the men that

were killed, he was sure that Hashem was not pleased with him. Perhaps the sacrificial sin offerings that were already begun in secret would remove the burden of sin that he felt.

But he hoped for more than that from the item retrieved last week. He hoped that it would turn away the forces of evil that were planning the imminent demise of Israel.

Chapter 34

*M*endez held a device in his hand that looked like a cell phone. He was using it to sweep for bugs, listening devices, in the airplane's cabin. As the former Staff Sergeant was finishing, Mac turned his attention from watching him to Bryce. The Montanan was sitting next to him with his laptop, monitoring the latest news – and there was a lot of it.

"Bugs Coop? Seriously?" Mac asked with a questioning look. "Just who do you think would be spying on a couple of geeks like us?"

Bryce turned his attention from the news and grunted. "More people than you know. Do you really think your supervisors were surprised when you told them that you opened a portal at the LHC? Or do you think they were already pre-positioned to move in, and shut you down once you completed your little task?"

Hand to chin in contemplation, Mac said, "Hummm... now that you mention it. They were there pretty quick. I wondered how they got so many men together so fast. It looked like a coordinated effort. Seems to me they were there in no more than a half-hour after I called."

"Ah huh... They were probably watching and listening to you all along. They pounced quickly because they didn't wanna take the chance of anyone talking about what you saw. Back in September 2008, a headline came out in the Austrian Heute. It said that a virus infected the LHC's computers after they saw a ghost type face appear on the consoles. Ring any bells?"

Mac had an enquiring look, "Operation Falling Star?"

"You got it... at least the first run through."

"But hold on," Mac said, "I didn't hear about it reaching the papers."

Bryce tightened his jaw, "They contained the news so it didn't get to the States. But there were other newspapers in Europe that picked up the story before CERN put the cabash on it.

"At any rate," he continued, "I think they learned from that incident. That's why they swooped in on you so quickly."

Mendez walked up to the men and said, "The sweep came up negative Boss. Looks like you can relax and talk freely."

"Thanks Danny. Can you go get the doctors Black? We'll be wheels up in about ten minutes."

"Sure, no problem. Be right back," Mendez said, as he spun around and headed for the door.

Turning his attention back to Mac, Bryce said, "Let's finish the conversation from my office. He hit a few laptop keys, "Do you know what this is?" Bryce asked.

Mac squinted at the photo on the laptop screen, "Looks like some kind of antenna array."

"Yup, but not just any array. That's HAARP's array... the one in Alaska."

"You mean the place you were contracted in that different timeline?"

"Yeah, one and the same. Now," he continued as he punched more keys and changed the picture, "do you know what this is?"

"I'd guess another array of sorts."

"Right, how bout this?" Again he changed the picture.

"The same."

"And look at this," another one in the snow.

"Okay Coop, I get it. You have pictures of a bunch of antenna arrays. What about em?"

"This is the same HAARP array system that Dr. De Aquino was talking about in that paper I showed you this afternoon. The next two photos were satellite photos of HAARPs in Russia and China. And that last picture is the one that just came on line a couple of years ago in Antarctica. And those aren't the only ones. There are enough HAARPs, ionospheric heaters, strategically placed all around the world to wrap it completely."

"Unbelievable," Mac said, shaking his head.

Bryce said, "Buddy, I hate to heap more onto your overflowing plate, but that's not all."

"More?"

"A lot more. And while I'd like to ease you into what I've found, I can't. Things are accelerating even faster than I expected. We don't have a lot of time. I... I don't know what this trip to Israel is all about, but..."

"But what?" Mac asked concerned.

Bryce looked down, then back to his friend, "But I think it has to do with answers. There's a reason why I have to go. And I think we'll find something. I don't know what... but something."

"What do you mean accelerating faster than you expected: You knew this was coming?"

Bryce smirked, "You think all I've been doing for the last four years is write books, lecture and do public appearances? You know me better than that. Almost every time I left the ranch for work, I went with ulterior motives."

"Ulterior motives?"

"Yeah, I used those trips as fact-finding missions. I was gathering info."

Mac shook his head, "Leave it to you Cooper. So what've you found out?"

Bryce raised his eyebrows, "Way too much to fill you in on all of it right now. But I can give you an outline over the next nine hours of flight time."

Mac's head bobbed up and down, "Okay, that'll do."

"Okay, first let's finish with HAARP. As I said earlier, there's ample evidence to conclude that... someone is spraying the skies with chemicals, i.e. Chemtrails, to try to manipulate the weather and change the atmosphere."

"But who would want to do that? Any ideas?"

Bryce snorted, "Oh I don't know Mac. Pick a name, the Illuminati, the Bilderbergs, The New World Order... Who knows, maybe all of the above... maybe none of 'em. Maybe all of those names are just aliases to keep us off the trail of who they really are. The point is that it isn't a single government. Otherwise they wouldn't be spraying Chemtrails and using ionospheric heaters all over the world. But whoever they are, I think they're moving into their end game."

"Why do you say that?"

"One word," Bryce held up finger, "Sulfur.

"As I said before, I think they're now lacing our atmosphere with sulfur to try to change it for whatever is coming."

"But that's crazy! They're gonna kill a whole lot of people," Mac protested, "Who's gonna be around to take out their trash and wipe their sorry butts! They can't kill off everyone."

Bryce narrowed his eyes, "You ever heard about the Georgia Guidestones?"

"No"

"My family and I had the auspicious honor," Bryce said sarcastically, "of visiting the site last summer. You can do your own research as to what it is and who put it there, but their first commandment is: Maintain humanity under five-hundred million in perpetual balance with nature."

Mac's mouth dropped open, "Five hundred... that's less than a tenth of the population now!"

"But it is... just enough people to take out their trash and wipe their butts... isn't it?"

"So... so what are they going to do? Just kill everybody?"

"I don't think they are spraying sulfur because they like the smell. And besides, based on what I've been tracking with Earth changes, Mother Nature may be giving them a little help."

"Huh?"

"Buddy, you just gotta trust me on this and do your homework later. Back before I first started looking into this stuff, I didn't believe in conspiracies. But that was before my personal experience of four years ago. There's talk that HAARP can be used for everything from mind control to even causing earthquakes."

"Earthquakes?" Mac asked.

Just then Ivy entered the cabin with Xavier in tow, still on the stairs. Eagerly she said, "That's right Mac, Earthquakes! That's what

Xavier needed to talk to him about!"

Mac and Bryce traded a look. The mutual silent thought was the hope that the couple didn't hear their conversation.

Both physicists rose to their feet. "Dr. Bryce Cooper," Mac said, "this is one of my oldest friends in the world Xavier Black, or X, and his beautiful wife Ivelisse Black, or Ivy, doctors both."

Bryce noted that X was as tall as Mac if not taller. He had blonde hair but without a hint of gray in it. This was curious to Bryce since he knew the man was almost as old as Mac. His serious eyes were steel blue but seemed hard and dull. His skin was fair and his hand was huge as he reached to shake Bryce's.

Xavier shook Bryce's hand and said flatly, "Nice to meet you."

"Likewise," Bryce said.

Ivy's shake was firm and sure. Mac was right, she was beautiful. She had long, dark brown, tight curly hair, which was tied back in a thick braid. Her skin was light, pale almost, and she had big green eyes. Her lips were thick and full, and he guessed that she stood almost six foot herself.

Sounding professional but distressed, she said, "Dr. Cooper, thank you for agreeing to speak with us on such short notice. We have urgent issues to discuss."

"Certainly"

Xavier said, "My wife is a geneticist at one of the leading pharmaceutical companies in the country. She's seen some very strange goings on... disturbing things."

"I'd love to hear all about it. But first please, my name is Bryce or Coop if you prefer, just not doctor, deal?"

The couple smiled and nodded. Ivy pointed to herself with her thumb, "Ivy." Xavier simply nodded, "X," he said.

"Secondly," Bryce said, "my plane is your plane. We're on our own for this flight so... head's right there," he pointed to the bathroom, "wet bar over there if you need a drink, and the galley is around the corner there. There's a microwave to warm stuff up and I believe snacks are readily available."

Just then Danny stuck his head in the door and said, "Boss, you're good to go," he made a thumbs-up sign, "Give me a call if you need anything."

Bryce waved, "Thanks Danny, see you in a few days."

Then he was gone and shut the airplane's hatch behind him.

Turning his attention back to the group, Bryce said, "Well folks, let's settle in." Just then the engines started.

After he stowed their bags in the forward storage closet, X took a seat against the cabin wall opposite Bryce. Ivy sat next to her husband, but in a perpendicular seat.

The couple was conversing between themselves quietly, when Ivy raised her voice slightly and said, "Tell him."

Bryce looked at the two, "Okay, you guys are busy professionals. I doubt that you agreed to a joyride halfway around the world because you don't have anything else to do. So... what's so pressing that you'd fly all the way to Israel just to tell me?"

Ivy prompted her husband again with a nod. He sighed and with a look of reluctance, said, "The Earth's crust is destabilizing... expanding. A lot of people are going to die if we don't warn them."

Bryce's mouth dropped open. "What?! I haven't heard anything about this! I mean, I've heard about the earthquake swarms... they're all over. And I've been keeping haphazard count of volcanoes going off... but not this," he said in shock.

Ivy nodded again at X. Bryce gathered that he really didn't want to talk about it.

"And you won't," X said. "That's the problem Coop. The USGS has been hit with a gag order from on high. Things are getting ready to really fall apart and our director, Dr. Young, is beside himself. Since Ivy wanted to come up here and talk with you anyway, I told him that I would try to find a way to get the information out."

Bryce traded a stunned look with Mac.

Before he could respond, Ivy added with a tinge of fear, "And Bryce, something else very strange is happening. Humans are being changed. I've seen this for myself and... I've seen the plans to make it happen on a grand scale. Mankind as we know it... is an endangered species."

PART THREE

NOAH'S DAYS

"BUT AS THE DAYS OF NOAH, SO SHALL..."

THE BOOK OF MATTHEW VERSE 24:37

∞

Chapter 35

Damascus, Syria – Present Day

$\mathcal{A}$ bdullah Abbas Tabak was a hero of legend to the people of Syria. It had long been rumored that he was found, as a newborn infant, in a well on the outskirts of Damascus.

If it were not for a poor, barren, farming couple, the wife from Iran and the husband from Syria, he would have surely died. Since no one else was seen on the small farm, neither the husband nor wife knew how the baby got there.

Considering themselves blessed with child, the couple, practicing Shia Muslims, raised the boy in the way of their religion. As a young man, Tabak alluded to a more Sunni belief. This was because at the time, the vast majority of Muslims were Sunni.

The Arab Spring of 2011 put whole nations into play. The Muslim Brotherhood gained control of no less than eleven nations, including Bahrain a Saudi stronghold, and turned them into budding Shia countries.

Although the main tenets of Islamic beliefs, and articles of faith, of the two sodalities were the same, the subtle differences between Shia Muslims and Sunni Muslims were very significant... and entirely lost on the West. These differences were more political than religious. But in the Muslim world, much blood was shed throughout history between these two distinct sects.

Sunni's believed that the Caliph, the Leader of the Islamic Nation, should come from the line of "elected leaders" after the Prophet Muhammad. The word "Sunni" comes from an Arabic word which means "one who follows the traditions of the Prophet".

The Shia Muslims, The Party of Ali, believed that the leadership of Islam, and the position of the Caliph, was to be passed down directly through the Prophet Muhammad's bloodline, thus through the Prophet's cousin/son-in-law Ali.

Tabak saw himself as a Shia, just as his adoptive parents were. As such, neither he nor the rest of the Shia recognized the authority of the Sunni elected leaders, but rather followed the line of Imams born in the bloodline of the Prophet himself. These ideological differences were important to "The Party" because many of them viewed the Sunni leadership, with their headquarters in Mecca, as apostate.

The idea of the Caliph is closely related to the arrival of the Mahdi, or the twelfth Imam. Shias also believe that the Mahdi, or Islamic Messiah, would not return until Israel was totally destroyed.

And soon, thought Tabak, *this hope would be turned into a reality.*

The Shia, if nothing else, were a shrewd lot. Through the clever and strategic efforts of both Syria's and Iran's Shia leadership, they wrestled away the majority of faithful from the grasp of their wayward Sunni brothers.

As Tabak walked and meditated on the truths that would guide him this day, his reverie was broken by Farouk as he approached.

"My apologies Your Excellency, but you told me to let you know when everything was set for this morning's news conference."

"Very good," he said in Farsi.

"Your morning briefing has been shortened in order for you to have ample time for the news conference. All of the major Western news outlets will be there and of course, our friends from the Arabic and Islamist newspapers and television."

"Excellent. Anything else I should know before I go into the briefing?"

Thoughtful for a moment, Farouk dropped his voice and said, "There is the one matter. The individual that you've asked me to keep under surveillance has registered a flight plan for our neighborhood."

A look of concern, "Oh? Specifically for what destination?"

Farouk cleared his throat, "It would appear that the flight will conclude in Tel Aviv."

"The Zionist State?" he asked, "For scheduled business?"

"No Your Excellency, not that I can see and..." the aide paused, as if trying to find the right words.

"And?" Tabak quickly prompted.

Farouk swallowed hard, "And it appears that the Subject boarded a private plane in Montana with the big black infidel from the LHC."

Tabak grunted, "This is quite bothersome. So the black dog fled to his friend's home in Montana after The Group closed down the LHC? And now they are headed for the Zionists?" Gazing at the rising Sun, he asked himself, "For what purpose?"

Looking again into the eyes of the shorter man, he said, "Farouk. We were warned about this one. What have we heard of the subject's intentions?"

Farouk looked uncomfortable, "I'm afraid Your Excellency that his flight was booked so quickly, that we were unable to plant our usual listening devices on the aircraft. And as you know, Dr. Cooper regularly sweeps his home. His friends are also very loyal and do not speak openly to outsiders. I am afraid that currently, we are at a loss to discern the reason for the flight to Israel."

Tabak stared hard at the balding bespectacled man, "This, of all days, is not the time for prying eyes. Circumstances dictate, that the problem be taken care of once and for all."

Farouk nodded without flinching, "How would you like it

done sir?"

In contemplation, with hands clasped behind his back, Tabak answered, "It matters not to me. However, understand that it must be done before that flight reaches Tel Aviv."

"Very well Your Excellency. I will make the arrangements," and he spun around to do the deed.

Left alone with his thoughts, Tabak stared at the last vestiges of the morning star. "Today we will make history."

Crawley Down, West Sussex, England – Present Day

Diggs took his haggard American group to Crawley Down, a small village not far from Gatwick Airport in London. The Professor slept while Stephanie followed the balding redhead Brit down the motorway to the quaint little Bed & Breakfast of Rowfant House.

Alvaro's wife, his two daughters, his granddaughter and their children were all safely in the other room. He sat heavy eyed on the bed talking to Diggs.

"Right then, it's settled. Dr. Cooper will charter a private jet and will fly your family back to America. At the same time, you and I will travel with him to Israel so you can speak with him on the flight."

Alvaro whistled, "A private jet? That's very kind of him."

"You do have your passports?"

Feeling his breast pocket, he pulled out his billfold and passport, "I was told to always keep it with me. I'm sure Zorida has hers in her purse. The girls brought all of their belongings with them from Cornwall."

"Splendid," the Brit said, rubbing his hands together. "So..."

Just then the door opened behind Alvaro. Diggs looked up and smiled, then blushed.

Judging by the look on Digby's face, The Professor guessed it was Stephanie.

"So..." Diggs continued, "your daughters," he nodded to the person at Alvaro's back "will be able to find their way home from Texas?"

"Yes..."

Stephanie erupted from behind him, "We're going back to the States? I'm not leaving you in this condition," she said angrily.

With a good deal of discomfort, The Professor turned slightly as she rounded the bed like a panther ready to attack. "Mija... It is not safe for you all to be with me right now. I need you girls to..."

She cut him off, "Don't Mija me. You're in no condition to travel by yourself. I'm coming with you," she said with an air of finality, as she crossed her arms and set her jaw.

With father-knows-best eyes, The Professor tried a different tact, "Tete," her nickname, "please. I need you to watch over your mother and sister and niece. You are older than Vanessa and Azlynn... I trust you."

She stubbornly shook her head, "No Papa. You know that Vanessa and Azlynn can take care of Mama. Plus they have children that they have to keep safe. I don't have kids and I still have a week left on my vacation! There's no way I'm going back to Goldman before my time's up!" She wanted to add that she was scared to go back to work, but didn't.

"Stephanie... be reasonable. Antonio would want you safe..."

His daughter hung her head. In the small voice of a child, she said, "That doesn't matter anymore. He... he doesn't even know I'm here."

"What?" Dr. Mora asked confused, "How can he not know you are..."

"I was going to tell you," she blurted out, "on this trip. I... I wanted to tell you in person... but not like this..."

"Tell me what Mija?"

"We were divorced six months ago," she shook her head, "He changed. Always angry and my... my work. I was always gone. It just fell apart," she said with misty eyes.

Alvaro wanted to stand up and give her a hug, but it hurt too much. Instead, he sat there and said, "It's okay Mija... things happen. I... I just wish you would've told..."

Then Stephanie's face hardened again, "Anyway Papa, it doesn't matter now. What matters is that you need someone to take care of you. I'm going with and that's final."

Dr. Mora lowered his head and blew out a long breath. He looked up to see Diggs quietly observing the standoff. Shaking his head, he said, "Digby... whatever you do, when you finally have kids..." he looked at Stephanie, "make sure they are boys. Girls are so much more stubborn!"

Chapter 36

New York – Present Day

C he last conference call of The Group before The Plan was to commence in earnest had just been completed. Everything was in place. Soon a ballet of events would start that would reshape the world in The Others' image.

The Banker glanced at his watch; nearly midnight in New York. That meant that in Damascus, ten hours advanced, the news conference was about to begin.

He walked to his windows that overlooked the lit city. His mind was afire with possibilities. The west coast was three hours behind him and he knew what tomorrow would bring for them. Meanwhile, in Washington, the President was told to wait by his phone.

He walked to his antique desk that sat in the corner of the room. He puffed his cheeks with air and blew out slowly. *Once we start, there is no going back*, he thought to himself.

It wasn't regret that The Banker was feeling. He couldn't care less about mankind. His concern was that everything was properly executed. If the timing was not right, The Plan could unravel. Were they ready? But he knew that things would begin to spiral out of control even without the launching. They must move now.

He snatched up the phone and hit the speed dial number for the private line that was pre-programed into the phone.

On the second ring, a voice answered, "Yes?"

In his calculating and monotone voice, the Banker simply said, "Your debt is being called in immediately. I can speak for your biggest debtors of China, Japan and the Federal Reserve as well. There is no more time. You will need to declare a Bank Holiday tomorrow to stop the anticipated bank run. Do you understand?"

"Tomorrow? I... I thought we would have more time. The

people will panic! They'll be rioting and looting. A terrible loss of..."

He cut off his whining and simply said, "That is why we have prepositioned troops throughout the country. In addition to the Bank Holiday, you will announce that under the Constitution, you are instituting Martial Law. It will stay in effect until such time as the New World Currency is available and stability is restored. Any questions?"

With forlorn in his voice, he said, "I understand. I will convene my staff right now and make arrangements."

The Banker hung up without any further discussion.

He started this phase of his mission a while back. The Euro and the European Union's economy had already fallen. They were on their way to the New World Currency and eventual One World Government. But before those things came about, he would need to take down the biggest obstacle to The Plan. After that, everything else would follow.

So the obstacle that he now set his sights on was - The United States of America... and its total destruction

International Airspace Over The Atlantic – Present Day

Mac felt like he was watching a tennis match. Xavier would shoot rapid fire geological facts toward Bryce and in turn, Cooper would lob rapid fire return questions toward X. This process went on for four hours straight until they were finally "feet wet" over the ocean.

Bryce, as he usually did, consumed the mass amounts of data that X brought him and committed it to his photographic memory. If he needed clarification or background on something, he would ask X to elaborate. Every once in a while, Mac would venture a question or make a comment. For her part, Ivy sat patiently by Xavier, waiting for her chance to share her concerns.

Mac got up to stretch his legs and motioned for Ivy to follow him to the galley.

"You hungry?" he asked.

She rubbed her concealed washboard stomach. "Now that you mention it, I'm famished," she said in a slight Spanglish accent.

"Well, what say we whip up some grub for everyone? If I know Coop, I doubt he's eaten since lunchtime in Montana." Shaking his head, he added, "Tunnel vision."

"Yeah, I know the feeling. X is that way too. But hold on, a plane as nice as this should have a flight attendant. What gives?"

Mac stopped peeling back the foil from an airline meal that he intended on putting in in the oven. He chuckled and said, "Well, there would be beeuuteeeful Flight Attendants waiting on us hand and foot if my redneck," he said pointing in the direction of Bryce, "hillbilly friend didn't call them off. He said he didn't want any prying ears! Paranoid," he added, shaking his head.

Ivy thought about what she needed to share with Bryce. It occurred to her that being paranoid was probably a good trait to have, given the volatility of the information.

"Same ol' Mac," she said grinning.

After a moment, her smile disappeared, "Do you think he'll be able to help?" she asked hopefully.

Mac just hit the buttons on the microwave to reheat the meal. "If anybody can, it's Coop. But sure sounds like there are people in high places that'll do whatever they can to keep this from the public." Then he added, "And just between me and you, Coop and I have been talking about some other things that just don't add up."

"Yeah, that's what I told Xavier."

Mac smiled, "If you listen to my friend tell it, he thinks there's a global conspiracy. Judging by the look on his face, he probably thinks this is another piece."

She swallowed hard, "If he thinks X's info is stunning, when I talk to you guys about what I've seen, you too might think it's a global conspiracy."

Then looking around she said, "I think I'm going to need something stronger with those meals than just coffee or tea." She reached over to the refrigerator and pulled out a chilled bottle of vodka and smiled.

Mac shook his head, "Same ol' Ivy!"

Chapter 37

Damascus, Syria – Present Day

Farouk caught his Charge's eye as he waited in the wings of the stage area. "We are ready Your Excellency," he said, with a slight bow of his head.

With a nod and deep breath, Abdullah Abbas Tabak put his best presidential foot forward and strode out to the podium on the center of the stage. As he reached the podium, he was assaulted by a barrage of blinding camera flashes and questions as reporters stood.

On the very front of the podium, where the State symbol should be, a simple black sheet hid something underneath. On that sheet was Arabic writing that read "Allau Akbar (There is no god but Allah and Mohammed his messenger)."

"Thank you for coming. Please be seated."

Reporters from all around the globe gathered for the news conference. The large room had exceeded its capacity and was full. In light of the withdrawal of Turkey from NATO and the "military exercises" of various Arab countries and the Russians, the world wanted answers.

"As you know, the world has been in a significant transition these last few years," he began. "Both economic and political change has understandably caused all nations to reevaluate their place in this new world order and... the relationships we foster. Syria is no different."

A murmur of agreement from the crowd was heard.

"First: As for Turkey's withdrawal from NATO - I personally spoke with the President of Turkey this morning. He told me that NATO's continued aggression toward Muslim nations, made it impossible for Turkey's continued participation in the unnecessary and outdated alliance.

"As you know, Turkey has demanded the immediate withdrawal

of all western troops from their soil. NATO was originally established by the West to counter, what they said was the growing threat from Soviet aggression. Since the Soviet Union has been defunct since the late 1980's, NATO has taken upon itself to be the Great Satan's policemen to the world!" he thundered as he pounded the podium with his fist.

An audible gasp could be heard from the crowd. Never before had Syria called the West, particularly America, "The Great Satan". Iran would occasionally use such rhetoric, but this language was not previously proffered by Syria. This was a new religious tone coming from Damascus and it was not lost on the news correspondents present. All of them were wildly scribbling on their notepads.

Tabak continued, "Turkey's President shared with me plans for an attack on yet another Muslim country. He would not say which one, but for Turkey, this was the final straw."

This statement caused an outburst of stunned disorder. Correspondents leapt to their feet shouting questions to the President, while others stood by looking confused by the revelation. It was a very strange and serious disclosure if true.

The President moved his hands up and down in a "be seated" gesture. Finally the group quieted again. "This aggression toward a fellow Islamic State will not be tolerated!" he said, as he slammed his fist onto the podium with authority.

The crowd of mostly Arab news reporters went crazy. Jumping to their feet, shouts of "Allau Akbar" could be heard throughout. Others were again hurling questions at the President. The scene developed into pandemonium with pent up anger focused against the West.

In the midst of the disorder, a small contingent of western reporters sat wide eyed and quiet. They were conspicuously slouched in their seats, trying to hide in plain sight. For them, the press conference took an unanticipated and hazardous turn. This groundswell of emotions could be dangerous to those Westerners in attendance, should the group turn violent.

Once again, the Prime Minister motioned for calm, "So, as of this morning, ten countries of the Middle East, including Turkey, are forming an alliance of our own. This new alliance is to be called the Islamic States for a New World, or ISNW. And to all the world, Syria as the founding nation, puts you on notice: Any aggression toward any member of ISNW," he vigorously tapped his finger on the podium, "will be considered aggression against all members of ISNW! And..." he paused glaring into the TV cameras present, "aggression shall be met with aggression! Especially against the Great Satan and her Zionist accomplices in Israel!"

The crowd roared and leapt to their feet. They pumped their fists and yelled "Allau Akbar!"

This time it took a few moments to gain control over the frenzied crowd. After a while, he continued, "Now to the economy. Throughout the modern era, our Arab neighbors have been blessed with riches of oil that lay beneath their feet."

A rumble of affirmation flowed through the crowd.

As he waited for the crowd to quiet, Tabak couldn't help but think of the Zionist pigs of Israel who recently discovered great deposits of oil and natural gas in the Mediterranean. His advisors told him that the find rivaled even the largest deposits of the apostates in Saudi Arabia. He would need to do something about that... sooner rather than later.

"As such, ISNW will not only be a... military and defensive alliance, but a new economic one that is designed to bring the entire world in servitude to Islam!"

The crowd erupted in cheers and euphoria. The frenzy seemed to be building toward a crescendo. The western correspondents present took this opportunity to slip away unnoticed.

Quietly standing in a corner, two large western looking men were observing without fear. But they were unnoticed by any human. However, there were plenty of nonhuman types influencing the journalists that were well aware of their presence. They sneered at them knowing that this frenzy was just the beginning: Their time was almost at hand.

Keeping their eyes on their adversaries, the slightly shorter of the two men said, "You will not be able to restrain them for much longer."

"No. You are correct. Their time is almost at hand. I have been ordered to slowly leave them to what they must do. And what of our friend? Have you contacted him? Does he know his part?"

"I will be on my way to see him when we are done here."

"Time is at an end," the taller one said.

"Soon," was the response of the shorter.

The two were again quiet as they listened to the Premier continue.

"For now, the initial membership of ISNW will remain at the established ten. When membership is opened, the rules for admission are as follows: One - no country will be admitted to the alliance unless it is Sharia Law compliant; Two – a country must be invited to join by an existing member State; Three – the applicant country must be unanimously voted into the alliance by all existing members.

"While the alliance will trade extensively between ourselves, we will continue to do business with all countries that wish to deal in fair trade. Perhaps... one day though... we will only do business with Muslim countries," Tabak said as if it were a passing thought.

The applause from the crowd was thunderous, although a bit more subdued.

"Lastly," Tabak continued, "on a personal note, as you know, it has long been rumored that I was found as a child in a well on a poor barren couple's farm outside of Damascus," he paused, "today I would like to confirm these rumors. They are true!"

A loud audible gasp went up from the crowd. *What could this mean,* many of them thought?

Seemingly reading their minds, Tabak said, "It is also true that my parents were practicing Shias."

Again a gasp; The Prime Minister never stated this publicly. It always appeared that Tabak was a practicing Sunni.

"And," Tabak continued, "I would like to formally announce that I and, according to a government census conducted last year, our country's majority are also Shias!"

Once again the crowd rose to their feet and cheered. The vast majority of Muslims in recent years became convinced that only a direct descendent of Muhammad could be the next Caliph. If what Tabak was saying was true, they could well be looking at the one who was promised in the Quran; the one who was to come up out of the ground and serve as the final Caliph.

This euphoric applause lasted for a long time. Initially Tabak took no action to suppress it. Finally he got them to stop and sit.

"In closing," he said with a slit of a smile, "as you know we in Syria have been transitioning to full Sharia Law. This week, the final implementations to Sharia Law have been instituted and I can proudly say that we are now a full Islamic State."

Again, applause began, but he quickly suppressed it, raising his voice over the shouts, "And... and my government and I believe it is only fitting to acknowledge our historical heritage."

He walked from behind the lectern to stand next to it. While standing there, he rested his hand on the Arabic inscribed black sheet. "Therefore, from this point forward," he shouted, "let it be known that our country will be called,," he paused for effect, then yanked the black sheet from the podium and shouted, "Assyria!"

The new national emblem of Assyria was fastened to the podium.

The reporters went wild. They jumped to their feet, shouting "Allau Akbar!"

Then, slowly at first, and then more pronounced, a new chant began. It continued from a rumble and turned into a deafening roar that bounced off the walls and ceiling.

In unison, the group yelled, "The Assyrian! The Assyrian! The Assyrian!"

The two quiet men in the corner looked at each other.

The larger one said to the smaller, "Come, let us go. There is much to do."

The shorter one nodded and they both disappeared.

Chapter 38

British Airspace – Present Day

*W*hite Orbs hung like festive patio lanterns throughout the sky. More and more began to appear and as he stood in front of the United Nations building. He watched in fascination as other types of UFO's or spaceships began to also show up, filling the sky with an otherworldly celestial display.

World leaders walked out of the UN to look up. People from around the city flooded out into the street. Many were gawking and pointing. Others were holding signs of welcome. Unabashed, some people on the streets were doing rituals and praying to the lights and ships.

As he was watching the scene, he noticed a slight hint of burning matches. At the same time, the sky began to change to reddish brown. Slowly, the sulfury smell began to grow and thicken until soon it was so pungent he could hardly stand it. Eventually the hue of the sky caused the Sun to flee from the day, leaving the sky dark, but without night.

The people on the ground were unaware of the changes to the sky or the air. Instead they gawked and reveled in the darkness.

And then, through the haze, he saw black holes open in the sky and on the ground. It started as a trickle. Out popped one creature and then two and then a torrent of ugly black sulfery creatures rose up out of the ground holes and rained down from the sky holes. But the people on the ground could not see them.

The red eyed creatures were a massive fifteen to eighteen feet tall and were soot black. They had wings that had sticky, pitch black feathers, but looked like bats wings. And their faces were a twisted contortion of rage and hate.

He knew exactly what they were. They were the same kind of creatures that Giovanni morphed into four years ago before his Reset. But now, instead of only one of them, there were... millions.

They swooped and swirled around the people, but the people remained ignorant to their presence. Instead, the crowds on the ground became agitated and restless. They began to push and shove one another. Fights broke out in large masses. Some of the people started breaking windows and setting buildings and cars on fire. All the while, the sooty black creatures circled and swooped around them.

His attention was drawn back to the holes, or portals, as he knew them to be. Joining the exodus from the portals were now other creatures. And these creatures were even more frightening than the first. They were swarms of strange flying shapes. Some of them looked like angry grey beings with big black eyes, elongated heads, no nose and a mouth. Still other creatures that he'd never seen flew into the sulfur red atmosphere.

But the most fearsome creature he saw emerge from the holes were grasshopper, locust beings. The front of their bodies looked like grasshoppers, but at the back of their bodies, were the shape of a scorpion's tail. As these creatures came out of the holes, some stayed by the UN but most began to spread out to the whole earth. As they flew, they stung the people with their scorpion tales and their stings were great.

Finally the people's eyes on the ground were open and they saw all of the creatures that were coming out of the holes. In terror, they stopped what they were doing and ran for their lives. But for many on the ground, including the world leaders, it was too late. The ravenous creatures swooped in and began to torture and kill them.

Suddenly in the midst of all the carnage, a blinding white

flash was seen and searing heat scorched everything on the ground. People were vaporized where they stood, buildings were erased from their foundations and in place of what was once the mighty city of New York, a huge mushroom cloud blossomed in the red sky like a terrifying flower.

As the fire rolled away and the dust settled, the people and buildings were gone, but the creatures, Orbs and ships remained.

With their work in this city done, the creatures left for other parts of the globe to continue their terrible celestial torrent.

The buzzing of Bryce's personal console woke him with a start. He was breathing heavy and sweating. He wiped his forehead with his sleeve and hit the answer button. It was the Captain telling him that they were a half hour outside of Gatwick.

The four scientists finally called it quits somewhere over the mid-Atlantic in hopes of catching a couple hours sleep before they landed. With full stomachs, each of them reclined in the plush leather seats and were fast asleep in a matter of moments. It had been a long day.

None of them could have guessed what the new day would bring.

Haifa, Israel – Present Day

The two men leaned on the rail overlooking the blue Mediterranean. To their right was a busy shipping harbor. On the water in the distance, they could make out an oil and gas platform. Regardless of the commerce, Joe noted how beautiful and peaceful the place was.

It was eleven in the morning and Zac was taking Joe around to the "non-tourist" sites of Israel. Currently they were standing in the onshore compound for the Leviathan Project.

"This," Zac said stretching his good arm out, "is the fuel independent future for Israel. No longer are we subject to our Arab neighbors who hate us."

Joe stood up, "It's very impressive. How much gas did you say is down there?"

"Almost two billion barrels of oil and nearly a hundred and twenty-five trillion cubic feet of natural gas."

Joe whistled, "That is some find."

"Yes it is my friend, but unfortunately it has raised the ire and envy of our enemies."

As if right on cue, two Israeli IDF F-16s loaded with full armament flew by at what Joe guessed was about a thousand feet off the deck, headed for the oil platform. Both men stood in awe as the thundering noise died down.

Back at the rail, Zac's head dipped. He said to the water in front of him, "Yes Josiah, Israel has many enemies and few friends these days. Even America is abandoning us."

Joe hardly knew what to say. He was a former Marine and had seen his share of conflict. But nothing could compare to this. It was as if tiny Israel was all on its own, surrounded by hostile forces. America, even in its most dire circumstances never contended with this.

The two men stood in silence for a moment. Joe finally spoke up and asked with a smile, "Just how did you get us into this compound? As far as I can tell, it's locked down tighter than a teenage daughter's bedroom window with her daddy standing guard downstairs with a shotgun?"

Zac chuckled, Americans and their euphemisms. He liked Joe and more importantly, he trusted him. He was genuine, with no agenda. He was just the kind of man in whom he could confide, had to confide, he corrected himself.

A coy smile crossed his face, "Let's just say that in my position with the government... I have access that others do not."

Joe chuckled, "You mean you break into places?"

Only half kidding, Zac started to say, "Who told you..." when his phone rang.

He fished it out of his pocket with his good hand and held up his index finger asking for a moment. He looked at the caller I.D. and Joe could swear that he swallowed hard. He punched the answer button and in Hebrew said, "Yes? No I'm with somebody and can't talk now... Okay, I'm listening."

And listen he did, for a long while with his head bobbing up and down, "Yes... yes, yes... okay."

Joe picked up some Hebrew in the three years that he'd been in Israel, although most Israelis spoke English. He didn't know what was said on the other end of the conversation, but could hear the obvious tension in Zac's voice.

After a few minutes, Zac finished the phone conversation by saying, "Okay, keep me informed if there are any new developments," and he hung up.

"Problems?" Joe asked.

Zac blew out a long breath. "It seems that our Arab neighbors are thumping their chests again."

"That bad?"

"Well Josiah, it is hard to tell. There is a cultural disposition of both our Arab and Persian friends to conduct themselves in this manner. In addition, they do not like us very much. So many times, it turns out to be more... how do you say... bluster than bite."

"Ah... yeah, I know exactly what you mean. So do you need to get back to the office or something?"

Zac waved dismissively with his good arm, "No, no. it is the day before the Shabbat, my day off. They will keep me informed and tell me if I need to report."

Joe looked at his friend sideways. He was a good reader of

people and he knew when someone was holding back. But it wasn't his place to push Zac. He would tell him when he was ready. He supposed that that was the reason for this little tour. He would wait to hear what his Israeli friend wanted to talk about.

"So!" Zac said with some enthusiasm, "Why don't I show you where to get the best Schnitzel on the Mediterranean coast?"

"That would be great! I'm starving."

Zac made an ushering motion with his hand for Joe to lead the way back to the car,

Little did either man know how exciting their afternoon by the sea would turn out to be.

Chapter 39

Tel Aviv – Present Day

*T*he rickety old man traversed the sidewalk in front of his and Joe's homes. With legs wobbly and hands shaking, he leaned on his crooked cane made of spindly hardwood. But his unsteadiness was not caused by his age or a feeble body. He was just plain scared.

It was one thing to see the new emperor of the Muslim hoard parading around like a peacock and making threats to the West. This, Islam had done for decades. No his concern was for a news conference that was still going on. He urgently needed to speak with his American friend to see what he thought.

With care and energy that belied his age, he was up the steps to Joe's front door in just a couple of steps. He rang the doorbell and waited.

After a few beats, the door slowly opened and he saw Ruby's normally cheerful face, now red and tear stained. She'd been crying.

"I'm sorry to intrude Ruby, but I was wondering if Josiah was available?" he asked gently.

Sniffling, she said, "I'm sorry Eleazar, he's not here, but please... please come in. I... could use the company."

Gingerly he crossed the threshold into the living room and he saw the television displaying the same news conference that he'd been watching next door. Apparently the U.S. President completed his remarks and the forlorn male news anchor was summarizing the announcement in a shaky voice.

"And so to recap," he cleared his throat, *"The President of the United States has announced from the Oval Office three important things:*

One - A bank holiday has been declared for the next five days. There will be no business conducted, withdrawals or deposits at any bank, anywhere on American soil. In addition, all stock exchanges, to include the New York Stock Exchange are officially closed, as well as all commodity exchanges,

Two – When the banks and exchanges do reopen, tentatively next Thursday, all transactions will be conducted in the new legal tender of the World Bank. This is only a target date for the banks and exchanges to reopen. This date is subject to change. The new currency is the same one that Europe has already been transitioning to and will eventually be used by all the nations of the world by the end of the year. It will also be the world's Reserve currency replacing the U.S. Dollar.

Upon the banks reopening, your dollars will automatically be converted by the banking institutions for the fair value of the new tender.

Three - All future transactions will be cashless and must be conducted with the new national I.D. cards that will be issued on Tuesday and Wednesday of next week. There is also an option to obtain the convenient new RFID chip under your skin for easy access to your money and information. All citizens

*are encouraged to obtain the RFID now as it will
eventually be mandatory for all sales and
purchases."*

The card and chip statement caused Ruby and Eleazar
to exchange a knowing, worried look.

*"Four – The President has instituted Martial Law in
the United States and its territories effective
immediately. He has stressed that rioting or looting
in the streets will not be tolerated. Shoot on site
orders are standing. All Americans are required to
turn in their firearms. Should a citizen not comply
with the firearm surrender order, military
authorities will conduct house to house searches on
registered firearm owners,"* the anchor looked down
at his notes, as he said, *"Deadly force is authorized.
To aid in maintaining social stability, military
leaders have recalled all of our troops from abroad.
This includes all troops around the world from areas
such as South Korea and the Pacific Theater, troops
from Europe and battle groups from the Middle
East."*

Both Ruby and Eleazar gasped at the withdrawal of the
last friendly forces from around Israel. It meant that The
Eretz was naked before her enemies. Israel was truly
alone. "God..." Ruby groaned, "help us."

*"Five - Lastly, FEMA (Federal Emergency
Management Agency) has set up Aid Camps
throughout the United States. These camps are safe
havens for those who need food, shelter and medical*

assistance in the coming days."

Under his breath, Eleazar said, "Safe havens! Ha! I know a concentration camp when I hear one."

"In closing, every American is encouraged to pray to whatever god you believe in for the welfare of the United States. Our nation has faced dark times..."

Ruby picked up the remote and turned off the TV. A new flood of tears pooled in her eyes and rolled down her cheeks. Helplessly Eleazar patted her on the shoulder and said, "Adonai! Help us."

Chapter 40

*C*he plane sat on the tarmac sipping new fuel from a snake like straw attached to a fuel truck. They were waiting for Diggs and his additional passengers. The four current passengers were huddled in the cabin, in the throes of serious conversation.

Bryce said, "Yes, I think that these Orbs are..." he exchanged a look with Mac, "Nephilim. More to the point, I believe that they are the harbingers of something... very unpleasant."

"Nephilim?" Ivy asked.

Again Bryce and Mac looked at each other.

Mac ventured, "Ivy, you know about the Nephilim?"

It was her turn to look down. When she looked back up, her expression changed to a woman who was all business.

X saw the look and knew that he couldn't stop the barrage that was about to happen. He leveled his gaze and narrowed his eyes at Bryce, but said nothing.

"Perhaps better than you two," she said cryptically.

"But ho..." Bryce started to say.

"Let me approach the subject from two different angles," she said sounding like a calculating scientist. "We don't talk about our faith much but at a bible study back home one night, the issue of the Nephilim came up. Up until then, we'd never heard of such a thing," she stole a glance at her stoic husband who slightly shook his head. She continued, "The subject was interesting enough, but as we started digging deeper, many correlations to my own work began to appear."

"Correlations?" Bryce asked.

"Yes... and those correlations are precisely why I needed to speak with you."

Cooper shook his head in confusion, "I don't understand."

"Do you know what it is that I do Dr. Coop... ah Bryce?"

"Not really. I know that you're a geneticist."

She nodded, "That's only partly correct. My Ph.D. is in Medicinal and Pharmaceutical Chemistry from USC. I graduated and went to work at a small lab. Amazingly a couple years later, I received an offer for the job of my dreams at a leading pharmaceutical company in Pasadena. Coincidently, I didn't know that Xavier was already working at the USGS also in Pasadena," she stole a look at him with a smile.

"As an aside, after a short engagement, X and I were married and we've been in Pasadena ever since. That's also where we go to church."

"That's all interesting, but I don't know..." Bryce started to say.

Ivy interrupted him with a rapid fire explanation: "Medicinal chemistry and pharmaceutical chemistry are disciplines at the intersection of chemistry, especially synthetic organic chemistry, and pharmacology and various other biological specialties, where they are involved with design, chemical synthesis and development for market of pharmaceutical agents, drugs.

"Compounds used as medicines are most often organic compounds, which are often divided into the broad classes of small organic molecules, as an example in atorvastatin, fluticasone, clopidogrel, and," she made quote marks with her fingers, "biologics, such as infliximab, erythropoietin, insulin glargine, the latter of which are most often medicinal preparations of proteins, also known as natural and recombinant antibodies, hormones, etc." She took in a breath. "Also useful are inorganic and organometallic compounds as drugs, as example lithium and platinum-based agents such as lithium carbonate and cis-platin."

She looked at Bryce who just blinked at her, so she tried a different tact, "In particular, medicinal chemistry in its most common guise, focusing on small organic molecules that encompasses synthetic organic chemistry and aspects of natural products and computational chemistry in close combination with chemical biology, enzymology and structural biology, together aiming at the discovery and development of new therapeutic agents. Practically speaking, it involves chemical aspects of identification, and then systematic, thorough synthetic alteration of new chemical entities to make them suitable for therapeutic use. It includes synthetic and computational aspects of the study of existing drugs and agents in development in relation to their bioactivities, biological activities and properties, i.e., understanding their structure-activity relationships, SAR. Pharmaceutical chemistry is focused on quality aspects of medicines and aims to assure fitness for purpose of medicinal products."

Although she could see the blank looks, she felt compelled to finish the barrage of details, "That is, at the biological interface, medicinal chemistry combines to form a set of highly interdisciplinary sciences, setting its organic, physical, and computational emphases alongside biological areas such as biochemistry, molecular biology, pharmacognosy and pharmacology, toxicology and veterinary and human medicine; these, with project management, statistics, and pharmaceutical business practices, systematically oversee altering identified chemical agents such that after pharmaceutical formulation, they are safe and efficacious, and therefore suitable for use in treatment of disease."

"Okay..." Bryce said scratching his head. "But medicine is not really my specialty. What are you trying to tell me?"

With a forced smile, she said, "The gist of my job at my lab in Pasadena is to develop chemical compounds that change human DNA. We also were involved in developing drugs that inhibit the rejection by the human body to animal and plant DNA after it's implanted in a human subject."

"What????" Mac asked stunned.

"You see, in the course of my work, I stumbled upon a Plan."

"A Plan," Bryce asked.

"Yes, a Plan. And I didn't understand the significance of it until I began to study the Nephilim."

Bryce didn't know what to say. He looked over at X who gave no indication of interest in the subject in the least. In fact, to Bryce, he looked like he didn't want to be there.

He looked back to Ivy, "So this Plan... it's the correlation to the Nephilim that you mentioned?"

She nodded once, "That's right. In my study of the Nephilim, as crazy as it sounds, I discovered that it appeared to be their goal to corrupt all flesh."

"I'd concur," was all Bryce said.

"In other words, they wanted to change what it meant to be human," she said looking for assent.

Mac and Bryce mumbled their agreement. X continued to sit passively off to the side.

"The correlation that I found in my work was that this Plan appears to be designed to use all of the techniques that I just mentioned in Medicinal and Pharmaceutical Chemistry, and more, to change what it means to be human."

"Come again?" Mac said.

"Gentlemen," she said, "When the angels of Genesis 6:4 began to integrate their DNA with mankind and began to corrupt our gene pool, God was so angry that he brought the flood to kill off all flesh because it was corrupted."

"Right..." Bryce said.

"In Matthew 24:37, I learned in this bible study that Jesus himself said that just before his return, we would see days like that of Noah."

"Been there, done that," Bryce said. "What are you trying to say? Where's the correlation?"

"I have found out about a plot to use chemicals, drugs, and technology to change, to corrupt, every man, woman and child's DNA on the face of the planet," she said with big eyes, "And it has already started."

Chapter 41

Gatwick Airport, London – Present Day

*B*ryce looked hard at Mac. This was what he suspected. There was a concerted effort by someone... or something to damage mankind. And apparently, it didn't matter if humans were killed or changed. So long as mankind was affected.

"You mentioned that this Plan used other means than just pharmaceuticals. What do you mean by that?" Bryce asked.

Ivy nodded, "Okay... I'm not an expert, but let me give you a couple of examples. Have you ever heard of GMO foods?"

Bryce nodded, "Yeah."

"GMO what?" Mac asked.

Directing her explanation to her former brother-in-law, she said, "GMO are genetically modified foods or foods that have been derived from genetically modified organisms such as crops, or fish whose DNA has been altered through genetic engineering."

"Okay, I think I've heard of them," Mac said. "Don't they try to make harvests more virile and increase the food supply?"

"Well," Ivy said, "that's what the big agricultural corporations will tell you. But the truth is it has the opposite effect."

"How so?" Mac asked.

"Well, I'm no expert on GMO foods, but there are two things that they primarily deal with: One, crops that withstand pesticides and two, crops that withstand herbicides."

"That doesn't sound too abominable to me," Bryce said.

A forced smile, "You wouldn't think. But here's the thing, the alteration of these foods appears to be passed down through both livestock and their offspring and humans and our offspring. As an example, there's documented evidence of a spike in spontaneous abortions in livestock that consume GMO feed. A study was done on the aborted remains of these animals and an astounding thing was found. Using an electron microscope, a whole new living organism was found in the intestines of the aborted animals."

"You're kidding," Mac said.

"No I'm not. Worse, it was discovered that it could be traced back to the GMO feed that the mothers were eating."

"What's the organism?" Bryce asked.

She shook her head, "No one knows. But they do know that it's the size of a virus and operates and works like a fungus. The worst part is that now there are trace elements of it everywhere: food, plants, air, and water."

"What are the health implications?" The Montanan asked.

"In humans we have seen links to autism and gut permeability."

"Gut permeability?" Mac asked.

"Intestinal disease like irritated bowel syndrome and such. You see, the idea is that pesticides and herbicides are introduced into the seed DNA of crops. What we are told is that it makes the specimen," she looked at Mac, "more virile, to use your word. The pesticide, as an example, is held within the DNA. If an insect eats it, their digestive tract explodes. Therefore, they won't eat it. But it is also very interesting that birds and wildlife won't go near the stuff either. Something about their animal senses I guess."

"Well hold on," Mac said, "If they eat it and their guts explode and we eat it... won't that make our guts explode?"

Bryce looked at him, "I guess that's where the intestinal problems come from."

"Right you are Bryce," Ivy said, "And this is all just scratching the surface. There's mounting evidence that it's affecting our food chain, i.e. our livestock and there is strong suspicion that that is what is killing off the bee population."

"I've heard they were dying," Mac said.

"Yeah," Bryce said, "And if there are no more bees to pollinate, what then?"

"Exactly," Ivy said. "And GMO foods are only one aspect of the Plan that I discovered. You ever heard of Chemtrails?"

Bryce and Mac looked at each other and nodded.

"We were just talking about them earlier," Mac said.

"Well," Ivy continued, "There is ample concern that Chemicals being sprayed are raining down and having negative health effects on the population."

Mac shook his head, "So they're attacking from the air and from the ground..."

"It would seem so," Ivy said.

"If those are tactics of this... this Plan that you found, they are fairly general. Do you have information on specific programs that are directly connected to the modification of people's DNA?" Bryce asked.

"As anecdotal evidence," Ivy said, "Have you ever heard of L.A. Marzulli?"

"Sure," Bryce said, knowing where she was going.

"Who?" Mac asked.

"L.A. Marzulli... he did a video series called The Watchers. He's also written several books," Bryce said to his friend.

"That's right," Ivy said. "In his early videos... now this is going to sound crazy..."

Bryce and Mac chuckled.

"Seems like it's been the day for crazy," Mac said.

"But in one of his early videos he dealt with people that experienced an," she made quote marks with her fingers, "alien abduction phenomena."

Mac narrowed his eyes. He was ready for crazy, but he didn't think she'd go there.

"These individuals came back and apparently found that something was implanted under their skin. So anyway, Mazulli takes these people to Dr. Roger Leir to try to remove whatever it was under their skin. But this proves a not too easy task and he has to devise a special surgical technique to get these things out of the victims."

"Okay," Mac said, unsure where this was going.

"When they finally get these things out, they look like little capsules not even a half an inch long. They want to analyze them to find out what they are and they go to cut them open, but find they can't. They're way too hard. So they take them to a machine shop to try to slice them open with their sharpest and hardest diamond blades," she shook, "They couldn't even put a scratch on them. So finally Mazulli takes these implants to a lab that uses a laser to cut them open and finally succeeds."

"That is some hard material," Mac said.

"Wait, it gets better. What they find in them is something akin to a mini supercomputer whose clock speed is faster than anything that mankind can do."

"What?" Mac said.

"But here's the crazy part. When Marzulli went back to Dr. Leir and asked him what he thought they were being used for, the doctor said that he thought these implants were changing their DNA!"

"You're right, that's crazy stuff, but what does it have to do with your work and the Plan that you said you uncovered?" Bryce asked.

"Have you heard of the RFID chip?"

"No," Bryce said.

"RFID stands for Radio-Frequency-Identification and it's a mini computer chip that can be easily implanted under the skin. The chip can store all of your banking records, your health information and anything else that you can imagine. This program is very close to being implemented today. If the program goes live, this chip would eventually be placed in every man, woman and child in the U.S."

"They couldn't do that," Mac said. "People would refuse."

"They may at first Dr. McNabb," Ivy said to her longtime father figure, "But if all of your banking and money was on that chip, it would make it really hard for you to refuse. Especially if you couldn't buy or sell without it."

"I see your point."

"But again, what does this have to do with the Plan that you're talking about?" Bryce inquired.

She smirked, "I was getting to that. It has long been suspected that these RFID chips can change your DNA."

"Hold on," Mac said, "Are you trying to tell us, that they are about ready to implement a plan that will force everyone's DNA to be changed, whether they like it or not?"

Ivy leveled her gaze at the two men, "Doctors, they've already started."

Chapter 42

Gatwick Airport, London – Present Day

"**A**lright," Bryce said, "I agree that all that's disturbing, but where is the connection to the Nephilim? By the job description you gave, you sound like you work indirectly with chimeras?"

A look of shame crossed Ivy's face, "Yes, that's right. I was getting to that."

"Ki.... what?" Mac asked.

"Chimeras," Bryce said. "A Chimera or chimaera is a single organism, usually an animal, which is composed of two or more different populations of genetically distinct cells. Chimeras are formed from at least four parent cells, two fertilized eggs or early embryos fused together. Each population of cells keeps its own character and the resulting organism is a mixture of tissues. Chimeras are typically seen in animals, but there are some reports of human chimerism."

Ivy gave Bryce an approving look.

Bryce shrugged and said, "Wikipedia... I read a lot."

"You mean, like half dog, half pig... and stuff like that?" Mac asked.

"Huh... try half human, half pig or dog or dolphin or... whatever else the mad scientists do in their labs in secret," Bryce said with an edge in his voice.

"Look," Ivy said, "I've done some things I'm not particularly proud about. But I'm a scientist. I was fascinated with seeing how far we could take this technology. Up until a few weeks ago, when we did that study on the Nephilim, honestly I was so excited, I didn't even give it a second thought. I was focused on the research. But... not now. Now I can see the correlation."

Bryce understood exactly what she was saying. When he worked at the LHC, before his Reset, he pushed the envelope as far and as fast as it could go. He didn't realize that he was working indirectly for The Others and The Fallen all along. He wondered if Ivy's epiphany about the Nephilim woke her up as it did him four years ago.

"Soooo..." he ventured, "it's your moral issues that has caused you to seek me out?"

Ivy was thoughtful, "Not only my moral issues about what they're doing, but there's something..." she searched for the right words, "wickedly nefarious about their intentions. And frankly, it scares the living daylights out of me.

"I've come to the conclusion," she paused, "that they're using this technology to make... modern day Nephilim. These creatures are not huge giants with oblong heads anymore. They look like you and me. But like their Nephilim predecessors, they have attributes and capabilities way beyond human. These beings seem to have an insidious evil that's hard to comprehend."

Bryce asked, "And why do you think that?"

With a look of resolve, she said, "Because they've been to our genetics lab. And we get all kinds of people going through there: Super Soldiers primarily, but we also see famous athletes, movie stars, singers, motivational speakers, many politicians, the rich and powerful, royalty, bankers and world leaders. I have not only personally seen them, but I was tasked with sampling and testing their DNA. I've looked into the eyes of these creatures. They are hollow, dark... not human, something else. But last week was the final straw. I knew then that I couldn't be a part of what they are doing any longer."

"What happened last week?" Bryce asked.

Ivy looked over at Xavier with sad pleading eyes. He was sitting in a seat, out of the way, and hadn't said a word.

When Bryce followed Ivy's eyes and saw her looking at her husband, he could swear that he shook his head almost unperceivably with a stern look on his face.

Ivy ignored his silent plea. She turned back with a set jaw, and said, "Last week I overheard a conference call between the Director of our facility and... they called themselves The Group."

"The Group?" Mac asked.

"Yeah," she nodded, trying to regain the memory, "that's what they kept saying... The Group this... The Group that... At first I thought it was a conglomerate of some kind, but there were way too many people on that call, from different walks of life. I'll explain later about that, but the point is that they were plotting and scheming. And there's something else," she said, just remembering, "they mentioned The Others."

Bryce flinched at the name, "The Others? Are you sure?" he asked urgently.

Surprised by his sudden change in demeanor, Ivy said, "Yes, yes I think so. They only said it one time... but I'm sure I heard it. They were talking primarily about The Group," she said with emphasis, "but they said that The Others made it possible for The Group to move forward with The Plan. You know these Others?"

From his seat off to the side, X's head was down, but he let out a heavy breath.

Mac looked at him and then to Bryce. "Same?" was all he asked.

Bryce nodded, "I think so."

"What am I missing? You know these Others?" Ivy asked.

Bryce was looking down and shaking his head, "Fraid so. You know them by a different name... the Nephilim."

Ivy's breath caught in her throat and she brought her hand to her mouth in shock. "Noooo...." was all she said.

"Did you hear anything else?"

Somewhat recovering, Ivy said, "They... they were talking about The Plan, like I said and they were also talking about some kind of event. They called it an arrival. But I'm not sure what that means."

"Arrival?" Mac asked as he looked at Bryce and thought of the Orbs. "Arrival of what?"

"I... I don't know, but those Orbs... I wondered if that's what they were talking about. But the scariest thing," she said, "was what the guy who was in charge asked our Director."

Bryce, "What did he say?"

"He asked if," she made quote marks with her fingers, "the troops were ready."

"Troops?" Mac asked.

Ivy nodded at him, "That's what he said... troops. I understood from the rest of the conversation that many of the study participants that I've dealt with were part of those troops."

The four lapsed into quiet while they digested the gravity of what they'd just discovered. Bryce broke the silence when he asked, "Ivy, did you happen to get any names from the conversation?"

She pursed her lips and said, "I did get a title from one of them."

"A Title?" Bryce asked confused.

"Yes, a title," she said in a small voice, "There was one individual that did most of the speaking and seemed to be in charge of the call."

"Who was he?" Bryce asked.

Ivy locked eyes with him, "The Prince of Wales."

Mac almost choked on his own spit and blurted out, "Prince of Wales?! As in England?!"

Unwavering, Ivy nodded, "The same."

"Wha..." Mac started to say, but was interrupted by Bryce.

"Any other names? Anything that might help?"

Ivy shook her head and looked to the ceiling as if the memory was written on it, "There was one other name... I think it was... Habit... or Abbot... something like that."

Shock registered on Mac's face and his mouth dropped open.

Bryce asked, "You mean Dr. Abbot? Dr. Lyn Abbot?"

"Yes, yes that's him! Do you know him?" she asked.

Mac groaned and put his hand over his mouth, "He's a Nephilim!" he choked.

Just then, lumbering up the aircraft stairs was Digby Stanford Williamson, distant relative to the Queen of England and the Prince of Wales. "Who's a Nephilim?" he asked.

Bryce's head dropped in near despair as he whispered, "Could this get any worse?"

Little did he know... it would get a lot worse.

Chapter 43

Jerusalem, Israel – Present Day

*T*he Rabbi's eyes were filled with tears. He waited his whole life to see this scene. Even more stirring would be the last part of this ceremony. Surely no one in Israel, except for a few select, knew what was to come.

In the last negotiations with Jerusalem's Muslims, Israel's Prime Minister negotiated away some more land in Israel for half of Har haBáyith, also known as The Temple Mount.

Although this information was reported in the local media, the planet seemed to be pre-occupied with the myriad of problems all around the globe. There were earthquakes and volcanoes erupting everywhere. Strange weather phenomenon which caused billions of dollars in damage and significant loss of life were almost common place.

Skirmishes between the Koreas, the Chinese and Taiwanese, India and Pakistan, Russia and her neighbors and broad civil unrest throughout Europe, Asia, Africa and even in the United States was routine. The latter was due primarily to dwindling food supplies, water shortages, high unemployment and economic depression.

These issues were always stealing headlines from Israel. In addition, violence in the last few months escalated all over the Earth; assaults, murder and rape occurred now with frequency even in the unlikeliest places. There were even wide spread reports of cannibals or "zombie", as people took to calling them. This criminal trend baffled police officials and they tried to credit the disturbing behavior to drug use.

As the Rabbi considered all of these things, he thought that it was no wonder the historical event that was about to commence went unnoticed by the world at large. No doubt there would be a mention of it on the back page of a newspaper or in someone's blog. But for the most part, even the Arab population of Israel were uninterested at what was about to occur. Or, the Rabbi thought, *perhaps they knew exactly what was happening and were only biding their time until their tanks began to roll through Israel.*

The small crowd on top of the Mount applauded as The Mishkan, or Tabernacle, was raised on top of the Mount of Olives. There was hardly a dry eye as the spectators were moved to tears by what Hashem had done. As the furnishings were brought up to the Mount by the Kohain, or Priests, and carried in front of the crowd into the Tabernacle, "oh"s and "ah"s were heard with each new piece revealed.

All of this, the Rabbi reflected, was only made possible because Hashem saw fit to provide his people with a Red Heifer as a sin offering. The ritual was conducted last night under the cover of darkness, least a disagreeing party try to stop the ceremony.

Per The Law, the heifer was slaughtered at least 2000 cubits outside the camp, east of the Temple, at the Miphkad Altar. The Rabbi was present to observe the sacrifice and marveled that the ancient site at the top of The Mount of Olives was once again used as it was thousands of years before.

Also according to The Law, the ashes of the Red Heifer were then used to purify the water. That water was used to purify more water, which was used to cleanse: The Temple Mount, the wall between the clean and unclean, all of the furnishings, all of the priests, and even the Tabernacle itself.

But all of this was only the beginning. There were immediate plans to build a proper house for Hashem; a temple to rival Solomon's great temple. *But one step at a time*, he reminded himself. *We need to get through this day without anyone dying.*

The Rabbi wasn't afraid of violence. *The Arabs were lovers of violence; it seemed to be in their nature,* he thought. Rather, it was the grand entrance of the remaining piece of the Tabernacle that gave him concern.

The item was retrieved five days ago in the successful secret operation in the Egyptian desert. It came at the cost of two lives and several wounded. The Rabbi couldn't help but think of his student Zechariah who led the raid. The old teacher wished that he could be here to see the fruit of his labor. But for political reasons, his student decided not to attend today's ceremony. *Too bad*, he thought.

He looked at his aged pocket watch. The hour neared. All preparations were made. He looked at the Priest who was standing at the edge of the Mount ready to signal the priests below.

Pausing, he thought about the two items that were not recovered. Prior to the raid, everyone, including him, was confident that these two very important items would be safely stored within the main item. However, after the High Priest carefully searched the main item, he discovered that they were nowhere to be found. This presented a whole new problem for the Rabbi and the Priests.

Israel's enemies were at that very moment surrounding her. And he knew her military were vigorous fighters. But the odds, as they say, were not in Israel's favor. Even Russia was massing their troops on Iran's border in what was described as military exercises.

His people knew better. He feared that Russia too would join the fight against the Eretz. If that were the case, Israel did not have the people or the supplies to sustain and win such a fight.

That is why the two missing items were of such great importance. Israel needed to hear from Hashem. With the main item secured, they now needed to be able to address the Creator of the Universe and ask for his divine direction. Then, with His help, they would surely be led to victory.

So, they were fortunate to have found out, with Zechariah's help, about the two substitute items that the American possessed. When he spoke to the man in Montana on the phone yesterday, he half expected him to deny he possessed the items. He was prepared to tell him everything in order to persuade him to donate them to Israel's cause.

But in the end, it wasn't hard to convince him. He said that someone told him to expect his call from Jerusalem; very curious. Instantly the American agreed to bring the items right away; given the urgency. Again, it was Hashem's provision. Once more he pulled out his old watch and looked at it. The American should be arriving anytime.

He took a last look at the skyline of Jerusalem; an ancient city, a proud city and once again, a city fit for Hashem's dwelling. He turned and with a simple nod of his head, the Priest waved his makeshift flag and then lifted the Shofar, Lambs Horn, to his lips. The sound of his mighty blast carried across the top of the Mount, and out over the city.

The group of onlookers by the Tabernacle knew the sound to be of significance. But even they could not guess how significant until the item came into view.

Chills ran down the Rabbi's spine and his eyes were filled with joyful tears. It was millennia since the item rested on the Temple Mount the last time.

An entourage of musicians and priests in traditional dress slowly emerged from out of a passage underneath the Temple Mount. The long procession traversed its way up the long walk leading to the top of the Har haBáyith. The spectators were craning their necks to see what all of the commotion was about.

And then suddenly, with the light of the Sun glinting off its gold fixtures... The Ark of the Covenant was revealed.

Chapter 44

<u>*Southern California Coast – Present Day*</u>

*A*s he bobbed up and down on his surfboard, Tim Ryan closed his eyes and breathed in deeply. He could taste the salt water in the air. It made him smile.

Leo Harper, his best friend and surfing buddy, broke into his ace moment and asked, "Just what are you gloating about?"

Tim opened his eyes. "Brah," raising his arms wide, "how could you not gloat over this!"

When the two men hit the waves, a transformation overtook them. Tim and Leo were not your average Beach Bums. Both were in their late twenties. Tim owned his own active clothing company with over six-hundred stores worldwide, plus a successful online store. Leo was the youngest partner at a flourishing Los Angeles law firm.

They were waterspiders (guys who surfed the waves and the internet), but on the beach, they sounded like every other hardcore surfer around the world.

It was Friday, usually a normal work day. But like so many Americans this first day of Martial Law and the Bank Holiday, they called in sick.

But because of the President's address in the early morning and the collapse of the U.S. economy, all business came to a standstill. People were scared. Armed troops were at virtually every street intersection. Most people, with the exception of rioters and looters, stayed indoors.

With the declaration of Martial Law, few people thought to go to the beach. Thus, the two normally busy and responsible buddies had the sand and surf all to themselves. It was still early in California. The water was cold and the fog hadn't burnt off yet, but it was still paradise.

"Weather sure has been crazy," Tim said pointing to the fog.

"Seriously," Leo agreed, "I've been checkin it out on the internet. It's not only here - it's all over the world!"

Tim grunted in agreement.

The two had yet to see a decent wave; mostly ankle snappers (little waves) and not worth riding – also an abnormality.

This place was one of their old haunts. Silver Strand Beach in Ventura County was a little more than an hour's drive up the coast from L.A. Only a mile long and well known for its killer surf, it maintained an infamous "locals only" policy. But the two young guns weren't bennies (someone not from there). They grew up in Oxnard, and Leo's parents still owned a place not far from the beach. That meant that they were welcome anytime – Which wasn't often enough if you asked them.

"The weatherman last night said it was supposed to be necter (perfect surf) today. I can't understand why it's so dead," Leo lamented. "And my internet was down this morning so I couldn't check it."

"That's weird, my internet's down too."

"You don't s'pose they took down the internet because of Martial Law do you?" Leo quizzed.

Tim shrugged and grinned, "No worries dude, this beats sittin in front of a computer any day."

Leo chuckled, "Yeah man."

The two, lost in their own thoughts, bobbed up and down on the unusually calm sea.

After a while, looking serious, Leo dropped the surfer accent, and like an attorney building a case asked, "Sooo... what do think is gonna happen? I mean, the economy, Martial Law, the country?"

Tim was the figurehead and businessman of the two. After a moment, he shook his full head of dark hair, "Don't know my friend... nothing to compare this to. You have second tier countries like Argentina, Russia and Turkey who have historically taken the step of devaluing their currencies... but never a country as big, wealthy and influential to the world's economy like the U.S. But that's exactly what the effects of QE3 (Quantitive Easing Three) was on the Dollar. Open ended printing of money by the Federal Reserve trying to get us out of a recession was like a drunk trying to drink himself sober – ridicules!

"What's worse is that the Dollar's the world's reserve currency; at least it was until this. But we were warned. The country's credit rating was lowered on three different occasions. We just didn't want to believe it. A lot of countries were already moving away from the dollar before this... backing transactions with gold or silver. All I know is that the repercussions of this default's gonna be huge... people got no clue."

Leo snorted, "Now I know how Greece and the rest of Europe felt when the Euro crashed and burned."

Tim simply nodded and the two men lapsed into silence.

This was the first conversation that they had about what the President announced in the pre-dawn hours of the morning. Both men watched the rebroadcast of the President's address at their homes before meeting up to surf. But it was so depressing, before they left for the beach; they made a pact not to bring it up again until they got back home.

Tim showed up at Leo's place with "The Beast", his raised four-by-four truck. On the drive to Silver Strand, the friends blared ear-splitting alternative and heavy metal music from the killer stereo system.

As a consequence of being "unplugged" they didn't hear about the other catastrophic events taking place. But this time the news wasn't coming from Washington D.C. It was coming from the top of the Ring of Fire and off the coast of North America.

The pair were unaware that a massive 9.5 subduction earthquake struck where the North American Tectonic Plate met the Pacific Tectonic Plate, near the Fox and Aleutian Islands - right under where the Orbs were hanging in the sky for almost a day.

Out of public view, one of those bright Orbs broke from the rest and settled over the long dormant volcano near the islands. Without notice, it dove straight into an old crater. After the eruption started, it popped out unseen and safe. The fuse was lit.

That eruption, and the 9.5 earthquake caused a catastrophic domino effect. Almost instantaneously, three others of the over one-hundred volcanoes in Alaska abruptly roared to life. The billowing smoke and ash instantly clouded the northern sky. And because of the plate shift, the stress ran south, down to where the plates met... setting off other faults along the way.

This caused the Cascadia subduction zone off the coast of Washington, Oregon and Northern California, to also incur massive slippage. That slippage produced another larger, 9.8 quake.

As a consequence, massive amounts of ocean water were displaced. Few would ever know where the tsunami started, but a wall of water, over one hundred and fifty feet high, raced to all points south, east and west. And geological cause and effect was not over.

Continuing the chain reaction deep under the Earth's crust, in order Mt. St. Helen's exploded in Washington State, the extinct Crater Lake Caldera in Oregon erupted and so too the long dormant Mammoth Mountain in the Sierra Nevadas in California blew up.

Death under or near by the volcanos was almost instantaneous for most of the victims. But between the tsunami and the consequential outbreak of earthquakes, millions of people would die this day. Like an out of control locomotive, the crust continued to splinter and eventually found the juggernaut: the San Andreas Fault, two hours after the first eruption.

Starting high in Northern California near Eureka, a strike slip 10.0 earthquake began to decimate everything in its path. Huge swaths of ground opened up and from San Francisco to Baja California, buildings crumbled and were set aflame.

All of this shaking caught Tim and Leo unawares. They were in the water. They couldn't feel it. To them, it felt like choppy ocean. And because Silver Strand Beach was secluded and lower than the cliffs, they also couldn't see the carnage occurring on dry land.

Still waiting for their first real wave, Leo gazed up into the sky.

The fog was burning off and he could make out a bright round object floating lazily in the exposed blue.

Leo pointed, "Check it!"

Tim craned his head around to see what Leo was pointing at, "Wow, that's weird. I heard something about Orbs this morning on the news. But I was in such a hurry to pick you up; I turned it off before it ended."

But Leo wasn't listening. He pointed at the cliffs on shore, "Dude, You see that?"

"See what?" Tim's eyes were coming down from the sky to look at what Leo was talking about when he was distracted by pulling water.

"That!" Leo said, as Tim drug his eyes from the water just in time to see a huge chunk of the cliff line break off and fall onto sand below.

"Whoa..." Leo said.

Tim wasn't listening. Once again he was focused on the water, "What's going on with the water? You feel that undertow?"

Mouth agape and still looking at the cliff, Leo asked distractedly, "What's that?"

"What happened to all the water? Look," Tim said pointing toward shore, "It looks like the tide has gone out again."

"Huh..." Leo shrugged, still looking to the sand, "And what happened to the few people that were on the beach? I don't even see any morning joggers."

Tim again looked around their boards. "Dude, that undertow is draggen us out to sea," he said with concern.

Leo's head began to swivel. "Brah this is meatball! (yellow flag that indicates no surfing)"

Tim stuck his arm in the water and felt the overpowering pull of the ocean. He looked up at the shore. The water receded so much that it exposed a good half of mile of extra sand.

"Leo," he said alarmed, "I... I don't like this. We better head in."

A wide eyed Leo said, "You don't have to tell me twice!" and the two men began to paddle wildly toward shore.

The now churning sound of the backward current filled their ears as they uselessly flailed their paddling arms.   But instead of moving forward, the ocean continued to pull them backward at an even faster clip.

Unexpectedly, far in the distance toward the disappearing shore, they heard a siren. It was steady and high. They stopped paddling and fearfully looked at each other with horrified understanding.

The crumbling cliff, the decreasing tide, and huge undertoe all made sense with that sound. They grew up here and in all that time, they'd never once heard... a tsunami warning. Its siren sounded a warning of the tidal wave that was generated more than two hours earlier, from over twelve-hundred miles up the coast.

They'd already spent much of their energy trying to paddle back. Leo and Tim were exhausted. They looked over their shoulders. Looming far out to sea, but building and increasing in speed was the biggest wave that either man had ever seen. Each of them knew it was easily a hundred feet if not more. And at the speed it was traveling, they knew it would be on them in seconds.

Shrugging his tired shoulders and accepting the inevitable, in a resigned tone, Leo said, "Lets shred it (surf aggressively)."

Tim nodded and reached over to fist bump his best friend.

As each man prepared to stand up on their boards, they knew that if they could catch this huge wave, it would be the ride of their lives.

The hundred and fifty foot wave slammed into them at over five-hundred miles an hour. They didn't stand a chance. And this wipe-out...

Cost them their lives.

Chapter 45

30 Miles South of Tel Aviv – Present Day

*J*oe hung up the phone with a grim look on his face.

He walked up on Zac who was waiting patiently. With a deliberate tone, he asked, "Did you know about this?"

Expressionless, the Israeli said, "Not exactly. We knew something was coming. But not this soon... and certainly not this bad. How is your wife taking it?"

Joe, pressed the issue, "Just what is it that you do for the government again? I mean, you wear the suit of a banker, but..."

Zac narrowed his eyes, daring the American to say what was on his mind, "But what?"

Never one to back down, Joe returned the look, "But you walk like a spook."

Zac was quiet for a moment. But then, a thin smile played on his lips. He shook his head, "Forever the American Josiah. Always speaking your mind. That is one of the things I like about you. One always knows where he stands where you're concerned."

Joe's look didn't change, "That doesn't answer my question. If... you know something... about what's going on. I'd really like to hear it."

The younger man was quiet for a moment. Then blowing out a big breath of reservation, he asked, "Does Ruby need you back home?"

"No, not really," he said reflectively. "She's worried about our family back in Montana, but she knows we can't do anything for them."

Zac nodded his head, and the corners of his mouth turned down. "Yes, we Israelis know a little something about feeling helpless in our circumstance."

His jaw set, he locked eyes with the younger man, Joe said, "I told her that we have unfinished business and would see her in a while. Was I right? Are we gonna keep doing the two-step or... are ya gonna tell me what you wanted to tell me?"

Zac sighed and gave a genuine smile, "Yes, it would do us well to spend a little more time together my candid friend. Come, the Ashkelon Kibbutz (farm collective) awaits." Then with a wave of his arm further south, he said, "The Prophet Ezekiel in chapter 36 of the Tanakh said that Israel would be more prosperous now than it was in ancient times. I showed you the oil and gas finds that makes this true. The Prophet Isaiah said in chapter 27 that the desert would blossom and fill the Earth with fruit... Ashkelon is doing just that... come see and we will talk," he said as he walked around and opened the driver's side door.

Joe grunted, but followed just the same.

As he started the car, Zac looked at the American and said, "Whether you know it or not Josiah, I have already been telling you what I need to. But before you understand fully, you must see that for which we Israeli's are really fighting."

Somewhere Over The English Channel – Present Day

Bryce's head was spinning. The marathon flight took on a life of its own. His stragglers consumed all of his brain capacity. It was all he could do to try and keep up with the immense amount of information that was being downloaded on him - And all of it was life or death.

The data transfer started even before the passengers took seats and the plane taxied. Mac, the astrophysicist of the group, and Diggs were primarily the ones asking The Professor questions. Bryce was relegated to a temporary bystander; a welcomed change from the last nine hours. As the discussion wore on, Bryce took the opportunity to pour over the massive amounts of data that The Professor brought. He found it very disturbing.

Perhaps most perplexing: None of the six scientists present previously heard anything even remotely close to this data coming from NASA or the science community. *If there was a hint of alarm, one of us would have heard something. But instead... NADA! -* Bryce thought.

Bryce picked up a yellow pencil and began twirling it in his fingers.

The silence from NASA was deafening. And it could only mean one of two things, he thought. *One: The story that The Professor told of both missing data and the attempt on his life were fabrications. But given Dr. Mora's lengthy and excellent reputation, his sheer knowledge and intelligence, and the presence of his injuries - it appeared that that possibility was... impossible. Two: The Professor was telling the truth. And that was one scary option, because it meant that there was an intentional and ongoing cover-up concerning the Sun's dangerous and increasing activity. It also meant that scientific and bureaucratic leaders around the world were intentionally keeping the whole world in the dark. In doing so, they were condemning millions to an unexpected early death.*

That thought sent chills down his spine and made his stomach burn. He looked out the window and saw that they'd left the English Channel and were now over dry land; Belgium Bryce guessed.

He continued to twirl the pencil in his fingers with the uncomfortable feeling that all of these things he'd talked about with Mac, and the things he'd just discovered, were all connected. Ivy told about this Plan that she overheard being talked about. With all of the different elements, it sounded like they were parts of the whole. And now this: Dr. Mora talking about how the Sun was acting like a blow torch. Suddenly he remembered that part of his vision. He shook his head. This was no coincidence.

Bryce was in the middle of trying to pull all of the pieces together when the pilot buzzed his console. "Sir, sorry to bother you but..."

"What is it Captain," Bryce asked tersely, irritated that his train of thought was interrupted.

"Well, I don't know if you heard the news from back home..."

"Look," Bryce said more forcefully than intended, "I'm... we're dealing with a whole lot of news right here and it is imperative, and I mean imperative that we are not interrupted until just before we land. Is that clear?"

"Yes, but I just..."

Unwavering, he asked, "Captain Is that clear?"

A beat's silence then, "Yessir, out," and then he was gone.

Bryce hated to be a jerk, but time was way too critical to worry about people's feelings. He needed to get to the bottom of this... this Plan and fast.

Unintentionally, Bryce's rebuke to the plane's captain cut him and his team off from news to the outside world. It wouldn't be until long after the plane came back down to earth that he and the other passengers would hear about Martial Law, the withdrawal of all American troops and the devastating Earth changes that occurred during their flight.

He again went back to twirling the pencil between his fingers. His eyes unconsciously drifted toward the forward storage closet that held The Package. He asked himself the same question that he already had at least a dozen times that day: How did the Rabbi know about The Package?

The only two people on the whole earth that he told were Uncle Joe and Aunt Ruby. They would never talk about it to anyone. Mac now knew, but he told him after the call. But how did the Rabbi know?

If it weren't for Mrs. Warkentin, he would have denied knowledge of The Package, but she was adamant:

"Bryce... time is very short... you must answer that call. It is a Rabbi who is building the third Temple in Jerusalem. He wants... he needs something that you have, desperately - something that no one else knows about. He's going to ask you to bring it Jerusalem. I didn't see this Package, but you need to do what he says. Time is very short. And you need to personally deliver the Package to Jerusalem... right away. There is no time for delays. Time is at an end. You must go,"

He believed her to be genuine: A "seer" able to use her spiritual eyes. There was no other way for her to know about his mother's favorite spot, or the vision he had in the morning. And if she was right about those things, then she must be right about The Package.

He again looked up from his laptop and set it aside while he focused back on the discussion. To his dismay, the analysis had turned into a free-for-all. Mac, The Professor and Xavier were all trying to talk over one another, each arguing their own perspective. Diggs, not one given to argument, simply sat back, shaking his head in frustration. Ivy and Stephanie were sitting next to each other, observing the male display of testosterone.

He rubbed his tired eyes. "Hold on! One person at a time!"

They didn't hear him.

He tried again, but more forceful this time, "Guys! You can't..."

They still ignored him.

"That's it," he said under his breath and he took two large steps back from the small group. Sticking his middle finger and his thumb in his mouth... he blew as hard as he could. Out blasted a loud Montanan whistle.

The piercing sound bounced off the walls of the Gulfstream's small cabin. Instantly the girls held their hands over their ears. In unison, the whole group turned to him in shock.

Wiggling his pinky in his ear, Mac asked, "What did ju do that for?!"

Bryce ignored him. "Look," he said with frustration, "we don't have time for this! We have to figure out what's going on! And we have to figure it out now! I know we all have our opinions, and our points that we feel are most important. But unless we work as a team," he looked each of them in the eye, "people are going to die."

He was quiet for a moment and then continued in a softer voice, "They need to be warned. And we need to see if there is anything we can do to slow all of this down."

He pointed a finger at each of them, "Look around," the group looked at each other, "There's a reason why we are all here. It's not by chance. It has to be by design."

"By design Dr. Cooper?" Stephanie asked with a confused look. "But, we just got on board and... and didn't know who would be on this plane. How could any of us know..."

A smile formed on The Professor's face, the first in a long time. In his Spanish accent he said, "Not designed by a man Mija." Then he looked at Bryce, "Correcto Dr. Cooper?"

Bryce nodded and Alvaro continued, "By someone who knows exactly what is going on. Entendido? (Understand?)" and he pointed up.

Bryce rested his hand on The Professor's shoulder, "Corregir El Profesor (Correct Professor)"

"So we're here for a reason. Now, let's quit arguing and see what we do know. Because as sure as I'm standing here, I think we are almost out of time."

Bryce couldn't know how right he was. Time was at an end.

Chapter 46

Ashkelon, Israel – Present Day

*T*he Kibbutz Yad Mordechai lay thirty-six miles to the south of Tele Aviv, along the deep blue Mediterranean Sea. The two men, both in linen white shirts, wide brimmed straw hats and dark Sunglasses, were sitting under the shade of an olive tree. Each were sipping on a cold fruit drink made from produce grown right at the Ashkelon Kibbutz.

"And," Zac was saying, "Ashkelon was also the place where Delilah cut Sampson's hair."

"Really?" Joe asked with interested dispassion. His anger at what was befalling America was simmering just under the surface. He was in no mood for a historic tour or games.

The two men lapsed into silence, sipping their drinks and lost in their own thoughts. The warm desert breeze could be heard as it whistled through the Olive tree above. Ocean air teased their nostrils and birds could be heard chirping and calling. For Joe, if it were not for the terrible news back in America, this would be a perfect day.

"Josiah," Zac said resolutely, breaking the long silence, "I owe you an apology."

Joe turned to him with a questioning look. His face appeared to have a frown on it, "Yeah? What for?"

"You were correct when you said that... how did you put it? That I walk like a spook?"

Joe's gaze was leveled on the younger man and he waited.

Zac continued, "You are right. I am one of nearly two-thousand Mossad agents," he said bluntly.

Joe looked back over to the fields, "Does that mean you didn't know about the financial trouble my country was in?"

Zac hid the surprise he felt. He was sure that the admission would produce a far different reaction than that of the American's question. Then again... his country just didn't go bankrupt and declare Martial Law. "That is not altogether correct. I am privy to special briefings on a regular basis, and I do have a desk at the finance ministry. But, I could not, as you can appreciate, disclose your country's problems to you even if I wanted to," then added, "But I am surprised that you didn't see it coming."

The Israeli had him there. He very much did see it coming. His nephew, Bryce, would talk to him about the impending fiscal cliff that the U.S. was approaching. And it was the strongest argument Bryce gave him when he converted all of his holdings to silver and gold.

Joe pulled a long twig from the tree and stuck it in his mouth. He sighed heavily, "Yeah, I guess I saw it coming. I just didn't want to believe it."

Zac nodded his head in understanding, "Yes... it is difficult for our countrymen to see the ugliest parts of our nation's future also."

Joe turned to look at the Israeli and cocked his head, "Somethin else you want to get off your chest Zecheriah?"

Zac's eyebrows raised at the use of his proper name. Since the very first day that he'd met Joe, he called him Zac. It was obvious to the Mossad agent that Joe was in no playing mood. But he ignored the question, "And since you have my confession, may I say that you do not carry yourself like the average cowboy from Montana."

"Ha... is that right?"

"Josiah, it is my job to keep my profession from people. Security you understand. My apology is not for keeping my profession from you. It is for what I did..." he looked down to the dirt and then back into Joe's eyes, "when I heard a stranger from America was moving in next to me."

Joe's face hardened. He didn't like the sound of this.

Because of the news back home, he was already itchin for a fight.

"You see, anytime my identity or position might be compromised, I must take precautions."

"Precautions huh?" Joe said as he spit out the twig and slowly got to his feet, brushed the dirt from his hands. "What sort of... precautions?" he asked intensely. He hadn't worked out in the dojo for a while. This Mossad agent with his secrets might just give the opportunity.

Zac, with his arm still in the sling, managed to grab onto a low lying branch and pull himself to his feet. "I did an extensive background check on you and your wife when you moved in... to make sure that you were not spies, sent to expose operations."

Joe's eyebrows became one tight knit wrinkle. It matched the scowl on his face. He swallowed hard, trying to contain his anger. "Is that right?" he asked, in almost an angry whisper. *He did what!*

Zac sighed, "But that still, is not what I owe you an apology for."

Joe began to casually circle Zac to the right.

Zac knew the signs of an approaching confrontation. With only one arm, he was at a distinct disadvantage. Just as casually he began to circle the other way. *No matter what happens, don't pull your knife,* he thought to himself.

"Sounds like an apology is in order I'd say," quipped the Montanan.

"No Josiah, as I said. That is normal operating procedure. But you didn't stay alive as long as I have without going above and beyond procedure."

"Whaat didju do?" Joe asked in a gravelly tone, unable to control the loss of a mask of normality.

In his long Mossad career, Zac had never felt as much shame as what he was about to tell Joe. He needed to tell him the truth before he found out on his own. But at the same time, his sense of self-preservation was screaming at him. The Montanan transformed from a jovial elderly man, into a wild animal on a chain that was ready to break it. Perhaps it was the news from back home that caused his friend of three years to morph into this creature. Or maybe it was a pre-sense of betrayal that he knew was to come. Regardless, wounded arm or not, Zac didn't think this encounter would be good.

Joe's hands came up in front of him, opened palm. He could see the look on Zac's face. Even without an explanation, the man looked guilty. And the Montanan was in just the right mood to dish out judgment and sentence.

Shame evident in his eyes, Zac said, "I put listening devices in your home before you moved in..."

Zac could swear that Joe growled at him.

The sixty-five year old Joe said, "You did wha..." and before he finished the sentence, in speed that belied his age, he jumped high in a forward motion to throw a "superman punch" square at Zac's jaw.

Narrowly seeing it coming, the Israeli ducked under the punch, and leveled a brutal body punch to the American's kidney in order to get him to stop.

But Joe didn't flinch. Rather, in one fluid rotation, he rotated in a three-sixty degree motion, swooped his leg around, and landed a high arching roundhouse kick right on Zac's jaw with the back of his heel. The force of the blow knocked Zac on his butt in the dirt and left his head spinning.

Joe jabbed his finger angrily at the downed man, "Now I forgive you!"

Zac sat in the dirt for the moment and rubbed his jaw as the world spun. Any other time, he'd normally bounce up from such a blow - If he didn't, he'd be dead. But this... this he had coming. And he knew that Josiah wouldn't really harm him... he was just angry.

"I am sorry," he said, looking up at the predator, "I didn't know you. If I had, I'd never invade your privacy. Just so you know, as soon as we verified that you were no threat, I had the devices removed."

Still circling, Joe said, "Hold on... what do you mean you had the devices removed? When I lived there?!"

Zac shook his head and held his jaw, "You do not want to know," was all he said.

Joe stared hard at him for a moment. Then his eyes softened and he dropped his guard. Shaking his head, he waved his hand, "Ah forget it. That was three years ago. Guess we can call it water under the bridge. Deal?" and he reached down to help Zac up with his one good hand.

Zac got to his feet groaning. The men shook hands and Zac said, "You kick like..."

Joe interrupted him, "A jackass?"

Zac chuckled, "I was about to say; like you've received some training. But now that you mention it, that moniker suits you."

For the first time since he talked to Ruby, Joe smiled. And then he started rubbing his side, "Well talk about training, I think I'm gonna be peeing blood for a week."

Zac was brushing off his paints when Joe asked, "What a minute. If that happened three years ago, why are you telling me now? If you'd never told me, I'd never know."

"Indeed," Zac said as he finished brushing himself off and pointing in the direction of the car. The two men walked slowly, "Before I took them out, something was overheard and a record of it was placed in your file."

"File? You have a file on us?"

"Your Mossad file," then Zac stopped and turned to face Joe. "We know about the Garments and the Urimm and Thumimm."

"You what?" Joe spit out.

"You and your wife were overheard talking about your nephew and what occurred at the LHC. It was shortly after that that I insisted that the listening devices be removed. To the potential detriment of my career I might add."

"Grreeaatttt, but you kept a file on me," Joe said sarcastically.

"Not I but..."

"I know. You said it was Mossad. But that still doesn't answer why you're telling me now."

"We have contacted Dr. Cooper and asked him to bring the Package with the Garments and the Urimm and Thummim straight away."

"Bryce is coming here? He didn't call..."

"We've asked him to be discreet. There are many prying ears."

"Yeah," Joe said bitingly, "I guess so. But hold on, you still didn't say why you wanted them. Besides, how did you get Bryce to agree? I would think he'd deny any knowledge of them. I can't think of one reason in the whole world why he would turn those things over to you. They're dangerous."

Zac started walking again and Joe followed, "Josiah, you know the gas masks and extra supplies that are being passed out all over Tel Aviv?"

"Of course, how could you miss 'em. We've even been instructed what bomb shelter to report to. But the government is saying that these are precautionary moves. I just assumed that this was normal given the hostilities around us."

"Josiah, this is not normal. There are more enemies surrounding us than even in 1967 and 1976 combined. These animals want to wipe us off the face of the Earth. We will never again allow another Holocaust. And because of that, we may be forced to use..." his voice dropped to a whisper, "weapons that would decimate all of us."

Joe stopped walking, "My God..."

"But," Zac continued, "there is one more chance. It is how I got this," he held up his arm in the sling briefly.

Joe shook his head, "I don't understand."

Zac's eyes grew big as he excitedly recounted, "We found it at the exact angle of 251.565 in Zuqba, Egypt just as the Torah Code said it would be! But we didn't have time to look around in the cave. If the Urimm and Thumimm were there, we missed them. And there is no way we would be able to pull off another successful operation to that location right now. But without the Urimm and Thumimm, we can't ask Hashem to get us out of this... this mess," he said raising his good arm.

Joe squinted his eyes at him, "Son... I'm sorry. Maybe I kicked you a little too hard. What are you babbling about? And what does this have to do with you bugging my house?"

Zac looked surprised at the American and said, "I'm sorry... you didn't know?"

"Didn't know what?"

With a faraway look in his eyes, Zac said, "Last week we recovered the Ark of the Covenant."

Joe flinched, "Wha..."

"And we brought it back to the Temple Mount. When the priests looked inside, there was no Urimm and Thumimm. Today there is a ceremony," he looked at his watch, "actually it's probably over by now, to set up the Tabernacle and take the Ark into its proper place in the Holy of Holies."

Joe's mouth hung open.

"But without the Urimm and Thumimm, the High Priest will not be able to go before the Ark and ask Hashem what we should do about our enemies that surround us. But he," Zac pointed to the sky, "has made a way. Your nephew, Dr. Bryce Cooper is bringing a Package containing the Urimm and Thummim and he has agreed to let our High Priest use them."

Joe began to feel his head spin and he needed to sit down. He put his hands on his knees and he took a few deep breaths, "The Ark of the Covenant..." he said shaking his head.

"Yes, that is why you needed to find out about the listening devices. Your nephew will be here with the Package within the next few hours. I wanted to tell you about it before you found out another way."

Joe was standing again, shook his head and said, "The Ark of the Covenant..."

Again Zac looked at his watch, "It is getting late. Come we must go. I have to be back before Sundown."

Chapter 47

Over The Mediterranean – Present Day

*A*s they flew over Athens, Greece, the pilot informed the passengers over the loud speakers that due to high winds coming from the north, approach to Ben Gurion Airport in Tel Aviv would be from the south. Thus, remaining flight time was stretched to two and a half hours.

This was Bryce's first fight with this captain. The public announcement, as opposed to buzzing his console, was probably due to the terse request he made to not bother the group. The physicist felt a pang of guilt and made a mental note to apologize after the flight.

As Bryce sipped on a hot cup of coffee, he surveyed the plane's cabin. X and Dr. Mora were in the middle of an intense discussion. The two women were sitting next to each other and chatting quietly. Mac and Diggs were looking at The Professor's data on a laptop while Diggs was animatedly explaining something to Mac.

Thousands of miles from home, he couldn't help but wonder what all of this would mean for his family. He was worried about them.

It was true that he had made preparations, but even he couldn't anticipate anything like this happening. If Dr. Mora and Dr. Black were right, things were about to get very dangerous for the people he loved.

Under his breath he asked, "Adoni, what are You doing?"

His thoughts meeting only silence, Bryce went back to watching his former co-workers.

As he did, he was reminded of a conversation between he and Diggs that only the Montanan remembered.

Geneva, LHC – Four Years Earlier

"In the research you had me do, I believe I found various examples of what you might classify as, encounters with interdimensional beings." With that, Diggs started to recount various biblical accounts between humans and non-humans. He also dug through some historical documents, of the same period, that gave the impression of other dimensional contact.

"Very interesting. I appreciate your efforts. As usual, you've been very thorough."

"My pleasure, but there is something more that I've needed to discuss with you."

"Fine, but before you do... what do you know about... ah... Noah's days?"

"Noah's days sir?" Diggs asked in surprise.

Bryce said, as if trying to strain to find a memory, "Yeah, that's what my mom told me. Something about angels... doing bad things... like in Noah's days."

Suddenly Diggs' demeanor changed and he became animated.

"Dr. Cooper, that's exactly what I wanted to talk to you about. But before I do, are you sure you want to delve into this. I know your disposition toward religion. If you would like to discuss this, you know I am happy to. But please understand, you may not like what I've found."

"What you have found? You mean you've already looked into 'Noah's days'?"

"Sir... I've wanted to discuss this very issue with you but... I didn't know how to broach the subject for fear of your reaction."

"What are you talking about? What could be so... horrible that I may not want to 'delve' into it? We are talking about science here, are we not? What would have me so concerned that you thought I'd not want to talk about it? Unless, of course, it was some religious mumbo-jumbo, and you already know how I feel about such things."

Diggs hung his head for a moment, trying to figure out how to tell his mentor. *Come on old boy! You can do it,* he thought.

Finally he looked up into Bryce's eyes and said, "I believe you are absolutely correct about other spatial dimensions being right next to ours. And that... we affect and... are affected by those same spatial dimensions," he said evenly.

Shaking his head, confused, Bryce said, "Yeahhh... sooo..."

Diggs held up his index finger as if to say, "wait a sec."

"Further, I also believe that there is historical evidence that beings from those other spatial dimensions have come... are here... and will, in the near future, make their presence known."

Bryce's mouth dropped open. "Come again?"

"Your mother didn't say 'Noah's Days'. She said 'as in the days of Noah'. Did you ever look it up?"

"Look up what?" Bryce asked frustratedly. "She was on her deathbed, pumped full of morphine for crying out loud. She probably didn't even know what she was saying. And no, I never went back to the bible... to look it up. In fact, I haven't cracked one open since. What in the world are you talking about?"

Diggs leaned forward, dropped his voice to barely above a whisper, and said, "The Nephilim."

"Dr. Cooper? Dr. Cooper..." Stephanie said.

Bryce's eyes refocused as he realized that he'd been standing there day dreaming. Stephanie and Ivy walked up on him and were trying to get his attention. "I'm sorry, I was thinking about something," he said embarrassed.

"Not a problem," Stephanie said with big eyes, "My father would like to speak with you, but first, Ivy and I need to tell you something."

"Yes?"

"We were sitting together chatting when I mentioned that I worked for Goldman Sachs."

"Sooo?" Bryce said not understanding the importance.

"Well Mora is my maiden name. My married name is Jackson."

"Okay"

"Antonio Jackson was my husband."

"Alright... but I don't see what this has to do..."

"We met a few years ago on our jobs at Goldman Sachs. I was his clerical assistant. We fell in love. But the company rules forbade supervisor and employee fraternization. So I became the manager's assistant and he went on to become a big-time broker. Meanwhile I progressed through the administrative ranks to eventually become the assistant to the President. You would know my ex-husband better as Tony. We divorced six months ago."

"I'm sorry about that but..." Bryce eyes lit up in sudden recognition. "Hold on... Tony Jackson was my broker at Goldman Sacs. You were married to that Tony Jackson?"

"Yes, that's right. I didn't know you were his client, but when I heard your friend say that you were from Montana and really smart, I remembered some of what Tony said about you. I just put two and two together."

"Wow... small world. He came out to the ranch a couple of times..."

"But that's not the most important revelation that I... we," she nodded at Ivy, "needed to tell you."

"Okayyy" Bryce said confused.

"Remember I said I worked my way up and eventually become the assistant to the President?"

"Yeah," Bryce said, not wanting to be rude, but wanting to move on. He looked over at the four men, who were looking at him and waiting.

"They call him The Banker and the thing is, when I say I was his assistant, I mean I did everything for him."

"Okay... I understand you were good at your job. But let me see what these guys need and we..." Bryce said as he started to walk away.

Ivy reached for his arm and said, "Wait for it."

Bryce looked down at Ivy's hand and then into her very serious eyes. He sighed and relaxed.

"Dr. Cooper, do you know how powerful of a man he is?" Stephanie asked.

Bryce shook his head frustrated, "Honestly no, can't say I do."

Stephanie's eyes were lit with fear, "He is arguably the most powerful man in the United States and one of the most powerful in the world."

"Ladies, please, that's very impressive but..."

Ivy spoke up, "You still don't get it. The President of Goldman Sachs was one of my patients at the lab in California."

Bryce felt as if a sudden shot of electricity hit him on the top of his head. He scanned the two ladies' faces, "Are you telling me that the President of Goldman Sachs has altered DNA?"

Ivy again looked at Stephanie. When she turned back to Bryce she said, "All I can tell you is I've seen his DNA."

"And..." Bryce said rolling his hand.

With a pained look, she said, "It isn't human."

Chapter 48

*B*ryce gathered additional information about The Banker, and Stephanie's association with him. He decided that it was best that he kept these details to himself, at least for the time being. The rest of the group was so focused on Earth changes; he didn't want to distract them.

Walking up on the group of four men with the two ladies in tow, he said, "Sorry, what's up?"

X caught Ivy's eye and stared at her with a sad look.

She shook her head slightly as if to say, "later".

"Dr. Cooper," The Professor said, "Dr. Black and I have been comparing notes. We believe that there is a definite correlation between our separate observations," The Professor said analytically.

Bryce looked to X and saw him nod in the affirmative.

"Finally," Bryce said, "Maybe we can make some headway. Whad a ya got?"

Xavier and The Professor looked at each other and Mora nodded at the younger man, letting him to go first.

"Okay," X said, "We know from the withheld empirical data from the government, that the crust of the Earth has become increasingly unstable. The evidence of this geophysical instability is increased seismic activity along fault lines, such as around the Ring of Fire, but also in non-plate adjoining areas. There are also other examples such as developed stress along the New Madrid fault line, the Yellowstone Caldera and the El Hierro Volcano in the Canary Islands."

"I'd never heard of that one," Bryce said.

Continuing, X said, "In addition, there are widespread reports of numerous large sinkholes developing virtually overnight."

"Sinkholes?" Diggs asked.

"Yes, sinkholes. Many of these holes have appeared in previously stable geological areas. Thus, their appearance is baffling. Along with those holes, there have been indications of venting from below."

"What can cause a sinkhole?" Mac asked.

"That's the million dollar question," X replied. "The simple answers are broken water mains, pockets of air in poorly compacted ground and even some minor shifting of topsoil. But these holes..." he paused and shook his head, "these holes are different. It's almost as if the Earth's crust is expanding, stretching the thin crust even further. The result are openings in that crust... sinkholes."

"X, you said something about venting?" his wife asked, "Like volcano venting?"

"Not exactly," the geophysicist replied. "If you think about it, the ground, or the mantel, beneath our feet is alive and active. There are pent up gasses that, when given the opportunity, try to escape. This can be seen in the form of steam, smoke or even sulfur and carbon dioxide. A good example of this venting is along the New Madrid fault line, which extends along the Reelfoot Rift."

"The what?" Bryce asked.

"The Reelfoot Rift. It's what formed after the North American continent split or rifted apart from the supercontinent of Rodina. That splitting, and others like it, seven-hundred and fifty million years ago gave us the existing continents we see today. But these areas are prone to instability. As an example, that rift was the fault that caused four mega quakes in 1811 and 1812. One of those quakes was so strong that it made the Mississippi River run backwards for a time."

"My word," Diggs exclaimed, "I'd never heard of that."

"Not surprising, but the point is that this is just one area from around the globe that's roaring back to life – And it's in our own backyard. Thus is the crux of our problem at the USGS. We see seismic activity growing exponentially and yet we are not allowed to report it to the public. It is so stunning that we also have observations of this venting coming up from the ground. What's worse is that the activity appears to be intensifying. It could get very ugly, very fast."

"Okay," Bryce said, "So we know that the Earth is throwing a temper tantrum. But what does that mean in real terms, and how does that relate to Dr. Mora's findings."

X hesitated. He came on the trip to keep an eye on Ivy. While he didn't mind sharing basic data, he hadn't anticipated the consonance of the unexpected scientific think tank connecting the dots.

Dr. Mora looked at the younger man and nodded. Xavier sighed and continued, "I believe that all of this data points to a Pole Shift which has already commenced."

Stephanie asked, "A... a pole shift? Like the North and South pole flipping?"

Again, there was a look between Xavier and The Professor. X nodded his head, "Yes... that's exactly what it means. Or at least significant movement of the poles I'm afraid."

"Wouldn't we see that coming?" Mac asked, "And... when was the last time one happened?"

"Good question," Xavier said. He reached for his laptop, punched a few keys and brought up a map that had a red X in the middle of Russia. "Do you know what this is?"

Mac bent at the waist with hands on hips to look down at the screen. "Looks like Russia to me?"

"Right. It is Russia. And that red X, in the middle of Siberia..." he looked around at the group, "...represents magnetic North."

"What?" Mac asked flabbergasted, "Magnetic north as in the North Pole?"

"Yeah... that North Pole," X said and he punched a couple other keys. The screen changed to a global view of Earth with a yellow dotted line straggling from the red X south, "And this is the anticipated migration path for the poles."

Gasps came from the little group as they were all stunned into silence. All that could be heard was the hum of the jet engines as each of them tried to imagine what would happen to a world torn by upheaval.

"The last pole shift is believed to have happened as little as thirteen-thousand years ago," Xavier said.

A serious Bryce asked, "How long?"

X scratched his chin, "A few months ago I might've said thousands of years, or maybe centuries."

"You said you would have said. How bout now?" Bryce pressed.

Shaking his head, Xavier replied, "Months, maybe weeks."

"And what does the migration of the poles mean in practical terms," Bryce asked, already thinking he knew the answer.

X was quiet for a moment. Then looking Bryce square in the eye, he said, "It means catastrophe of biblical proportions."

Chapter 49

North of Ashdod, Israel – Present Day

*T*he gentle breeze of earlier in the day had developed into a strong headwind from the north. Concealed behind an outcropping of boulders, just North of Ashdod, The Assassin, dressed in his desert fatigues, crouched low behind the rock. The IDF patrolled this road, especially now, and he still hoped to live after the strike.

Ashdod was between Ashkelon and Tel Aviv, and was the furthest southern point of Israel. He got there from Gaza by hanging on to the underside of a family van, with his weapon taped across his back. Route 20, along the Mediterranean, was the much used highway that traversed the coast all the way from his home of Gaza to Tel Aviv, and all points in between. His victim would follow this route.

With the windblown sand now peppering his face, he covered it using his keffiyeh (traditional scarf). Then he reached into his pocket and pulled out the goggles that he had the foresight to bring.

His Lookout, who also snuck out of Gaza, was up the road. He would call him with advanced warning of the target. Pulling back his sleeve, he looked at his watch. Then he took out a bottle of water and took a long pull - Anytime now.

Route 20, Between Ashkelon & Ashdod – Present Day

Behind the wheel, Zac could feel the headwind buffeting the car. They were moving at a leisurely pace down Route 20, on their way back to Tel Aviv. Few cars could be seen on the road and Zac thought it was probably due to the looming war. *Even now people's lives are changing,* he thought.

"So I don't get it," Joe said making conversation. Forgotten was the tussle under the Olive tree, although both men would be sore from the incident. Even now as he talked to him, Joe could see the deep black and blue bruise on Zac's jaw where his heel connected.

"What do you not get Josiah?"

"Well... you're Orthodox, right?"

"Yes, of course."

"So I imagine that the setting up of the Tabernacle, and placing the Ark of the Covenant in it would have been both of historical importance to you and very spiritually significant. Especially since you had some skin in the game," Joe said pointing to Zac's arm in the sling. "So if you knew about the ceremony, why didn't you go?"

Zac was thoughtful, "Obviously if I were to go to Jerusalem for the ceremony, it would be instantly noticed that a representative, from Israel's government showed up."

"So... I'm sure that there were many officials there," Joe countered.

"True," Zac nodded as he looked from the road to his friend and back again. "But those individuals went in their official capacities to represent the government on this historic day. I, on the other hand, am a member of the Finance Ministry. Do you suppose that a government official from a department that has nothing to do with the Temple would tend to... how do you say... stand out?"

"Well... I suppose. But as a Jew, you could be curious and just wanted to see what was going on."

"I coouuldd," Zac nodded in agreement, "but then perhaps those in my own government might wonder if I had Orthodox leanings," he shrugged. "Such a disposition in my capacity with the Mossad may give the appearance that I am weak. And it would not be long until those in my own agency might wonder if I had the capacity to conduct operations."

"Hold on... let me get this straight. You're saying that if they thought one of their spies was too religious, they'd think he was a wus and couldn't do his job?" Joe asked sarcastically.

Zac smiled, "That is exactly what I'm saying my candid American friend."

Joe shook his head, "And they say the CIA is too political." Then pointing to the town in the distance, he asked, "Is that Asdod?"

"Yes it is."

"Do you think you can pull in somewhere? I need to take a leak," then he added with a smile, "You know us seniors. We are weak and feeble and we have even weaker bladders."

Zac smirked and rubbed his bruised chin, "You mean that you are an old goat that can still kick?"

Mediterranean Airspace – Present Day

Bryce puffed out his cheeks and blew out a heavy breath. "Well that's not too encouraging," he said to Xavier. "So how bout you Professor? What do you see on your end?"

The older man looked grim, "Not much good news I'm afraid Dr. Cooper. Now," he said in his Spanish accent sounding like a teacher to students, "everyone knows that the Sun operates on eleven year cycles. "These cycles entail the Sun moving from an active period to an inactive period." The group nodded. "But what most people do not know is that the Sun also flips its poles periodically."

"Wow," Ivy said, "I did not know that."

"Understandable my dear. Unless you are interested in things to do with the Sun, it is easily missed."

"So how does this affect the Earth?" Bryce asked.

"Yes, this I will get to in a moment. But for now, I would like to direct your attention to this," he said pointing to his laptop. He hit a few keys and up popped a picture of a raging Sun.

Bryce was the first to see it and his throat sunk into his stomach. "Professor, I looked at all of your data, but never once did I see this image," he said in a shaky voice.

Stephanie was standing behind the crowd, trying to see what was so interesting. Finally getting a glimpse she asked, "Dad, is there something wrong with the camera or something?"

"No Stephanie, there is not. You are seeing the Sun as it is at this moment."

"But... where'd all those holes come from. What are they?"

"Those are called coronal holes."

"Coronal holes?" she asked.

"Yes" The Professor said, "Coronal holes are areas where the Sun's corona is darker, and colder, and has lower-density plasma than average. They're linked to unipolar concentrations of open magnetic field lines. During solar minimum, that's one of those cycles that I was talking about, coronal holes are mainly found at the Sun's polar regions. But they can be located anywhere on the Sun during solar maximum. But here is the dangerous part. Fast-moving solar winds travel along open magnetic field lines that pass through coronal holes. So with all of those active regions that we are seeing, it means that the Sun is acting like a blow torch in every direction."

"And how is that different than solar flares?" Ivy asked in a quiet voice.

"Very good question," The Professor said, "Solar flares are plasma filament, coronal material if you will, that develop on the outside of the Sun and look like long crooked strings. Sometimes this filament will snap off and eject massive amounts of plasma into space. These can be more dangerous than the solar winds coming from the coronal holes."

"Professor," Digs said, "I've never seen so many coronal holes... where did they all come from?"

Dr. Mora shook his head, "I don't know Digby. There is no precedent for this. This is beyond a simple cycle change or pole shift for the Sun. It appears to be increasingly unstable."

Diggs fixated on the picture, "It almost looks like... cheese cloth, or..."

"Sackcloth?" Bryce asked, as a sheen of perspiration beaded on his forehead despite the cabin's cool interior.

"Yes, yes that's right," Diggs said, "Sackcloth."

"I was hoping," Bryce said looking like he was going to be ill, "That I was the only one making the connection."

While interesting and disturbing to the other scientists, the reason for Bryce's discomfort was for far more than just an unusual scientific observation. The physicist from Montana was looking at a picture of the Sun in his vision.

Chapter 50

Mediterranean Airspace – Present Day

r. Mora stuck out his lower lip, "Yes, I suppose it does look like sackcloth."

Bryce coughed in his hand, trying to get his equilibrium back. He looked at his student from another life and said, "I know where you're going Diggs. But let's hope it's not time for Revelation 6:12 just yet."

"Revelation 6:12?" Mac asked.

Bryce looked to his newly believing friend, "Yeah, it says:

> *'And I beheld when he had opened the sixth seal, and, lo, there was a great earthquake; and the Sun became black as sackcloth of hair, and the moon became as blood...'*"

Mac's eyes got big, "That doesn't sound good."

"No it does not," The Professor said with a worried look, "I am familiar with the passage and frankly I have thought the very same thing."

"And those strings on the side of the holes? What are they?" Ivy asked.

"Those are the plasma filaments that I spoke of," Dr. Mora said.

Diggs asked, "And you think this is the reason that they've changed all the data?"

"Yes Digby. Both the solar winds and the charged particles discharged from a solar flare can be tracked on the Magnetometer. But that data too has been falsified."

"The Magnetometer?" Ivy asked.

"Yes, this is an instrument that keeps track of those particles and tells us how they are affecting our Magnetosphere, annnddd," The Professor stressed, "how the particles may break down this protective shield in our atmosphere."

"And what is the Magnetometer telling us?" Mac prompted.

"Well," Dr. Mora said shaking his head, "If you look at the

readings that they changed, it tells us nothing! Everything is normal! Look, I have it here." He punched a few keys on the laptop and everyone gathered around for a look. "But that is the information they doctored. This," he said, tapping other keys and changing the screen, "is the data that they tried to kill me over!"

The little group gasped in unison. It was obvious by the numbers that the Magnetosphere was eroding.

"What the data suggests," Alvaro continued, "is that the Magnetosphere is breaking down, and thus our protection is breaking down. This is allowing high doses of gamma radiation to bombard the planet. In the long run, the effects of such an increase in gamma ray radiation will cause a definite rise in the rate of cancers, accompanied by unexplained rashes and animal die offs."

"Or human die offs," Mac said under his breath.

"Hold on," Bryce said, "I've been reading about animal die offs all over the planet. And would this also account for the terrible droughts that we've seen?"

"Exactemente!" The Professor said, "And as a result of the droughts, we are now seeing food shortages on a massive scale. That is why most of the rioting has started. They are food riots. And it is only going to get worse."

"Professor," Ivy choked, "What Dr. McNabb just said about humans dying off... is this a real possibility?"

Dr. Mora nodded his head weakly, "I'm afraid so. That could be the worst case scenario. Never before have we seen the Sun do these things. And to top it all off, we are in grave danger of a massive solar flare hitting Earth. With our weakened Magnetosphere, if a significant X-Flare, that's the largest type of flare," he said looking at Ivy, "hits us, it could cripple our electrical infrastructure and communications network. This damage would not be repairable for many years and, aside from the deaths that it would surely cause, those who are still living would be thrown back into the Stone Age," he said grimly.

"But I don't understand Dad," Stephanie said, "Why would

anyone want to cover up this information. They can't keep going back to all the servers and erasing data. Surely someone would find out eventually. They couldn't hide this forever."

The Professor shook his head, "I don't know Mija. You are right. It doesn't make sense."

Again silence fell.

"Unless," Bryce broke in, "unless they were just biding their time... and they only needed to keep it quiet for a while. If things went beyond a certain point, it wouldn't matter what eventually came out."

Mac looked sideways at his friend, "What are you getting at Coop?"

There was a faraway look in Bryce's eye as he formed his hypothesis aloud, "What if whoever is doing this is looking to a point of no return. What if they have already begun to put into place their... their new vision for the world and once that Plan gets beyond a certain point, it'll be too far along to stop."

He looked at Ivy, "You said that the voices on the conference call were talking about this Plan moving forward and... the Arrival? Did you hear anything about how soon this might be?" Bryce asked trying to pull information out of her.

The geneticist furrowed her brow trying to remember even a little detail that might help. Finally she said, "No... no. Not a date. But now that you mention it, I got the feeling that this Plan was already underway and that this Arrival that they were talking about was soon."

Again the group lapsed into silence as they pondered what might be. After a moment, Mac asked, "Professor, how does all of this relate to the earthquakes and volcanic activity that Xavier shared with us."

"Yes... yes, that is right. Thank you. I almost forgot," Dr. Mora said. "The Sun operates on eleven year cycles. Toward the end of these cycles the Sun's activity increases and then we know that a Sun polar reversal is about to occur. After the reversal, the Sun's activity wanes and thus we see less solar activity, Sun flares, coronal holes, etcetera."

"But that's not what's happened?" Mac asked.

"No it is not," Dr. Mora said. "Actually the opposite is true. Sun activity has not decreased, but increased and it appears that the Sun itself has entered a new, distinct phase that we on earth have never seen."

"And then there's this," Xavier said almost begrudgingly as he punched a few keys on his laptop bringing up an article.

"This is an excellent abstract written by Marilla Tavares and Anibal Azevedo out of Brazil in February of 2011. It sites numerous studies throughout modern scientific history that give credence to the belief that the Sun's activity is directly linked to seismic activity. This and other scientific work lend Dr. Mora and I to believe that the Sun and the Earth are tied inexplicably together, and this bond is now tearing our planet apart."

Bryce looked like he was in the final round of a heavy weight fight. He'd been emotionally and intellectually battered for the last twelve hours and now his opponent just landed a right cross directly to his chin. His legs were wobbly.

Just then, over the intercom they all heard the Captain say, "Folks, we are on final approach to Tel Aviv. Please take your seats and buckle up for descent. And thank you for flying with us today."

As he took his seat and buckled in, Bryce asked under his breath, "Could it get any worse."

It did.

PART FOUR

CELESTIAL TORRENT

"AND KNEW NOT UNTIL THE FLOOD CAME, AND TOOK THEM AWAY..."

THE BOOK OF MATTHEW VERSE 24:39

∞

Chapter 51

Geneva – Four Years Earlier

"*N*ephilim? What is Nephilim?"

"Dr. Cooper, it's not what the Nephilim is, but who are the Nephilim."

"You often like to quote Hynek and Vallee when they say that UFO's are not 'intergalactic' but 'inter-dimensional' right?" Diggs asked.

"Yeah, so," Bryce said wearily.

"I submit to you Dr. Cooper that those very inter-dimensional creatures that Hynek, Vallee, and you yourself, point to as being 'inter-dimensional' are, in fact, Nephilim hybrids."

"Nephilim wha..."

Without pausing, Diggs continued, "Further, I believe that they have access to our dimension, because they themselves are from a lower dimension in your dimensional stack.

"I believe that they move back and forth between dimensions while masquerading as 'aliens' from other planets."

"Say what?" Bryce asked dumbfounded.

"I promise you Dr. Cooper, this is about physics and your own dimensional theory... just bear with me."

"Alright..." Bryce said sighing again heavily. "I'll bite. What does any of this have to do with physics?"

Diggs smiled and asked, "Do you know who 'the sons of God' *(In Genesis 6:2)* are referring to?"

Diggs was quiet, waiting for him to connect the dots.

"So you're saying that... that these Nephilim are the half breed offspring of fallen angels and humans?" Bryce asked incredulously.

"That's right doctor. That's exactly what I'm saying... if you can accept it," he said, before dropping the real bombshell on him.

Intensely staring at his mentor, Diggs said, "And there are other places in the bible where they show up. But I understand how you feel about the bible, so let me defer to other writings."

"Such as?"

"There are other writings called the Book of Enoch, the Book of Jubilees and the Book of Jasher. These are ancient texts, pseudo-books, found with the Dead Sea Scrolls. Each, describe huge beings that were massively strong. There were accounts of them having six fingers and six toes. Most were said to have blonde hair, the precursors to the 'Aryan Master Race' that Hitler was trying to duplicate. Other stories said that they had flaming red hair. But the one constant to all of the tales is that the Nephilim were easily provoked to anger. They were also known to have huge appetites and eventually became so blood thirsty that they had to leave the Earth, or go into hiding."

"Honestly Diggs, I don't have time for fairy tales. We have a news..."

"Speaking of fairy tales, do you remember all of the Greek myths of gods and such?"

"Sure, but I don't see..."

"And do you remember hearing the urban legends of werewolves, vampires and Big Foot?"

"Son, did you hit your head or something? What are..."

Diggs made a few other keystrokes and swung his flat screen monitor around for Bryce to see. "Take a look at these."

"What in the world?"

"No Dr. Cooper... not of this world is my point.

"These are skeletal remains found in and around Greece. There is no explanation for them, nor do archeologists know from what time period they came. And there are similar findings in other parts of the world."

Bryce was instantly intrigued.

Diggs, made a few more clicks with his mouse. "These are ancient axes recovered from the Sumerian era of ancient Babylon."

"They're huge! How could anyone swing one of those?"

"That's the point doctor. No 'man' could swing them, but it was said that the Nephilim were over twenty feet tall."

"Come on Diggs, if there were creatures like that roaming the Earth, why didn't they leave their mark on history."

"Dr. Cooper, they left their mark more than you know." Diggs changed the screen. "These are some hieroglyphics from the pyramids.

"The pyramids? That looks like..."

"So let's talk about the building of those same pyramids. Despite the best efforts of archeologists, no one can give a satisfactory explanation of how ancient peoples, with simple tools, could build such great monuments. The precision alone was beyond the knowledge of those people. Even with our technology, we would be hard pressed to duplicate them.

"Just look at the physical aspects of cutting stone. And, what of moving those massive stones over great distances with people who barely discovered the wheel? It would take our generation, with all of our technology, and huge machinery, many years to build those structures. And yet, they did it with rickety wooden carts? What's harder to believe? That they accomplished all of this on their own, or that they had outside help?"

Diggs made a few more keystrokes. "These are the Abydos-Hieroglyphs depicted on the walls of the ancient temple of Abydos in Egypt."

"Holy moly! That looks like a helicopter," Bryce said taken aback. "And that looks like a plane... hold on... is that a spaceship?" he asked dumbfounded.

"And these glyphs are not just in Egypt. There are plenty on Mayan temples as well. Look here," Diggs said with a few more keystrokes and a couple of clicks with the mouse.

"What in the world?" Bryce said shell shocked.

Giving Bryce no reprieve, Diggs pressed on, "And you know how the Mayan's made human sacrifices?"

"Sure..." Bryce said, still staring at the computer screen.

"What if the Nephilim left because they were blood thirsty as I've mentioned? And what if, because those primitive people knew the Nephilim, or gods as they called them, to be blood thirsty, so they sacrificed humans, spilling their blood like chum for sharks, to draw them back?

"And look at this," Diggs said, as he made a few more clicks that pulled up a map of the world with various ancient ruins listed on it.

"The pyramids are located at the very geographic center of the world. How did the Egyptians figure that out? But wait, there's more.

"And look at these. These are ancient ruins all around the world whose builders are also questionable." Diggs pointed to the screen, which showed a topographical map of the Earth, with ancient ruins superimposed all over it.

"Okay," Bryce said.

"Now watch," Diggs made a few keystrokes and a line appeared connecting all of the sites, all over the world.

Those lines on the map formed a mirror image of the constellations in the sky.

Bryce's mouth was agape, "No way..."

Diggs now rammed his point home, "I believe... that these creatures still interact with us on a regular basis. I believe that these and others are interdimensional creatures that are not bound by our physical laws. As such, I believe that they operate in that spatial dimension right below our own in your theorized dimensional stack. And, I believe that they move with impunity in and out of human sensory range."

"I'll be a... So are you saying that these... these... angelic beings mentioned in the bible are really Nephilim?"

"No, those angelic beings are not Nephilim. Remember, Nephilim are half breeds with human DNA. I believe that that is why they need to travel around in 'space ships'. Because unlike their angelic cousins, they are somewhat bound by the same physical laws that we are. The difference is that they have the technology to overcome the dimensional barrier.

"Angels on the other hand can move back and forth with impunity without such assistance. In addition, I believe that the Nephilim are relegated to the shallower dimensions in the stack. From what I've read, angels are able to travel into the stack relatively deep."

"Hold on a second. Are you telling me that you think the stack of dimensions lead to heaven... and... and... God?" he said skeptically.

"I promised you doctor that we would keep this discussion scientific. Let's just say that whatever is over there... in the other dimensions... isn't us, and leave it at that.

"But getting back to the Nephilim and UFO's," Diggs said, spinning his monitor back toward him. "The ancient depictions of these creatures have them disappearing up into the sky. As crazy as it sounds, it seems that UFO sightings have increased over the last few years. The UFO craze has even been made popular and acceptable by Hollywood science fiction movies.

"As you know, through your own research, the investigation of UFO sightings has become a quasi-science. I've read instances where astrophysicists go into flattened down crop circles looking for evidence of electromagnetic residue that..."

"Hold on a sec. Did you say... electromagnetic residue?"

"Yes... amongst other things..."

Bryce picked up a pencil on the desk and started twirling it in his fingers. Diggs knew this to be a sign that his mentor was thinking and digesting. As crazy as the story might be, he knew that Dr. Cooper as a Dimensional Theorist didn't automatically dismiss things that were out of the ordinary. He weighed all factors and tried to postulate an answer or reason.

Bryce, now fully engaged, seriously asked Diggs, "Have you given some thought as to what the reason was behind this magnetic residue?"

"As a matter of fact, I have given it some thought. It could be something to do with the changing of electromagnetic fields that enables them to move between dimensions. The bigger the magnet, the deeper in the stack they are able to go."

Bryce went white as a ghost. He looked as if he were going to be sick.

"Are you okay Dr. Cooper? You don't look so good."

"I was afraid you were going to say that; the bigger the magnet, the deeper the penetration..."

Bryce was stunned into silence by the revelation. Slowly a look of recognition came across his face. He was holding the pencil in his hands so tightly that it snapped in half with a "crack".

"Uh-oh."

Chapter 52

<u>***North of Ashdod, Israel – Present Day***</u>

*T*he wind blew strong and steady from the north. He made a mental note, knowing that he would have to compensate when he aimed the weapon. Letting down his keffiyeh, he took another long gulp of his lukewarm water and re-covered his face to protect it from the blowing sand. Startling him, his cell phone vibrated in his pocket.

Seeing it was his Lookout, he hit the button. "Get ready! They are coming!" the Lookout said in an excited Arabic whisper.

"Allau Akbar!," the Assassin whispered.

"Allau Akbar! May you be blessed with victory," the Lookout responded and the line went dead.

The Assassin pocketed his phone. He said one last prayer and asked for success. Then he turned and pulled the heavy shoulder fired weapon out of its case. Looking down at the weapon, he turned off the safety. Steadily, careful to keep his finger away from the trigger, he got on one knee and rested the heavy weapon on his shoulder. Only then did he stick his head around the big boulder to locate his target.

With the target not yet in sight, he waited in the blowing sand.

In addition to Joe's bathroom break, the neighbors decided to sit at a popular café and have some coffee. Finally they got back on the road.

"Thanks for the pit-stop and the coffee. You're right, it's some of the best I've tasted since we've been here," Joe said.

"My pleasure Josiah. My father used to treat me to Ashdod's strong coffee when I was growing up. It is a tradition that I have maintained even after his death," Zac said.

Joe was quiet for a moment, and then cleared his throat. "I meant to ask you; was it the Mossad that contacted my nephew? And how did he take it?"

Zac looked sideways at Joe. Normally he would tactfully rebuff such a question, but the American deserved an answer. As he spoke, he smiled, "The information made it to a very influential Rabbi, who also happens to be my Rabbi."

"Ah huh"

Zac interpreted the look on Joe's face, "No Josiah, I did not plan it that way. I wasn't the one who told the Rabbi about the Package. That information came from someone else at Mossad. However, I must say if someone needed to break the news to Dr. Cooper that his secret was out, Rabbi was the best one to tell him. He is truly a servant of Hashem."

Joe looked skeptical but let the explanation stand, "And how did he take it?"

"That was the most baffling part," Zac said shaking his head. "When I asked the Rabbi the same question, he said that your nephew was expecting the call. He was not surprised, or angry. Nor did he try to deny that he had the Package. Rabbi said that he agreed right away to bring the Garments and the Urimm and Thummim to Israel without protest... very strange."

"Was this the same Rabbi from TRM who was responsible for the setting up of the Tabernacle today?"

Zac simply shook his head in the affirmative.

Now seat belted into their padded leather seats, Dr. Mora finished his dissertation loud enough to be heard over the increased sound of the jet engines.

"What I have not told you about is the FTEs," The Professor nearly shouted to be heard.

"I've heard about 'em." Bryce shouted over the engines.

"Yeah," Astrophysicist Mac chipped in nodding.

"FT... what?" Ivy asked.

Looking at the geneticist, The Professor raised his voice and said,

"An FTE, or Flux Transfer Event opens every eight minutes over the Earth. It is a literal magnetic portal, or conduit, that connects the Sun to our Magnetosphere. Through this conduit, high energy particles flow to our planet from the Sun."

Diggs and Stephanie were sitting next to each other and simply nodded. They'd heard this at Stonehenge.

Looking at Bryce and Mac, an animated Dr. Mora said, "But what you do not know is what I believe was another reason for that data being erased from the helio servers worldwide. It was to hide what has been traveling inside these... these portals."

"But we know that: High energy particles," Bryce said confused.

"Yes, Dr. Cooper. That is true. But what I observed was different... much different," The Professor shouted.

"How so?" Bryce pressed.

Dr. Mora's hands were moving wildly in explanation, "After slowing down the data feed, I have detected some anomalies."

"Anomalies?" Mac asked.

"Yes..." Mora said. "Within those portals..."

The mechanical sound of the landing gear added to the noise. Bryce pinched his nose and blew to pop his ears.

The Professor continued, "I believe that I have evidence of some sort of vehicles... ships of some kind... using those portals to come and go to and from Earth."

X who was quiet up until now, shook his head and said, "Come on doc, you're not talking about spaceships?"

The Professor bobbed his head up and down in certainty.

Mac looked to Bryce and asked, "Did he just say portals?"

Bryce was white as a ghost. "Yeah, I'm afraid he did."

The Assassin locked his eyes on his prey. He'd just abandoned the shelter of the rock outcropping. He planted his knee squarely in the sand and raised the weapon to his shoulder.

"What do you Israeli's know about horses anyway?" Joe said as the two men were lost in a macho game of bantering.

"Are you joking? Our horses are raised in the desert and much more..."

Suddenly, Joe pointed and yelled, "Hey! What's that? Look out!"

Zac saw the weapon mounted on the shoulder of the Assassin, as he kneeled by some large boulders.

The Mossad agent's training kicked in and he turned the wheel hard, and slammed on the breaks. The tires squealed in protest as the car did a power slide diagonally.

But he was too late.

The Assassin pulled the trigger.

The missile leaped out of the canister like a viper lunging for its victim. His aim was true. The Assassin knew his target would be dead in less than a second.

Chapter 53

Damascus – Present Day

"You are certain that the problem will be eliminated?" The Banker asked.

Tabak did not like answering to Westerners, no matter how much they assisted him. "I have my best man on it. He assures me that the threat will be eliminated within the hour."

"Very well then. I will let The Group know that we are able to move to Phase II," the Banker said.

"Alright. We'll talk soon," The Assyrian said and he hung up.

He shook his head. He had a nagging feeling inside, but didn't know why. *It would seem that the Banker wants to take the lead in The Group. Are we not all equals? What is going on that he should only now begin to try to assert himself?*

A knock at the door interrupted his train of thought.

Sitting down and clasping his hands together, he said, "Enter!"

The door cracked open and through it slithered Farouk.

Seeing the look on his Charge's face, he asked, "Is something wrong Your Excellency?

Somewhat defensive, and more forceful than intended, he snapped, "Nothing's wrong. Why do you ask."

Farouk knew the look. The man's eyes were as thin as slits and his face was reddened. He'd seen Tabak's infamous temper in action, but had never personally felt the full weight of it... nor did he intend to now.

"You have been working rather hard Your Excellency. Any man would be oppressed by the weight of your schedule. The new alliance needs you. I am just concerned about your wellbeing."

Sighing, he realized that his anger was misplaced. His loyal servant Farouk should not feel its brunt. "I am fine. Perhaps when time allows, I will be able to go to the seashore and relax. But for now there is much to do. Where are we with our problem from America?"

"Our man is in place and the ah... problem will be eliminated within the hour."

Tabak was resting his elbows on the desk with his hands in a diamond shape. "Are you certain of this?"

Farouk raised an eyebrow at the question. Never before did The Assyrian doubt his efficiency. "Yes Your Excellency, as sure as I can be until I hear a report back."

"As soon as you hear anything, let me know. Things are moving quickly and we do not need the distraction. Do you understand?" he asked with menacing eyes.

The hardhearted Farouk was not given to fear. But the look on Tabak's face sent an involuntary shiver down his spine and his mouth instantly dried up. "Yes..." he cleared his throat, "Yes Your Excellency. Will there be anything else?"

Turning his attention back to the work in front of him, Tabak said, "No, not right now."

"Very well Your Excellency," and his assistant turned to go.

As Farouk slithered back through the door, he had the distinct feeling that something was weighing on his Charge. Apparently the problem from America was more of an issue than he initially thought. And because it weighed on his Charge, it weighed on him like a giant lead ball.

Tel Aviv – Present Day

"Here you go," Ruby said, as she handed Eleazar a cup of tea. He was sitting on Ruby and Joe's couch watching the developing news from the west coast of North America.

"Thank you my dear," the gentle elder said as Ruby sat down next to him.

This day was full of news: All of it bad. The forty-six inch flatscreen TV had been on all day, revealing scene after scene of destruction and death. For a break, the news stations would switch back to financial or political news. It didn't matter. It seemed that the world was abruptly covered with a dark foreboding blanket of gloom.

Currently news helicopters were filming the scene from the Oregon, Washington border:

"Stan, you can see that whole seaside communities have been washed out to sea. Trees have been uprooted and completely removed. In some areas, like there (the camera panned a cliff area) the tsunami was high enough to breech even that raised cliff and wash inland. Loss of life has to be tremendous and the situation is still so fluid that emergency personnel have yet to reach many of the affected areas. The National Guard has..."

"I just don't understand how this could happen," Ruby lamented. "How could all of those people just be... gone." She used the tissue in her hand to dab her eyes.

"Does Josiah know about this?" Eleazar asked.

Ruby tilted her head in thought, "I... I don't think so. I was so upset over Martial Law that I didn't mention it to him. And he didn't say anything. So I'm guessing not."

"And how far is your family from all of this my dear? Surely Montana is safely inland from the tsunamis?"

The old man shook his head. Things spiraled out of control after Oregon. The top of the San Andreas Fault fractured all the way down to Baja California. In turn, volcanoes all along the southern portion of the Ring of Fire were triggered. Nearby faults slipped and more devastating earthquakes were wrought.

If there was any silver lining the old man thought, it was the fact that the tsunamis generated from the crumbling earth fizzled out after reaching Southern California, Japan and Hawaii. However, while the waves further south were nominal, the loss of life further due to earthquakes was still in the hundreds of thousands, perhaps millions. It was mankind's worst day on so many levels.

Eleazar's question about how far Montana was to the coast brought fresh tears to Ruby's eyes. "Well, Montana is far from the coast, so my immediate family is okay..." she started, but couldn't continue as her words evaporated into painful sobs.

The old man reached over and gave her another tissue. As he patted her hand, he said, "There, there dear, you don't have to talk about it."

After a moment, she regained control. "No, it's fine. It's just that..."

Eleazar could see she was trying to be brave.

"It's just that we have such a big family... many of them live in California, Oregon and Washington." Again she dabbed her tears. "But with all of this," tissue in hand, she motioned to the TV, "I wouldn't even know how to contact them."

Eleazar knew the feeling. Although it was on a smaller scale, when the war broke out and the Nazis began herding his extended family into cattle cars and gas chambers, he lost touch with many of them in the midst of the crisis.

His train of thought was interrupted by a breaking story from a different part of America.

"Stan, we are here in St. Louis, Missouri and are witnessing a most unusual sight. High in the sky," the reporter said as she pointed and the camera panned, "we are seeing the same kind of Orbs that were hovering over the Pacific yesterday. And it is being reported that these Orbs are present along what is considered," she looked at the notes in her hand and swallowed hard, "towns and locations along the New Madrid fault zone. The President and State Governors are telling people not to panic, but say they want to study..."

Whispering under his breath in what could only be classified as a guttural moan, Eleazar said, "It's not over."

Chapter 54

Pasadena, California – Present Day

$\mathcal{T}$ he offices of the USGS resided twenty-five miles from the coast of Southern California. Because of the numerous foothills and dense construction between the tsunami waters and their location, they were able to escape the onslaught of tidal wave after tidal wave... but just barely.

The water stopped just blocks from the offices of the United States Geological Survey. But that did not mean that the building, nor the people inside it, were unscathed. During the mega quake, the roof and several walls collapsed on the scientists and researchers inside the building. So violent was the shaking that the quake... nearly spilt California in half.

In fear for their lives from the tsunamis, civilians and many rescue workers fled to the high ground of the nearby Pasadena foothills. With the all clear given, they were only now returning to the city to dig for survivors. What they found looked like a warzone: Utter devastation.

Government help was yet to arrive. Those who'd escaped and returned now scoured through the wreckage with their bare hands - looking for survivors. Two such people were digging in the area of what was once Evan Young's office.

As the Director of the USGS, Young would be essential in the coming days to try to make sense of the trembling Earth. They hurried, hoping to find the missing Young alive. One of the men muscled a large piece of caved in ceiling from an area; he saw a foot. He called out for help and a large group of survivors ran to the rubble heap. Slowly they strained and grunted and were able to tilt up a large jagged piece of the concrete that covered a body.

Dr. Evan Young's crushed and lifeless remains were revealed. Still in his hand was a cell phone. The rescuers figured that he was trying to sound off a warning with his last breath.

In tears and distraught, the workers covered the body with a coat. What would they do now when the head of the USGS was not there to guide them through the terrible days that were sure to come?

Understandably the workers never looked at the number on the cell phone's screen. If they had, they would have seen that it was a final warning call of impending disaster to the USGS's second in charge: Dr. Xavier Black.

X never got the call.

LHC, Topside, Geneva – Present Day

Abbot was seated at his old desk, in his favorite position - Leaning back in his big overstuffed desk chair with his huge feet on the corner of the desk. As was his habit, he rubbed the outside of his hand, next to his pinky, where the extra sixth digit was removed as a child.

The phone was nestled between his unusually large oblong head and his shoulder. "Are you confident that the problem is out of the way in Israel?"

The Banker refrained from blurting out an expletive to the Scot in response. He always considered him, although bright compared to the humans, genetically challenged in comparison to himself and younger Others – and therefore obsolete. No more were The Others large, slow witted and cumbersome. Rather, those like him were designed to fit into human society. He decided to take the high road and not respond to the big man's ignorant insolence.

"Of course my large friend," he cooed, "I believe that we are ready for the next step. This is already progressing faster than we'd hoped."

Abbot strangled the phone in his hand, imagining it was the Banker's neck. He hated to be placated, especially by the snooty Banker. But as in any good chess match, one must counter move.

Thus, his response was equally patronizing, "Of course. You always do know best."

That got to the Banker, "Of course I do!" he snapped, "The humans think that they are in control. They will be so surprised as the Plan unfolds. I want to see their faces when they find out that I'm not one of them."

Abbot couldn't help but smile at the uppity one's outburst. But back to business: "Should we be concerned that things within the Earth are deteriorating faster than anticipated?"

"Of course not. You need not concern yourself with the trivial. The more that suffer and die, the better. The Earth changes will just usher in the endgame that much sooner. And how is the restart coming?"

"On schedule. The modifications are relatively minor compared to what we had the humans do. We'll be ready."

"When will you make the trip to Tehran?" Abbot asked.

"I'm leaving straight away. The Assyrian will fly out shortly. Let's move to Phase Two."

"Alright, I'll do my part. A simple phone call will get the deed done."

"War it is," The Banker said with amusement.

Through a devious smile, Abbot agreed, "War it is."

Jerusalem, Israel – Present Day

The Rabbi reached into his breast pocket to retrieve his antique pocket watch and checked the time. He could hardly contain the anticipation he felt inside. He breathed in deeply, taking in the sweet smell of the Temple Mount and surrounding Israel. He placed the watch back in his vest pouch and looked up to observe all that had been accomplished thus far.

He was not a Kohanim and thus could not participate in the priestly ceremonies. However, he took great satisfaction in knowing that his hand was significant in the restoration of the

Tabernacle and Ark.

He surveyed the land in the distance. Although he could not see them, but imagined Israel's enemies lining up in formation, ready to invade. He looked back to the Tabernacle, a cloth tent, rippling in a strong wind from the north. They needed answers. They needed help. And very soon, they would have in their possession the Urimm and Thummim so that the High Priest could approach the Ark and ask of Hashem what they should do.

Under his breath, he whispered, "Hurry Bryce Cooper."

Geneva – Four Years Earlier

Sounding very much like a lawyer cross-examining a witness, Bryce said, "The last time we spoke, you said that the High Priest had to be barefoot in the Temple, is that right?"

"Yes, the temple was considered Holy Ground, so as a sign of respect, they were barefoot."

"And briefly, I understand that the Ark of the Covenant had the... Presence? And that it, the Presence, came right down from the sky, through the roof of the Temple and into the Ark, is that right? And that this so called presence was in the form of a... ah..." Bryce looked down consulting his notes, "was in the form of a pillar of fire, but it never burned up anything?"

"Yes, right on both counts. My... you have done your homework. What's this all about?"

Bryce continued, "And the clothing of the High Priest was fabricated using pure gold and cloth. As you know, that gold in their outfit was made from sheets of pure gold and then cut into fine wire, and used as thread. In other words, the gold thread through these religious Garments was an electrical conductor, placed on the bodies of men who were barefoot and grounded!"

Eleazar shrugged his shoulders as if to say, "so?"

"I submit to you... that that conduction, combined with the High Priest's grounding, made them..." Bryce paused for effect,

"...walking lightning rods! Since electricity wasn't invented yet, they would naturally attribute electrical conduction to something religious. They didn't have knowledge to do otherwise!"

"And yet," Eleazar said with a knowing smile on his face, "how would they know to become... lightning rods without Adonai's omniscient, all knowing direction?"

"My, my Bryce, you certainly have done your studying," said the fatherly old gentleman.

Now it was Eleazar's turn to point out the obvious. "It certainly sounds like you have got your facts straight. But none of what you've said changes anything about how Adonai spoke to His people. The fact remains that He, in His infinite wisdom, found a way, before the invention of electricity or... or... har... harrrmonnics, to communicate. I don't see why you find any of this important for anything other than spiritual truth?"

"Believe me when I tell you, this... these factoids of modern science are important old friend. I'll elaborate in a moment, but is there anything else of significance to the Garments. I mean... ah... other than regular cloth material?"

"Of course there were two of the most important items, the Urimm and Thummim. They were placed in the pockets of the breastplate. The historical description of these items is very limited. But the translations for the words come from the old Hebrew roots for lights or perfection."

"Huh... I hadn't heard of those... What were these Urimm and Thummim used for exactly?"

The old jeweler smiled big and said, "Historically, it was through these two items that the priests guided the people about critical decisions, such as going to war or not. In other words, that's what they used to talk to Adonai with."

"What were they made of?"

"That is the ah... 'million dollar question' as you Americans say. Some historians say that they were colored stones that lit up with Adonai's answers. Some say that they were letters on parchment scripts that illuminated, giving Adonai's answers.

"But the fact is, no one really knows. They were lost in the Babylonian destruction of Solomon's Temple, never to be seen again. They didn't even have them after the second temple was constructed. Thus, they had not been utilized since Solomon's Temple," he shrugged.

Chapter 55

$\mathcal{T}$he car skidded to a stop in a diagonal position about twenty-five feet from The Assassin. Almost before the vehicle's forward momentum halted, Joe opened the door and crouched behind it. Then, he watched as the scene developed in slow motion.

Immediately both men noted that the Assassin was not aiming the rocket at them. He was pointing it at something in the air. Because the shooter was so focused on his target, he didn't even see them. This was their chance.

They saw the rocket jump out of the tube spitting fire out of the end with a loud swoosh. Then they saw the Assassin pump his arm and yell, "Allau Akbar!"

Zac also jumped out and pulled his Jericho 941 Baby Eagle from its holster. He rounded his door and came to a shooter's kneeling position at the front driver's side fender. Using his only good arm, he leveled his gun in the direction of the Assassin. The man was still by the boulder and looking up.

He was just about to pull the trigger when automatic fire erupted from somewhere behind him. He could feel the car shake as the "tink, tink, tink" of bullets strafed the length of the Mazda, from back to front.

Only inches from him, the window of the still opened driver's side door exploded as glass and ricocheting metal buzzed by his ear.

Without a second thought, like a tumbling gymnast in the Olympics, he launched himself over the hood of the car to its opposite side just in time to hear bullets spray the fender he was just leaning on.

Now Zac was on the same side as Joe who was now on his butt, well behind his open door and guarded by the body of the Mazda. The inside of his open door, where he was crouched a moment ago, and the seat where he'd been sitting were riddled with bullets. Had Joe still occupied the space, he surely would have been dead.

Zac felt precipitously naked. In front of him was someone shooting with an automatic weapon. But his back was exposed to the other terrorist who just shot a rocket and could be armed with a gun.

He had only one pistol... and nowhere to go.

From the moment the car stopped rolling; Joe fixed his sights on the Assassin. He was still looking at him when he heard machine gun fire. At the sound of the car being slammed with slugs, he fell back and scooted on his butt, just as he saw Zac acrobatically roll over the hood to his side of the car. Instantly the front passenger seat was chewed up by bullets as was the door where he'd just been. Then the passenger window shattered spraying him with glass.

He looked at the Israeli, now a few feet in front of him. His focus was in the direction of the machine gun fire. And he was the only one with a gun.

Without a weapon, he couldn't do anything about the person shooting on the other side of the car. But he wasn't going to just sit here and die. He got back in a crouch and put a bead on the Assassin.

Joe saw the Assassin pump his fist and heard what he thought was an explosion in the sky. But he didn't look up.

Instead, he exploded from his crouch in a dead run like a track star from the blocks of a race. Paying no mind to the machine gun fire, he headed straight for the Assassin.

The shooter firing the machine gun was the Lookout who called the Assassin on the phone.

He was also hidden by some rocks, up the road more than a hundred yards from where the Mazda stopped. As he watched the sky, he heard the car's squealing tires. He came around from his hiding place just in time to see the car halt and the doors begin to open.

The Lookout was a teenager, but he was also the fastest of all of his friends. Seeing the scene unfold, he knew he had to do something. So he grabbed his AK-47 and set out in the fastest run of his life in the direction of the Assassin.

He crossed the hundred yards in almost nine seconds flat. But even before he was in range, he began to fire wildly at the man closet to him on his side of the car.

The Assassin's enjoyment over his success was short lived. Just as the rocket hit the starboard wing engine of the plane, he heard machine gun fire from behind him.

Instinctively he dropped the empty rocket canister and reached for his weapon.

Turning around, he saw a blur of motion. Someone

had taken a running jump with his foot aimed right for the Assassin's head. He ducked just in time.

Zac was still looking south and could see the Lookout, with automatic weapon in hand, running in his direction at full speed.

But because he was running, his shots were bouncing all over the place wildly... and he was without cover.

Very stupid my friend, Zac thought.

Zac blew out a long breath to steady his good hand. And he willed himself to wait.

The Assassin ducked under the blur's foot just in time.

The man nearly flew over him, but his other knee caught the Assassin on the shoulder. It knocked him off balance and he dropped his rifle.

Judging the maximum range for his pistol, Zac figured he needed the attacker to come closer by another ten yards.

The attacker closed the distance quickly and he continued to fire wildly as he ran.

Unexpectedly the Lookout's weapon made a "click, click, click" sound. The teenager blurted out an expletive. He realized that in his haste, his finger had stayed on the trigger the whole time he ran. He'd emptied the entire magazine.

He slowed his stride, bouncing his eyes from the rifle to the car. He had taped two magazines together at opposite ends. Continuing to run and focused on the AK-

47, he ripped the magazine out, flipped it over and jammed the other one in. Then he pulled back the operating rod to load a round into the chamber.

A brief sense of pride came over him since he was able to reload so quickly and still run. But what he would never realize... is that as he reloaded, he closed the gap between him and the car by ten yards.

Zac saw the attacker run out of ammo. He saw him curse and yank the clip out. He saw him flip the clip around and jam it back into the rifle. And he saw him pull back on the operating rod and raise his weapon to continue firing.

But Zac got his ten yards.

With the steady hand of a marksman, the Mossad agent gently squeezed the trigger. The 9mm spit once... then twice - A precise double tap.

Joe landed on his feet and was now face to face with the Assassin.

Recovering quickly, the Assassin pulled a huge curved knife from his waist sheath.

The two men looked at each other. And Joe started to circle him, counter clockwise, away from his knife welding right hand.

One of Zac's bullets hit the Lookout in the eye and the other in the forehead.

The Lookout's head snapped back as it exploded in a puff of red. Immediately his momentum stopped and he fell lifeless, face first to the asphalt.

Remembering he was not alone, Zac spun around just in time to see The Assassin lunge at Joe with a knife.

He raised his pistol. But the men were too close in their dance of death. He couldn't risk hitting Joe.

Chapter 56

Jackson, Mississippi – Present Day

$\mathcal{P}$ ristine... that was the only way to describe the beautiful Mississippi afternoon. It was so beautiful that Doug and Lisa nearly forgot that the country was in the middle of the worst constitutional crises in its history.

Although originally a native of Alabama, Doug's last duty station before he retired from the Air Force was in Florida. But it didn't really matter. Pensacola, where they now lived, was a short drive to his home town and other Southern points in between.

The Hemphills had family all over the South. Now that he retired, they visited them often. They were on one such road trip down in Jackson, Mississippi when the President declared Martial Law. That's when their problems began.

Martial Law meant curfews. They couldn't drive at night. The "Bank Holiday" also caused most businesses to close: Including gas stations. So they couldn't buy gas to get home anyway. They were stuck.

Fortunately, their relatives were happy to put them up for a few more days. But the upheaval to their country and their lives put Lisa in a recognizable funk. With the devastation out West and an uncertain future, depression swept over her like dark clouds moving in on a sunny day.

Watching the change, Doug felt helpless for his wife. Then, in a spontaneous show of support for humanity, an announcement came that promised to be the one bright spot in the midst of all the gloom.

One of Lisa's favorite bands, Ground Zero out of Jackson, Mississippi announced that they would hold a charity concert for disaster victims out West. Admission to the concert was free, but they planned to take donations throughout the evening. Gold and silver items were preferred, but even the now defunct Dollar would be accepted and exchanged for new currency later.

Instantly Lisa's attitude improved. The show would be at the fairgrounds in the Jackson Mississippi Coliseum. Her clouds of depression seemed to move away. That afternoon, the happy couple headed for the concert.

Mississippi National Guard was out in force. Considering the riots, violence and lootings throughout the rest of the country, Doug was grateful for the additional policing.

Although it was summer, the climate was unusually mild for Mississippi. The air had yet to turn to the humid soup that the area was known for this time of year. And the temperature was uncharacteristically cool. Doug's window was down as he traversed through mid-town traffic. Neither one of them spoke; both were lost in their own thoughts.

The blaring local radio station made around-the-clock announcements about the charity concert that afternoon. They also continually encouraged the populace to attend by playing various selections from Ground Zero's numerous hits. But at the moment, the playlist was paused as a reporter brought Jacksonville up to speed on the unending string of bad news:

> "... and in related news, small earthquake swarms have been felt all along the New Madrid fault line. These tremors, no bigger than 3.2 on the Richter Scale, have been noted as far north as Chicago, Illinois, as far east as Nashville, Tennessee, west as Little Rock, Arkansas and even in our southern metropolis of Jacksonville.
>
> However, geologists at the USGS local office have stated that it's not unusual for a fault to let off stress with small tremors. When we contacted them, we were told that another large trembler like the 1811-1812 along the New Madrid Fault is not anticipated anytime soon."

Lisa reached over and turned down the radio. Doug saw the fear on her face.

"The New Madrid what?" she asked with concern. "I've never heard of earthquakes in the South before?"

Doug tried a reassuring smile as he glanced at his wife. "I wouldn't worry about it babe," he soothed in his southern drawl. "That was a long time ago."

Lisa shuttered. Images from television of the horrible scenes in California flashed through her mind. "Have you heard about earthquakes down here?"

"The New Madrid earthquakes?" he asked.

"Yeah"

"Only that it was a long time ago. The stuff of folklore really. But I seem to recall that one of those quakes made Reelfoot Lake. In... Tennessee... I think."

Lisa scrunched up her face, "Your... kidding right? Earthquakes don't make lakes."

"No really... true story," he raised his right hand.

The fairgrounds were in sight. The Mississippi Coliseum rested in the center of the fairgrounds of the Gulf Coast community. Overlooking the town, it was set on top of a hill, easily the highest point of the city.

To himself, Doug thought: *And that fault line stretches all the way down here...*

But he didn't want to share the thought with his wife. Tender hearted Lisa cried a lot of tears over the last couple of days. While he would freely admit that he was the anxious one, Lisa was the one that empathized with people.

Since their daughter Sarah grew up, married and moved out, they spent a lot more time together. Both were in their fifties and considered themselves still young. They may be grandparents, but their carefree retirement felt good... at least it did.

Seeing the look on his face, she asked, "What-a-ya thinkin? Come on. Out with it!" she said, playfully punching his arm.

"Nothin," he quipped.

But she knew better, "Come on, really. I know this isn't

California."

"Well..." he said warily, "I was thinking that that fault line runs down through here."

With big eyes, she asked, "Here?"

Nodding his head slowly, "Yeah, I think so. As a matter of fact," he pointed to the Coliseum at the top of the hill, "If I'm not mistaken, that there's no ordinary hill."

They were the first car stopped at an intersection by a red light. A long line of cars heading into the fairgrounds for the concert was beginning to grow.

"Whad-a-ya mean?" she asked with concern.

He patted her hand. He could see the look in her eye. But he couldn't stop now; she would press him until he told her what he was thinking. "It's okay. I was just goin to say that it's an extinct volcano."

She looked at him sideways and smiled, "Come on... a volcano? Get outa here."

Doug chuckled, "I kid you not. Been dormant thousands... heck, maybe millions of years. It's just ironic."

"Ironic?"

"Yeah, ironic," he said, "Jackson is the only city in America to be built on a volcano," he shook his head.

"Why's that ironic?"

He smiled at her, "You don't see the humor? Ten-thousand people will be listening to Ground Zero on the top of a volcano. Crazy huh?"

She smiled big and nodded, "That is ironic."

The light turned green. But before the traffic could move, the Earth jolted violently. Neither Doug nor Lisa understood what was going on.

They saw that the cars on all sides of them were bouncing up and down. Doug looked over at his wide eyed wife, "Earthquake!" she screamed.

Green light or not, they stayed put. Doug stomped down hard on the brake trying to keep them from moving. But the effort was useless. The car's bouncing motion caused it to skid from side to side, banging into the other cars around them.

In a panic, a few cars in the other lanes tried to make it across the intersection. They were rewarded by being slammed into by other foolish drivers.

Power poles, street lights and stop lights began to twist and topple. Huge fissures and cracks opened in the asphalt. Buildings were demolished. The car next to them was swallowed by a giant hole that opened up in the road.

Holding on as best they could, Lisa shrieked loudly. Doug looked around helplessly trying to figure out what to do.

The shaking lasted for four minutes straight. Then, as quickly as it started, it stopped. Doug was sure that the earthquake was at least an 8.0 or more. And the evidence was the devastation around them.

His windshield was cracked from flying debris. As he looked through it, he saw cars overturned in the intersection. Next to them, the whole lane collapsed into a sinkhole – The cars were gone.

Hardly a building was left standing; the ones that did, looked like they were about to collapse. People were crying and screaming all around them. Car alarms were going off all over. The air was filled with a cloud of dust so thick that it reminded him of the scene from New York City on 9/11.

He tried to console his hysterical wife, "Shhh... it's over. It's over. We're safe. We'll be..."

Suddenly, as he was in midsentence, a high piercing noise blasted all around them. It sounded like an amplified train whistle.

Glass that hadn't been broken by the earthquake now exploded from the high pitched tone. They both immediately reached for their ears to cover them. Doug could feel the fullness of the whistle inside his chest and he felt his body vibrate.

Then, the noise stopped. It was dead quiet. No one said anything. They were all stunned into silence.

After a moment, Doug reached for the door handle to let himself out. Lisa grabbed his arm, "No!" she said fearfully.

He looked at her, "Shhhh... it's alright. I'm not going anywhere. I'll be right here."

Again he tried the door handle, but the door was stuck. Doug put his shoulder into it: Nothing, one more time, still nothing. Then one final time, with all his might, he threw himself sideways into the door. It flew open with a groan of protest. He stumbled out.

What he saw was something akin to a Hollywood disaster movie. There was death and carnage everywhere. And worse, they were stuck. All the roads were blocked. The only way out would be on foot.

His mind switched to the best routes to take. Suddenly a huge rumble could be felt beneath his feet and a visible wave rolled under him, coming from the direction of the Coliseum. And then it stopped.

Wide eyed he looked to the hill. Without warning - the Coliseum exploded as the hillside, with thousands of happy concert goers, was instantly vaporized.

In its place spewed thousands of tons of rocks and sprays of lava. A massive amount of earth was being launched hundreds of feet in the air in an awesome display of Mother Nature's power.

Doug stood mesmerized by the scene, unable to look away. As he watched, orange and red molten lava began to pour down the sides of the hill.

Doug snapped out of it and bent down to look at his wife, "We've got to get out of here!"

Lisa started to move, but then a secondary explosion, exponentially bigger than the first, blew up what remained of the hill. Right behind the explosion, a wall of pyroclastic flow raced toward the couple at over seven-hundred miles per hour.

With no time to react, Doug reached for Lisa's hand.

The Jackson, Mississippi's volcano was dormant no more.

Chapter 57

*J*oe knew that the strike was coming. The years of trained Aikido muscle memory came back in a flood and he instantly calculated his counter strike.

The first slash was aimed at his throat and he jumped back just in time. The next was a wild arc of the blade that almost connected with his chest. That slash was dangerously close. He looked down to see a neat horizontal line cut through his white linen shirt, but no blood. The Assassin sneered at him.

Too close, Joe thought, *time to end this.*

At the attacker's next lunge, Joe moved with lightning speed. He grabbed the wrist of the Assassin's knife hand as it went by. Holding onto it with a mighty grip, he bent it in awkwardly. Using all of his weight, he took two huge steps forward, closing the distance between them and bumping into the attacker while driving him back.

At the same time, he slammed the underneath edge of his forearm on top of the attacker's forearm in a leverage move. Then, in one fluid motion, using all of his strength, he swept his left leg under and through the attacker's feet.

What happened next was just physics.

The Assassin now had no legs to support him. His body was going one way, and his wrist was going the other, while his arm was going another. With a loud "crack!" the Assassin's wrist and elbow snapped in unison. He immediately yelped and dropped the knife.

Instinctively, Joe went to finish him.

Just as soon as the Assassin hit the ground, Joe stomped on the prone man's chest with his foot and held him down. He then pulled his already broken arm, straight and twisted. The Aikido third degree black belt was rewarded with a "pop!" as the Assassin's arm dislocated.

Lastly, Joe raised his leg straight out without bending his knee, and brought his heal down in a scissor kick on the man's groin.

Instantly the Assassin curled up in a ball of agony.

Joe kicked the knife away and took two steps back, as he stood in a ready stance.

The broken Assassin was withering and crying in pain – he was done.

Zac saw the whole confrontation. It took less than ten seconds for the American senior to destroy the attacker. Unconsciously he rubbed his bruised chin as he slowly approached the two men with his gun drawn.

The fog of conflict dissipated and Joe became aware that the Israeli was standing next to him. He dropped his guard.

With appreciation that only a professional could give, Zac shook his head and said, "I have never seen a man your age move so fast! And..." he looked down at the writhing man without sympathy. Then he looked back at Joe, "...disarm an assailant so efficiently." He added with a smile, "And here I thought you were just an old retired American Cowboy."

Joe blew out a tired breath as the adrenaline of the moment bled off. He wiped his sweaty forehead with his sleeve, then leveled a narrow gaze on the Israeli, "Son, who you calling ol..."

Just then they heard a huge rumble and crash.

Both men lifted their eyes just in time to see a plane crash in shallow water up the coast.

North of Ashdod, Israel – A Few Moments Earlier

"Folks, we are next in line to land. If you've not already done so, please secure the cabin and... What the?! Mayday! Mayday! Mayday! This is Charlie Delta 479... we've just been painted and fired upon..."

Bryce was sitting on the left side of the plane with his seat back against the cabin wall. As if in slow motion, through the cabin windows, he saw a huge explosion and fireball. Instantly the right wing was shredded and ripped off.

At the same time, shrap metal from the torn wing sliced through the fuselage opposite him, on the right side of the cabin. It punched a large jagged hole through the bulkhead, just behind Xavier's seat. The cabin immediately filled with smoke and high pitched alarms screamed danger. Yellow oxygen masks dropped from the cabin's ceiling, adding to the surreal scene.

Xavier was buckled in a seat across from and facing Bryce. The Montanan saw the geophysicist's eyes grow wide in surprise. Because he was buckled in, he couldn't turn around to see the huge hole behind him. But X knew that the sudden thunderous roar and rushing air to his rear was bad news.

Bryce felt like he was watching a movie that was being played slowly in front of him. First, X's seat began to wobble. Then it began to twist and turn. Finally, as if a giant hand reached inside the plane and grabbed it, the seat twisted a full one-hundred and eighty degrees and was suddenly ripped from its mooring off the cabin floor.

Helplessly the physicist saw Xavier's seat tilt back. Instinctively Bryce reached for him from his own seat belted position. But it was no use. With a curious look of anger rather than fear, X was sucked through the plane's gaping hole, seat and all.

Ivy screamed and also reached from her perpendicular seat, as her husband of seven years fell more than a thousand feet to a sure death in the ocean below.

To compensate for the loss of the starboard engine, the Gulfstream IV's remaining engine instantly roared with an ear piercing whine. The plane jerked in the direction of the remaining engine in the beginnings of a death spiral.

As Bryce felt the plane violently yank to one side, his mind again went to a distant memory.

Across the Dimensional Divide – Four Years Earlier

Bryce asked Gabe, "Am I dead? Is this what being dead is like?"

For the first time he could ever remember, Gabe smiled. He replied, "No... you are not dead. You were snatched away a moment before the explosion. You are simply away."

"What do you mean away?" Bryce asked.

Gabe said in a reassuring tone, "You are our guest. You are visiting. With the help of the Garments, the Urimm and Thummim, and your LHC, you were snatched away just before the explosion.

"Because you have not come to us in the usual way, it will be necessary to place you back in your proper spatial dimension; out of harm's way of course."

"If I'm not... not dead... what is this place?" Bryce asked with confusion registering on his face.

Gabe said, "This is what has been called 'the third heaven'. To put it in terms that you will understand," he said with a gentle wave of his arms, "this is what you might call the tenth or eleventh spatial dimension.

"The Fallen are able to move freely in," he pointed off in the distance, "the fifth and sixth spatial dimensions. That is how they have confused and deceived mankind."

"The Fallen?" Bryce asked. "You mean... the Abbot creature... the ah... Nephilim?"

"You are partially correct," Gabe said. "The Nephilim are the offspring of our fallen brothers. Your Abbot was a descendent of them.

"The Nephilim have technology that readily enables them to move freely between those dimensions. Humans have seen their technology in the skies as alien space ships and UFOs. You have also seen the work of their hands in some of the ancient monuments that are on Earth, whose origin is not yet satisfactorily explained."

"And what of your... your fallen brothers?" Bryce asked.

"They are able to move freely between those allotted dimensions without the help of technology. Your physical laws, and the fourth-temporal dimension of time, do not bind them. They are only bound to the physical laws of the sixth dimension, and thus cannot penetrate deeper into the other dimensions like here."

North of Ashdod, Israel – A Few Moments Earlier

Like a crack of lightning, he swooped in on the side of the aircraft's gaping wound. He reached the right side broken wing just in time to see one scientist sucked through the hole, and fall a thousand feet to the water below.

Grasping the remaining part of the damaged right wing, he clamped down with hands like vice grips. Furiously he flapped his massive white wings, replacing the engine and wing that was blown away. But the plane acted like an uncooperative stubborn and wounded whale. He desperately fought to keep it from corkscrewing in a cartwheel of death.

Finally, after what seemed to be an eternity, but was only fractions of a second, he righted the airship, and pointed it into a gradual decline for controlled crash. Nearing the water, he flapped his wings even harder, pushing the plane in the opposite direction to slow its momentum. Still holding on, he let it kiss the ocean in a spray of sea foam and smoke.

To an observer on the ground, the crash would have looked like little more than a controlled landing without the gear down.

As the aircraft hit the waist deep water, a loud thud was heard and the crumpling of sheet metal as its underbelly gave way. The splashdown caused the plane to slide fifty yards, pushing a huge wake of displaced ocean along the way. With the tail section on fire, it finally screeched to a smoking stop in the shallow water, just a few feet from shore.

When the plane stopped moving, the huge white being took a few steps back, with his hands on his hips. He surveyed the wreckage and saw that the tail section was on fire. The emergency door was already popped open and out. He was sure that the rubber emergency slide would soon follow. While the remaining passengers would be scared and shaken, most of them would live. It could have been much worse.

He looked at the sand and road a few hundred feet away from where the plane sat. Already a car was nearing the scene. Although the crash was spectacular, no one saw his frantic, invisible efforts.

Then he disappeared.

Chapter 58

North of Ashdod, Israel – Present Day

$\mathcal{J}$oe and Zac exchanged an urgent look that didn't require speech. In unison, their eyes shot down to the still howling terrorist that just brought down a plane.

"GO!" Zac said, "I'll deal with this!"

That's all the encouragement Joe needed. He nodded and sprinted to the still running car.

Looking at the Mazda as he ran up to it, he thought it looked like Swiss cheese. Bullet holes were riddled down its side and most of the windows were shot out.

Shaking his head, he hopped in and gunned the engine, letting forward momentum close both open doors.

North of Ashdod, Israel – A Few Moments Earlier

As the plane jerked to a stop, smoke and fire were already filling the cabin. Bryce was instantly out of his seat and ran over to a middle left side cabin window, above the remaining wing, that doubled as an emergency exit. He popped it out.

Cupping his hands by his mouth, he yelled, "Everybody okay?!"

To his brief relief he heard a chorus of groans and cries to the affirmative.

"Come on! Everybody up and out!"

The fog of smoke blurred his vision, but he could hear seatbelts unhooking in the scramble. Ocular ability in the burning plane had already greatly diminished. He felt his way to each person, pointing them to the door. Then he came to The Professor.

"Daddy!!! Nooooo!" Stephanie screamed standing over her father. "Are you okay? Say something!"

Even through the smoke's haze, Bryce could see that a long piece of metal had impaled Dr. Alvaro Mora. He guessed that it was probably a good two and a half feet and was sticking through a bloody hole in his stomach. Although conscious, he was pale, dazed and nonresponsive.

Flames were flooding into the plane from the hole on the side. Likewise fire was creeping up from the tail section.

Looking over his shoulder, at the advancing flames, Bryce said, "Come on! We have to move him!"

"But..." Stephanie protested.

"NOW!" Bryce yelled.

He undid Dr. Mora's seatbelt and tried to stand him up. As Cooper pulled on his shoulders, the astronomer cried out in pain and didn't budge.

Bryce took his hand and ran it down between The Professor's back and the seat. The physicist quickly realized that the rod went all the way through his body and literally pinned him to his seat.

He didn't want to take out the rod all the way. Bryce was afraid that Alvaro would bleed to death from the gaping wound. Instead he yelled to Stephanie, "Hold him down!"

"What?! Noooo I can't!"

"HOLD HIM DOWN NOW OR HE'S GONNA DIE!" Bryce yelled as he again checked his back for the flames – They were spreading in their direction.

"Like this!" he said, as he pushed Mora's shoulders back to the seat. The Professor again cried out in pain.

Stephanie looked at Bryce, then the flames, then her father, "I'm sorry Papa!" she said. She shoved his shoulders all the way back into the seat as hard as she could and held him there.

Alvaro writhed in pain, crying and calling "Jesus!"

Bryce put his foot on the arm of the seat for leverage. He grasped the rod firmly with both hands, quickly rolled it back and forth while pulling on it - like he was unscrewing it. He continued to do it while Alvaro cried out. Finally, after he backed it out about two inches, he stopped.

He told Stephanie to let go. Instantly The Professor slumped forward – he was free.

"Let's get him on his feet!" he yelled.

Each of them lifted him by his arms gently. "Exit! Hurry!" Bryce said, as the flames began to burn the ceiling a few feet from them.

They dragged The Professor to the window. Because of the long metal pole sticking out of him, they had to be careful. They handed him through the narrow window, head first, to Mac who was standing on the remaining wing. As the top part of his body went through, Mac had to bend it up to get the rod through and the rest of his body. Dr. Mora screamed in agony.

Everyone else was already off the plane. He looked at Stephanie, "You next!"

She straddled the window and then was out.

Looking back to where they were just standing, Bryce saw flames engulfing the seats. He looked around. He knew the plane was about to explode.

He turned back around and saw Stephanie climbing off the wing. Mac was already wading through the waist deep water, carrying the Professor around the plane to dry land. Bryce took one last survey of the burning cabin – And then he remembered.

"Come on Dr. Cooper! Hurry! It's going to explode!" Diggs called.

But rather than coming through the emergency exit window, Bryce disappeared from view.

He hurried down the aisle toward the front of the plane.

The front nose had buckled and there was now a distinctive bump on the floor, with the nose of the plane angled awkwardly down.

When he got to the forward storage closet he looked back. The seat he was sitting in was now fully engulfed in flames. Acidic smoke bellowed from the tail section.

He tried the latch on the storage closet – stuck! Using both hands, he pulled back on it with all of his might. It still didn't budge. He looked toward the flames. They now covered the exit hatch... his escape route.

He looked back at the storage door and beat on it with his fists – Nothing.

"I'M NOT DYING HERE! NOT TODAY! NOT THIS WAY! JESUS!!!"

He stepped back and with all of his strength, he gave the door a forward kick using the bottom of his foot.

It crumpled.

He pulled the ruined door from its hinges and threw it in the aisle behind him.

There was the package, just where he left it. He grabbed it.

The smoke gagged and chocked him. It was so thick, he couldn't breathe anymore. He pulled his shirt over his mouth. It was nearly pitch black and he began to lose his sense of direction.

The flames were now racing toward him. He couldn't go back toward the hatch. Fire was all around it. He had to get out now!

He looked forward. In a split second decision, he ran to the cockpit door.

Bursting through it just in time, he slammed it with the flames licking at his heels.

As he turned around quickly, his head smashed into the low ceiling. The blow made him even dizzier and the world spun. He wagged his head hard trying to clear it.

He looked down and saw that the co-pilot was bloodied and still sitting in his seat. His eyes were open in death, but Bryce checked his pulse anyway. He was gone.

The side window on the pilot side, like the rest of the nose, was askew and unsealed. It was tight, but there was no other way out. He felt the door behind him. It burned his hand and he shook it off.

He climbed in the pilot seat. Using the dead co-pilot for leverage against his back, he kicked up with both feet against the side window. One... two... three... with every kick, the window loosened until finally after about the sixth kick, it popped out completely.

The cockpit was now filling with smoke. "That'll have to do! Time to go!"

Cooper, crouched on the pilot's seat, stretched out his arms and with the Package in hand, lunged himself head first through the opening.

Chapter 59

LHC, Topside, Geneva – Present Day

"Noo (Now)," the voice said in a thick Scottish brogue. "Dae ye kin exactly whit ye ur supposed tae dae? (Do you understand exactly what you are supposed to do?)" and then he added, "Ah woods hate tae see whit woods happen tae yer fowk if ye failed, (I would hate to see what would happen to your family if you failed)."

Ahmed shivered involuntarily. They'd been over it many times. What he was supposed to do and the consequences for not being successful. And it was true; while he found it immensely difficult to understand the Scot's accent, he understood a threat.

He was doing this for his family. His mother had too many mouths to feed. His father was gone, killed by the army in the uprisings against the King. He was the oldest and therefore responsible. He knew that it was probably a suicide mission. But nonetheless, it had to be done.

"Yes... I understand and... I will not fail," he said solemnly.

"There... that's a guid laddie. Ah shaa be waitin' fur bark oan yer success. min', th' present main be darlivred tonecht. onie questions? (There... that's a good lad. I shall be waiting for news of your success. Remember, the Present must be delivered tonight. Any questions?)"

There were tons of questions. Like why the Present had to be delivered at all? There was so much hope and promise with the Assyrian and the new Islamic Coalition. But to ask such a question, especially to a man like this, might get his family killed anyway.

"No... no questions. But how will I know if my mother got the money?"

He could hear the smile in the Scot's voice. "Ay coorse laddie. we hae awreddy paid 'er. wa don't ye caa 'er tae fin' it? (Of course lad. We have already paid her. Why don't you call her to find out?)"

"You've already paid her?" Ahmed asked with amazement. "But... but you said I had to do this thing first?"

"Ah thooght it micht gie ye more... incentife. yoo're nae thinkin' ay backin' it an' runnin' awa' wi' uir bunsens ur ye? (I thought it might give you more... incentive. You're not thinking about backing out and running away with our money are you?)"

Again, chills. "No! No! I will not run. I will deliver the Present tonight..."

"Guid laddie, (Good lad)," the voice cooed. "Why don't ye caa yer maw? I'm sure she woods loch tae hear frae 'er hero son. (Why don't you call your mother? I'm sure she would like to hear from her hero son.)"

"Yes, yes I will. And you will hear news. I swear!"

"Fine... we'll bide tae hear fur bark. (Fine... we'll wait to hear for news,)" the voice said in finality. Then the line went dead.

He hoped forgiveness would find him for what he was about to do. But he needed to take care of his family. Surely, the Koran spoke of this.

Looking into the late afternoon sky, he thought about the person he would have to help him. His friend was also first born of a very large family with no father. He was sure he would help.

But first, he needed to call his mother.

Tonight would come only too soon.

North of Ashdod, Israel – Present Day

The Mazda groaned in protest as Joe floored the accelerator of the battered car. As he sped off in the direction of the downed aircraft, the backend fishtailed wildly from shot out tires.

His adrenaline abated after his tussle with the Assassin, but was once again spiking as he neared the crash. Across the sand he could just make out what looked like a wounded whale billowing smoke in shallow water. From what he could see, the tail was cracked and sagging. And he could tell that three quarters of the right wing and engine were missing.

He felt for his phone, but he didn't have it.

Probably dropped it in the fight, he thought.

He wondered if Zac left his in the car. He took his eyes off the road for a moment and scanned the console. He was just about to look in the glove box, when he glanced up. A large man was standing in the road, directly in front of him, waving him down.

Joe stomped on the brakes and the car shuddered and squealed. It stopped just two inches from the man.

"What the?!!!" Joe yelled, as he hit the steering wheel angrily with his fist.

The young man walked up to his shattered window and in English, said, "I'm sorry sir. Are you going to help that aircraft?"

"Are you crazy?! You were almost road kill! You can't just..." He stopped in midsentence. There was something about this guy. He couldn't put his finger on it.

The young blonde haired man had piercing blue eyes, and broad stout shoulders like a weight lifter. He was at least 6'5" and Joe wondered who would fare worse if he ran into him: the young man or the car.

"Sir?" he asked again.

Finding his voice, Joe asked, "Do you always walk in front of moving cars?"

"I'm sorry sir. I was in a hurry to get to the plane... are you going there?"

Still at least a mile from the site, without a second thought, Joe gruffly said, "Get in!"

As the young man rounded the front of the car, Joe noticed that his big frame moved with speed and grace.

Very strange for someone so large, he thought.

The young man opened the passenger door and slid in. Joe punched the accelerator.

Chapter 60

Lazy Hoof – Present Day

*G*abby wondered how the whole world went crazy all at the same time. She was sitting in the ranch office, watching the news on the television. There were horrific pictures coming out of the west coast and even Central and South America. Casualties were estimated in the millions. There was still very little help getting to the affected areas. Many roads were impassible, and the sheer volume of dead and injured instantly overwhelmed local, state and federal officials.

Looming in the back of her mind was the announcement the President made about Martial Law - Just before the disasters.

Gabby shook her head at the thought: *It was like he knew exactly what was coming. Could the collapse of the dollar just be a smoke screen? But how? How could he know?*

In addition, there was breaking news from the Midwest and the South about another massive earthquake in the middle of the country. *How could he know?*

Martial Law would have far reaching implications not yet grasped by the citizenry because of their focus on the disasters. But Gabrielle knew what Martial Law meant.

It virtually gave the government unlimited control over all natural resources, food and water, fuel, etc., as well as the ability to conscript private property and people for federal use.

Once again her brilliant husband amazed her, even in his absence. He saw all of this coming. He often spoke about the need of being prepared for such contingencies. When they moved back to the Lazy Hoof four years ago, he started gathering huge stores of food, water, guns and ammunition. He started a hydroponics garden in their new underground shelter that he'd built. He even went so far as to discreetly have large gasoline station fuel tanks, with both gas and diesel, buried on the property. He said that there would be a time when they couldn't get gas. He was right.

And then of course there was the gold and silver. Only she and Danny knew that he had stores of precious metals in a vault in the underground shelter. He collected the metals in small enough coins so that when the time came, the gold could be used as currency to trade.

He studied the world's economies and told her that simple mathematics indicated that they would collapse. *He was right about all of it,* she thought shaking her head.

With the collapse and disasters, society broke down all over the country. There was widespread rioting and looting in the streets. Violence had also erupted in Missoula. She fought off fresh tears.

She was scared. She needed Bryce and desperately wanted to hear his strong reassuring voice. But she'd tried his cell phone several times before the breaking news and only got his voice mail. Now all the phone services were down and reaching him was impossible.

So she did the only thing she could do. She, as she'd heard Bryce say to their son, had to "suck it up" and push on. Until he got back, she had to keep the Lazy Hoof and its people safe.

That's why she told Danny and Goose earlier to lock down the Lazy Hoof. It was one of her husband's contingency plans if things happened while he was away. So Danny, posted sentries in key places around the ranch. Those guards, and the technology that Bryce installed, gave them the ability to cover most of the ranch's borders.

And also, just as her husband hoped, somehow people instinctively knew that the Lazy Hoof was a good place to come. They'd already gotten many stragglers looking for safety and shelter. That too was part of the contingency.

Bryce wanted to make sure that people would look to the Lazy

Hoof as a "safe haven". The plans called for them to take in as many peaceful people as possible, converting the guest cabins into dorm rooms for the needy.

Nowhere outside of an armed compound like the Lazy Hoof was safe. Even with all of Bryce's preparations, they weren't guaranteed safety. If the military rolled up wanting their guns, food and water, like they did during Hurricane Katrina, they'd have to oblige. They couldn't fight the military.

Always thinking, Bryce planned for that contingency also. The secret underground bunker was directly under the main ranch house and it contained additional weapons and ammo, as well as the bulk of their food stores.

If government troops did come and demanded their weapons, everyone was told to surrender the guns and ammo that were on their person. If food and water was also demanded, they were to surrender that too. But when the troops left... that was a different story. They could go down into the bunker to rearm and bring up more food. Bryce had thought of everything.

She hadn't spoken to him since he left last night. While she didn't think the worst, she desperately wanted to hear his voice. Phone service was down, along with the internet. There was a short-wave radio in Bryce's office. If the services didn't come back up soon, she may have to resort to using it.

As she was pondering this thought, a strong contraction pulled at her belly and she moaned with pain. She breathed rapidly through her mouth until it was over. After a moment, the pain subsided.

She looked down at her eight month bump of a belly. Because she wasn't full term, she just assumed when the contractions started that morning, that they were Braxton Hicks.

Braxton Hicks contractions were false labor pains that could start at six weeks of pregnancy. But those contractions were usually irregular. Her brow wrinkled at the thought that her contractions were very regular and seemed to be building to a crescendo. And that last one was a duzzy. She focused back on the television to take her mind off of a new problem she didn't need right now.

Murders and violent crimes increased dramatically in the last twenty-four hours. People were killing each other unabated. And not just for food, but many times for no reason at all - Just senseless acts of violence. Perhaps the strangest violence was the unexplainable increase in cannibalism. Some people started calling it the new "zombieism". She shook her head at the scenes unfolding on the news. It seemed that a dark blanket of evil had befallen the country and the world.

She was thinking about going down to Bryce's office to try to raise Uncle Joe on the short-wave. But as she got up, it felt like her pants were wet.

She looked down. Her chair was soaked. There was water all over the floor.

The radio call would have to wait.

Her water just broke.

Chapter 61

*B*ryce did a belly flop in water that was at least five feet deep. When his head came up he saw Diggs and Ivy crying and calling to him at the now fully engulfed escape hatch. Apparently they didn't see him bail out the front.

He yelled, "Everybody! Get away from the plane! It's going to blow!"

In unison, Diggs and Ivy said, "We can't! Dr. Cooper is still in th... Dr. Cooper?"

"Come on!" he shouted, waving his hand.

The pair didn't need to be asked twice and waded over to him.

Digby's arm appeared to be broken and Bryce, took his weight and helped him get to shallower water. Physically unhurt, but emotionally pained with tears in her eyes, Ivy was trudging alongside of them.

As they got to the shore, Diggs and Ivy advanced further up on the sand.

Bryce stood staring at the crash, with Package in hand, in the ankle deep water. The plane was now fully engulfed in flames. He shook his head, turned around, and said, "I don't get it. I really thought it would ex..."

The plane exploded in a thunderous orange and yellow fireball.

The blast's concussion hit Bryce in the back like an NFL Defensive Tackle. So strong was the explosion that it lifted him off his feet and threw him like a ragdoll, face first, into the wet sand.

While the plane exploded for a second and then third time, Dr. Bryce Obadiah Cooper lay unmoving.

Lazy Hoof – Present Day

The contractions were coming in waves now. Gabrielle sat on the wet chair, moaning in pain.

Her eyes were glued to the television again. It happened to be the local news showing rioting and looting in Missoula.

Shaking her head in disgust, it felt like the screen was saying to her, "No you can't go into town to the hospital! It's too dangerous!"

"Grreeaattt," she grumbled, and hit the remote's off button.

She struggled to her feet and groaned in pain. Reaching for her walkie talkie, a match to the ones she handed out to the staff that morning, through gritted teeth she barked, "Ranch Man (Mendez), this is Lady Liaison (a reference to her old job at the U.N.), come back."

No response.

"Ranch Man! This is Lady Liaison, come back!" she snapped.

Still no response.

She screamed with another contraction.

"Danny Mennnndeeezzzz... you better pick up that radio or else!"

After a pause, Danny came on the line, "Yeah, yeah I'm here." he said hurridly. Gabby could hear strange popping sounds in the background.

"Danny! I need..." she paused. "What's that sound? What's going on?"

"Can't talk right now Mrs. C. Got a problem. People shootin'," he said distractedly. "Armed men... want what we got. They ain't asking nice... Just started shoot... Hey lookout!" she heard him yell to someone.

After a moment, he hurriedly came back on the line, "Sorry! Can't talk now! Call you back..." and the line went dead.

She looked at the radio in shock. It was one thing to see violence on TV. It was another to have it at your front door. Now she realized what the sounds were in the distance; the "pop, pop, pop" of gunfire.

Another contraction - She moaned and slapped the top of her desk over and over with her open hand. Finally it ended.

I just can't sit here, she thought.

After a moment, she hit the house intercom button on her desk,

"Lisa! Come to the office! Right now! I need you!"

One way or another, this baby is coming, she thought.

And then, looking back up at the now silent TV, she said, "But to what kind of world is he coming?"

North of Ashdod, Israel – Present Day

Abruptly he found himself in the beam tunnel of the LHC. He was standing by the Collision Chamber. There was a surge of bluish light above him. It began to pull like a tornado sucking him up into the dark blue hole. Frantically he grabbed for a handhold on anything. But the pull was too strong. Instantly he went feet first into the hole.

A dark blue hue with veins of lightning was all around. He was tumbling and spinning like he was in a washing machine. He realized that he was in a tube of some kind... a conduit. All at once, he was at the end of the churning tunnel and he was spit out to the hard ground.

He got to all fours and looked around. He realized that he was dumped by... the control panel of HAARP. The very place he last was - four years before.

"What's going on?" he asked himself in bewilderment.

Gingerly he got to his feet. He was sore, but nothing was broken. He looked around and scratched his head. The machine was off and no one else was around.

Recalling his last visit to that place, he remembered that he'd gotten sick on the floor. But the ground was free of the blood and puke that he'd deposited back then.

The Reset, he thought. *Of course it wouldn't be there.*

As he stood there, trying to understand what was happening, without warning another vortex opened above him.

"Noooooo" he said, just as he was sucked back up into the hole.

From there, he was taken to ancient Mayan ruins. He didn't understand what was going on. Then he was sucked up again. He was spit out at another ancient site and again vacuumed into the vortex. Time and time again he journeyed to both ancient locations and to laboratories and machines all over the world. Each time he was there only briefly and then sucked back up.

He realized that he must be moving through wormholes, conduits that were connected to what he now knew to be portals or stargates.

Instantly he was spit out into space. But it wasn't dark where he was. He realized that he was floating, without a space suit, in front of a burning hot star. And, although he didn't know how he knew, he knew that it was... the Sun.

The Sun looked as it did in the vision he'd seen when he fell off his horse. It had holes all over it like Swiss cheese and where there weren't holes, a flaming spider web could be seen encompassing all around it.

Only this time, as he watched, a UFO of some kind hurled itself at the Sun. But instead of crashing, one of the honeycombed holes opened up and absorbed the ship right into the Sun. He didn't know where it went, but he knew it didn't crash.

As he was pondering what he'd just seen, without warning, one of the dark holes opened up and spit out another ship, different from the first. It was headed right for him at an amazing speed. He drew to the side just in time and watched as the ship sped off to a blue dot in the distance.

"What's going on here," he wondered aloud. Instantly, the vortex opened above him again. "This is getting old," he said.

He was sucked back up into the wormhole. And again he began to tumble and roll. But this time he was spit out on a dusty mountain, different from all the rest of the locations.

He coughed and groaned, as he picked himself up out of the dirt. He was slapping the dust off his jeans when he realized that he was overlooking Israel.

As he stood, what he saw stunned him. Below him, on the valley floor, armies of many different countries were surrounding the Jewish State. These armies had creatures amongst their ranks that didn't look human.

But that isn't right, he thought. They were only partly human. These creatures were chimeras.

And he knew that this allegiance was... ready to attack.

Unexpectedly, his eyes were opened. His scientific mind instantly understood that he was now seeing into one of the adjoining spatial dimensions that his former research talked about.

He saw dark ugly holes open up all across the sky and the ground. Out of the portals flew huge bat like creatures by the hundreds of thousands, or perhaps millions. Bryce rubbed his eyes. They were flooding out so quickly and in such great number that they resembled just one long big black blur.

And then his perspective abruptly changed. No longer was he on the mountain top. He now had a bird's eye view of Earth from space. As in his previous vision, he saw the same blur of black... coming out of all the portals all over the world.

Fear began to well up in his heart. The crystal blue planet began to grow darker and darker, until... it was completely covered in a black ubiquitous blanket. Darkness had fallen onto the Earth. And he knew it was because the black winged creatures now covered the whole planet. And that darkness... was evil.

Instantly he was aware of a heavy presence floating next to him. The hair on his arms and his neck stood on end. He knew that the presence was more evil than all of the dark beings covering the Earth, combined. As he was just about to turn his head to look at it, the presence shot down to Earth like lightning.

He didn't see what it was. But he needed to see what it was. So... he took off after it.

He got there just in time to see this presence drive into a black, lightless ball of stone. The stone was about the size of a basketball and no light came from it.

Not understanding what he just saw, he pondered what occurred. Suddenly, the image blurred away.

He opened his eyes as he coughed and gasped. He turned his head and he wretched in the sand.

His eyes began to focus. He was lying on his back on the beach. Two battered faces stared anxiously down at him.

"You alright Coop?" Mac asked.

Bryce sat up. Diggs, who was standing next to Mac, was holding his arm gingerly. Dr. Mora was laying prone in the sand with something under his head. Stephanie was looking down at her Dad and speaking softly. He could hear a woman wailing in pain somewhere and realized that it was Ivy. And then he remembered X.

He looked at Mac. He was covered in blood. "Are you okay?" he asked his friend.

Mac saw the look on his face and then looked down to his blood stained clothes.

He shook his head, "Not mine," and pointed with his chin to The Professor's direction.

Kneeling over The Professor, Bryce saw the back of a broad shouldered man he didn't recognize.

Smelling acidic burning plastic and metal, he remembered where he was. He groaned and looked around Mac to the burning plane, "Wha... what happened?" he asked.

"I'll tell you what happened," a familiar voice said, "You nearly gave me a heart attack!"

Bryce turned his head in the direction of the voice. And he came face to face with his Uncle Joe.

Chapter 62

New York – Present Day

"**C**ome in here please," The Banker said to the intercom. "Yes sir," the timid Temp replied. A moment later there was a knock at the door, and the Temp entered the Banker's office.

Pad in hand, she asked, "Yes sir?"

The Banker was rifling through his desk distractedly. Without looking up, he said, "I need you to clear my schedule for the next five days. I'm flying out of town."

"Clear your schedule sir? Do you mean that you'll only be available for phone conferences?"

The Banker abruptly stopped filling his open briefcase. He looked up with burning eyes and face contorted. In a voice that sounded like a snake hissing, he spat, "I mean cancel my appointments. Meetings and conference calls. Do you understand?"

He had had enough. Stephanie would have known exactly what he meant. Nor would she have been so rude as to question his judgment. Why did he ever grant her leave right now?

"I must fly out to Dubai tonight. I'll be out of touch for a few days. Thus I will not be able to speak with anyone," he said, looking up with hollow eyes.

The transformation of the Banker's face startled the Temp. It looked otherworldly. And for the briefest of moment, she could swear that his eyes turned to reptilian slits. She involuntarily took a step back.

"Yes... yes sir. Will there be anything else?" she asked hurriedly. She suddenly felt very uneasy. She didn't know why. But she wanted out of that office.

"No, that will be all," he said, as a means of dismissal and went back to filling his briefcase.

"Yessir, very good sir," she quickly said, as she turned tail and headed for the door.

Breathing heavy in the safety of her own outer office, she walked up and held onto her desk to steady herself. She looked down at her hands. They were shaking. Then she glanced at the Banker's door and shivered.

She'd been the President's Administrative Assistant for a number of years at Lehman Brothers. After their collapse in 2008, she submitted her impressive resume to the temp service to get herself through to retirement. It was difficult for someone of her age to be picked up by another firm... especially in a down economy. But after this experience... she hoped that the collapse of the U.S. economy didn't wipe out her retirement. She'd made her decision. She was done. She would quit working for good and wouldn't be there when the Banker returned.

Staring at his door, she thought: *Since when do they not have phones in Dubai? That wasn't like him... to be out of touch for any length of time. It was almost like he didn't care anymore?*

And then another thought hit her: *Maybe he doesn't care... what does he know that he's not telling anyone?*

Lazy Hoof – Present Day

"AAAAhhhhhhhhhhh!" she moaned.

"Don't push yet!" Lisa said, "The baby's not in position!"

"Youuuuuuu don't push! I want him ouuuuutttt!" Gabrielle cried.

"Just a little longer... breathe!"

"He he ho, he he hooo," Gabby breathed. "Heeee! Oh youuuu breathe! I'm going to push!"

Lisa raised her head up from between Gabby's legs. "Sweetie, you can do this! Just a little longer.

Gabby's cry for help caused Lisa to come running from the kitchen. She found here at her desk moaning in labor pain. That was an hour and a half ago.

Now, Gabrielle was lying on her office floor with her back against the sofa. Cushions propped her up for support and Lisa placed other cushions under each of her legs.

Neither woman wanted to talk about the gunfire in the distance. Danny and Lisa's husband, Goose, were in the middle of the fray. Lisa couldn't raise Goose on his radio either. After Danny's abrupt hang-up, both women knew that the situation at the front gate was bad.

Focusing on Gabby's labor gave them a needed distraction. The shooting stopped fifteen minutes ago and they feared that bad people would rush into the lodge to take whatever they wanted... or worse.

As a contraction ended, they heard the front door noisily spring open, "Gabby! Lisa!" Danny called out.

"Here!" Lisa shouted.

A few seconds ticked by and they heard stumbling, banging and scratching... like someone was being dragged.

All of a sudden, the office door burst open part way. Danny Mendez entered back first. He was covered in blood.

Somewhere in The Middle East – Present Day

"Yella! Yella! They're coming!" his friend, acting as lookout, whispered in Arabic.

Looking back over his shoulder at his nervous Companion, Ahmed replied, "If I don't do this right, it will not matter will it? Now shut up and let me work!"

A few moments ticked by. Although the night air was cool, beads of sweat rolled off the Companion's brow. He continued to nervously move his head between looking at Ahmed and off to the distance for the guards.

"Done..." Ahmed said with a sigh of relief.

"Fine... but now we have to get out of here without getting seen!" the Companion reminded him.

"If it is his will," Ahmed said. "Besides, if we are caught, they will surely inspect the whole area. If they do, they will find our little Present... and our mission will be for nothing."

"Let's go..." the Companion said as the two young men ran off in a crouch.

Left behind in the bushes was a small suitcase with a timer. It was counting down from two hours.

North of Ashdod, Israel – Present Day

Bryce's vision began to clear and the ringing in his ears subsided. "Uncle Joe? Is that really you? What are you doing here?"

"Yeah son," he replied with relief evident in his voice. "You gave us quite a scare."

Bryce realized that his back hurt like someone beat him across his shoulders with a baseball bat. He felt his head. There was a golf ball size lump on it. He tried to get up.

"Easy boy," Joe said. "Let's make sure nothin's broken."

He grunted as he got up on one knee. "Ah... I'm alright," he said, as he stood on unsteady feet. Joe held his arm so he didn't fall over.

Bryce started looking around and desperately searched the sand.

"Looking for this?" Joe asked, holding up the Package.

Bryce sighed, "Yeah, it almost didn't make it. I had to go back and get it."

Joe looked at is nephew and for the first time noticed that all the hair on his arms was burnt off. His hands were blistered, and parts of the hair on the top of his head were singed.

"Are you sure you're okay," Joe asked again in concern.

"Yeah," Bryce said balancing the Package in his hands. "Hey, how did..."

Joe didn't let him finish, "I'm sorry son..." he said with remorse in his voice. "We didn't tell them... they found out..."

Bryce could see the pain in his uncle's eyes. He knew he or Ruby wouldn't tell anybody. He put his hand on Joe's shoulder, "Ah, forget it. It's just good to see you."

Joe nodded in grateful understanding. "You too," then he joked, "But next time... call ahead so we can have you over for dinner at least."

Bryce smiled, and then remembered what just happened. He began to look around and asked, "Is everybody okay?"

To that, Mac who was trying to splint Diggs' arm, looked up and shook his head. His eyes went over to Ivy who was sitting in the sand sobbing uncontrollably.

What a dumb question, Bryce thought.

He looked at Diggs who read his mind. "Broken, I think," he said.

Bryce nodded.

Walking up to where The Professor was laying prone, Stephanie looked up at him. She was at her father's feet. She shook her head and began tearing up again.

The back of the big man with broad shoulders was still to Bryce. As he limped up to them, he saw the long rod sticking out of The Professor's stomach. He could tell that Dr. Mora's breathing was shallow. His shirt was stained with blood and his eyes were closed.

As Bryce looked on, the astronomer's eyes briefly fluttered open. When they did, they settled on the large man kneeling over him. Instantly his eyes grew wide and a look of recognition crossed on his face. Dr. Mora realized that it was the same man that gave him a ride after someone tried killing him in England. But then, before he could ask why he was there, Alvaro passed out again.

"Are you an EMT or something," Bryce asked the back of the stranger. "Is he going to be...?"

The stranger's head turned and he stood up to his full six-five height. Bryce's mouth dropped open in recognition.

He'd come face to face with... Gabe.

Chapter 63

Geneva, LHC (Topside) – Four Years Earlier

*B*ryce hurriedly walked out of the P1 entrance, still barefoot with boots in hand. Under one arm was a substantial sheave of papers, in the other, his beat-up old, soft sided briefcase, so stuffed it looked ready to explode.

He shook his head and muttered aloud, "I must be losing my doggone mind!"

His thick rimmed reading glasses were still pushed up on top of his head and slightly askew. His tattered brown tweed sport coat, with patches on the elbows, was wrinkled and looked like it'd been pulled on hastily with the collar disheveled.

Bryce had the look of a man in distress. Events had swept him up in a torrid of lunacy, and that stress was beginning to weigh on him. His forehead had distinct worry lines, and there were dark circles under his eyes. He hadn't gotten more than four hours sleep a night for months.

He was hurriedly walking to his car. He needed to get away from there so he could think. Just then his phone rang in his pocket. Looking down and still moving, he tried to switch his briefcase to the same hand holding his boots so he could answer the phone. He nearly dumped the sheave of papers under his arm and struggled to keep it from falling.

Crossing the large expanse of asphalt parking lot, looking down, and in a hurry, Bryce didn't see the person impeding his path until he bumped into him.

"What the..." he said frustrated and surprised. As he looked up, he was flabbergasted to stare into an increasingly familiar face.

"Hey! What are you doing in here? This is a secure compound!" he said, spouting off the first thing that came to mind.

"My apologies Dr. Cooper, but I needed to speak with you," the young man with the melodious voice said.

"Well, make an appointment like everybody else!" Bryce said sarcastically. "And... hold on a second... how did you know my name?" Bryce said scrutinizing the young man's face. *Boy, this guy really looks familiar*, he thought. "How did you get in here? What-are-ya, a stalker or somethin?" he said with a perturbed look on his face.

The young man with his melodious voice patiently answered, "I'm sorry for the intrusion and your confusion..."

Uncaring, he dumped his papers and dropped his briefcase. He had enough, and exploded, "You're dog-gone right I'm confused!"

Steadily and calmly, the young man said, "Really... I'm here to help.

"...we had already assigned your son a Protector. He was there this morning to hinder the Other's attempt on your son's life."

Bryce was befuddled and the expression on his face showed it. Words spilled out in a frustrated rush, "What do you mean assigned a Protector? And who are... The Others? For that matter, who are you? What the heck is going on?!"

"Dr. Cooper, you will not understand what is occurring. And I cannot explain it all to you. But I can tell you this much; we will protect your son and we will help... within reason... with the progress in your scientific efforts.

Again shaking his head and fully in a daze, he looked up with pleading eyes to the young man. "Will you please tell me what you're talking about? What is going on?" he asked his voice low and small, like that of a frightened child.

"In time... you will have your answers Dr. Cooper, but not now. Now you are not ready for answers. I will talk with you again soon. But now I must go."

"Wait... please..." Bryce said in a small whispering voice. "I don't understand... I... I don't even know what to call you... your name," he said quietly.

"You can call me Gabe."

North of Ashdod, Israel – Present Day

Bryce looked over his shoulder to see where Joe was. His uncle was talking to Mac and Diggs. Looking down at The Professor again, he could see that his eyes were closed and Stephanie, still at his feet, looked to be praying.

Ivy, although not outright sobbing, was sitting in the sand, teary eyed and in a daze. The pilot was also sitting in the sand. Clearly he was in shock as he sat there staring at the burning aircraft.

He turned back to Gabe, "I'd say that it was good to see you after all these years, but if you're here, it's probably not good."

Leaning into Bryce's ear, Gabe spoke in his melodious voice and said, "Dr. Cooper, I have always..."

"Yeah, yeah. I know. You've always been with me." He pointed to the plane, "But what's this all about? Judging by the exploding engine, I'd say we should probably all be dead!"

Answering the unasked question, Gabe said, "Yes, you are correct. I kept your plane from crashing. But more importantly, I came to give you a message."

"Does it have to do with Xavier's or The Professor's data. Or more to do with this?" he asked, as he held up the Package.

Gabe leveled his gaze at him, "All of it."

Bryce shook his head, "I... I don't understand."

"Time is at an end."

"Hold on," Bryce said shocked. "What did you say?"

Gabe looked deeply into his eyes. "Time is at an end."

"Where have I heard that?"

Gabe said nothing.

"Of course! Mrs. Warkentin said that. Time was at an end."

After a moment, Gabe said, "Dr. Black's and Dr. Mora's data point to things that will happen. Those things that were written about long ago are about to be fulfilled. The things that you have seen, yesterday and just now, are part of that end. The Restrainer is being pulled away."

With his mind's eye, Bryce saw exactly what Gabe was talking about: 2 Thessalonians 2:6 & 7. It talked about "The Restrainer".

"I... I don't understand. I thought I stopped them four years ago?"

"They were trying to gain an unfair advantage and launch a surprise attack."

"You mean they were trying to cheat," Bryce said deadpanned.

Gabe nodded.

"And the darkness that I saw when I was knocked out?" Bryce asked pointing to the sand.

"Darkness is falling upon the land. Time is at an end. But the One who created all things will hold His. They will be true light during the difficult times to come."

Bryce was quiet for a moment as the gravity of the words sunk in.

"There are many among you who will try to explain away

these things," Gabe said, "You must tell them that these are signs of His return. The Others are ready to launch their greatest deception. You must help them to see even as you have seen."

Bryce knew Gabe was right. He had seen The Other's in action.

Overcoming his shock, Bryce said, "So... I... ah..." Bryce was looking at the chamber, he had to get closer, "So you are a... a Nephilim?" he asked.

"That's right human. I am a Nephilim, he said proudly. My ancestors, my cousins, were the fallen angels who took human women and had their way with them. I come from a generation of Nephilim, genetically manipulated to fit right under your noses in your puny little society without notice," the creature said, twirling the meat in his hand for emphasis.

"Some of us 'come down in space ships' or 'UFOs'. You humans are so gullible. One day, you'll welcome us as the solution to all of your earthly problems. And in doing so, you will set up your kind for the Great Deception," he said, as he hideously laughed again.

Finally, Bryce said, "And the... portals. They're opening?"

Gabe again nodded, "What you saw is what the world will become. The Others have been preparing this dimension for the Fallen. The membrane that separates your reality from the Fallen's is thinning quickly. Your people will begin to see things that they will not understand. Many will be deceived and I'm afraid... many will die."

"And... and I helped them," Bryce said somberly.

"Dr. Cooper, you have been chosen. These things would

have happened anyway. But you have been placed in a position to have an impact on the end of time and the human race. In the short time that is left, there is much for you to do."

Gabe continued, "You will not understand these things now. When the time comes, you will know what to do."

"What... what am I supposed to do?" Bryce asked. Then he turned around to look at the burning airplane. "And when and where am I supposed to do it?"

From behind him, Gabe said, "You will know, but for now I must go to put things in order."

"Is my family o..." Bryce turned back around, but Gabe was gone.

Chapter 64

*L*isa screamed, "Dave!" assuming the blood on Mendez' clothes were her husband's.

Danny looked down at his blood soaked shirt in confusion.

"What?!" a voice said from the other side of the door. Goose popped his head around, "No, no April E," her nickname, "I'm fine! But this guy isn't."

It was a surreal moment. Gabrielle's back was against the couch. Lisa was between her legs; ready to catch the baby. The office door opened in and bumped up against the end of the couch. As such, the door shielded the women's view of Danny and Goose, until they came fully into the office.

"Aaahhhhhh," moaned Gabby as the contractions got closer.

Mendez backed into the office dragging someone. Goose had the guy's feet and they deposited the unmoving body on the office floor.

"This guy needs a doctor!" Danny said emphatically.

Instantaneously Danny's eyes got big and he looked at Goose who was equally stunned. The two men realized that the matriarch of the house laid in a prone position with her back against the couch. She was covered in sweat. Her face was ghost white. Between her legs with her back to them was Lisa. Most embarrassing was the fact that Gabrielle had her legs spread wide open. Both men simultaneously averted their eyes.

Gabrielle screamed again in labor agony, "Aaahhhhhh!" And then in a growling guttural voice she said to the two men, "Well tell hiiimmmmm to take a numberrrr! Ahhhhhhhhhh!"

Both men dared not look her way. Instead one was looking at the ceiling and the other the floor. "Sure, sure. Okay," Mendez said lightly.

Lisa's position actually blocked the men's view of Gabby, so their embarrassment was for naught. She yelled, "Well, don't leave him there! Take him to the front room. Get the vet to work on him!"

"Sorry Lisa," she's working on some other guys at the front gate.

"Great!" she said sarcastically. "I'll get to him between contractions! Dave... go get the first aid kit in the kitchen!"

"Oh... okay," Goose said, as he began to drag the man back out to the front room by his feet with Danny holding him by his shoulders.

Sounding more like an NFL coach instead of a midwife, Lisa looked at Gabrielle, "One crises at a time. Now lady - let's do this. Are you ready? PUSSSHHHHH!"

Jerusalem, Israel – Present Day

"Very well then... we will wait," the Rabbi said, as he hit the end button on his cell phone.

He turned to look at the tense faces of the small assembled group, "That was my Mossad contact. Their airplane was attacked..." a collective gasp was heard, "but miraculously most of them survived. Coincidently our man was in the area. While he was unable to stop the attack, they have the attacker in custody. They are interrogating him now."

"And what of the Package?" an older rabbi asked anxiously. "Is it safe?"

"Yes, yes," the Rabbi patted him on his shoulder, "It is safe."

"And what of the American?" the High Priest asked.

The Rabbi played with his beard, "That is the curious thing. He is fine but..." and he turned to look at the night sky through the window.

"But what?"

The Rabbi turned back, "He risked his life for the Package?" he said more as a question than an answer. "This Dr. Cooper... is very strange. How he obtained the items remains a mystery."

Another of the small group said suspiciously, "Perhaps he managed to sneak them out of the Egyptian site?"

The Rabbi shook his head, "I do not think so. If that were the case, our men could not have snuck into the site. The Egyptians would have been on alert. No... there is something else about this man. He is a Gentile. And now we hear that he guards the Package with his life. It makes no sense."

Another priest present said, "He is a follower of the Nazarene. They do not understand our ways. Yet they see significance for their set of beliefs. It is probably nothing more than that."

The Rabbi looked at the lower ranking priest and said, "While that may be true of most... followers of the Nazarene, it does not hold true for this one."

"How so?" the High Priest asked.

The Rabbi leveled his gaze on the man, "He may be Christian, but he has the same blood running through his veins as you do. He has traced his bloodline to Aaron. We have confirmed this."

A murmur swept through the group.

The Rabbi continued, "While he is considered a Gentile because of his religious belief, there is a strong sense of destiny in this man."

"And your point?" another rabbi asked.

The Rabbi turned to look at him, "My point is that I believe that Hashem himself has brought him to us - If for no other reason but to safeguard the Urimm and Thummim."

"But we do not even know if they are genuine. How can you be so sure?" asked another dissenting rabbi.

The Rabbi looked at him, "You do not know what I know. This man has seen things... did things. Those things are of Hashem. That is all I can say."

"But he is still a Gentile," insisted the High Priest, "And because of that, we will need to cleanse all of the contents of the Package when it gets here."

A chorus of agreement could be heard.

The Rabbi gathered with a collection of the leading rabbis and priests in Israel. This secretive group was primarily responsible for what occurred on the Temple Mount earlier in the day. Combined, they had powerful connections in the Israeli Knesset, the Israeli legislature.

Like so many other times in history, Israel found itself surrounded by its enemies. But this time, the odds against them were overwhelming. This group of religious leaders was tasked to find a supernatural solution to Israel's desperate situation.

In ancient times, the Ark of the Covenant was used, with the Urim and Thummim to speak directly to God in order to receive direction on a pending war. Although they found the Ark of the Covenant, they did not have the Urim and Thummim in order to go before the Ark and ask the questions.

Dr. Bryce Cooper's provision of the Urim and Thummim gave them the instruments that they and their government so desperately needed. As soon as Bryce delivered The Package, the plan was to have the High Priest go before the Ark of the Covenant and beseech Hashem for his favor and direction. The tension in the room was palpable. The future of the State of Israel, and millions of lives, were at stake.

The Rabbi started to say, "Gentile or not..."

Suddenly a bright light filled the small room in which the meeting was being held. The men tried to shield their eyes from the piercing light.

As they were trying to gather their senses, a voice, full and strong, filled the room, "Listen to me!" it said.

All of the men fell on their faces from terror. Cries of fear rippled through the group. They laid there in silence for a few beats.

Finally the Rabbi was the first to speak, "Who... who are you?" he asked in a shaky voice.

The brightness dimmed enough for the men to look at the source of the voice. What they saw was a massive angel standing fifteen feet tall.

His arms were as strong as ancient tree limbs. His color was whiter than snow. His wings were thick and strong. Feathers covered his wings, but his skin looked like that of a man's except white in color. He wore what looked to be a loin cloth and sandals.

His chest, stomach and legs were bare, displaying rippling muscles. At his side, he wore a sword that sparkled.

"I am Gabriel."

Murmurs of fear rolled through the prostrate group, "Gabriel the archangel!", "What have we done?", "Have mercy on us!", "Are we to be judged?" they said from the floor, while averting their eyes.

"I am not here to harm you. I am here to give you a message."

More murmurs, "A message," "he's not here to kill us?"

"Please tell us lord," the High Priest said.

"This man that is coming, the American."

"Yes lord,"

"He has been chosen."

The group was silent.

"He is bringing the Urimm and Thummim."

"Yes lord."

"I came to tell you that I gave them to him."

More murmurs.

"They are real."

More murmurs.

Gabriel pulled his sword from its sheath. The rub of the blade echoed loudly in the small space.

All of them cried in fear thinking they would fall by the sword.

"Fear not," Gabriel said. Then he took the sword and pointed to the north, "Your enemies are at the gate," to the east, "they are surrounding you," to the south, "you cannot see them," to the west, "but I already see them."

The men began to wail, "Please protect us."

"He, the American, is only a man. But he is a man that has been chosen," Gabriel said with his sword at the ready, "You will not understand why I am telling you what I will tell you. But you must trust the One who sent me."

And Gabriel began to tell them what must be done.

The Rabbi listened quietly. When Gabriel was finished, he asked, "And what if we do not do what is requested?"

Gabe looked down at the men with a sad expression. He remembered the many times their ancestors would not listen to what Adonai told them. He put the sword back in the sheath with finality and said, "Then you will not hear and you will perish."

And then he disappeared.

The men lay prone on the ground weeping and mumbling for some time. Finally one, then another and then the rest got to their feet. No one spoke.

After a while, the High Priest looked at the Rabbi, "What are we going to do?"

"I do not know..."

Chapter 65

Lazy Hoof – Present Day

*G*abrielle rested comfortably on the leather couch. Pillows were stuffed behind her back. She couldn't help but smile warmly at the newborn cooing in her arms. In spite of being a month premature and delivered at home, he was perfect in every way. She was thankful.

Gabby liked the name Aaron. Bryce remembered an old friend that didn't remember him, and chose Eleazar. Thus, their new son was christened Aaron Eleazar Cooper.

Staring down at her new son, she found the moment bittersweet. He looked so much like Bryce. She wished she could have shared this experience with him.

Her eyes started misting again. She realized that it could be a long time before Bryce would be able to meet his son for the first time.

Not wanting to cry, she looked up from Aaron, with a serious look on her face. "What happened out there?" she asked Danny.

Danny already changed clothes and washed off the blood. He shook his head and said, "Unbelievable... One minute Goose and I are talking with the guys up front about perimeter security. All of a sudden, this group of about a dozen nasty looking armed men pull up. They stopped about thirty feet from the closed front gate. Our lookout on the wall waved and asked if they needed help.

Without so much as a warning, they piled out of their vehicles and started unloading on us. It was like something out of a movie," he shook his head again.

"They didn't even talk to you? Didn't they make any demands or anything," Gabrielle asked incredulously.

"Nope, not a word. If they asked for help, that'd be a different story. The Boss had me prep the cabins for town refugees. Lisa Duckett's prepared in the kitchen to cook in quantity, cafeteria style. Our veterinarian can act as a doc if she has to, but this..." he looked dazed, "... this was an assault. They didn't want help. They wanted what we got. And they didn't care who got hurt.

"It's just a good thing that you had the foresight to implement our security procedures when the President declared Martial Law. Plus Betsy helped," he said with a smirk.

"Betsy?"

"Yeah, Betsy. That's one of the old 50 caliber machine guns that Dr. Cooper had me make a mount for on the front gate's wall. Part of our proceedures was to set it in place."

All the levity drained from his voice, "They didn't know what hit 'em. Shredded their trucks. Killed a few. Wounded a bunch too," he shook his head as he played back memory. "The others ran off on foot, dragging their wounded. But that guy," Danny said, pointing to the other room, "They left him for dead."

Danny looked down at the ground. Gabby saw a tear fall in front of him. "Are you okay?" she asked with compassion.

Still looking down, he wiped his eye and sniffed, "Never killed a man before."

Gabby looked at him a moment. She said, "Danny?"

He looked up.

She nodded to the newborn sleeping on her chest, "I know it was hard. But we thank you. If you guys didn't do what needed to be done, we'd all probably be dead."

That helped. After a moment, he cleared his throat and pulled himself together, "Looks like the military's coming to town."

"The military?"

"Yeah. National Guard I think," he pointed to the road, "a whole convoy was moving real fast down the road. That's why that bunch didn't want to fight anymore. They saw them comin and took off."

"Headed to town?"

He nodded, "Didn't even slow down. There's a ton of smoke coming from the city now. It's like the whole town's on fire. We've had a lot of stragglers. They're sayin that there are fires and looting all over. And a bunch of dead lying in the street. All hell's broke loose down there. The Guard's probably got orders to quell the violence."

The office door opened and Goose walked in. He hadn't changed yet and was still covered with dried blood. The look on his face said it all. He shook his head slowly as if to say "he didn't make it", referring to the man they'd brought in.

Danny nodded his head in understanding and said, "Give me a minute."

Goose's head bounced once and walked out, leaving the door open.

Gabrielle looked down to the covered newborn baby. "Ecclesiastes says that there is a season for everything. A time to be born, and a time to die." Her eyes started welling with tears.

Danny was quiet for a minute, not knowing what to say. After a bit, he asked, "Any word from the Boss?"

Gabby wiped her tears on the baby blanket, "No... no word. Phones are down. Don't know what's going on. He should have landed in Israel a few hours ago. Hopefully he'll use Uncle Joe's shortwave radio..." she paused, "Danny do you think you can send somebody down to the basement to monitor the radio? Just in case he calls?"

"Sure, no problem," he was thoughtful for a moment, "Got just the man for the job. LJ is dying to help with something. I'll put him on the radio."

She smiled weakly at the thought of a son waiting to hear from his father half a world away. "Good idea. He can play games and watch movies down there while he waits. But Danny?"

"Yeah"

"Make sure he uses the back stairs. I... I don't want him to see any of that," she said pointing her chin to the front room, "until we can clean it up. I get the feeling that he'll have an eyeful in the coming months. No need to rush it."

With a solemn look, "Sure thing Mrs. C," and then he was out the door.

She looked down at her new son. A flood of tears began to drip down her checks. "A time to be born... and a time to die. God please help us."

Ouside Terhan, Iran Airspace – Present Day

The specially modified Gulfstream G650 had larger fuel tanks and more thrust capacity. What that simply meant to the Banker was that its top speed was Mach 1.25 and was easily the fastest private jet in its class in the world. Traveling at 51,000 feet, with nominal air traffic, he made the trip from New York to Tehran, Iran in a little over six and a half hours without refueling.

Iran suffered under a U.S. embargo for years because of their failure to curtail their nuclear aspirations. As such, there were no longer direct flights from America - public or otherwise.

When his nosy temp asked him about his location for the next few days, he couldn't very well tell her that he was breaking the embargo. So Dubai was an easy replacement.

After all, it was in the same general direction.

Although The Group did not know it, total Phase II implementation of The Plan could not happen until the Present was delivered to The Assyrian. It was absolutely necessary for success.

The Captain's voice came over his personal console, "Sir, we are on our final descent. We'll be on the ground shortly.

"Very good," was all that he buzzed back.

Phase II was almost at hand.

Chapter 66

Tel Aviv – Present Day

*I*t had been hours since the airplane crash. All the IDF (Israeli Defense Force) got out of the Assassin was that someone high up in the Assyrian government ordered the attack. He said he didn't know who, or why, but that it was part of the next step... whatever that meant.

At the urging of Joe, Zac secured a Mossad "safehouse". But that was accomplished only after a compromise. Bryce was expected in Jerusalem to meet with the Rabbi and the High Priest. The other scientists, even Ivy, didn't want to leave his side. The reason, they said, was "unfinished business". When asked what kind of business – they refused to volunteer any information.

Bryce understood how they felt. He felt the same way. The more information that they dug up, the more questions they had. He too wanted to finish what was started on the long flight.

Plus Bryce was alerted by Joe that he and Zac saw someone intentionally shoot down their plane. Something that they were discussing was so crucial: people were willing to kill them for it. The physicist was stubborn enough to take that as a sign that they were on the right track and should keep digging.

So the compromise that was arranged - All of them would go to the ancient city of Jerusalem, near where Cooper was supposed to have his meeting. That way, when he was done, he could get back and finish what they'd started.

Stephanie confided in Bryce that she was worried about another attempt on her father's life, and she wanted him close to the group. So the Montanan made the arrangements. The Professor was flown by an Israeli Med-Evac flight to Hadassah Medical Center. Diggs joined The Professor on the transport to have his arm set at the hospital in Jerusalem.

The MBB/Kawasaki BK 117 helicopter, with a top speed of one-hundred and sixty-three mph, flew them the forty miles in fifteen minutes. By the time they landed on the roof of the hospital, the surgical suite was already prepped and waiting for Dr. Mora. He would have a fighting chance.

Stephanie called from the hospital and told the safehouse guard to relay a message to the scientific team when they awoke. It was simply, that Dr. Mora was still alive and the doctors gave him a fifty fifty chance of survival. She promised to call if things changed.

Add to all of the trauma of the day, because Bryce insisted that the pilot not disturb them, the team was unaware of the great devastation and political upheaval that occurred all over the world in the brief twelve hours they'd been in the air.

As if surviving the attack on their plane wasn't enough, the remnant of the group was shocked and sickened by the news. In particular, the news from America; the devastation on the west coast, the great loss of life along the New Madrid Fault, the sudden collapse of the economy and the institution of Martial Law was almost more than any of them could take.

And judging from the other pictures coming out of world news outlets, the whole world was now in turmoil with rioting and fighting in the streets. But this scientific group knew that it was only the beginning. And Bryce knew that darkness was falling.

Like gasoline to the fire of the world's accelerated destabilization, the U.S. recall of their military from around the world caused countries who were at odds with one another for decades to take advantage.

China was poised for war with Taiwan, both India and Pakistan were now on their highest alert, Russia sent troops to the border of neighboring Georgia, North Korea was massing its army along the DMZ and a dozen other skirmishes looked to be ready to break out in full scale war.

In the scientist's estimation, those conflicts paled in comparison to their own predicament. They found themselves at the center of the mother of all battles: Israel versus the rest of the Arab world. Worse, they couldn't leave. Air travel was now grounded.

The Israeli Navy scoured the section of ocean where Xavier fell. They had yet to retrieve the body and called off the search after a couple of hours because of higher priority military needs. Ivy couldn't fault them. Even though the ISNW was still calling the massive troop moments around Israel a simple military exercise, everyone felt that war was imminent.

Besides, with her husband falling from well over a thousand feet, she knew it was more of a mission to recover his remains rather than conduct a rescue. In her heart, she knew that he was dead - A human couldn't survive a fall like that.

When Zac dropped everyone off at the safehouse, he told Bryce that he would give him a few hours to rest and freshen up. Later in the evening, he said he would return to pick the physicist up for the meeting with the Rabbi and the High Priest.

Bryce hadn't spoken to Gabrielle since he left the States. With all that was going on in the world, he was worried. But up until his downtime at the safehouse, he didn't allow himself the luxury of thinking about his own problems: Millions of lives were at stake and he couldn't be selfish.

But now... now as he sat and considered all of the ramifications of world events, he desperately wanted to speak with his wife and children.

Unexpectedly, as if in answer to an unspoken prayer, Zac offered to take him by an IDF Station House not far from where their meet was going to be. There, he said, Bryce could try to raise his family on a shortwave radio.

In the hours since, Diggs also arrived at the safehouse with his arm in a bright new cast. Forgoing food, he went straight to his room and was fast asleep. Mac had been asleep since they arrived. Ivy was in her room, but Bryce doubted if sleep could find her in her mourning. Stephanie was staying at the hospital with her father. Once he was out of the woods, the plan was for her to join them in their new temporary housing.

Although Bryce lay on his bed and went fast to sleep, his subconscious mind continued to prick at him. After only being asleep four hours, he found himself lying wide awake in bed, staring at the ceiling, and trying to put the pieces together.

Why would someone want to kill us? And who knew we'd be coming to Israel? How did they know? I didn't even know until yesterday... was it really only yesterday?

Finally he gave up on sleep and got up to make a pot of coffee.

For the first hour, he sat in the front room, cup of coffee in hand, thinking. He mulled the events and facts he'd learned over and over in his mind. Then shifting gears, he thought he'd give his brain a break and catch up on the news.

He was shocked and sickened by what he saw of the devastation in America. The news continued to show morbid shots, flipped between the west coast to the New Madrid Fault area. Scenes from all over the world showed rioting, looting and senseless violence.

After an hour of depressing news, he shook his head in disgust, hit the remote's off button and angrily threw it on the couch.

An hour later, one by one, each of the scientists ventured from their rooms. The last out was Ivy. She looked as if she rested and had freshened up. But her eyes were still puffy from crying. There was no other way to put it Bryce thought: She wore the painful grief stricken look of a new widow.

When he heard his friends stirring in the back room, Bryce took the liberty of making scrambled eggs, toast and fruit for everyone. After a few minutes, the group of four found themselves around the dining room table. Everyone was hungry, even Ivy.

They conducted small talk for a while, avoiding the overwhelming subjects that all of them knew they were facing. But finally Diggs said, "Doesn't it seem odd that all of these things are happening at the same time. Like it was some kind of..."

"Plan?" Ivy proffered.

Diggs looked at her and nodded. It was the first word that she'd uttered since they were rescued on the beach. "Yes, precisely. All of it has the feel of an orchestrated effort."

"Yeah," Bryce said, pointing his fork at Ivy, "It fits with what you heard on that conference call."

"Yes it does I'm afraid," she said, pushing her half eaten dish of eggs and fruit aside.

"I guess we have our answer," Mac said, shoveling eggs and toast in his mouth. Bryce remembered how his friend could eat, so he made him an extra portion.

"What answer is that?" Diggs asked.

"Huh..." Mac reached for his glass of juice and took a big drink. Dabbing his mouth with a napkin, he said, "We were wondering how far along they were in that so called Plan. I guess they were further than we thought."

"Apparently," Ivy said with misty eyes.

Changing the subject, Diggs asked Ivy, "Have you ever seen that documentary..." his face scrunched as he tried to remember the name, "Motorway Madness on the M6 or something like that?"

"It doesn't ring a bell," she said.

"It was a BBC film I believe, in 2008. But I saw it on youtube. It was about two tall and very attractive Swedish sisters that displayed very odd behavior, were very, very strong and were both run over by a lorry and a car. They hardly had a scratch on them when they should have been killed. Eventually, one of them committed a senseless murder and was found innocent by reason of insanity. That just speaks to the strange behavior they displayed."

She shook her head, "No, doesn't ring a bell. But I think I know where you're going. It certainly sounds like the kind of behavior one would expect from transhumanism research like what we've conducted."

"You mean... you think they're Nephilim?" Diggs asked in a shocked tone.

"I don't know about Nephilim, but there are hidden and underground labs all over the UK. It wouldn't surprise me if a couple of their experiments escaped and went wild. You ever heard of R.A.F. Lakenheath?"

"Why yes, of course. I have a cousin, Percy, that I grew up with that obtained a position there a few years ago. Come to think of it, I haven't heard from him in a while," he said scratching his red head.

"Did you know that there was an underground facility at that base?" she asked pointedly.

"Underground facility. No..."

"Well, we have representatives, geneticists, that have went there to assist them in some of their ah... studies."

Diggs' mouth dropped open, "Did you say geneticists?"

"Of course, from my company. Why?

Diggs' hand went to his mouth, "Because that is what my cousin Percy is: a geneticist."

Just then, there was a knock at the door.

There were two guards posted outside and one sitting by the door reading. The inside guard looked through the peep hole and unlocked the door.

In walked Zac.

Looking at Bryce, he said, "It's time to go."

Chapter 67

Tehran, Iran – Present Day

*T*he Assyrian, Tabak, came to Tehran for the first time in his unofficial capacity as the Emperor of the New Ottoman Empire, or otherwise known as ISNW (Islamic States for a New World).

The secret meeting was a high level gathering of the Islamic, both Sunni and Shia, leadership under the auspice of discussing the current military exercise throughout the Middle Eastern military theater.

The afternoon was filled with plotting whispers against the Zionists in Israel and the Great Satan, which was already beginning to weaken. However, The Assyrian considered their containment enough for the time being. As a skilled politician, he elected to bide his time and then strike after his power was truly solidified.

Nonetheless, should some kind of provocation occur, the countries of the ISNW and their allies, would instantly rally behind him. If that were the case, he would kill both proverbial birds with one stone: The annihilation of Israel and his personal rise in power.

The first official state dinner was scheduled for the evening. The Assyrian donned military dress with emblems of both the new Assyria and the ISNW. He was the keynote speaker for the event that hosted dignitaries from every Arab country throughout the Middle East and Northern Africa. Even the President of Russia was in attendance, as were representatives from Nicaragua, Cuba, El Salvador,

Argentina, China and other ISNW friendly countries.

A knock on Tabak's door drew a curious look from Farouk. The assistant walked over to the door and opened it. The shock on Farouk's face was immediate, but he said nothing. From behind him, Tabak said, "Please come in."

"Your Excellency, thank you for seeing me on such short notice this evening."

"Of course. You are a welcomed friend," The Assyrian said.

"As I mentioned on the phone; I wanted to give you this Present before you took to the podium tonight and addressed the gathering in your new capacity."

"That is very generous of you. But why could it not wait until later?" he asked with a hint of irritation in his voice. But the Assyrian knew that he had no real choice in the matter. The Banker was one of the most powerful men in the world, if not the most powerful. If he wanted an audience, you gave him an audience.

The Banker smiled warmly and continued, "Your Excellency, there could be no better time to bestow such a gift on you than just before you take the reins of what will be the greatest power in the world."

Now the Assyrian was curious. For the first time he noticed the round metal case in The Banker's hand.

"Indeed, your assessment is right about ISNW. Now you have my interest peaked. Your friendship and assistance has been instrumental in the union's development. What better gift can there be than that?"

"May I?" The Banker asked, slightly raising the case and pointing with his chin to a waist high table in the middle of the room.

"Please" The Assyrian said.

The Banker walked across the marbled floor, his heels making a sharp clicking noise with each step. "What is," he asked, "the one thing you wish was different, as a Shia, in the world of Islam?"

Tabak thought for a moment, and in almost a whisper said, "That is easy. I would wish that Mecca was not in Saudi Arabia, but in Assyria."

A thin slit of a smile came to the face of The Banker. "I knew you would say that. But it is not Mecca that you seek, is it?"

Again a thoughtful look, "No you are correct. Mecca is only the place that pilgrims go to worship. But they are worshiping the Black Stone in the Kaaba."

"Ahhhh, and if you had," The Banker asked with anticipation, "your own Black Stone, could you not set it up in Assyria and change the pilgrimage to your homeland?"

As the new Emperor, Tabak knew that in time he could do anything he wanted. But first he must have such a stone. And moving the Black Stone from Mecca would be very untidy. "Of course," he simply said and took a step toward the case.

The Banker undid the clasps on the round aluminum piece of luggage with a "click, click". "My gift to you, my old friend," The Banker said with suppressed enthusiasm, "is" he lifted the lid of the case, "a Black Stone of your own!"

Both Tabak and Farouk, who had been observing quietly from a distance, gave an audible gasp.

"This stone," The Banker explained, "is an exact duplicate

of the Black Stone in the Kaaba, only smaller. And on this most important day, I place it in your hands," The Banker said as he picked it up out of the case.

Tabak's mouth was open as awe sparkled in his eyes. He could see that the stone was round and bigger than a basketball. It was blacker than night and although perfectly smooth, it gave off no sheen at all. By the way The Banker was holding it; he guessed that it was relatively heavy.

He reached out for the stone, but then hesitated from fear, slightly pulling his hands back.

"Go on my friend. It is yours. It belongs with you."

Again he stretched out his hands, but this time he took the Black Stone from The Banker.

Suddenly there was a flash of white light, a spark and then a surge of electicity through the air of the room, like lightning.

Above The Assyrian appeared a dark ubiquitous cloud hovering over him, which slowly descended. It enveloped him and seemed to wrap itself around him until all of it permeated into his being.

Initially he screamed, but then went silent as the change began.

His body vibrated and shook. His face shifted and contorted into a thousand different shapes. Over it rolled every feature of evil caricature that the world had ever imagined. From the gory to the grotesque, The Assyrian's face vibrated and rolled with evil.

Farouk was frozen in fear. He watched in fearful fascination at what was happening to his Charge. In the midst of Tabak's contortions, his eyes burned fiery red and that was enough for Farouk. He screamed and ran across the large suite's floor to the door, ready to escape. But still he remained. He stood by the door, observing from a distance.

Finally the movement stopped. Tabak stood there, head down and still.

The Banker was the first to break the silence: "My Master," he said, as he fell to his knees.

The Assyrian raised his head. His face looked like the same Tabak, but there was something different about him. The skin appeared to be almost plastic and his eyes were deep empty pools of black.

He looked in the direction of Farouk, shaking by the door. Suddenly his eyes burned like fire. "Come here!" he shouted in a low guttural, otherworldly voice as he reached out his hand in the direction of the beady eyed man.

Farouk was lifted off his feet and flew across the room into the grip of The Assyrian. The assistant found himself held in the air by one squeezing hand around his neck.

As he struggled to breathe, he looked into the Assyrian's face. It was contorted with rage and hate, different than the man he willingly served. He held his breath, not because he was being choked, but because of the eyes.

The Assyrian's eyes were burning red. Where the white of his eyes should be, they were pitch black, almost like they were hollow.

"Mas... master... please..." Farouk choked.

The Assyrian dropped him with a "thump" to the ground. Farouk quickly recovered and sprawled out before him prostrate with his face to the ground, "Yes my lord."

They remained there, The Banker and Farouk, head down in worship as The Assryian cackled and laughed. His voice thundered through the penthouse suite, vibrating the walls and furnishings.

The Banker and Farouk, an odd combination to be the first to worship... The Beast.

Chapter 68

Jerusalem, Israel – Present Day

Bryce followed Zac through the creaking, ancient looking door. As they emerged into the room, he saw that a small group of white bearded men were standing and waiting for them.

"Shalom Rabbi," Zac said, as he slightly bowed to the man at the front.

"Shalom my friend," the Rabbi said.

Zac looked over the crowd and again bent at the hips and said, "Shalom."

A chorus of shaloms could be heard from the group.

"This is the man whom you have heard about, Dr. Bryce Cooper."

Bryce was standing to the side and slightly behind Zac. He reverently held in his hands the Package. Bowing his head slightly, he said, "Shalom."

Again, a chorus of shaloms could be heard.

Zac directed his attention to the bearded man in front, "This is my Rabbi."

"Very nice to meet you sir," Bryce said without offering his hand. On the way over in the car, Zac briefed Bryce on what to expect. He said that he would introduce him to the men, but that he should not touch any of them; especially the High Priest. Rules of cleanliness were strictly followed.

"And this," Zac gestured to the man next to the Rabbi, "is the High Priest."

Again Bryce slightly bowed his head and said, "It is an honor to meet you as well sir."

The High Priest and the Rabbi exchanged a look.

In a heavy guttural Hebrew accent, the Rabbi said in English, "Dr. Cooper thank you fer coming."

Bryce nodded but said nothing.

The Rabbi continued, "Iz zat de Package?"

"Yes it is," Bryce said quietly and stretched out his arms to hand it to him.

The Rabbi gestured to the High Priest, "Please," he said as a way of telling Bryce to give it to the priest.

"I understand zat you rissked your life for ze Garments? Is zish trrue?"

Bryce cocked his head and nodded, "They are important," he said as a way of confirmation.

The Rabbi's hands were grasped in front of him, "Yes, very important." Then he looked at the High Priest and nodded. "May we?" he said asking to open the Package.

"Please," Bryce said.

The High Priest moved toward an old wooden table. The group of rabbis and priests remained silent behind him but moved as one, following him. Zac gestured with his hand for Bryce to follow.

The High Priest's hands were shaking as he cut the twine that held the sooty brown paper together. He gingerly unwrapped the paper. Revealed was something in a plastic bag. The High Priest looked to Bryce as if questioning "why?"

Understanding his unspoken question, Bryce said, "I didn't want them to get wet or soiled. As it turns, the brown paper ended up going in the ocean during the crash. But as you can see, everything inside is dry."

Zac translated.

The High Priest's eyebrows raised and he nodded his head in appreciation. Then he went back to unsealing the plastic bag and paper that covered what was inside.

Finally a piece of the Garments was revealed that caused the whole group to gasp in awe at the sight.

He carefully picked up the main part of the Garment and held it up. He said something in Hebrew. Zac whispered in Bryce's ear, "Exquisite he said."

Then the High Priest started speaking animatedly to the Rabbi, gesturing with his chin back to the Garments. The Rabbi said a few things in Hebrew back to the High Priest. Other members of the group commented excitedly. One of the others from behind the group handed the High Priest a measuring tape. The High Priest began to measure the Garments. Then the High Priest spoke rapidly to the Rabbi.

To the American Bryce, these men sounded angry like they were arguing. He stood there with a confused look on his face. Finally Zac turned to him with a smile and said, "They are very curious. The High Priest says that the Garments are an exact match to the specifications in the Torah. He wants to know how you were able to duplicate them so perfectly."

Bryce looked at Zac, unsure of how much he should say. Then he looked at the Rabbi and the High Priest and simply said, "Adonai."

This drew a collective gasp from the group. The High Priest pointed to the sky, nodded his head and asked, "Adonai?"

Bryce simply nodded.

Immediately, wild conversation rippled through the small group. The Rabbi was gesturing with his hand to the Garments;

the High Priest was animated and responding. Others in the group spoke amongst themselves excitedly.

To Bryce it looked like disorder and chaos, but he knew that it was their way.

Bryce wrapped each of the items that made up the several pieces of the Garments separately. The High Priest went one by one, unwrapping each of them. Each time the excited reaction was the same.

Again the High Priest's hands shook as he unwrapped the last item - the Ephod. The Ephod was a breastplate made of gold and several precious stones. There were also two pockets on either side of it. These contained the two most important pieces for the ceremony that the rabbis and priests hoped to conduct. In those pockets were contained the Urimm and Thummim, two crystal like items that were used to communicate with Adonai.

This time however, the men's reaction was very different. As the item was unwrapped, they gasped. But when the High Priest did a visual inspection of the pockets, without reaching inside them, he turned to the group and nodded. All of the men, including Zac began to weep for joy. After all of these centuries, the Urimm and Thummim returned to Israel.

Not understanding what the men were saying, but clearly seeing the significance of the moment, Bryce felt his eyes tear up as well. The men stood there for a long time crying and giving praise to Adonai.

After a while, the Rabbi wiped his eyes, cleared his throat and asked, "Dr. Cooper, please tell us. How did you find these items?" he said, referring to the Urimm and Thummim.

Bryce knew that the question would come. He wasn't sure

how he would answer it until that very moment. Solemnly he said, "They were given to me."

"Given to you, you say? By whom?"

Bryce searched the expectant faces of the men before him. He looked back to the Rabbi, "By... an angel."

A loud gasp was heard. Quiet whispers and exclamations were heard.

"An angel? Do you know what angel?"

Bryce looked from Zac, to the Rabbi, to the High Priest. Time seemed to stand still. Finally he said, "Gabriel," again a gasp, "the Archangel."

Quite unexpectedly this answer brought moans and cries from the group. Bryce thought the information would stun them. But the disclosure seemed to frighten them. He wasn't sure why.

The Rabbi looked at the High Priest who nodded to him. Both men turned around in what Bryce thought looked like a huddle in football. They were talking quietly in whispers so Bryce couldn't hear what they were saying. Not that it would have mattered. They were speaking rapid Hebrew.

Bryce looked at Zac who shook his head and shrugged his shoulders, indicating he didn't know what the group was discussing. The debate from the center of the huddle grew loud as if a few of them were protesting. Finally the voice of the Rabbi and then the High Priest could be heard over the dissenters.

Many minutes of debate went by while the American and the Mossad agent stood there. Finally, the huddle broke up and the Rabbi and the High Priest turned back around to face the two men.

The High Priest looked to the Rabbi who nodded. The priest cleared his voice. In a very serious tone, he began to say something in Hebrew to Bryce.

The normally pokerfaced Mossad agent's eyes got wide and he put his good hand to his mouth. He looked back to the High Priest and asked a question. The priest nodded and gestured his chin to Bryce.

"What's wrong?" Bryce asked. "Is there something wrong with the Garments?"

Zac, recovering, cleared his throat and said, "No, the Garments are exactly as they should be."

Bryce shook his head, not understanding. "Then why are they all worked up?"

With a pained look of uncertainly, Zac said, "Dr. Cooper. They need something else from you."

Chapter 69

Hospital, Jerusalem – Present Day

*S*tephanie fell asleep in the only chair in her father's ICU room. He hadn't woke up since they took him away in the ambulance. After his surgery, the doctors placed him in a medically induced coma to try to let his body heal. But with harsh honesty, they told her that his chances of survival were less than fifty percent.

Last night she contacted her family back home and told them what happened in the crash. Her mother, Zoraida, wanted to fly to Israel to be with Dr. Mora. Stephanie talked her out of it. The doctors said they would know within the next twenty-four hours if her father was going to make it. She reasoned with her mother that she and her family back home would be better off praying for the patriarch.

She hadn't eaten anything and was thinking about going to the cafeteria to get a bite. Abruptly the monitor above The Professor's bed sounded an alarm.

In rushed the nurse. She looked hard at the monitor and saw that The Professor's blood pressure was dropping and his heartbeat was erratic.

Stephanie asked, "What is it?! What's wrong?!"

The nurse ignored her, stuck her head out the door, and called to the nurse's station for help. As the doctor ran into the room, The Professor's monitor sounded a high pitched "eeeeehhhhh".

Instantly the doctor barked orders out in Hebrew and a flood of hospital staff came rushing into the room, shoving Stephanie off to the side. She saw what could only be a "crash cart" brought in. Her father's heart had stopped.

"What happened?!" she demanded. No one listened.

Suddenly, an orderly spoke to her in Hebrew and ushered her out of the room.

As he was closing the curtain around her father's bed, she was shocked to see the same large blonde headed man that had kneeled over her father at the beach. Now he was standing at the head of the bed observing. He looked at her with a passive face. And then the curtain closed.

Her heart was in her stomach as she listened to the sound of the "eeeeehhhhh". Then she heard someone say "clear!" Then there was a thump and quiet. Again, she heard the "eeeeehhhhh" and then there were shouts and orders again.

She stood there crying hysterically as another nurse came out from behind the desk and ushered her out of the ICU to the Waiting Room.

Before the door shut, she continued to hear the monitor scream, "eeeeehhhhh" and someone yell, "Clear!"

LHC, Geneva, Switzerland – Present Day

"Is everything prepared?"

"Just like riding a bike," Abbot replied.

The Banker asked, "How soon?"

"We are already at full power. Just waiting for word."

"How did you…"

"You are not the only one who knows the schedule of the Arrival."

The Banker bit his tongue. "So what are you waiting for then? Start the collision."

"I thought you'd never ask," Abbot said and hung up the phone.

"Thank you Dr. McNabb," the Scot said to himself.

Dr. Grover Washington McNabb completed the modifications to the LHC before the experiment was shut down. While Operation Falling Star started the process years before, he and his team were the ones to complete the modifications leading to the next step – This step.

After McNabb and his team were dismissed from the LHC a few days ago, Abbot came back to the facility to oversee the implementation of additional modifications.

But this was no experiment. This was purposeful. Nephilim technology permeated every aspect of the LHC. But up until now, the collisions were done with protons.

In his short time back, Abbot modified the machine for the collision of a new element, or subatomic particle, previously unknown to man. This element, the Klarion, always existed in Earth's three dimensions, but could only be observed and captured with the proper equipment and technology.

With Abbot's guidance, the Nephilim collected just enough klarions for the collision that was just about to occur. That collision would be the mother of all collisions.

With a collision of klarions at slightly below the speed of light, the portal, the main lock of the LHC, would be opened. From there, all other portals around the globe would be unlocked and also opened.

Darkness was falling.

Tehran, Iran – Present Day

The next morning in Iran consisted of strategy sessions and closed door meetings. But all everyone could talk about was the Assyrian's speech of the night before and the change that had come over him.

It was said that he metamorphosed into the Caliph, the twelfth Imam, overnight. The power that now emanated from him was infectious and every leader in the new ISNW was eager to throw their support behind him. Even the non-Muslim members attending were in awe of the new leader of the world.

Mecca, Saudi Arabia – Present Day

"Hey! You can't do that!" Alim shouted. A boy, much bigger than he, just shoved him down and stole the ball.

As he ran off, kicking the ball in front of him, Ghalib looked over his shoulder and laughed.

Alim picked himself up out of the dirt. The tears in his eyes made long lines of mud from the dust on his face. But he wasn't crying because he was hurt. He cried because he was angry.

It was always the same story. He was younger and smaller than all the other boys in the neighborhood. Because of that, he was often picked on and ridiculed. Even in this street football (soccer) match, his small stature haunted him.

But his mother always told him: "You may be small, but in your heart sleeps a lion." For his part, his father would always tell him not to take abuse... to fight; regardless of the size of his opponents. And fight he did... often.

The opposing team had been turned away. They were now headed for his team's goal. This was his chance for revenge.

He spied the bully Galib a few yards away. He was trailing the boy with the ball and not looking toward Alim.

The lion inside woke from his sleep. He began to stalk Galib, matching his strides. Soon the game would be called and the children would have to return home. This was his last chance.

He might be small, but Alim was extremely fast. With a burst of speed, he ran toward Galib, as swiftly as his legs would carry him. Just before he got to the bully, Alim slid feet first into the legs of the larger Galib. He took his legs right out from under him.

Galib fell face first into the dirt with a crunch.

Alim jumped to his feet. He backed up in fear. He didn't mean to hit the bigger boy so hard.

Galib writhed on the ground in pain with the wind knocked

out of him and a bloody nose. Slowly he stood to his feet. He cried as he held his nose. He rubbed the dirt from his eyes with his palms.

Slowly his vision cleared. He saw Alim standing a few paces away. A smirk rested on his face.

Murderous rage rose up in Galib. The bigger boy wanted to extract his revenge on the runt. He took a step toward the still stationary Alim.

The policeman's eyes were wide with fear. He'd only just found the present that Ahmed and his friend had left a short distance from the Masjid al-Haram, the mosque that was built around the Kaaba, the holiest site in Islam.

Instinctively he unclipped his radio from his belt to call his superiors. But he stopped himself from pushing the transmit button.

His knees grew instantly weak. He realized that he was watching red numbers count down: fifteen... fourteen... thirteen... twelve...

Rather than calling, the policeman turned and ran. It didn't do any good.

"You!" Galib screamed, "You did this to me?! Now you will pay!"

Alim turned to run and took two steps with Galib on his heels.

Without warning, a thunderous roar and bright light punched both boys in the face and they stopped in their tracks.

Instinctively they threw their arms up to shield their eyes... but it was no use.

The heat of the thermonuclear explosion instantly disintegrated the nearly two million people living in the city. Every living thing in the nearly two-thousand, six-hundred square miles of Mecca was vaporized.

A huge mushroom cloud bellowed over the city. It could be seen for miles.

The Israelis and Westerners would be blamed for the destruction of the beloved site.

And just as the Plan called for... The Assyrian had his provocation.

Chapter 70

Lazy Hoof – Present Day

anny and Goose were standing by the front gate. They hadn't had any more trouble from roaming gangs. But the stragglers that came looking for refuge told horrible stories of looting and murder in town.

Worse, it was rumored that the National Guard troops started firing on the regular army troops. It didn't take long for both sides to pull out the big guns and artillery. Air strikes were decimating whole parts of town as American fought American.

Danny and Goose watched jets go fast and low over the town, dropping ordinance and firing their cannons. Up until they heard about the National Guard and the federal military fighting each other, they'd just assumed the ammunition was directed at civilian dissidents. But the dog fight they were watching confirmed the outbreak of civil war.

Four planes, all with U.S. markings, were involved in live fire, air to air combat just in the distance. Two planes were pursuing two others when both trailing planes launched missiles and blew the lead planes out of the sky. Danny, Goose and the rest of the sentries were in shock.

"What is going on out..." Danny started to say when somewhere high in the atmosphere a huge blue ball of lightning and static erupted.

"What the?" Goose said. "There's not a cloud..."

Just then, the two planes who just won the dogfight were in a slow bank and headed back in the direction they came from. Instantly after the flash, the planes lost all power and control and dropped to Earth like lead bricks. Only one pilot ejected. The other was lost in the ball of fire that consumed his aircraft when it hit the ground.

Goose and Danny looked at each other. "What's going on?" Goose asked.

"I don't know, but it looks like a good time to take shelter!" Danny replied.

He reached for the radio at his side. Unclipping it, he brought it to his mouth. Pushing the button, he said, "Mrs. C, it's Danny at the front gate... come back?"

No response, "Mrs. C... you there?"

Still no response.

Danny keyed the radio a few times, but it didn't make a sound. No click, no static, no nothing.

He looked to Goose, "It's dead... try yours."

Goose's radio wouldn't click either. He made sure it was on, but there was no juice. He shook his head, "It's dead too."

"I don't like this," Danny said. Then he looked at his watch. It was stopped.

"Goose, your watch working?"

Goose looked at his watch. "What the..." he thumped it hard a couple of times. "Nope... it's stopped."

Danny stood quietly thinking. After a few beats, a look of fear gathered on his face. His eyes were huge. He looked at Goose, and then sprinted for the truck that was parked near the gate.

"What's wrong?" Goose asked urgently.

Danny ignored him.

He got behind the wheel of the old pickup truck, pumped the gas and turned the key... nothing. Not even a "click".

He jumped out of the truck and slammed the door.

Moving wild eyed toward the men on the wall, Goose grabbed his arm and said, "Danny! Talk to me dog-gone-it!"

Danny stopped and faced his friend. His eyes cleared and he found his voice, "EMP" was all he said.

"What?!!" Goose asked irritated.

"It's what took down those planes... broke our radios... stopped our watches. That truck won't even click... it's fried." He started moving again toward the men and was about to say something, when Goose grabbed his arm and spun him around.

"Will you talk to me?! What are you talking about? EMP?"

Slowly Danny's demeanor changed. Recovering from his initial shock, he breathed in deeply before speaking again. When he did, it was in full sentences and steady. He had to lead these people. He couldn't let himself freak out.

Looking into the stocky man's eyes, he said, "EMP stands for Electro Magnetic Pulse. It's a weapon that we have long suspected that our enemies had and would use if given the chance.

"Its purpose is to fry every electrical circuit in an area. Because we are so dependent on technology, our military leaders have long feared that it would render our forces deaf and blind.

"It would also make it impossible for us to repel an advancing force or retaliate for a nuclear strike," he said deadpanned to Goose.

"A... a nuclear strike?! How... how do you know all this?"

Danny started moving again toward his men, "We were briefed on it up in Alaska. It was always feared that it would fry everything we had. I guess somebody thought that today was the day to use it."

Danny called up to the man on the wall, "Memphis, get down here. I need you. Gather your men. I need to talk to everyone!"

Goose grabbed his arm again, "You guess who would use it," he asked through clinched teeth.

"Come on! Over here! Hurry!"

Danny looked at his friend, and under his breath, said, "Only countries that have that capability are Russia, China, maybe North Korea and possibly Iran."

Goose's eyes got big, but Danny wasn't finished.

Still talking in an urgent whisper he said, "Only reason they would use that kind of weapon was so we couldn't retaliate when they attacked."

Goose's mouth fell open and he went white as a ghost.

"Okay boys! Listen up," Danny shouted to the gathered twenty or so men around him.

"It seems that we're having radio and communication problems. We need to implement our shelter in place plan. Do you hear me? We are going to shelter in place!"

Stragglers augmented the Lazy Hoof's security force. Ranch Hands had been briefed on what it meant to "shelter in place". To them, using the term was an indication of how bad things really were.

Murmurs from a few stragglers immediately sounded: "Shelter in place? I thought that's what we are doin?", "What's goin on?", "What was all that dogfighten?", "What was that blue light?"

"Look!" Danny said with authority, "There's no time for questions! Vehicles are not working either. Memphis, I want you to send out some runners to the guard shacks on the perimeter. Get to the barn and grab some horses. You boys gotta ride like your lives depended on it! When you get back, take the saddles off where you stand and let the horses run free. Then you get your butts and the lookouts into the below ground shelter! You got it?!"

The head guard Memphis barked a few orders of his own and seven guys took off on a dead run toward the barn.

Danny pointed, "I need you four to go over and shut off the artesian well!"

"Shut off the well?"

"No questions! Just do it! And then make sure that you close the recycle baffle so the water can't flow below ground. When you're done, head to the bunker!"

Another four men peeled off in a dead run for the well.

"The rest of you! I want you to scour the guest cabins and the main house. Tell all those people to head down to the shelter. Now! I don't care what they're doing! They have to go now! And they can't bring anything with them! Go!"

The rest of the group took off in a dead run toward the main house and the outbuildings.

Danny looked at the cloud of dust that the men made as they ran off. He looked over his shoulder. He walked to the main gate and locked the bolt. No one else was getting in. He turned back around to see Goose standing there in shock.

He quickly walked over to him, "Come on... we got work to do."

Goose didn't move.

"Come on!" he yelled as he hit Goose on the shoulder as hard as he could.

Instantly Goose recoiled and then went to lunge at Danny. Mendez held out his hands, "Okay, okay! Are you back?"

Goose backed down and shook his head, "Yeah, I'm back" he said as he rubbed his arm.

Danny started off in a trot with Goose matching him stride for stride.

"Soooo," Goose said as he ran, "You really think they'll bomb us?"

Danny shook his head as he ran, "Hard to say... But I really don't want..."

Just then there was a huge flash from behind them. The men stopped dead in their tracks. They turned to see what the cause of the flash was. But they couldn't see anything."

Both men shielded their eyes from the Sun. "What was that?" Goose asked.

"I don't know..." but just as he finished his sentence, a huge mushroom cloud could be seen growing in the northeast.

"What is that?" Goose asked.

Danny swallowed hard, "That's the answer to your question - Great Falls and Malmstrom Air Force Base was just wiped off the map."

Goose swallowed hard, "Ya... you mean the missile base?"

"Yeah"

"How far is that from here?" Goose said as he started to walk backwards.

"Bout a hundred and seventy miles."

"Well," Goose said as he started trotting again with Danny following him, "could be closer."

Danny looked at his friend, "Might even get closer depending on the way the wind blows the radiation."

Almost in a dead run, Goose said, "Guess we better get below ground."

"Great minds think alike," Danny said as the two men sped off to the main ranch house.

What the two men in Montana could not see was tens of thousands of paratroopers dropping into Canada and Mexico, breaching U.S. borders in their initial invasion. On the coasts, Russian and Chinese destroyers and aircraft began to pummel the east and west coast in preparation for a sea assault.

The battle for what remained of the United States of America had begun.

Chapter 71

Jerusalem, Israel – Present Day

$\mathcal{D}$iggs, Mac and Ivy were sitting in the front room of the safehouse chatting. All had coffee in their hands and were discussing current news. Bryce hadn't been back the whole evening. But he phoned and said that he would arrive late in the day and that they could continue their discussion.

They hadn't heard from Stephanie at the hospital since yesterday. She left a message with the guard while they slept saying that The Professor made it through surgery and had a fifty percent chance of survival. They later learned that he was in Intensive Care in a drug induced coma - Nothing since then.

Mac got up and went to the kitchen for another cup of coffee. Diggs and Ivy were standing by the front door with the guard, pleading their case to him. They wanted him to let them go visit The Professor at the hospital.

Ivy thought they were making good progress when there was an urgent banging on the front door.

The guard drew his weapon and ordered them across the room. He turned and looked through the peephole.

It was one of the two guards who was standing post outside. His partner's eyes were so big, that the inside guard thought they'd pop out of his head.

"Let me in!" he shouted through the door.

The inside guard figured that he urgently needed to use the bathroom. So he quickly unlocked the deadbolt and door lock. As he went to turn the handle, the door burst open, knocking him down. His weapon slid across the room.

In a blur, he saw his partner's head turned by two huge hands so quickly that his neck snapped with a crack. Then his lifeless body was hurled in the direction of the kitchen toward the right.

Standing just inside the threshold was a hideous monster.

The Mossad agent was so shocked, that it took him a moment to reach for his spare gun in his ankle holster. In that brief second, the nine foot tall creature closed the distance between them and punched him in the face with a massive blow.

The creature's fist traveled through the guards face to the other side. When the creature quickly pulled his hand back, the guard crumpled dead to the floor.

With both hands to her face, Ivy screamed in terror.

The creature's black eyes had no white in them, which made them look like deep dark tunnels to nothing. Its muscles were huge and bulging, and its skin was pasty grey. Its hair was blonde and it appeared to have fangs. Its face was contorted in rage as it slowly crept toward Ivy.

Ivy was backed up against the wall. She was about to scream again when something stopped her.

The monster's clothes were normal, more than normal. They were tattered and torn, but she knew they were the same. They were familiar... they were her husband's.

The creature moved like a quirky and rhythmic wild animal. But Ivy instantly noticed some of its mannerisms - also familiar.

The beast continued to stalk his prey when he stopped, only inches from Ivy's face. He said in a sad tone, "I told you we needed to think this through. I told you that you shouldn't go around telling people the things you saw in your lab. I warned you... You were the one who they were trying to kill on the plane. They couldn't let you talk about the things you saw and heard. You could have brought their whole Plan down. But you didn't die like you were supposed to. Now you have given me no choice. I'm sorry Ivy."

Ivy's mouth dropped open. It was the voice of her husband. He was alive... and... he was a Nephilim.

Tel Aviv, Israel – Present Day

Joe and Eleazar were sitting on Joe's front porch as was normal for their morning routine. Over strong hot coffee and strudel, they spoke of events half a world away in Joe's America.

Violence had escalated and the news was reporting that civil war had broken out between a coalition of Arizona, New Mexico, Texas, Oklahoma, Colorado, Wyoming, Kansas and Nebraska in the center of the country. They were pitted against federal forces who they felt were using Martial Law to eradicate liberty.

The break-away States' National Guard units were under heavy fire from the federal government. Details on the news were sketchy at best and it was unknown who started shooting first. There were also sketchy reports of foreign troops breeching America's borders and coastlines. But these reports were yet to be confirmed.

China moved on Taiwan with an invading force. Russia had overwhelmed Georgia and was said to be launching attacks on other former Soviet Union Block States. Eleazar told Joe that he'd heard that India launched a nuclear missile against Pakistan. Reports on the news said that Pakistan was fueling their missiles for a retaliatory strike.

It was also reported that North Korea breached the DMZ. South Korea launched a counter offensive using tactical nuclear weapons to repeal the attack. Casualties were in the hundreds of thousands and the civilian population on both sides suffered terribly.

Ruby stuck her head out the door to ask the men if they needed more coffee. As she was just about to open her mouth, air raid sirens began to blare all over the city of Tel Aviv.

"What's going on!" she screamed.

Joe jumped to his feet. "I don't know!"

Instantly the street was filled with people running. Most of them were civilians with automatic rifles. Many of them had gas masks on. Husbands, wives, children, young and old, were all running in one direction.

Joe raced across his lawn to the street. He yelled, "What's going on?"

Nobody paid attention to him.

He tried a different tact. A young girl, no more than sixteen, was racing by with rifle slung over her shoulder. She was trying to pull on her gas mask while running. Joe grabbed her arm tightly and the girl practically spun around.

"What's going on?" Joe shouted over the sirens to be heard.

The girl was frightened, but realized that Joe was no threat. She pointed in the distance. "The ISNW! They're coming!"

Joe looked shocked and he let go of the girl, "What?"

She started backpedaling while talking and pointing, "A few minutes ago... they broke through the lines! You must go to your shelter!" and then she turned and ran off.

Joe, regaining his senses, turned to tell his wife to get their gas masks so they could go to their shelter. But he stopped dead in his tracks.

High in the sky above him, he heard the distinctive whistle of an inbound missile. He was about to tell Ruby and Eleazar to take cover when the missile, set for an air burst, exploded in a blinding flash of light.

Joe was thrown to the ground.

He lay there momentarily and then he got to all fours. Lifting his eyes to the sky, he saw that the blast turned it from blue to a yellowish green. That fog began to descend on the city.

Joe, Ruby and Eleazar were there when Tel Aviv became the first metropolis in the history... to be wiped out by a chemical weapons attack.

Chapter 72

Jerusalem, Israel – Present Day

*T*he ground vibrated, shook and swarmed with mini-earthquakes, moving and pulsing. The charged air smelled fresh and crisp, like after a thunderstorm, ionized from raw electrical power.

His body twitched and tingled with static shocks throbbing up out of the ground, through his bare feet. Current traversed his body to the crown of his head. The sandy brown hair on his arms stood straight up on end. And he shivered at the goose bumps that ran down his arms and back.

Although he'd experienced something like this, never had he experienced this. His skin was cold and clammy, yet sweat beaded on his forehead. It tickled as it dripped down his face. He dare not wipe it away with the Garment's sleeve.

His head was thick and swimming from the dizziness he felt. His mind was fuzzy and his eyes blurry. His vision was unfocused and he struggled to stay conscious. He wagged his head violently, trying to clear it. The low drone of the electrical hum began to build, vibrating through his ribcage.

As he progressed to the curtain, he saw clear waves breaking up through the ground, bending and distorting the air as they rolled and crashed. He rubbed his eyes hard with his fists trying, but failing, to remove the wisps, swirls and spirals of bending air that filled the room. He pressed on.

Pausing only briefly, he looked over his shoulder from where he'd come. The strange sights seemed familiar, but not quite. The sound... the sound was even louder than he remembered. It was building and threatened to become an ear piercing roar.

In his previous experiences, he never thought about what was occurring. It was different this time. This time - think he did. And those thoughts threatened to paralyze him and halt his progress.

He pushed them aside, and focused on one thing: *I must complete my mission; I must get the answer; the people... the nation... the world... they are depending on me!* He turned forward again and pressed on.

He willed his feet to move, each step exceedingly heavier than the last. The pressure in the room felt like a pile of stones heaped on his shoulders, threatening to collapse him.

He reached the thick curtain, a barrier between worlds. It really did sound like many waters behind it. It was a roaring and rushing sound that seeped under and around the sides of the curtain.

Even here, he could barely stand. In front of the curtain divide, his senses were overwhelmed. He licked his dry chapped lips as they moved, uttering his petition. If it was so heavy here, what would it be like on the other side of the curtain, he wondered?

He reached to part the thick curtain, its fabric densely laced with pure gold. As he drew his hand close, there was a sudden snap and flash as static electricity jumped off the curtains and bit into his fingers. He yelped and recoiled in pain, rubbing his stinging hand.

With dreaded anticipation, he closed his eyes, gritted his teeth and again reached for the fabric. Again a snap and bite, but this time he fought the urge to pull away. He hung onto the cold fabric, not letting go.

With a handful of the thick material, power surged off the curtain into the flesh of his hand and traversed his body. He shivered violently as small shock waves coursed through him.

Slowly and deliberately, he pulled back the stiff heavy curtain. Cautiously, he moved into the veil and was swallowed up in its thick, cold fabric. And then... suddenly... he was through.

Bright blinding light slapped him in the face as he broke through to the other side. He raised his hand quickly, shielding his eyes from the assault of the light.

With mouth agape, he viewed the light that was before him. It was brilliant white and beamed pure and hot, but did not burn. It pervaded the space, soaking into every part of the small room and permeated even into him. It washed over him and through him.

The light originated from the pillar of what seemed to be unexhausting white fire in front of him. But at the same time it was all around him. It filled every crack and crevasse, leaving no room for shadows or darkness.

The sound of many waters that he heard muffled on the other side of the curtain was now a bone-rattling roar. He fought the urge to cover his ears. He needed his hands.

His breathing was shallow and quick. His heart was beating wildly. His body was rocked by the combination of the sound and the light, as his insides vibrated with the roar.

Constant thunder of pure power filled the small room. It was coming from the light. He'd always assumed that the light was pure electricity. But this... this was something more. While it had characteristics of electricity, it wasn't that simple. It was power: The power that held the universe together.

He stood, frozen while taking in the sight. No man had been in this room, in this way, for thousands of years. His hand up, still shielding his eyes, he scanned the space. It was a perfect cube, 10x10x10. Although small, it was not cramped.

At the back of the room, dominating the space, was a large wooden vessel with gold accents: The Ark of the Covenant.

Before him, the brilliant white light was channeled into a pillar of raw power. The pillar came down from the sky, through the roof of the building, and rushed into the Ark.

Amazingly, the pillar showed up just before he entered the Tabernacle. He assumed it was the same pillar that the ancient

Hebrews saw.

Its roar was deafening. He stood there, wanting to move forward but afraid to approach. He tilted his head to the side slightly. He heard another sound, distinctive from the rest. It sounded like the sound of someone's rhythmic breathing; slowly moving in and out.

He realized that it was coming from the Ark itself. He squinted and strained his eyes, still shielding them with his hand as he looked beyond the brilliant white light. He could see the vessel's wooden sides, moving in and out in concert with the breathing sound. Realizing what this was, his knees grew weak from fear. He wanted to run. He wanted to hide. But he was frozen in fright.

He wasn't supposed to be here. He wasn't Orthodox. Although he went through the cleansing ceremonies, he couldn't help but wonder if Adonai would be angry at him for his presence in this place. But he had to get an answer for the people.

Once before, the Creator of the universe turned back the clock for him in the Reset. Would he do so again? During the cleansing ceremonies, he heard whispers of the attack on Tel Aviv. He'd also heard that things were very bad in America. If the World ever needed a Reset, it was now.

His own shivering from fear brought him back to the present. He forced himself to take a few paces forward toward the Ark. The heaviness of Hashem's presence was so thick in the small room that he felt like a semi-truck parked on his shoulders. Unable to stand any longer, he dropped to his knees and then to his face.

He realized that he couldn't complete his task if he were lying flat. He'd come so far and he knew he must get an answer. The people, the World, were depending on him.

He struggled to get up on all fours. Slowly, he pushed himself up to a vertical kneeling position. He was exhausted and spent. His hands were trembling, but he couldn't help it. Slowly he raised them against the unseen weight and he reached into both breast pockets.

Gingerly, he pulled out a clear crystal cylinder from each side of the Ephod. The cylinders were the width of a man's hand, tapered on one side and flat on the other. His hands were shaking and he held onto the crystals tight, careful not to drop them.

The High Priest told him through Zac that the Archangel Gabriel visited the group of rabbis and priests. Gabriel told them that the Urimm and Thummim that he delivered in the Package were made only to work for him. And therefore, it was he and not the High Priest that would need to go before the Ark and petition Adonai.

There was much dissent amongst the little group. He was a Gentile and not a practicing Jew. Yet, Gabriel told them that they had to trust Adonai. The Angel told them that he was chosen. So they asked him to come.

With hands now occupied, his eyes were defenseless against the bright light. He paused taking in the view of the awesome power before him.

Kneeling on the cold floor, he closed his eyes and forced himself to relax, breathing deeply. Then, in reverent whispers, he made the people's petition, repeating it again and again. Finally, after a moment, with shaky hands, he brought the crystals chest high, flat sides facing each other.

One last time, he opened his eyes to this world with a look of steely determination on his face. He nodded and closed his eyes again. His lips quivered as he resumed his petition for Israel.

And then... he uttered his own personal petition, "Adonai, please give me wisdom, courage and the ability to hear your voice *As The Darkness Falls*."

Taking one last deep breath and holding it, he grimaced and

touched the Urimm and Thummim's flat ends together.

There was a loud snap, and out of the pillar, a brilliant ark of light, shaped in the form of a hand, reached out for him.

And then... Dr. Bryce Obadiah Cooper was gone.

THE BEGINNING
OF
THE END

About The Author

Daniel Holdings is a successful businessman and award winning public speaker turned author.

He often jokes that he "just woke up" a few years ago and experienced a massive paradigm shift in his thinking regarding "reality" verses our perception about the world around us.

His stories are birthed from the extensive research that he conducts on the numerous subjects. These seldom heard truths provide the backdrop for his books, which are designed to educate as much as entertain.

While his books are not designed to be "religious" or faith based, he's been a Believer in Yeshua, Jesus, for more than thirty years. As a result, his stories evolve out of this worldview.

Regarding his faith, he tells the story about how a few years ago he began to dissect the history and tenets of the Christian faith. He shares that through this search for the historical Jesus and Christendom, he's gained a deeper love and assurance from a living God, Yahweh, which carries him, even in these challenging times.

Currently he is working on the next installment of the series featuring Dr. Bryce Cooper and lives with his longtime wife and teenage daughter in the Southern California Area.

Follow him on Facebook
&
Be sure to check out the interesting articles and tools at his website:

WWW.DANIELHOLDINGS.COM

Made in the USA
Charleston, SC
22 March 2015